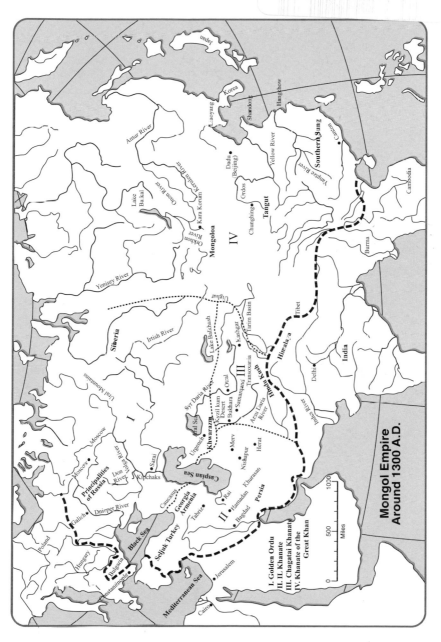

Mongol Empire Around 1300 A.D.

I. Golden Ordu
II. Il Khanate
III. Chagatai Khanate
IV. Khanate of the Great Khan

Miles
0   500   1000

Regions and places:

Siberia, Mongoloa, Tangut, Korea, Southern Sung, Cambodia, Burma, India, Tibet, Himalaya, Hindu Kush, Persia, Transoxania, Khwarazm, Seljuk Turkey, Georgia, Armenia, Principalities of Russia, Siberia, Kipchaks, Poland, Hungary, Bulgaria

Cities: Laoyang, Shandong, Hangchow, Canton, Dadu (Beijing), Ordos, Chunghing, Kara Korum, Kashgar, Delhi, Kaifeng, Otrar, Samarqand, Bukhara, Merv, Nishapur, Herat, Khurasan, Hamadan, Rai, Baghdad, Tabriz, Ungench, Sarai, Galich, Moscow, Moscow, Jerusalem, Cairo, Constantinople

Rivers and water features: Amur River, Onon River, Kerulen River, Okhon River, Yenisey River, Irtish River, Yellow River, Yangtze River, Syr Daria River, Amu Daria River, Indus River, Volga River, Don River, Dnieper River, Ural Mountains, Lake Baikal, Lake Balkhash, Aral Sea, Caspian Sea, Black Sea, Mediterranean Sea, Kyzil kum Desert, Caucasus, Tarim Basin, Uighur, Kara kum

GENGHIS KHAN

The World Conqueror

VOLUME II

By

Sam Djang

Printed in the United States of America

ISBN-13: 978-0-9846187-0-5 (Volume I, case bind)
ISBN-13: 978-0-9846187-1-2 (Volume I, perfect bind)
ISBN-13: 978-0-9846187-2-9 (Volume II, case bind)
ISBN-13: 978-0-9846187-3-6 (Volume II, perfect bind)

Library of Congress Control Number: 2010932313

Contents

CONTENTS

Preface

Human history could be distorted. The intentional, or
unintentional, distortion of history has happened in
the past, present and, possibly, in the eternal future. The exact
reasons for this are varied, but one important explanation is
that people tend to try to understand history from their own
point of view. A respectable person to one group of people
could be a sworn enemy to another; a historical and greatly influential figure to some could be meaningless to others. Someone identified as a hero in a certain era could be perceived as
anything other than that in times that follow. Once we accept
it as truth that self-protection and selfishness are a basic part
of human nature, we will realize how hard it is to accept historical facts that could be detrimental to our own sense of self,
community and culture. It is also hard to pass fair judgment on
historical facts of which we have no eye witness.

One year, in the 1990s, I had a chance to see the Genghis
Khan exhibit on display at the Natural History Museum in Los
Angeles. Within this exhibit, I had a chance to see historical
relics, remains, photos and records related to Genghis Khan.
Observing these historical artifacts and information inspired
the writer in me. Immediately following that experience, I
began intensive research on Genghis Khan, his history and his

lineage, which took me eight years to complete. During my period of research, I took numerous trips to Mongolia, Russia, China and related countries. My research in these countries led me to read hundreds of articles and related books, and to interview numerous people in Mongolia, including scholars and college professors. After all this effort and time, I finally arrived at a conclusion regarding the life of Genghis Khan, which happened to be the exact same conclusion the American historian Owen Lattimore had declared years ago. He proclaimed that, "The greatest conqueror in human history is Genghis Khan."

I think the history of Genghis Khan has been distorted, belittled and depreciated in many ways. Some of the ignorant accusations describe him as "the Scourge of God," "the Destroyer of Civilization" or "the Warmonger." Anyone who looks at his in-depth history will inevitably discover that none of those descriptions are accurate. How could there be such vast and negative misconceptions of this man? One explanation is that most of his recorded history was probably written by his enemies. In many parts of the world it is still taboo to even mention his name, for a variety of false reasons. When we compare all the great conquerors and their empires of the past, Genghis Khan and his Mongol Empire are outstanding. He was the greatest among all Emperors and no other nation, besides his Mongol Empire, has made as great an impact on the world. He was the only successful one and a true victor in the end.

The size of the land he had conquered in his lifetime was 2.2 times bigger than that of Alexander the Great, 6.7 times bigger than that of Napoleon Bonaparte and 4 times bigger than the Roman Empire. Also, the Mongol Empire, which his descendants continued to expand in later times, was the biggest empire in history by the time of A.D. 2010. The actual size of the Mongol Empire was 13,754,663 square miles (the potential conquered land was 14,493,569 square miles) and the 19th-century British Empire comes in second, in size, at 12,788,632 square miles.

The kingdom of Alexander the Great was torn to pieces by his generals after his death, Napoleon had been exiled to the island of St. Helena after losing the battle at Waterloo and Hitler's glory did not last more than three years. The Mongol Empire continued to grow after the rule of Genghis Khan because of the strength of the empire he built.

The greatness of the Mongol Empire is represented by their success in opening trade between the East and the West. The most meaningful and influential items in human civilization, such as paper, gunpowder and the compass had been transferred from the East to the West. Among many other important items are Arabic numerals, the concept of mathematics, astronomy and the manufacturing technique of glasses that went from the West to the East. Marco Polo's visit to the city of Dadu (Beijing), which had marked the turning point of Western history, was made during the Kubilai Khan's time, the golden age of the Mongol Empire. The voyage of Christopher Columbus, which introduced the existence of the American continent to Europeans, after all, was related, directly or indirectly, to Marco Polo's travels.

Before the emergence of the Mongol Empire, it was considered very unsafe to travel from the Italian Peninsula to the city of Dadu (Beijing) in China, in a small group, which Marco Polo, his father and his uncle made frequently.

This book was written in the form of a historical novel, and yet, 90 percent of its contents are based on the sensible, true story. The only elements that have been fictionalized are the areas that recorded history does not tell, mostly in the early part of his life. I sincerely hope the readers of this book do not judge or measure him based on our modern standards. If so, this could lead to further misunderstandings about him. Thank you very much for reading.

CHAPTER FORTY-TWO

Jamuka Elected as the Guru Khan

The political climate of the Mongolian Plateau was simple. If one tribe or group became bigger and unnervingly stronger, all the others would join together to resist and eventually break them down. All the tribes and clans on the Mongolian Plateau had, at some point, joined together as friends and at other times, turned against each other as enemies, making constant alignments and realignments. There were many motivations for this, but the foremost was that the petty chieftains, or heads of each tribe and clan, didn't want unification of the Mongolian Plateau. They were enjoying their independence. What they feared most was that someone strong might emerge and subjugate all the others to him.

If they established a friendly relationship, it would only last as long as it remained beneficial to both parties. If their political views became antagonistic, their friendship was dissolved at the same moment. This was widely accepted as something natural and expected. For these reasons, conflicts between them had never ceased and it was very clear that they never would unless someone of unprecedented strength took them over and set up a complete new order. Sometimes they built up a huge union or coalition and elected a khan of khans, but his power was limited and the union or coalition could collapse over night like a sandcastle.

Jamuka, of the Jadarats, was not the only one who had been feeling uneasy about the emergence of the combined power of Temujin and Wang-Khan, who destroyed half of the Tartars, conquered the Jurkins, and completely destroyed the mighty Taichuts and Buyiruk of the Naimans. It caused quite a stir across the plain to see what Temujin had accomplished: successive victories and fierce and destructive battles, which they had never known before.

They gathered around Jamuka saying, "Jamuka is the only one who can put a rein on Temujin."

It was quite natural that everybody was turning to Jamuka, who was believed to be the best strategist of his generation and the only one who had beaten Temujin and put him into utmost misery.

Some time ago, Jamuka allowed an audience to Achu Bagatur and Qodun Orchang of the Taichuts, who were asking for acceptance. They came to Jamuka with only a few of their soldiers. Jamuka deeply regretted he hadn't chased down Temujin to the end at Dalan Baljut when he heard he had completely destroyed the Taichuts.

Looking down at the two men who were kneeling and begging for acceptance, Jamuka pondered a while whether he would accept them or cut their heads off and send them to Temujin in an attempt to reconcile. Jamuka knew Temujin well, just as Temujin knew Jamuka. Their ultimate goals were to unify the Mongolian Plateau. Unless one of them gave up their dream, their clash would be inevitable. They might be unable to coexist under the same sky. Having come to this conclusion, Jamuka decided to accept Achu Bagatur and Qodun Orchang. He knew they were outstanding warriors.

"From now on, do your best to find and regroup the scattered Taichuts and their former subordinates."

Later, Achu and Qodun Orchang gathered about 4,000 of the Taichuts and the ones who were with them before. Jamuka put them into his regular troops.

Jamuka decided to remove Temujin before it was too late. His first step was to gather all the anti-Temujin powers or groups and make a new union. That was part of his original plan. Temujin and Jamuka were both well aware that they needed power for unification, and yet they had different opinions on the source of this power. Temujin thought the main body or source of power were the karachus, the Mongol commoners, the majority of the population and the free men, even though they were not allowed to participate in decision-making.

On the other hand, Jamuka believed that the elite groups and the aristocrats were the main source of power. He used to say, "The karachus are like livestock. The horses are for riding and the sheep are for wool. They can be molded into whatever form you want them to be. They are satisfied with meat and women. They want no more and they simply want someone to lead them. They are not the history makers and this is the will of heaven."

First, Jamuka sent out messengers to all the chieftains of tribes and the heads of groups who were most likely to join him and his future union. These were Baqu Chorogi of the Qadagins, Chirgidai of the Saljiuds, Qajiun Beki of the Dorbens, Jalin Buka of the Alchi Tartars, Tuge Maka of the Ikires, Chanak and Chakaan of the Gorolas, Toktoa Beki and his son Qutu of the Merkids, Quduka Beki of the Oyirads, the Naimans and even the Onggirads, the home people of Temujin's wife.

Upon receiving Jamuka's messenger, the Onggirads disputed each other in a high tone. The chieftain of the Olqunuuds, the sub-clan of the Onggirads, who was also the father-in-law of Temujin, Dey Sechen, and his son Alchi, were against joining Jamuka.

Nonetheless, most of the chieftains of the other clans were afraid of Jamuka's power. Ala Qus, the final decision maker of the Onggirads, made a remark after listening to all the opinions presented.

"Temujin will never beat Jamuka. In the past, he has already been defeated by Jamuka once. We'd better not offend Jamuka, who will be the most powerful man on the plain. We'd better choose the safer way."

The Onggirads made the decision to join Jamuka and notified him.

The next spring, all the chieftains and the heads of groups who were willing to join Jamuka's plan gathered with their own troops at the riverside of the Ake Nuke Green Stream, a branch of the Ergune River, located at the northeastern side of the Mongolian Plateau. It was the biggest convention ever seen in the Mongolian Plateau. On the field near the Ake Nuke Green Stream, countless military tents had been put up, and numerous soldiers as well as horses swarmed. Jamuka sat with all the representatives of the tribes and groups in a huge tent that had been set up as the interim headquarters, near the small stream coming from the valley of the nearby mountain with thick pine forests. It was the first general meeting of the union, with almost all the tribes and groups, a meeting of which Jamuka had dreamed.

After the confirmation of the presence of all the representatives, about 200 in total, Jamuka got to his feet and began to speak.

"I welcome all of you, as one of the participants. Thank you very much for coming. We are here with only one mind and a single heart. Now we are experiencing and facing the destruction of our current stable order in this land, and our peaceful coexistence is being disturbed and threatened by newly emerging menaces. They have shown us their extreme destructive nature and brutality, which we have never experienced before. They are the combined group of Wang-Khan and Temujin. We have to stop them. We have to protect ourselves, as well as our traditions. We have many witnesses here who have already seen or experienced this. Let's take some time to hear about their experiences."

After Jamuka, Jalin Buka of the Tartars stood up and spoke, "Toghrul and Temujin attacked my brothers. They had violated our nomads' taboo to bring in foreign power. They killed Megujin, who was like my real brother. In return, Toghrul received and rather happily accepted the title of Wang, given by the Juchids. I don't call him Wang-Khan. They are betrayers to all of us nomads."

After Jalin Buka's remarks, this time, Achu Bagatur of the Taichuts got on his feet and spoke, "Temujin's atrocity and wickedness are beyond description. He put an end to my people, the Taichuts. He even killed six- and seven-year-old boys. It's true that we have been in endless conflicts among ourselves, but we have never experienced genocide like this before. We surely have to get rid of them."

After Achu's remarks, Jamuka got on his feet with a smile of contentment on his face and said, "I think that is enough. We don't have the whole day to talk about their wrongdoings. Now we have to talk about the most important item on today's agenda. We gathered here with lofty ideas. We need a leader, like we have the sun in the sky or the head of a family in each and every household. I encourage you to honestly recommend anyone who you think is best for the job."

As Jamuka sat down after finishing these words, Qodun Orchang, who had become one of Jamuka's puppets, stood up and said, "I recommend Jamuka Sechen as our leader, who I believe to be the best strategist of our generation and the protector of our traditions."

Everything was planned, organized and arranged by Jamuka, so no one else could be recommended. They elected Jamuka as their leader unanimously. Jamuka stood up again with a broad smile on his face.

"Thank you very much for choosing me. I know the importance of this position. I will do my best. The first job we have to do is destroy the Wang-Khan–Temujin power, as soon as possible. We will make a detailed plan within the next few days."

The next morning, at daybreak, they all gathered at the triangular-shaped river basin, an island made by two rivers, the Ergune and the Ken, at their diverging point. While there, they had Jamuka's inaugural ceremony as their leader. They gave him the title "Guru Khan," which meant khan of khans. That was the moment when Jamuka's lifelong dream came true.

A ceremonial altar was arranged at the northern tip of the triangular-shaped river basin and, below it, all the chieftains and the heads of the groups with their selected soldiers holding their banners lined up in order. Quduka Beki, the chieftain of the Oyirads and a shaman as well, was the master of ceremonies. After praying to heaven and earth, Quduka Beki blessed Jamuka. A white stallion and a white mare were pulled out in front of the altar by several axmen and butchers. The axmen and butchers cut off the heads of the two horses by the order of Quduka Beki. Jamuka and all the chieftains and heads of the groups pledged allegiance to the heaven and the earth.

Oh! Gods of the heaven and the earth!
Listen to our pledge of allegiance.
If we break our own pledge,
Making the existence of this alliance endangered,
We shall suffer and bleed
Like these animals.

Jamuka, now Guru Khan, began to take a step toward his attack on Wang-Khan and Temujin.

CHAPTER FORTY-THREE

Battle at Koyiten

Temujin was stationed on a plain below the Mountain Kurelku, his base campsite. One afternoon a man was galloping toward Temujin's ordu like a gust of wind. Temujin's soldiers on sentry duty saw the approaching man on the horse. Mounting their horses, armed with spears and scimitars, the soldiers set out to stop the man.

The stranger began to shout, while his horse kept running, "An urgent message! An urgent message to Temujin Khan!"

The man, who stopped in front of the sentry soldiers, was drenched with sweat and covered with dust; he seemed to come from a distant place. Actually, he had been galloping his horse for almost 500 miles. Both man and horse were panting and his horse moved around as if it couldn't stay still from excitement.

The stranger kept on shouting, out of breath, "I am Qoridai of the Gorolas. Take me to Temujin Khan."

The sentry soldiers took him to the khan's tent, escorting him in front and in back. Receiving the report, Temujin allowed a reception. Qoridai gave his report in front of Temujin.

"Jamuka has been elected as Guru Khan. Jamuka and his allied troops have already begun their march to attack you."

Qoridai was Temujin's man, a spy in the Gorolas tribe. Temujin was fully aware of the importance of collecting information and espionage, and was the one who took advantage of it most. The Gorolas were Jamuka's allies. Society is a complicated entity and woven with many different elements, and so there will always be those unhappy with their own society, even if it is an almost perfect one. Temujin's spies were planted in almost every tribe on the Mongolian Plateau.

"In this extreme feudal society, a piece of information could save a man's and tribe's life."

Temujin used to say this.

Temujin was well aware of Jamuka's movements, based on his spy network. Temujin offered Quoridai a seat and ordered his servant nearby to bring him a cup of fresh milk.

Temujin asked, "What is the size of the troops and from which direction are they coming?"

Taking a sip of the milk, Qoridai answered slowly, "I don't know the exact number. In my estimation, it could be more or less than 50,000. They were moving toward the northern side of Quelen Lake."

Temujin nodded. Temujin gave an order to his servants to give him food and beverages, water to clean his body and accommodations.

He said to Qoridai, "Today, take a good rest. After this operation, you will be the number-one man of merit."

Just as he chased down his enemy to the end of the world and rooted him out, he never forgot to give a reward to someone who rendered distinguished service or was a man of merit.

The sound of a huge horn, telling of an urgent, impending situation, echoed through Temujin's ordu.

At the same time, Temujin dispatched messengers to Wang-Khan's ordu in the Black Forest. Upon receiving Temujin's urgent messengers, Wang-Khan mobilized his troops immediately and joined Temujin. Temujin discussed tactics and strategy with Wang-Khan over the map.

Wang-Khan asked Temujin with a worried look, "What would be the best way to crush them?"

Temujin gave him the reply.

"The two key points in this operation are time and supply. We have to stall for time. A stalling tactic will work in this operation."

Temujin explained over the map, "Jamuka's allied troops moved from the Ergune River. They are combined troops from all different areas. Many of their groups are far from their homeland. Supply would be their weakest point or their biggest problem. We have to delay the decisive battle until their food stocks are running low. The best spot for a stalling tactic is here."

Saying this, Temujin pointed to three high grounds that were located about eighty miles from Quelen Lake to the west-northwest direction. Those were Chiqurqu Mountain, Chekcher Mountain and Enegen Hill.

"They will pass through these three high grounds. We have to take those three before they pass through. If not, it will be hard."

Wang-Khan nodded. Temujin dispatched Altan, Quchar and his uncle Daritai with 2,000 horse soldiers each, as vanguards, to seize the three high grounds. Wang-Khan also sent out his vanguards, Nilka Seggum, Jagambu and Bilge Beki, to support Temujin's troops.

Temujin explained to his vanguards, in a strong and high tone, the importance of their mission.

"The key points for victory in this operation are the three high grounds. It depends on who will take those three high grounds first. Don't forget my words! Rush to the place with maximum speed. Take those three before they do! When you encounter the enemy, try not to fight with them until our main body of troops have arrived."

Temujin's vanguards were successful in taking over the three high grounds. They galloped at full speed without a single pause and arrived there before Jamuka's vanguards. Moments later, Wang-Khan's vanguards arrived and they tried to find a campsite. At this moment, the warning sound of the horn blowing came from the soldiers stationed on top of Chiqurqu Mountain. Altan, Quchar, Jagambu and Senggum talked with each other about how to handle the situation.

Jagambu said, "Temujin Khan said not to fight until the main troops arrive."

They let the soldiers shout toward the enemies.

"It is getting dark! Let's fight tomorrow!"

The approaching enemy was Jamuka's vanguards, Achu, Qodun Orchang, Toktoa Beki's son Qutu and Quduka Beki, four in all. They were surprised because they never expected Wang-Khan and Temujin's troops to be there. They also decided to wait until Jamuka's main troops arrived. It would be no exaggeration to say that this was the decisive moment in the battle that would decide the most powerful man on the Mongolian Plateau.

Temujin was exultant upon hearing the news when he arrived late at night with Wang-Khan and his main troops. On the other hand, Jamuka was in great despair. He never expected Temujin and Wang-Khan's troops to move so fast.

For about a month from that moment, fierce battles continued to take over the high grounds. Whoever was occupying the high ground had enormous advantages over the ones under their feet. They could see every movement of the enemies on the ground, and conversely, the ones on the ground could never see over the hill. The arrows shot from the high land were more destructive than the ones shot from ground level up to the high hill.

Jamuka's allied troops were about 50,000 in number and Temujin and Wang-Khan's side were about 40,000. The amount of food that Jamuka's 50,000 men consumed each day was enormous. The nomads usually moved together with their family members and livestock when they were going into war.

However, there were some exceptions, such as when they were attempting a surprise attack, when they needed to make urgent movements or when it was an unnecessary security risk. Temujin and Wang-Khan's troops didn't have much of a problem with their supply line, but it was different for the Oyirads and the Merkids of the allied forces. Their homelands were just above and below Lake Baikal, which was too far from their battleground. And between the two places were many high and rough mountains, so it was impossible to get additional supplies.

Disharmony began to creep in among them. The biggest complaints came from the Oyirads and the Merkids. They were very unhappy with the original food supply plan. To make things worse, the other tribes with enough food refused to share with them. Jamuka released emergency provisions, but there was a limit to that.

Quduka Beki, the chieftain of the Oyirads, suggested "jada." "Jada" meant some kind of magic to bring rain, a gale or a storm to favor them on the battleground, by incantations and certain arrangements of stones that were believed to have magical powers. Quduka Beki was a shaman. Upon his request, Jamuka frowned, but he couldn't refuse him due to his strong voice in the alliance. With permission, he did what he wanted to do.

As nothing happened, he turned around to his troops and shouted, "Heaven is not on the alliance's side! We will go back!"

Enraged, Jamuka unsheathed his sword to cut his head off. At this moment, Jalin Buka, who was standing next to him, held his hand and stopped him, "No! If we fight each other here, we will all die!"

The time was right for Temujin. After noticing their disharmony, Temujin launched an all-out attack.

The allied troops, with disharmony among their tribes and an uncertain line of command, were completely destroyed. It was Koyiten, near Chiqurqu Mountain. The dead bodies of the allied troops were strewn across the vast field. The chieftains, with their remaining defeated troops, scattered in all directions. That was the end of Jamuka's short-lived power and the moment that his dream was shattered completely. It was 1201 and the year of the cock.

CHAPTER FORTY-FOUR

Jebe, Temujin's New Man

The defeated soldiers of the alliance group were running away toward each of their homelands, led by their chieftains or leaders. Wang-Khan chased down Jamuka. After losing more than half of his troops, Jamuka tried to escape along the Ergune River. As Wang-Khan's soldiers were nearing, Jamuka and his soldiers fled into the nearby thick mountain forest. Wang-Khan's 25,000 soldiers encircled the mountain. After five days' resistance, Jamuka at last gave up, descended the mountain and surrendered.

Meanwhile, Temujin tracked down the Taichuts, Achu Bagatur and Qodun Orchang. They took the route of the Onon River. Eventually, Temujin's troops caught up with them and landed the final blow. Achu's head was cut off by Bogorchu's scimitar and Qodun Orchang's waist was speared by Mukali. Temujin's soldiers cut off fallen Qodun Orchang's head. This was the way that the remnants of the Taichuts were completely annihilated. The dead bodies of the Taichuts were covering the Onon River banks and nearby field, and thousands of crows, drawn by the smell of human blood, were covering the sky, making a deafening noise. It was evening and dusk was falling.

Early the next morning, Temujin lined up his troops. They had set up camp not far from the battlefield. Temujin was inspecting the troops, which were lined up in due order with their banners in front of them. Kasar, Bogorchu and Jelme followed him. The rising sun was pouring its strong morning light over them. At this moment, suddenly, the whizzing sound of an arrow hit Temujin's eardrum. Reflexively, he ducked his head. Next, with a dull thud, an arrow lodged deeply in the middle of the left-hand side of his horse's neck. After being attacked, his horse stood on its hind legs, neighing, and then fell down on its side. Temujin fell down too with his horse. It caused a big stir among the soldiers.

Kasar, Bogorchu and Jelme, who were joining the inspection, dismounted their horses and covered Temujin with their bodies to protect him from a possible second attack.

A while later, Bogorchu and Jelme helped Temujin get up and asked, "My lord, are you all right?"

Temujin answered, dusting himself off, "I think I am all right."

Kasar and several dozen horse soldiers dashed toward the pine forest on the nearby hill, from where the arrow came.

Temujin shouted at them, "I want him alive!"

Temujin's horse kept on screaming from the pain, and the wound continued to bleed. Strangely, the animal couldn't move its front or hind legs at all, or the rest of its body.

The horses name was Qula and it was a fine steed. It was covered with smooth, shiny, golden hair all over its body, with a white muzzle and a pitch-black mane and tail. Qula was amazingly swift and persistent; he could run twice the distance and at twice the speed of any other. He was the most beloved of Temujin's and was the one Temujin spent the most time with on the battlefield.

Temujin summoned the military veterinarian specializing in horses. Qaraldai, military veterinarian as well as horse breeder, checked the wound and shook his head.

"My lord, bad news! His neck has been broken. He cannot move below his neck."

Temujin closed his eyes and took a deep breath. He knelt on one of his legs and said, smoothing its head, "Thank you very much, Qula. You have helped me a lot."

The animal continued screaming in pain. Standing up slowly, Temujin told his men with a sad look, "Relieve him of his pain."

At this moment, the suspected sniper, with his hands tied behind his back, was being dragged in front of Temujin by Kasar and his soldiers. Temujin watched him carefully. Even though he was tall, he looked young, about fourteen or fifteen years old.

Temujin said to Kasar, "I will question him myself. Bring him to me."

Temujin questioned him in a sunshade tent, with all four walls rolled up and open. Temujin looked at him carefully as he was kneeling with his two hands tied behind him.

"What was your motivation to kill me, while all of your fellow soldiers died on the battlefield like men?"

The sniper raised his head and answered in a clear voice, looking straight at Temujin, "I wanted to accomplish my mission."

Temujin asked him, looking into his eyes, "What is your mission?"

He answered without hesitation, "To kill Temujin Khan."

The staff soldiers around Temujin's chair seemed to be frustrated and stirred by his straightforward answer. They looked at each other. The boy seemed to be fearless, in spite of the fact that he would lose his head within a few moments.

Temujin regarded him for a while and then asked him in a low, gentle voice, "How old are you?"

"Fourteen."

"Aren't you afraid of death?"

The boy answered in a clear voice, "I am afraid of death, like others. However, there's something I fear more than death."

"What is it?"

"Failure to fulfill my duty."

Temujin seemed to be amazed. Temujin sat straight without taking his eyes off the boy. What a boy! He is just a fourteen-year-old boy! That was what Temujin thought.

Temujin looked into his eyes. His two eyes were shining with boldness, determination and even some kind of dignity. Temujin began to think that killing him would be a loss. Temujin asked him again, "What made you think that killing me was your duty?"

The boy answered, "My master was killed by Temujin's soldiers. So, I think it is my duty to kill Temujin."

There was another stir among Temujin's staff. Temujin asked in a soft voice, "Who was your master?"

"He was Todogen Girte."

"Are you a Taichut?"

"No, my parents were Besuts."

The Besuts were serfs to the Taichuts. In earlier days, the Taichuts conquered the Besuts and enslaved them. The enslaved tribesmen and women would take care of the livestock of their masters and lend their hands to household chores and to all the other hard and dirty work. And, in wartime, they had to fight for them as part of their troops. At that time, on the Mongolian Plateau, the slaves were the lowest group of people in the social structure, with no freedom.

Temujin asked him, looking straight into his eyes, "Did you know your parents were slaves to the Taichuts?"

The boy answered, avoiding Temujin's eyes, "I knew. But Todogen Girte was my master."

Temujin was impressed by his loyalty. Loyalty was the most important quality Temujin considered when he evaluated his men. Temujin whispered to him, "We don't have slavery among ourselves. Why don't you join us?"

The boy gave a little thought and answered, "I am sorry. I am not ready for that. I am not ready to accept a new master."

Temujin got on his feet and said abruptly, "You will be beheaded. Is there anything else you want to say?"

The boy said determinedly, looking straight at Temujin, "You can take my life, but not my mind."

Temujin let out a loud guffaw. A moment later, Temujin asked the boy, wearing a serious look, "What is your name?"

"Jirkodai."

Temujin ordered his men to set him free and to let him have a horse, three days' food and a bagful of sheep's milk. Temujin said to him upon bidding him farewell, "Go! You are free now! Your loyalty to your master is admirable and praiseworthy. Find a new master and don't change your mind."

Temujin watched him disappear into the far distant horizon.

Three days later, the boy came back. As Bogorchu reported the boy's return, Temujin let him in.

"Why did you come back?"

The boy answered, kneeling and lowering his head, "I am here to give my mind and body to you."

Temujin was glad. A true mind always brings in true minds. Temujin accepted him, "From now on, your name is Jebe. You need a new name because you are reborn."

"Jebe" meant arrowhead in Mongolian. Temujin's keen sense and eyes allowed him no mistakes in the evaluation and judgment of his men. Later, Jebe became the head of first 10, then 100, 1,000 and finally 10,000, for in Temujin's troops and society only ability and competence mattered. Eventually, he became one of the leaders, along with Subedai, in the conquest of Russia.

CHAPTER FORTY-FIVE

Last of the Tartars

Since the beginning of time, seemingly, the Tartars had ruled the eastern side of the Mongolian Plateau. At one time, they were the most powerful and richest tribe on the plateau. Their population was about 350,000 to 400,000, or 70,000 households, and their homeland was the place around Lake Kulen and Lake Buyr, which were located between Khingan Mountain and the Kerulen River. They had such an abundant natural source of silver in their area that they made everything, tools, kitchen utensils and even baby cradles, out of silver. They had been well-known to the outside world since the eighth century, so "Tartar" became the name representing all the people on the plateau and even the people of central Asia as well. They were a strong rival to the Mongols and had been competing for the control of that area for a long time. The discord between them had dramatically worsened since the Tartars captured Ambakai, the second khan of the primitive Mongol nation, in a secret agreement with the Juchids of the Chin Empire, and handed him over to the Juchids. They were strong, rich and aggressive in nature, and yet, fractioning into many small clans and a lack of harmony among themselves had weakened their power.

Temujin was victorious. Now he decided to move to the next step in his plan for the unification of the Mongolian Plateau. That was to remove the Tartars. Temujin knew that, as long as they remained, his movements wouldn't be easy. Years ago, Temujin had removed some of their power by killing Megujin Seultu, with Wang-Khan and Wanyen-Xiang of Chin, but their main powers were still strong. Temujin knew it would be a tough job. He also knew he needed thorough preparations. After coming back from the Koyi-ten, Temujin passed the winter hunting around the Kurelku Mountains. When spring arrived, Temujin began to take action. Temujin estimated six months for preparation. The very first thing he had to do was convince his people that they could win.

> *Heaven allowed me the power*
> *To rule this land.*
> *By the will of heaven,*
> *And with the power of heaven,*
> *I will defeat the enemy.*
>
> *My troops are invincible,*
> *And the ones gathered under my banner,*
> *Will be immortal.*
> *Their armor will be lance-proof,*
> *And the arrows will miss them.*

In front of my followers,
Will be only victory and glory.
And their children will enjoy
The endless prosperity,
Generation to generation.

Temujin's rules for his troops were draconian. The deserters were beheaded. Someone who refused to obey an order from their superior on the battlefield was beheaded. When a unit of more than ten soldiers made a dash at the enemy, and if more than two of them were far ahead of the others, the rest of them should follow them to help. If not, the delayed ones were beheaded. When the troops were moving forward, if someone dropped his weapons or belongings, the next person behind him should pick them up and hand them back to him. If he ignored it or didn't give them back, he was beheaded. The commander of a unit, small or large, who intentionally made false reports, or hid his faults was beheaded. All these rules were reinforced and subdivided into details as Temujin's troops grew bigger and bigger. Temujin set up an accurate promotion system within his troops based on their ability, competence and capacity. The one who rendered the most distinguished service got the leader's position. They could be replaced in their position by someone more deserving at any time.

Each of Temujin's soldiers received two bows, a quiver, a spear, a lasso, a scimitar, a dagger, a battle-ax, a mace, a round shield, two sheepskin bags for beverages, an awl for fixing leather products and a small hand knife. All these things were kept and maintained like the soldier's own body and were ready at any time. Random and occasional inspections were done by Temujin or high-ranking generals, and if any problems were found, not only was the owner punished, but also his commander.

The combat rations were mainly dried beef, which could last several years without spoiling. They could eat it as was or boil it. Temujin ordered short stirrups for his soldiers, which gave them more freedom with their body movements when they were engaged in man-to-man combat on the battlefield. All of his soldiers were supplied with silk underwear, which delayed the speed of the poisonous effect when they were shot with a poisoned arrow, and at the same time made it possible for them to remove the arrowhead easily, with only a slight wound. This was possible, because, in many cases, the silk cloth was lodged, along with the arrowhead, inside the soldier's body, slowing the absorption of the poison.

In the autumn, Temujin marched on the Tartars. Temujin's drummers signaled the opening of the war, beating their nacaras, or tin drums, all together. Temujin's troops were composed of 7,000 of his own men, 5,000 of Altan's, 4,000 of Quchar's, 3,000 of Daritai's, 2,000 Uruuds of Julchedai, 2,000 Mangkuds of Quyilda, making a total of 23,000. The Tartars had 30,000 men from five different clans, and those were the Alchi Tartars, the Chagaan Tartars, the Tutaut Tartars, the Aluqay Tartars and the Tete Tartars.

Temujin had a meeting with the leaders of each group and his high commanders. After the meeting, Temujin gave important instructions.

"This war could be a tough one. We need to move under one direct order line. That is the way we can keep ourselves strong. Individual movements won't be allowed. Until the complete destruction of the enemy, no group can step out of the line for any reason. After the war, distribution will be done fairly."

Until that time, when many tribes were joining the same war, each tribe or group would tend to come out of their line in pursuit of their own benefit. Their main target was war booty. Temujin continued.

"In case our tactics are not very successful, we have to come back to the original starting point. That is how we can regroup and retry. Anyone who tries to run away shall be beheaded."

Temujin and his troops marched more than 500 miles eastward, and then crossed the Khalkha River near Lake Buyr. They met the Tartar troops at the riverside of the Dalan Nemulges, a branch of the River Khalkha. The Tartar troops were strong, yet they couldn't stand against Temujin's well-organized troops. They were crushed and retreated to the Ulqui Selugejid riverside, their home base, leaving countless dead bodies of their fellow soldiers. Temujin chased down and destroyed their main force, but found out later that too many defeated Tartars had escaped to ignore. Temujin tried to continue to chase them, but Altan, Quchar and Daritai didn't follow him. Since their main target was war booty and loot, they busied themselves taking the livestock and property that the Tartars had left, ignoring Temujin's warning. Temujin couldn't move on. Enraged, Temujin sent Jebe and Qubilai to seize all the booty that they had taken.

"Khan's order! We have to seize all the booty you have taken from the Tartars. We will keep it all until the khan's next instructions."

Jebe and Qubilai faithfully carried out the khan's order. Altan and Quchar began to resent that they had supported Temujin as their khan. They began to believe that Temujin was trying to break down the old traditions and violate the sovereignty of each clan or group as an independent entity. Only Daritai came to Temujin to apologize for not keeping his promise. His apology was accepted, yet, later, he had to pay for disloyalty.

Temujin had a secret meeting with a very few people to discuss the future plans regarding the remaining Tartars. Temujin asked for their opinion.

"We have to talk about the remaining Tartars. What shall we do with them? If you have any opinion, let me know."

Daritai spoke his opinion.

"The Tartars have been our sworn enemy for generations. They don't deserve our mercy. We have to treat them the same way we did the Taichuts. The ones who are taller than the wheel of the cart should be removed."

No one was against Daritai. They all agreed not to accept the Tartars' surrender, which meant they would annihilate them, killing all the male Tartars taller than the wheel of cart.

About ten days later, after regrouping his soldiers, Temujin marched toward the place where tens of thousands of Tartars were gathered. The Tartars had already built up a strong fortress on a high hill, about eighty miles from the spot where Temujin began his march. After looking at the fortress, Temujin knew intuitively that they would have short-term suicidal resistance because they built their base on top of the hill, where water was scarce. Temujin tried attacks from all different directions, but their resistance was fierce. Temujin suffered heavy casualties. The number was bigger than any of the previous two battles. Temujin decided to try a deceitful tactic. Temujin's soldiers began to shout to the hilltop fortress.

"Surrender! Then you will be saved!"

Yeke Cheren, the last Tartar chieftain, snorted when he heard that. He made his men shout back to Temujin's soldiers at the foot of the hill, "Don't make us laugh! We know your khan's decision not to accept our surrender! We will fight to the last man!"

Temujin was shocked to hear that. How do they know our top-secret decision? Who let it out? Who is the betrayer? Only eight men attended the secret meeting, including Temujin. They were Temujin himself, Altan, Quchar, younger brother Kasar, half-brother Belgutai, uncle Daritai, younger brother Kachun and younger brother Temuge Ochigin. However, Temujin didn't start his quest to find the betrayer right away.

Temujin simply waited until the Tartars were running out of water. Several days later, in the morning, they opened the gate of the fortress and made an all-out attack. After a fierce battle, the fortress fell into Temujin's hands; however, Temujin suffered great casualties. Many of the enemy soldiers were hiding among the dead bodies of their fellow soldiers, and then attacked with daggers hidden inside their sleeves, when Temujin's soldiers stepped into the fortress. Temujin lost one high-ranking general and numerous soldiers. All the Tartar males taller than a cartwheel were killed. That was the last of the Tartars.

CHAPTER FORTY-SIX

Temujin Meets Yesui

Temujin received the report of the war results from Kasar. The estimated number of enemy deaths, 50,000; Tartar women and babies captured, about 90,000; the number of Tartars that escaped, unknown; seized horses, about 20,000; camels, about 7,000; cattle, 5,000; sheep, about 200,000; goats, 10,000. And the weapons, jewelry, gold and silver products, animal furs, hides and horse equipment were stacked like a mountain, impossible to count. The death toll for Temujin's side was 1,200 of Temujin's men, 600 of Altan's, 400 of Quchar's and 350 of Daritai's, making a total of 2,550.

Temujin asked Kasar, "What about the Tartar chief, Yeke Cheren?"

Kasar answered, with a look of embarrassment, "His whereabouts are unknown. We couldn't find his dead body. It seems he has escaped with his wife and a son. However, his two daughters are in our custody."

Temujin thought a moment and then told Kasar, "Bring his two daughters to me."

A moment later, two of Yeke Cheren's daughters were presented to Temujin. They looked young, about eighteen or twenty years old, intelligent, and were extremely beautiful. Temujin took a good look at the two women. Though they looked tired from the long-lasting disturbances of the war, they still had the elegance and dignity of noblewomen. Temujin offered them a seat and ordered nearby servants to bring some tea. As Jelme was trying to frisk them for possible hidden weapons, Temujin stopped him, "It's all right. Leave us alone."

Temujin offered them the tea the servants just had delivered. Temujin was looking at the soldiers and horses passing in front of him and sipping the tea, under a tent for shade with all four walls rolled up. The bright morning sunlight was pouring over the soldiers, horses and over the camp.

Temujin took one more sip of the tea, made from jasmine touched with fresh milk, and then asked the two women, "What happened to your parents?"

The woman that appeared to be the elder answered, "We really don't know. We tried to find them ourselves, but couldn't."

Temujin asked, "How about your own families? Are you both married?"

This time the younger-looking one answered, "We both are unmarried. However, my elder sister has a fiancé."

After one more sip of the tea, Temujin asked, "Where is he?"

The elder sister answered, "I don't even know if he is still alive. He was with me until some time ago."

Temujin kept silent for a while, and then asked, "What are your names?"

The younger one answered, "Her name is Yesui and mine is Yesugen."

Temujin told them as he was sending them back, "Go back and wait. I will call you back soon."

Temujin ordered Jelme to provide them a separate yurt, four serving women and special meals, along with ten guard soldiers to protect them.

The foul odor from the decaying dead bodies filled the air, making it hard for Temujin and his soldiers to breathe while still on the battlefield. Temujin's soldiers cremated some, and dug a huge hole and buried others. Temujin held a mass funeral for his fallen soldiers. On a hill with a view of the endless field that was the battleground, an altar was arranged with a huge bronze incense burner. Kokochu, the official priest of Temujin's troops, prayed and burned a sheep as an offering, sending its smoke into the sky. Next, Temujin took off his helmet and belt and said his prayer:

> *The history of mankind is the history of wars.*
> *Tab Tenggri, the owner of everything,*
> *Is in the place too high above,*
> *And the mother earth remains silent.*

Though a fistful of days are given to the mortals,
Only the one who dies with a sword in his hand,
Shall complete his life.

Always there are followers and those disobedient
Of heaven's will,
Which make this world a never-ending battleground.
They are trembling with fear,
With their own fate,
Which they can never escape.

Oh! Tab Tenggri, the greatest one.
What is your truth?

After the ritual, all the warriors walked between the two huge columns of flames, for purification and protection from the evil spirits. The Mongols held the fire sacred.

Temujin and his soldiers left the battlefield and, after almost a whole day traveling, they picked a campsite about 100 miles from their starting point. They celebrated their victory there. They built up campfires, barbecued, drank and danced. Here and there, wrestling matches were being held. Temujin arranged a table outside and was watching a wrestling match, drinking with Yesui and Yesugen on his left and right sides. Many onlookers gathered around and enjoyed watching the wrestling matches, shouting and shaking their fists in the air, rooting for their side.

At this moment, Temujin noticed Yesui was getting nervous and irritable for some reason. Occasionally, she even sighed deeply. Temujin looked around carefully. Temujin found a man, not far from his table, casting side-glances at her rather than watching the game. He seemed to be trying to send some kind of message to Yesui. He looked young, handsome and elegant. Temujin called in Bogorchu and Mukali and gave an order,

"Make them form a line, tribe by tribe."

The wrestling matches were temporarily interrupted. By Temujin's order, Bogorchu and Mukali had the people around Temujin's table line up with their own tribe. There was a line with only one man. It was him. Temujin ordered them to find out who he was.

The man told Bogorchu and Mukali, who came up to him, "I am a Tartar. I am betrothed to Yesui, Yeke Cheren's daughter. Now the war is over, so I came to pick her up."

This absent-minded man had run away from the battlefield and come back without noticing that all his tribesmen had been annihilated. And more, he was asking for his fiancée. When Temujin heard this, he was dumbfounded. He couldn't believe his ears. Temujin stood up slowly and walked up to him. Staring into his eyes, Temujin said to him, "Don't you know your tribe has been completely destroyed? All of your tribesmen taller than a cartwheel have been killed. Where have you been and where did you run away to? All your tribesmen fought until the very last man. You are not even a Tartar! You are just a maggot!"

Temujin shouted at Bogorchu and Mukali, "Take him out of my sight!"

The man was dragged out of the place by Bogorchu and Mukali and was beheaded. Unable to conceal his displeasure, Temujin got on his feet, emptied his wine goblet in one swallow, and said to Yesui, "I am sorry!"

Temujin left there and went back to his tent. That night, Temujin couldn't fall asleep. Sometimes people don't even understand themselves. While Temujin was tossing and turning in his bed, the low shouting of a guard soldier reached his ears. Even the guard soldiers couldn't step into the khan's tent; instead, they had to shout from outside to make a report. When this rule was violated, they were beheaded.

"A woman wants to see you, my lord! What shall I do?"

Temujin shouted back toward the door, "What's her name?"

"She said her name is Yesui."

Temujin let her in. Yesui knelt in front of Temujin's bed and said in a low voice, "I am here to give my mind and body to you, my lord. I never realized that my former fiancé was such a coward and so unmanly. If you accept me as even your lowest servant, it would be a great favor to me."

Temujin watched her silently while sitting on his bed. Her image under the Arabian lamp was beauty itself. Her shining, dark-brown eyes under her eyebrows, which created the image of flying seagulls, showed that she was telling the truth.

Temujin got on his feet and offered his hand. Holding her hand, Temujin helped her to stand up. Temujin embraced her, "Oh! Yesui."

Temujin slept with Yesui that night. It was a long night. Later, Temujin accepted Yesui as his second wife, standing next to Borte. A man can love more than one woman.

Temujin's New Enemies: Altan and Quchar

After Temujin returned to his base campsite on the plain near Kurelku Mountain, the first thing he had to do was distribute the war booty, rewarding and punishing based on merits and demerits. In Temujin's system, if someone had a merit, he was rewarded and, conversely, someone who had a demerit had to prepare for the punishment that would surely come. He perfected this system.

Temujin began his secret investigation to find out who was the betrayer who revealed the top secret. First, Temujin considered the possibility of Altan, Quchar and Daritai, who acted contrary to their own promises and his order. However, Temujin could not find any possible direct motivation for them. They were the ones who, from the beginning, were focused on the Tartars' annihilation. Next, Temujin thought about anyone who had connections to the Tartars. In that regard, Belgutei came first on his list. Belgutei's wife was a Tartar. Others might think Belgutei could do it, but Temujin's sixth sense told him he did not. Then who had done it, and why?

Temujin met with Belgutei directly, instead of having Kasar, the spy chief, meet with him. Temujin sat face to face with Belgutei. Temujin asked Belgutei, looking into his eyes, "Was it you who revealed the secret?"

Belgutei looked down at the ground for a while without saying anything. He then raised his head slowly and said with a gentle voice, looking straight at Temujin, "Temujin, if I had it in my mind to betray and harm you, I would have done it a long time ago. Especially when you killed my brother Bektor, I could have considered you my enemy. If you suspect me now, there is no way I can disprove it. I just feel sad."

Temujin held his hands and said, "Belgutei! I don't think you did it. However, I need your help. Just pretend you did it. The punishment is very light. And don't ask me why; that's the way you can help me."

They looked at each other. At last, Belgutei nodded, as if he had read Temujin's mind.

The next day, Temujin had an official meeting with about a hundred chieftains, group leaders and high-ranking warriors for the reporting of war results, achievements, rewards, punishments and distribution fundamentals. Kasar reported all the statistics of casualties of the war by the groups and tribes.

Temujin issued the following decrees in the name of the khan:

1: The war booty will be distributed to the soldiers equally, regardless of their origin of tribes, clans or groups.
2: The families of the fallen soldiers will get triple the amount of distribution.
3: The amounts given to the chieftains, or group leaders, will be allotted based on the numbers of their soldiers that joined the battle and how many died on the battlefield.
4: Altan, Quchar and Daritai had stepped aside for their own selfish plan against the khan's order, and so half of their shares will be seized.
5: The seized articles will be retained as common property.

After the official meeting, a separate kinsmen council was held by Temujin to punish Belgutei, who was believed to have revealed the secret decision.

"Belgutei leaked the secret decision by mistake, and it eventually reached the enemies' ears. As punishment, he is not allowed to attend the kinsmen council for one year and is also not allowed to drink otok for one year from today."

Otok was an alcoholic drink that the Mongols used in their ancestral memorial ceremony. They used to drink it after the ceremony in order of importance or position in the lineage, to confirm themselves as one of the kinsmen. Belgutei accepted this decision without objecting.

Altan and Quchar had a secret meeting. They grumbled to each other about Temujin's policy and the way they had been treated by him. Altan said, "Temujin is trying to assert himself as king over us. It's ridiculous! Who supported him to become the khan? We did! How can he treat us like this? If we leave him, he is just like an eagle without wings or a tiger without claws. I hope he knows that."

Altan grumbled and Quchar sympathized with him.

"He is trying to take our independence away. That is the trouble. I think it is the time to leave him."

At that time, on the Mongolian Plateau, the position of the khan meant no more than a conductor of operations on the battleground. When they were faced with mutual enemies or were pursuing common gains, they elected their leader, and named him the khan. The elected khan would be invested with certain powers over the joined tribes, but it was very limited and each chieftain would still hold the absolute power over his own people.

Altan said to Quchar, "If we leave Temujin, where should we go?"

Quchar gave this some thought and then answered, "I think we'd better join Wang-Khan."

"Wang-Khan is no different from Temujin. Aren't they in the same group?" Altan asked back, giving a dubious look.

Quchar explained, "Actually, we are joining Jamuka, who is under Wang-Khan's command. I heard that he is still doing fine, even though he has been deprived of military power by Wang-Khan. If we join him, I am pretty sure we will be welcomed. He is the one who acknowledges the independence of each tribe."

They agreed to join Jamuka.

Jamuka welcomed Altan and Quchar. He received them with cheers, raising his two arms high and hugging them.

"Welcome to both of you! I really appreciate your coming and not forgetting me."

Jamuka touched their cheeks with his own, one after another, three times, each of them, which was a greeting that was only possible between two parties with complete trust. Yesterday's enemy was today's friend. Jamuka offered them seats and also offered green tea touched with fresh milk, which was just delivered by servants. After taking a sip of the tea, Jamuka said to Altan and Quchar, with a broad smile on his face, "I knew you two gentlemen would come join me. Temujin is not the right one for you. I know him very well. He is trying to get all the chieftains in his hands and enslave them. We must stop him."

Quchar opened his mouth and said, "Since we have left him, his power should be weakened. However, he is too close to Wang-Khan. That could be a problem."

After another sip of the tea, Jamuka said, "That is right! To remove Temujin, we have to separate them first. As long as they are together, nobody can stand against them. Moreover, more, we have to make them fight each other. After they have battled each other to the end and become dog-tired, it will be easier than picking up dried, cow dung to remove them."

At Jamuka's remarks, all three laughed together. After a moment, Altan asked Jamuka, with a serious look, "Do you have any idea how to separate them?"

After picking up the Chinese teapot and filling his empty cup slowly, Jamuka took another sip and said, "Leave that to me. I have every idea and plan in here."

As he was saying this, Jamuka narrowed his eyes and tapped his head twice with his right index finger. All three, again, let out a loud guffaw.

That evening, Jamuka held a welcome dinner party for Altan and Quchar. The guests entered Jamuka's tent one by one, in the order of their arrival. Jamuka introduced all the incoming guests to Altan and Quchar. The first one was Qachiun Beki of the Qadagins. The Qadagins were the enemy of Temujin and they previously supported Jamuka as the guru khan. They exchanged greetings by touching cheeks, one by one. The next guest was Ebugejin of the Noyakins. He did the same thing with Altan and Quchar. The following guests were Sugeetei, one of Jamuka's confidants, and Tooril, who used to be Temujin's man, but later betrayed him and joined Jamuka. Lastly, a middle-aged man, with a thick beard and mustache on his face, stepped in with a young man in his twenties. Jamuka cautiously introduced them to Altan and Quchar. They were Yeke Cheren, the former commander-in-chief of the Tartars, and his son Narin Keen. After losing the battle, Yeke Cheren had successfully escaped with only his wife and a son. He joined Jamuka. When he faced Altan and Quchar, instead of saying hello, he tried to grab their throats and yelled. Jamuka had already prepared for this by holding all their weapons before they stepped into his tent.

"You bastards! How could you fight against me?"

Yeke Cheren kept on yelling at them, his face flushed with anger. Jamuka and others stepped in between them and tried to stop Yeke Cheren.

"Easy! We are now friends! We are not enemies of each other anymore. Did you forget that the enemy's enemy is your friend? The past is the past. The present is more important than the past. We should cooperate with each other to remove our common enemy, Temujin. All this happened because of Temujin."

Jamuka calmed them down and offered them their seats. Jamuka ordered his servants to bring wine and food quickly, trying to change the mood.

After confirming everybody had his own wine goblet, Jamuka raised his and said, "It is not an easy job to remove Temujin. However, it is not impossible either. If we work together, we will surely get what we want. Let's have a toast for our future success."

They all raised their wine goblets. Yeke Cheren and his son also raised their goblets, hesitantly. The men all talked, discussed and had many drinks until late in the evening.

Wang-Khan Refuses Temujin's Hand

Another new spring had arrived. It was 1203 and the year of the boar in the Mongol chronicle. Temujin was now thirty-six years old. Temujin and Borte had four sons and five daughters. Temujin named his four sons Juchi, Chagatai, Ogodei and Tolui. Juchi, the firstborn son, was now seventeen years old and began to join his father on the battleground and hunting field. He already showed his talent and valor as an excellent hunter and an outstanding warrior. Like the first son should, he became a good companion to his father.

One day, Temujin called Juchi while he was with Borte. In his yurt, in his comfortable Mongolian del, Temujin was enjoying his green tea on his sofa after breakfast. Borte was next to him and in front of her was a silver cradle in which a year-old daughter was sleeping, wrapped in silk swaddling clothes. Borte now had crow's feet around the outer corners of her eyes and yet they did not detract from her original beauty. Though it was early spring, the weather was cold and the wood chips were burning in the bronze stove, throwing occasional orange flames up like they were dancing. A few serving women were moving around to clean up the table and to organize things in the yurt.

Temujin said to Borte, "Fujin, I am going to ask Wang-Khan for his daughter, Chaul Beki's, hand in marriage for our Juchi. What do you think about that?"

Fujin was the title given to noble women and the official name for Borte was "Borte Fujin." Temujin had some plans for the new spring. He wanted to do what a Mongolian father was supposed to do, find future spouses for his children who had reached marriageable age.

"I saw her once, too. If it's her, I wouldn't mind. However, do you think they will say yes, my lord?"

Wang-Khan's daughter's official name was Chaul Beki and Beki was also a title for a man or woman in a high social position. Chaul Beki was Wang-Khan's only daughter and Nilka Senggum's sister.

Temujin answered, "I don't know. But you know that I have to find somebody for Juchi."

After saying this, Temujin put his teacup on the table and guffawed.

This time, Borte asked Temujin cautiously, "How about letting our Qojin Beki marry Tusaqa, Nilka Senggum's son, under the condition that we are asking for Chaul Beki's hand? I think that would make things easier, my lord."

Qojin Beki was Temujin's fifteen-year-old firstborn daughter, and Tusaqa was Nilka Senggum's first son. Temujin gave a little thought about that and then nodded. Double marriage between two families was quite acceptable in Mongolian society and was common at that time.

A report came from the guard that Juchi had arrived. Juchi had rushed to his father's yurt, leaving his work behind, when he heard his father wanted him. Borte gave him a broad smile, as if she were very happy with him. As the baby began to cry, Borte called out to the serving women to take care of the baby.

After looking at him for a while, Temujin allowed him to sit on the dark-brown chair near his sofa.

"Is Chagatai still teasing you?"

Temujin asked Juchi. This was because of the gossip going around that questioned whether Juchi was Temujin's real son or Chilger Boko's, who had abducted Borte for a while. At one time, Temujin decreed that anyone who talked about this topic should be beheaded. Nonetheless, with the lapse of time, suddenly Temujin's thirteen-year-old son, Chagatai, began to tease him on many occasions, saying, "The Merkid bastard!" Temujin, who considered this serious, tracked down the source of the gossip and cut off the heads of an old man and a serving woman, with his own hand, for starting this gossip.

Jealousy among siblings is a primordial instinct. It is seen in a newly hatched eagle chick pushing the other un-hatched eggs from the nest. Brothers and sisters can be best friends or worst enemies. Temujin knew that. Temujin had heard numerous times from his mother, Ouluun, the lesson of the five arrows. Now it was time for Temujin to tell the same story to his children.

To his father's question, Juchi answered with smiling face, as if it were a matter of no importance, "No, he is not."

Temujin nodded, relieved, and said, "You are my first son. Always remember that!"

Temujin emptied the tea in his Chinese porcelain cup and called the serving women to take it away. He then said, "You have reached the marriageable age. You are seventeen now. I married at seventeen."

Mongolian men were supposed to get married when their age was an odd number, according to their custom. That meant if he didn't get married at seventeen, he would have to wait until he was nineteen.

Temujin continued, "My son, a good man always has a good woman behind him. I was lucky to have a good mother and a good wife to be your mother. I always thanked God for that. To find a good spouse is very important. You will be heard soon. You'd better get ready for that emotionally."

This time Juchi asked anxiously, "Father, who is she?"

Since Temujin couldn't answer quickly, Borte did, instead.

"She is Wang-Khan's daughter, Chaul Beki. You saw her before. We are just going to ask for her hand."

Juchi kept silent. Chaul Beki was seventeen years old, the same as Juchi. Her mother, the first official wife of Wang-Khan, after giving birth to Nilka Senggum, couldn't have another baby for a long time. Then suddenly, she got pregnant again after she was forty years old, and died after childbirth. The second child was Chaul Beki. Wang-Khan loved this daughter very much and Nilka Senggum also treasured her as his only sibling.

Three days later, Temujin sent out three messengers to Wang-Khan's ordu. After receiving Temujin's messengers, Wang-Khan summoned Nilka Semggum. Wang-Khan said to Nilka Senggum, "Temujin is asking for Chaul Beki for his son, Juchi. This is under the condition that he will give his daughter, Qojin Beki, for our Tusaqa. What do you think?"

Temujin was not to Nilka Senggum's liking. It had become worse since Wang-Khan declared Temujin as his number-one official successor. Temujin's proposal didn't appeal much to him, with his emotional nature. Nilka Senggum moved his chair close to Wang-Khan's sofa and said with a displeased look, "Father, I cannot accept his proposal."

Wang-Khan regarded him with surprise and asked him bluntly, "Why? Juchi is a good one. I saw him a few times."

Nilka Seggum tried to explain to his father with a more displeased look, "Father, Temujin is the number-one official successor of our Keraits. He and his family members wouldn't think much of our Chaul. If his daughter is coming to us, she will sit at the north, looking to the south; on the other hand, if Chaul goes there, she will sit at the south, looking at the north."

Inside the Mongol yurts, without exception, the north side was for the head of the family and the southern side was for the servants. The Mongols considered the north side more important than the south, just like the right side to the left. They used to put the ritual utensils for ancestor-worship service, which were considered to be the most important items in every household, on the northern table, and, on the southern table, they put the kitchen utensils or minor things.

Wang-Khan sat back in his sofa, letting out a moan. He pondered a while and then said to his son with a distressed look, "Now I know your thinking and so I won't talk about that any more. I will refuse his proposal."

Wang-Khan gestured him to leave.

At that time on the Mongolian Plateau, the matrimonial matters among the ruling class were closely related to politics. If one tribe or clan wanted to forge a close relationship with another, the shortcut was to make a marital relationship. If everything went smoothly, it was good for both; if not, sometimes it started a war.

Upon receiving the reply of refusal, a dark cloud passed over Temujin's face and he was very displeased.

Temujin Khan,
Even though you are the first in line

Of the Keraits succession,
You are still just one of my vassels.
How can a subordinate ask for his master's daughter's
hand, first?

That was the first incident that soured the relationship between Temujin and Wang-Khan.

CHAPTER FORTY-NINE

Jamuka's Strike Back

J amuka made a visit to Nilka Senggum with Altan, Quchar, Sugeetei, Tooril, Qachiun Beki and Ebugejin. Nilka Senggum was staying on the plain near the Berke Ravine of the Jejeer Range, on the northeastern side of the Mongolian Plateau. Wang-Khan was at the Ergune Riverside, which was about 30 miles from Nilka Senggum's campsite.

Nilka Senggum met Jamuka and his company in front of his tent. As Jamuka and the others dismounted their horses, the guard soldiers took over the reins and took them to a place with a manger for food and water. The other group of guard soldiers, in front of the tent, disarmed Jamuka and his company. Jamuka raised his two arms high and greeted Nilka Senggum, "Hello Senggum, long time no see!"

"Hi, Sechen, it's been a while. Good to see you!"

They hugged and touched their cheeks, one side after another. Jamuka's official name was Jamuka Sechen. Sechen meant wise man and Senggum meant general. Therefore, in the case of Nilka Senggum, Nilka was the real name and Senggum was the title. However, people around him usually called him "Senggum" in a friendly way. The Mongols did not have family names. They just put their title in the front or back of their names if they had a title. Nilka Senggum welcomed all the others, too. He had already heard about Altan and Quchar leaving Temujin and joining Jamuka.

Clean water was provided for Jamuka and his company to wash their hands. The Kerait serving women came up with silver basins filled with water, one for each guest. Behind them, another group of women was holding white cotton towels. Nilka Senggum showed his guests into his tent. The huge tent was decorated with luxurious and expensive items, and the floor was covered with high-quality carpets from Bukhara. Nilka Senggum offered them a seat and ordered the serving women to bring the beverages. Surprisingly, kumis was offered to them, even though it was early spring. Normally, kumis is available in the summer time only. Nilka Senggum, a regular drinker and a wine-lover, let his cooks develop year-round kumis, with the same quality and taste as the summer kumis.

Nilka Senggum raised his golden goblet high and said to them, "Let's have a toast! I appreciate your coming from such a far, distant place."

They had a toast. Soon after, the Kerait women in their silk garments stepped in with large silver plates stacked with various cuisines, and served their master and guests. As Jamuka highly praised the quality of kumis, elated Nilka Senggum proudly remarked, "I have 40 cooks in my kitchen and some of them are specialists in brewing kumis."

They exchanged idle chitchat about food and wine for a while and then Jamuka suddenly changed the subject, "Have you ever been to one of Temujin's dinner parties?"

At Jamuka's question, Nilka Senggum replied with a displeased look, "He doesn't know how to enjoy his life. He does not drink and he eats slave food. I wonder what he is living for."

Jamuka guffawed and asked again, "Is it true that Temujin asked for the big brother's daughter's hand for his son?"

Jamuka used to call Wang-Khan big brother. The relationship between Temujin and Wang-Khan was foster son to father; on the other hand, Jamuka to Wang-Khan was younger brother to older brother. Nilka Senggum gave an answer with a more displeased look, "That is true. I gave him a flat refusal. I do not like Temujin. I would rather burn my sister than send her to Temujin's."

Nilka Senggum gulped down his kumis nervously, as if he was angry at something. Jamuka looked at him quietly and then asked in a calm tone, "Senggum, do you know why Temujin asked for your sister for his son?"

Putting his goblet on the table, Senggum looked into Jamuka's eyes quietly. Jamuka continued, "He wanted to solidify his position as the ranking, number one successor of the Keraits' throne. If you refused it, you did the right thing."

Having heard this, Nilka Senggum squinted his eyes and shook his right, clenched fist, "Is Temujin keeping his eye on the Keraits' throne? Never! As long as I am alive, it won't happen!"

Jamuka remarked, with a serious expression, "But, your father already officially declared Temujin as his ranking number one successor. Didn't he?"

To Jamuka's remarks, Nilka Senggum spat out his words, "That's my father's decision! Not my decision!"

Their conversation was stopped temporarily when two Kerait serving women with carafes in their hands began to fill up their empty goblets, one by one. Nilka Senggum picked up one piece of venison in front of him and put it into his mouth.

Chewing the meat, he asked Jamuka, "What do you think, Sechen?"

After a sip of kumis, Jamuka answered, "Well, I am the third party ... so, hard to say. But, if I was in your situation, I would try my best to retrieve the number one succession rank, as soon as possible."

With an attitude of deep concern and interest, Nilka Senggum took a sip of kumis and then asked Jamuka, looking into his eyes, "My father approved Temujin as the number one ranked in succession. What can be done, when my father is still alive?"

Jamuka regarded him with pity and then said, "The decision has been made by your father, so it should be changed by him, while he is still alive. If not, even though you retrieve it later, it cannot be legitimate. It simply would be usurpation."

Nilka Senggum suddenly seemed to lose his appetite. He stopped eating and drinking and sat back in his chair. He sat there staring into space for a while. Jamuka watched him silently and then said to him, tapping on his shoulder, "Senggum, persuade your father."

At these words, Nilka Senggum sat straight and said angrily, "My father never takes back his decisions. What shall I do with my mouth and tongue?"

Jamuka sat closer to Nilka Senggum and whispered, "Remove Temujin; that is the only absolute way. Tell your father this, 'The Keraits should be ruled by the Keraits.'"

After these words, Jamuka gazed at him for a while. Then he continued, "Senggum, look, these two decent men, Altan and Quchar were with Temujin for years before they left him. They are now strongly against Temujin. This shows clearly that Temujin is unreliable and untrustworthy. Once he has the Kerait people in his grasp, he will surely enslave them and use them as a war-machine for his dark plan. The safety and well-being of the Kerait people can hardly be expected under his rule. All these people here, today, gathered with only one common goal, which is to remove Temujin. Help us, and retrieve your future Kerait throne."

Nilka Senggum sat back in his chair again. A moment later, he nodded slowly.

Jamuka continued, "I don't have troops. You know that your father took over my commandership. However, once the battle starts, I will support you from the side with all these people. And I will persuade your father in my own way, too."

After dinner, they moved to a round table and discussed the plan over tea.

A few days later, Nilka Senggum sent out a messenger to his father, who was staying at the Ergune Riverside. Wang-Khan was enraged when he heard the message from Sayqan Todeen, Nilka Senggum's messenger.

"What? Remove Temujin? Who said that? Senggum did? Go back and tell Senggum we would not exist without Temujin! He is the back-bone of our Keraits!"

Wang-Khan kicked out Sayqan Todeen. As if he were tired from his anger, he sank into his sofa and ordered the serving woman to bring sheep's milk.

He pondered a while, and then called one of his men, "Go and tell Jamuka to present himself here, right now!"

Wang-Khan thought that Jamuka was the only one who could tempt Senggum into this. Jamuka arrived at Wang-Khan's tent late in the afternoon of that day. As Jamuka showed up in front of him, Wang-Khan drew out his scimitar and readied himself to cut off his head.

"You, rat! You lured Senggum into this, didn't you?"

Jamuka answered, kneeling on one knee, "Yes, I did, big brother! But, please, listen to me for one moment. You can cut off my head after my words. It won't take long."

As Wang-Khan was hesitating, Jamuka began to talk.

"Big brother, I know Temujin very well. I know what is in his mind clearly. He plans to have all the tribes on the Plateau in his hands. There are no exceptions! Even the Keraits!

Originally, he was with me. But, one day, he left me without even a single word. Then, he became my enemy. Is there any guarantee that it won't happen to you?"

Wang-Khan put his scimitar back into his sheath and sat in his chair.

Jamuka continued, "Big brother, Temujin is like a bilduur. He migrates from one place to another in each season. I am a qayirukana, which stays in one place and never moves to another because of weather."

The bilduur, which Jamuka mentioned in his remarks, was a migratory bird, like a wild goose, and the qayirukana was a lark. Wang-Khan began to suffer from emotional conflict. He sank himself into the chair, put one hand on his forehead and gestured with the other for Jamuka to leave.

Senggum sent out his second messenger, and yet, he still could not get the approval from his father, so he made a visit in person. Wang-Khan yelled at his son when he saw him.

"Don't you know Temujin is our main supporter? Thanks to him, we have made it so far! Against all this, if we try to remove him now, we won't be loved by the Heavens anymore!"

However, Senggum was ready for this, "Father, Temujin does not think much of us. He asked your daughter first! What kind of manners is that? That happened while you are still alive. When you are no longer in this world, what in the world will happen? It is very clear to me!"

Wang-Khan calmed himself down and tried to persuade his son in a soft tone, "We don't need to remove Temujin. We only need to weaken his power. He is still useful to us."

After these words, Wang-Khan gestured him to come closer and whispered to him, "Temujin's brother, Kasar, is helping us. If we can separate them, Temujin won't be a threat to us anymore."

Kasar's wife was a daughter of the chieftain of a certain tribe, which belonged to Wang-Khan. For this, Kasar was a frequent visitor to Wang-Khan's ordu. Wang-Khan and Kasar got together on several occasions in private. Wang-Khan noticed that Kasar was as ambitious as his brother, Temujin, and so he began to take advantage of it.

However, Nilka Senggum's main concern was to retrieve his number one ranking in the succession list. He knew that he had to remove Temujin to reach that goal.

"Father, my main concern is who will be your successor. Temujin is not a Kerait! How could a non-Kerait, like him, become the ruler of the Keraits? Why are you going to hand this nation as a whole over to somebody else, which you and your father, Kyriakus Khan, had taken pains to build up? You have two choices, father: Approve my plan or take him off the succession list."

Wang-Khan burst out again, "You really don't understand! Without him, we can stand no more! I can approve nothing!"

Getting on his feet, Nilka Senggum let out his ultimatum, "Father, this is the last between you and me. I am not your son anymore!"

Senggum kicked out the door and left. Wang-Khan suffered from heavy emotional pain. Senggum was his only son. He spent the whole evening and night, agonizing over whether to approve Senggum's plan or not. He concluded that his appointment of Temujin as his successor had been made not by his own will but by the inevitable situation. What you have in your mind will decide who will be in your mind. At last, Wang-Khan approved Senggum's plan to remove Temujin.

CHAPTER FIFTY

Munglik's Advice

A group of people gathered in Jamuka's tent. Besides Jamuka and Senggum, they were Altan, Quchar, Sugeetei, Tooril, Qachiun Beki, Ebugejin and Yeke Cheren. They sat down around a round table and began to plot how to remove Temujin from the plateau forever.

Jamuka opened his mouth and started, "The best way to win is to win without fighting."

All the attendants kept silent, pondering the complexity of his meaning.

Jamuka continued, looking at Senggum, "To catch a poisonous snake safely, you have to hold the head. If you hold the middle or the tail part by mistake, you will get bitten."

Since Senggum shrugged and kept silent, Jamuka guffawed and explained, "Without Temujin, they are just an unruly mob. If we remove Temujin, they will automatically collapse."

After these words, Jamuka gazed at Senggum with a serious look and said, "Invite Temujin, and we will do the rest."

Since Nilka Senggum asked for a more detailed explanation, Jamuka replied in a slow and clear voice, "Send messengers to Temujin through your father. Tell Temujin your father has happily approved the marriage of his daughter, Chaul Beki, to Temujin's son Juchi. Invite them for an engagement ceremony and they will surely come!"

After these words, Jamuka looked around inside the tent cautiously. Two men were standing straight at the left and right sides of the northern wall, and two other men were at both sides of the southern door, making four in total. They were all wearing round metal rings on their necks, the symbol of a slave. In response to Jamuka's eye movement, Senggum quickly said, "Don't worry, they don't have tongues. And nobody can come close to this tent until the end of our meeting."

They discussed until late in the evening and made a detailed plan. During the celebration banquet, at a signal from Senggum, Jamuka and all the others would step into the banquet hall. Ebugejin and Qachiun Beki would hold Temujin's hands and legs and then Altan and Quchar would hit him on his head and chest with axes. That was their scenario, and they also decided to put sixty axmen around the banquet area, just in case.

It was a fine spring day. The Wang-Khan's emissary and eight other members arrived at Temujin's ordu. They were clad in formal, light-colored silk dresses with luxurious designs and wearing short, cylindrical, black sable caps. One of them was holding Wang-Khan's golden, triangular banner with an eagle's image on it. Temujin put on a formal dress and received Wang-Khan's emissary.

"Greetings from the honorable Wang-Khan and his family! Wang-Khan and his family gladly accepted your proposal to tie two families together through marriage. The last day of this month could be an auspicious day, and so an engagement ceremony will be arranged on that day. Temujin Khan and the future bridegroom are cordially invited to attend, to make this celebratory event happen."

Wang-Khan's emissary recited this message and handed over the engagement gift box, wrapped with red silk cloth. Temujin showed them into the visitor's tent and they were served tea and cookies. Temujin and Borte opened the box in their yurt. They found a golden belt and a milk-colored pearl necklace, presumably for Temujin and Borte. Borte touched it and had the feeling of the bright and shining pearl necklace for a moment and then asked Temujin, taking her hand off it, "My lord, I wonder what has motivated them to change their minds?"

Temujin kept silent for a while and then answered, looking at Borte, "People change their minds all the time. It looks weird to me as well, but I am not in the position to refuse this."

At that time, Mongolian custom allowed the bride's family to pick the date for the engagement and wedding ceremonies, and all the events took place at the bride's home. There was nothing wrong with Wang-Khan's invitation. If Temujin refused the invitation without good reason, it would be a big humiliation to Wang-Khan and his family. Temujin forced himself to accept the invitation, regardless of Borte's suggestion to delay the event with an excuse.

Temujin set out on his journey to the north, in the direction of Wang-Khan's ordu, with his son Juchi and about only ten guard soldiers. They left early in the morning and in the late afternoon, they arrived at Munglik's camp town, which was on their way. Temujin decided to stay overnight there. Munglik was the long-time retainer for Temujin's family, and Yesugei, Temujin's father, had personally asked him to take care of his children before he had passed away. Since then, he had been loyal to Temujin's family, except for one incident, and so Temujin treated him like his own father.

The nomadic people on the Mongolian Plateau, moved around from one place to another with each season, and, in many cases, scattered around in a wide area even though they were in the same group. That was mainly because of the grazing ground. The bigger the group and the more livestock they had, the larger the grazing ground needed.

That evening, Temujin had dinner with Munglik and his sons. Kokochu, Munglik's fourth son and the official chief priest of Temujin's ordu, happened to be in his father's camp town, and so he joined the dinner. His nickname was Tab Tenggri, which meant the highest heaven.

Munglik said to Temujin, "Temujin, there's something fishy about their invitation. At first, they refused it, and then later, they approved it. The reason they refused your proposal was because they don't trust you. There's no reason they would change their minds. There could be a dark plot in this. I think you'd better not go."

After his father, Kokochu added, "My lord, I think my father is right. A few months ago, I got a message from Wang-Khan that he wanted to see me on a personal basis. I couldn't see any reason to see him, so I ignored it. I think he has some kind of intention to separate us and eventually weaken our power. I also think it would be better to reconsider."

Temujin stopped eating and gazed into space for a while. Temujin's decision was quick. He decided to accept Munglik and his son's advice.

Temujin picked two men out of ten, and sent them out to Wang-Khan's ordu as messengers. They were briefly trained to explain why Temujin couldn't make it. The two messengers, Buqatai and Kiratai, delivered the message in front of Wang-Khan, exactly the way they were told to.

"Temujin Khan tried to attend the ceremony at first. However, since this is the early part of spring, he thinks it is not a good time to have such an important event. He said nowadays he is very busy feeding the horses, which were weakened during the winter. So, he ardently wishes to reschedule the engagement ceremony at some other time when things are much easier."

After listening to this message, Wang-Khan shouted, hitting the handle of his chair with his fist, "What? Temujin has refused to come?"

There was a stir among the men who were standing around Wang-Khan. Jamuka approached Wang-Khan and whispered,

"Big brother, it is very clear Temujin has sensed our plan. We have to take action immediately."

Wang-Khan jumped up from his chair and shouted, "Take them into custody!"

Wang-Khan summoned all the chieftains and generals under his rule and had an urgent meeting.

Badai and Kishlik, the Sheepherders

At Wang-Khan's urgent meeting, besides Jagambu and Senggum, all the chieftains and generals under his rule were present. However, the ones who were with Jamuka, including Altan and Quchar, were not allowed to attend the meeting, with the exception of Jamuka, who was acknowledged as a talented strategist by Wang-Khan. Wang-Khan looked around and said, "War is inevitable with Temujin. If you have any ideas, tell me!"

Jamuka, who was sitting next to Wang-Khan, opened his mouth and said, "The best strategy at this time is to dispatch the troops and surround him as soon as possible. If possible, we'd better depart this evening and attack him early tomorrow morning. We have to hurry. Time is on his side."

Wang-Khan asked, "What is the size of Temujin's troops? Has there been any change in his numbers?"

Senggum answered his question, "Temujin's own troops are just about 7,000. But it is presumed that he lost many of them in last year's battle with the Tartars."

Jamuka added, "Temujin has recovered a lot. Probably up to 6 or 7,000 now. However, some other tribes with him could be the trouble."

In response to Jamuka's answer, Wang-Khan asked, "Who will be with him?"

Jamuka answered, "The Uruuds and Mangkuds will be with Temujin. Their numbers are only about 2,000 each, and yet they are formidable ones. They are well-organized and each of their soldiers is highly trained with many different kinds of weapons."

Wang-Khan gave a little thought and said conclusively, "Our vanguard will be the Jirgins. Qadak! Where are you?"

At Wang-Khan's calling, one man jumped to his feet and answered, "Yes, my lord! Qadak is here!"

The Jirgins were well known for their valor, and Qadak was their chieftain. Wang-Khan appointed Achik Shirun of the Tubegen as the backup troops for the vanguards, in case they were broken down. The head of the third follow-up troops was Olon of the Dongqayids, and the fourth was Qori Shilemun Tashi, the chief of Wang-Khan's royal guards. The commander of the center force was Wang-Khan himself, with Jamuka as his advisor. Wang-Khan decided to mobilize a total of 40,000 cavalry. They set out immediately.

After the meeting, Jamuka met separately with his participants, Altan, Quchar, Sugeetei, Tooril, Qachiun Beki, Ebugejin and Yeke Cheren, and let them know the decisions and plans about the upcoming war. They all decided to join Wang-Khan's operation.

Yeke Cheren hurriedly returned to his yurt to get ready for the departure. He didn't have any troops, so he agreed to join Qachiun Beki's troops.

Returning, he said to his wife, Alak Yid, "Get ready to move. I am joining the battle. We have to leave early in the evening, so hurry and pull down the yurt and pack up!"

At that time, when they joined a big battle, their whole family moved with the troops. Usually, the families followed behind the troops.

His wife, Alak Yid, gazed at him for a while as if she were dumbfounded, and then said, "Did you forget you don't have any troops? All you have now is me and your son!"

Embarrassed, Yeke Cheren tried to make her understand, "Wang-Khan of the Keraits has already started taking steps to remove Temujin. He and his troops will leave this evening to attack him. I am joining the battle with Jamuka."

Alak Yid responded, with a look of unhappiness and insult, "Wang-Khan is going to remove Temujin? What's in it for us? You have already lost all your people. You cannot bring them back! It wouldn't make a difference! It's their war, not ours!"

She spat these words nervously and muttered to herself, "I heard Yesui became Temujin's second wife. To remove Temujin now is only to make our Yesui a widow."

Yeke Cheren just stood there, because he didn't know how to answer.

Badai had overheard all this from beginning to end as he was carrying a wooden bucket filled with fresh sheep's milk and trying to deliver it to the yurt. When Yeke Cheren visited

Jamuka after he had successfully escaped from the battlefield, Jamuka helped him with forty sheep, two camels and two slaves. Badai and Kishlik were the slaves sent by Jamuka, and they were sheepherders.

Badai realized that he had just heard very important information. He went out to the field to look for Kishlik. Badai met him in the field where he was tending sheep and asked for his opinion on what he had heard.

"If it's true, it is very urgent and important information for Temujin Khan. What shall we do?"

As he was saying this, Kishlik studied Badai's face.

Badai said to Kishlik with a firm, definitive tone, as if he had already made up his mind, "Kishlik, we must help Temujin Khan. Do you know why? We are slaves. To remove the bondage of slavery we are wearing, we have to go to Temujin Khan and join him. Temujin Khan doesn't allow slavery in his system. I have heard what he eats and wears are not much different from what we do now. Who do you want to help?"

Kishlik answered, holding his hands firmly, "Right! You just said what I wanted to say. I am with you. However, since this is very important information, we can't make a mistake. We'd better double-check."

Badai nodded. Kishlik walked to the yurt with the wooden buckets in his hands. Narin Keen, Yeke Cheren's son, was sharpening arrowheads in front of the yurt and yelled at Kishlik when he caught sight of him.

"Where have you been? I have been looking all over for you!"

Kishlik walked up to him and asked, "Yes, my master, what can I do?"

Narin Keen said to Kishlik, as he continued his work, "We are going to war. Before sunset, finish packing up, bring the horses back from the field and put the saddles on them!"

Kishlik asked, "Master, if you are going to war, does the whole family move, or only you and your father?"

Narin Keen answered, continuing to sharpen the arrowheads, "This evening, only my father and I are leaving. You and Badai have to take my mother to Wang-Khan's ordu early in the morning. There, you will find Jamuka Sechen's family. Just join with them. Do you know where Wang-Khan's ordu is?"

Kishlik answered, "Yes, I know, master. Is it that urgent that the whole family cannot move together? Which soldiers should I be careful of while I am taking your mother to Wang-Khan's ordu?"

Narin Keen briefly stopped his sharpening and then answered, restarting his work, "Wang-Khan is going to attack Temujin. We are on Wang-Khan's side."

Badai and Kishlik galloped at full speed without pause. They were riding fine steeds with the names of Merkidei Chakaan and Chakaan Keer, which were owned by Yeke Cheren and his son, Narin Keen, respectively. The steppe aristocrats used to give names to their horses. They were swift. They arrived at Temujin's ordu about two or three hours later. Temujin was about to go to bed early, after dinner. Temujin got an urgent report from the guard soldiers. Since Temujin didn't know the two men, he ordered them to make the report directly from outside the yurt in a loud voice.

"An urgent message for Temujin Khan! We have information that Wang-Khan's troops will leave this evening to surround Temujin Khan and attack early tomorrow morning!"

Temujin jumped to his feet. After picking up his scimitar from the table next to his bed, he went out. Temujin took a torch from a guard soldier and lit up the two men's faces. They were not familiar to Temujin. "Who are you?" he demanded.

To Temujin's question, Badai answered, "Originally, we belonged to Jamuka Sechen. However, since last autumn, we are with Yeke Cheren and his family as their servants. We have heard, today, early in the afternoon, that Wang-Khan's troops will leave early in the evening to attack Temujin Khan at day-break tomorrow."

Temujin eyed them carefully.

When Temujin's eyes turned to the two white horses they had brought, he immediately summoned two Tartar women who used to be with Yeke Cheren. The two women fully recognized the two white horses.

"These two horses belong to Yeke Cheren and his son Narin Keen."

The two women even knew the names of the horses.

Temujin accepted Badai and Kishlik's words. Temujin proclaimed a state of emergency. The sound of horns blowing and drumbeats echoed through Temujin's ordu and the fire arrows and the whistling arrows were continuously being shot into the sky to tell his widely spread troops that an urgent situation was upon them. Temujin kept on shouting, "Retreat to the south at full speed! Give up all the property and livestock! Pick up only your horses, weapons and emergency food!"

Temujin retreated to the south at maximum speed all through the night. It was an impending crisis and Temujin was on the brink of being exterminated.

Jurchedai and Quyilda, the Warriors

Temujin galloped all through the night with his troops and his people. In many places, they couldn't speed up because of darkness and unfavorable road conditions. They had to find their way with torches. The dim light of the crescent moon was falling on their heads and shoulders like fog. The night air on the steppe was cold; nonetheless, they had to keep on wiping the sweat from their foreheads. Temujin arrived at Mau Height, which was about eighty miles from their starting point, when the silhouette of the high and low eastern hills began to show. Temujin appointed Jelme as the head of the rear guards, whose function was important when retreating. Temujin put two sentries on top of Mau Height. Even after daybreak, Temujin kept on galloping and around noon, they arrived at Qara Haljin, the hill covered with dark forests. Both men and horses were exhausted, so they decided to take a break and eat.

While Temujin was taking a break, two sentries from the rear were galloping towards Temujin, creating tails of grey dust. They kept on shouting as they neared.

"The enemies, the enemies are coming!"

Temujin mounted his horse and looked back. On the horizon, he could see countless men and horses beginning to show up, making huge clouds of dust. Temujin retreated twenty more miles and set up his war camp against the background of the huge Khingan Mountains. It was favorable for Temujin, in case of a retreat, for him and his troops to hide in the mountains. Temujin and Wang-Khan's troops faced each other between several small hills and streams. It was also important for Temujin when he had to deal with the enemies, who outnumbered his troops four to one.

A choking, tense atmosphere hung between them and death was in the air. Temujin had the experience of many tough battles, but he still felt a sense of urgency. Temujin knew this was the decisive battle either for himself or Wang-Khan. For Temujin, who lost his father at an early age, Wang-Khan had been like his own father. He relied on, trusted and treated him like his own father. Now Temujin was facing him as his enemy. Temujin was sad. However, Temujin also knew sentimentalism was taboo on the battlefield. On the battlefield, only the victors will remain. The losers will vanish. Justice, freedom and the right of choice were the privileges left to the winner. Even truth and history are left in their hands.

Suddenly, an arrow came from Wang-Khan's campsite with a loud whistling sound. It lodged into the ground in the center of Temujin's camp. There was a little stir among the soldiers. A soldier brought it to Temujin. It was a godori, with an arrowhead made of cow or goat horn with many holes in it to make a whistling sound when it was shot. It was usually used for communications, not for killing. It came with a message. A small piece of rolled paper was firmly tied to the end of the arrow. It was written in Uighur letters on Chinese paper.

Temujin,

> *The Keraits' troops will attack in waves.*
> *The vanguards, 2,000 Jirgins—commander, Qadak*
> *The second attackers, 2,000 Tubegens—commander,*
>   *Achik Shirun*
> *The third attackers, 2,000 Dongqayids—commander,*
>   *Olon*
> *The fourth attackers, 2,000 royal guards—commander,*
>   *Qori Shilemun Tashi*
> *The center force, 30,000 troops—commander-in-chief,*
>   *Wang-Khan; second-in-command, Senggum; the*
>   *advisor, Jamuka*
> *The rear guards, 2,000—commander, Jagambu*
> *Be careful.*

Temujin called a meeting based on the arrival of this message. Many of the generals doubted the truth in it. However, Temujin's sixth sense told him who the sender was.

Temujin said, with a light smile on his face, "I don't know who the sender is, and yet, I think I can presume. I will take this information into consideration. If their tactic is to attack in waves, we will destroy them with the same tactic. Who wants to be the vanguard?'"

Jurchedai of the Uruuds stood up.

"I will be the vanguard with my 2,000 warriors."

However, before he finished speaking, Quyilda of the Mangkuds stood in front of him.

"I want to be the vanguard. I will fight to my last breath. Please, take care of my orphaned children after my death."

Quyilda showed his determined resolution. He became the vanguard. While the meeting was still going, an urgent message arrived that the attackers were approaching. Quyilda mounted his horse immediately and galloped out with his 2,000 warriors.

The 2,000 Jirgins led by Qadak were approaching like a roaring wave. They were fierce and valiant, worthy of Wang-Khan's vanguards. In Temujin's camp, the drummers began to beat nacaras, or tin drums, all at once, signaling that the attack had commenced. During the earsplitting drumbeats, Quyilda dashed towards the enemies with his 2,000 warriors. Quyilda was in front of his men and met with Qadak, who was also in front of his troops. The two veteran fighters dueled for a while. Each time their scimitars hit together, blue sparks came off with a clanging sound. In a short while, more than half of the soldiers in both troops fell from their horses after being cut in half or pierced through their chests or abdomens by spears. The horses that lost their riders scattered out into the field in all different directions. The fallen soldiers who could still move hooked the enemy riders down from their horses with their hooked spears and then speared them deeply in their chests or backs. Those that were doing this had their heads crushed in with maces by riders dashing around. As time went by, the picture became clear as to who was the winner. The Mangkuds had many more soldiers still on their horses.

Quyilda of the Mangkud and Qadak of the Jirgin never knew retreat. They had never been defeated. Victory or death was their only choice. At this time, Wang-Khan's second attackers, the Tubegens led by Achik Shirum, had arrived. Quyilda had to deal with these newly arrived attackers. In the meantime, Qadak and his remaining troops had retreated. Quyilda was too tired to handle the new enemy, Achik Shirun, who was full of energy. He was speared through the waist and fell down from his horse. The Mangkud warriors swarmed around to save him. This was the moment when Jurchedai, with his 2,000 Uruud warriors, arrived. Jurchedai faced the enemies while his soldiers were saving wounded Quyilda. Achik Shirun retreated after losing more than half his troops.

At this moment, Wang-Khan's third group of attackers, the 2,000 Dongqayids led by Olon showed up. Olon dashed to Jurchedai with his spear firmly gripped. He thrust his spear forward, fiercely, but it did not do decisive damage to Jurchedai. His spear tip had just touched Jurchedai's armpit. Instead, Jurchedai's battle-ax cut both Olon's helmet and skull in half, making the blood and brain tissue spurt out. Losing their leader, Olon, the Dongqayids retreated.

Next, Wang-Khan's fourth attackers, led by Qori Shilemun arrived. Soon, Qori Shilemun's neck had been cut by Jurchedai's battle-ax. Qori Shilemun's head was still with his body, but connected only by a few layers of skin that managed to stay intact.

Knowing that his attack-in-waves tactic had failed, Wang-Khan launched an all-out attack. Temujin also had to send all his troops, but a four-to-one ratio of inferiority in numbers was hard to overcome. Temujin's fate seemed to be sealed. Casualties from either side were increasing in numbers as time went by, and the fields and hills were strewn with dead bodies. At this time, something happened that influenced the direction of the war. An uchumak arrow, or an arrow with a three-pronged arrowhead, shot by Jurchedai, hit Senggum on the cheek. Senggum fell down on the ground, losing consciousness. The Kerait soldiers swarmed to save him. It was the time of the day when dusk was falling, so both sides had to retreat.

Temujin retreated to the southeast, near the forest, and waited for daybreak. Temujin reinforced his guards against possible nighttime enemy attacks. Temujin took the roll call in the darkness. He found that his ten-year-old third son, Ogodai, and his two generals, Bogorchu and Boroqul were missing. Temujin repeated the roll call, and yet there was still no answer. Temujin was gloomy. All of Temujin's soldiers slept on their horses. Near daybreak, a horse was walking slowly towards Temujin's side from the front line area. Temujin's guard soldiers tried to identify the man on the horse with their torch lights. He was like a ghost of war. His helmet was gone, his armor had been torn apart, and yet he was still holding his blood-stained spear firmly. He was Bogorchu. He looked extremely tired. Temujin helped him dismount his horse and gave him his arm to hold.

"Bogorchu! Are you all right? I have been worried about you."

Temujin ordered his men to bring something to drink. Bogorchu, holding a sheepskin bag upside down, gulped down the sheep's milk and said, "My lord, I am all right. I am just a little tired."

After these words, he guffawed. Temujin, patting his back, smiled at him. Bogorchu had had a hard time when his horse had fallen down from enemy arrows, and yet, eventually he made it, tracking Temujin's footsteps with an enemy horse he had taken.

At dawn, another horse was approaching. The man on the horse was Boroqul. He was carrying a boy in front of him who could have been either dead or alive. Both corners of Boroqul's mouth were stained with blood. The boy was Temujin's third son, Ogodai, and he had been wounded in the neck by an enemy arrow. Since the Keraits were using poison arrows, Boroqul had to suck the blood from the wound to keep him alive.

Temujin took his son down from the horse and examined the wound. A military doctor was called to take care of the wound. Having set up a fire by the soldiers, the doctor put his dagger in the flame to make it red-hot and then seared the wound with it. The boy's body was shaking vigorously as he let out horrible screams of pain, but Temujin's tough hand covered his mouth and other helping hands stabilized his body. This lasted for a while, but at last, the boy became quiet. He fainted. The doctor checked his pulse and said, "He is all right. Let him have a good rest. He will wake up."

The doctor finished his job with medication and bandages. Temujin ordered his men to take good care of his son.

At sunrise, Temujin retreated about thirty miles more to the south, arriving at the Dalan Nemulges riverside, which had been the battleground with the Tartars. They could still see decaying, dead bodies, broken war wagons and discarded weapons all around. The dead bodies had been half-eaten by wild animals, vultures and crows and the rest were weathering from natural forces. Temujin regrouped his troops there to get ready for Wang-Khan's second attack. He confirmed the remaining numbers of his troops. The number had been decreased from 11,000 to 4,600. He had lost more than half of his troops.

Temujin's Message to Wang-Khan

Wang-Khan had a meeting in his war camp to decide whether to continue the war or retreat. Wang-Khan's side had also suffered terrible damage. He lost about half of his troops, and more, his son, Senggum, was still unconscious. Against Jamuka's strong insistence that the battle should continue, Achik Shirun presented a different opinion.

"My lord, before we make a decision whether we should continue the war or not, think about what caused this war. It was because of your son, Senggum. He insisted on this war to retrieve his future khanship and the Keraits' dignity. He is still unconscious and nobody knows when he will wake up. At this point, if we continue the war, what does it mean to us? The most important thing right now is to make him wake up, and to make sure he is all right. It is clear that Temujin's troops have been badly damaged. Most of the Kyat Mongols are with Jamuka now, Altan and Quchar; the rest of Temujin's group won't be a big threat to us. Continuing the war will only weaken us."

Nobody spoke out against him. After a short silence, Wang-Khan opened his mouth slowly and said, "Right! At this moment, the most urgent thing is to make Senggum wake up. Be careful when you carry him and the doctors should do their best to make him wake up as soon as possible. We will go back."

Wang-Khan decided to retreat. They slowly moved back to the north, through Mau Height.

Confirming Wang-Khan's retreat, Temujin moved his troops to the west, through the Qalqa riverside. Since they had run out of food, they had to hunt. They picked a forest, presumably a good habitat for wild animals, surrounded it and drove the animals into the circle. While Temujin and his generals were directing and supervising the hunting operation, a huge boar broke through the encirclement and began to run away. At this sight, Quyilda rushed to chase down the boar because it was his part of the encirclement. Temujin shouted at him, trying to stop him, "Quyilda! No! Your wound has not healed yet!"

Temujin was right. Two or three days were too short for his deep wound to have healed. While he was chasing the boar, his wound reopened and the blood began to gush out. The doctors tried to stop the bleeding, but they were not successful. Enormous amounts of blood kept gushing out of the wound and he soon lost consciousness. Having checked his pulse, the doctors shook their heads, saying that he had already passed away.

Temujin buried him on top of the Keltegey Qada High Hill, near the Qalqa River. They put his favorite weapons and belongings together in his tomb. At dusk, Temujin and all his generals gathered around his tomb and bade him farewell.

Here lies a symbol of man.

> *His vigor moved mountains,*
> *And shook the heaven.*
> *Now, his body, by the will of God,*
> *Embraced by the arms of Mother Earth.*
> *And his high spirit,*
> *Like a free bird,*
> *Will be flying over the plain,*
> *Forever.*

Temujin kept on marching along the Qalqa River. Around the Qalqa River estuary to Lake Buyr lived a group of people who were a clan of the Onggirads. Even though the Onggirads were the tribe of Temujin's first wife, Borte, in the past they had joined Jamuka's allied forces. Temujin summoned Jurchedai and gave him instructions.

"Enter the Onggirads' territory. If they are cooperative, do not touch them; if they are resistant, hit them."

By the order of Temujin, Jurchedai entered the territory with his 1,000 Uruud warriors. Terge and Amel, the chieftains of the Onggirads in that area, quickly noticed Temujin's troops entering their land. They accepted Jurchedai's troops without resistance. Temujin led his troops into the Onggirads' territory. Before his move, Temujin gave a strict order to his troops that the Onggirads should not be touched and should not be looted. They were not hostile to Temujin at all. Temujin reminded them, when he met Terge and Amel, that he was a friend to the Onggirads based on marital relations.

At Temujin's remark, Terge guffawed and said, "We know! That's why we are welcoming you."

Terge sent somebody to inform Dey Sechen and his son, Alchi, of Temujin's arrival. Temujin met again with Dey Sechen and Alchi. Dey Sechen said, holding Temujin's hand, "I am sorry for the other day. That happened because our decision maker, Ala Qus, and some other chieftains had been afraid of Jamuka and his power. Alchi and I tried to persuade them, but we were not successful. Anyway, things have changed now. I think they will be different for days to come."

This time, Alchi said to Temujin, "I want to be with you someday. Call me! I will be there!"

Their words comforted Temujin. However, Temujin knew they couldn't be of any help at that point.

Temujin left the Onggirads' territory and continued his march. He arrived at the Tungge Stream, a branch of the Qalqa River. He set up his base camp there. Once everyone was there, he issued an official statement denouncing Wang-Khan, Senggum, Altan and Quchar. He picked Arqai and Sukegei as messengers to deliver his messages to Wang-Khan and the others. Temujin tried to make them realize their wrongdoings and thereby demoralize them.

By their customs at that time, messengers should not be killed on any account. Since they didn't have a writing system at that time, the messengers had to deliver verbal messages. Temujin's message to Wang-Khan was this:

What about the promise you made to me
That you will never make any decision
Until we talk with each other face to face?

I have been your loyal follower,
And have never betrayed you.

If one of two wheels of a wagon breaks down,
How can it move forward?

If one of two shafts of a cart breaks down,
How can it be pulled forward?

For your poor judgment and unwise decision,
I, your foster-son, am lamenting deeply.

Temujin also sent a message to Altan and Quchar:

I became the khan,
Not by my request but by your will.

What about your pledge you gave me?
If you fail to follow my orders,

You pledged to cut your heads off
And throw them away in a field.
Do you still remember?

You are now with my foster father, Wang-Khan.
You all know how loyal I was to him.
Now you see clearly what has happened to me.

Do you have any guarantee,
That this won't happen to you?

Temujin also sent a message to Senggum. By the time Seng-gum received Temujin's message, he was completely recovered from his wound.

My friend,
My foster-father, the khan, has two sons,
One who was born with clothes,
And the other who was born without clothes.

My foster-father loved and cared for both these sons.
Whichever he loses, he surely will suffer.
Stop bothering your father.

Even for the sheep we tender, we have two kinds,
One for milk,
And one for wool.
Consider this.

All three provided different responses to Temujin's messages. Wang-Khan agonized, Altan and Quchar snorted and Senggum got angry. Senggum yelled at Temujin's messengers.

"What? Friend? Since when did he call me a friend? Did he call my father, the foster-father 'Khan'? Nonsense! He may call my father 'the old butcher' behind his back! Sheep for milk and sheep for wool? Didn't he call me a shaman with the sartakchin sheep tail on his back?"

The sartakchins were giant sheep that lived on the Mongolian Plateau at that time. Their tails were enormously thick and long. Their tails were so big, in many cases they could completely fill the whole cart. Some shamans put this tail on their backs when they performed the rituals. Of the ones that did this, many of them couldn't even walk very well because of the weight and length of the tail. The Mongols at that time described a man who was holding a position greater than he could handle as a "shaman with the sartakchin sheep tail on his back."

Senggum said to Temujin's two messengers, "I will not accept Temujin's words. Go and tell him that the war will continue!"

Temujin's two messengers, Arqai and Sukegei, left Wang-Khan's base camp. But Sukegei didn't feel like going back to Temujin; he thought Temujin was doomed. He gave up going back to Temujin and joined Tooril, who was with Jamuka. Arqai, alone, returned to Temujin and reported everything.

CHAPTER FIFTY-FOUR

The Baljuntus

Temujin decided to hide himself for the time being. What he needed was time. The Mongolian Plateau was not a safe place for him anymore. It was another big trial for him since the loss at Dalan Baljut. Nevertheless, it never disheartened him. He headed for the south with his remaining troops. They crossed plains, deserts and went over the hills silently. Since they had run out of their rations, they had to find a way to provide for themselves. They picked up small animals on the plain to alleviate their hunger and on some lucky days, they caught wild camels. Many of his soldiers gave up the painstaking, hopeless, long march and deserted. The number of followers at the beginning of the march was reduced by half by the end.

After about 250 miles of marching, Temujin and his troops arrived at Baljuna Lake, a remote area located at the southeastern end of the Mongolian Plateau. It was at the southern end of the Khingan Mountains and close to the border with Chin. Temujin picked Baljuna Lake as his hiding place. He looked around the lake. It was small and connected with swamp area and forests at one side. He could see the light-blue image of the faraway Khingan Mountains to the northeast. The water in Baljuna Lake was not clean, it was muddy. It was a place where caravans occasionally stopped by to water their livestock. Even the caravans who were traveling the desert did not stay there. In the summer, a foul odor from the lake made it hard to breathe, and swarms of mosquitoes and flies bothered, even tormented, both men and animals. However, Temujin did not have a choice.

After rounding the lake, Temujin said to his men, "We are going to stay here for the time being. This may not be a good place to live, but it could be a good place to hide."

Temujin let his soldiers cut the trees from the nearby forest and build up a tent town. A while later, Temujin heard a commotion and went out to see what was happening. A group of soldiers had gathered at one corner of the lake, talking to each other and pointing at a certain area of the lake. Temujin walked up there. Temujin could see some dead horses and other animals through the muddy water. It was presumed that the carcasses had been there quite a long time, because many of them were mere skeletons. Temujin looked around the lake. He could see some birds were swimming on the water, while some other wild animals were drinking water at the other shore.

Temujin comforted his soldiers, "It is all right. It may be muddy, but it is not toxic. We can use this water after boiling it."

In the evening, Temujin and all his generals and tribal chieftains sat side by side around the campfire. He ordered one of his soldiers to bring a big cupful of muddy water from the lake.

With the cup in his hand, Temujin got on his feet and said in a strong voice, "I am giving my sincere appreciation to everybody here for sharing these ordeals and hardships with me. I promise that I will share with you all the glories, joys and sorrows, together, from now on. If I break my own word, I will be like the animals in the muddy water."

After these words, he took a sip of muddy water and passed it around. They all took a sip of the same muddy water, in turn. They all got on their feet and pledged allegiance to Temujin.

"We swear our allegiance to Temujin Khan that we will never give you up, in any situation, whatsoever, and will share the destiny and be loyal to our last breaths."

A total of nineteen generals and chieftains pledged. Later they were called the Baljuntus or the "muddy water drinkers" and they became the core members of Temujin's staff.

Temujin gradually began reconstructing his power while there. One day, about a month after his arrival, numerous sheep and camels were approaching the lake from the southern side, led by about ten people. Temujin sent somebody out to identify them. They were Muslim caravanners. They were on their way to the Onggut territory, which was not far from there, driving about 1,000 sheep for trade. They were coming to the lake to water their livestock. They planned to barter their sheep for sable furs. One of them, a man with a thick beard and mustache, wearing a white robe and a turban on his head, walked up to Temujin, who was watching them on the shore. When he arrived in front of Temujin, he gave the Islamic-style greeting, bowing and touching his forehead with his right hand.

"Greetings Temujin Khan! It's been a while since I last saw you."

Temujin eyed him carefully and searched his memory. He was the Muslim caravanner, Jafa. Temujin remembered that he had seen him many times before, in Wang-Khan's court. At that time, Temujin had a very good impression of him; he could speak several languages, including Persian, Mongolian and Chinese. Most of all, he was well acquainted with international politics. Jafa had also been fascinated by Temujin's character and saw him as the future ruler of the Mongolian Plateau. They had built up a friendship, staying overnight together and talking the night away on many topics, especially international politics.

"Jafa! I am so glad to see you again, after all these years!"

They hugged and touched each other's cheeks with their own. They rejoiced in their reunion, patting each other's back.

"I have been hearing about you, but I would have never imagined I would see you in a place like this."

Temujin showed him into his yurt. As before, they had a long talk over tea. Temujin heard many things about international situations from him. Jafa promised Temujin that he would support him instead of Wang-Khan, even though his present situation was very uncertain. Jafa was one of the men who had foreseen Temujin's future. He was also a very practical man. He knew how to behave himself to be a successful caravanner. Noticing Temujin's difficulties, he happily donated 1,000 sheep he had brought for trade. Later, Jafa helped Temujin in many other ways and became one of his important staff members.

People began to gather around Temujin again. One of them was Yelu Ahai, the Khitan. Yelu Ahai's ancestors were the Khitans, but since Liao, the Khitans' empire, was overthrown by the Juchids of the Chin Empire, his grandfather and father had worked for the Chin Empire. Yelu Ahai was the Chin ambassador to Wang-Khan's court. Temujin saw him many times in Wang-Khan's court and had established a good relationship with him. He, also, was one who highly valued Temujin's character and ability, and saw him as the future ruler of the Mongolian Plateau. Although he should be with Wang-Khan, in view of his position, he came to Temujin with his brother, Tuka. However, Temujin never trusted anybody at the beginning. Sometimes, it took a very long time to gain Temujin's confidence. Yet, once Temujin found their truth, he gave them almost unquestioned confidence.

"Welcome! Let's work together, for our bright future."

Temujin welcomed them. Yelu Ahai, like Jafa, was fluent in several languages, and was an expert in international affairs. He was a talented diplomat. Temujin talked with him a lot about situations in China and other countries over dinner one evening.

"What is the political and social situation in Cathay?"

In response, Yelu Ahai gave him his opinion that Chinese civilization was on the decline, their power had been weakened and they were moving toward becoming a decadent society.

"Their society has been impoverished in many ways. Honesty was considered stupidity and all strangers are enemies."

Before the downfall of any society, the collapse of the moral standards and the confusion of true value come first. Yelu Ahai told Temujin that the politics and governments of the Chin and Sung Empires were only for the aristocrats and the eunuchs, not for the people. Temujin listened silently.

"It is about time for them to start a new era," Yelu Ahai concluded. At that time, the human world was being carried by a two-wheeled cart: one wheel, the Chinese civilization, and the other, the Persian civilization. Nobody knew that, at that moment, Temujin made up his mind to conquer both civilizations and steer the human world in a new direction. Later, Yelu Ahai and his brother, Tuka, pledged their allegiance and became new Baljuntus.

Temujin had unique characteristics among other leaders. First, he was a leader of generosity and broad-mindedness. He accepted anybody who followed him and had his same aim or will. He did not discriminate against their ancestry, their race, their language or their religion. The only things that mattered to him were loyalty and honesty. He rewarded his men for their service, big or small, without fail, and conversely, he destroyed his enemies completely. He refused luxuries, and ate the same foods and wore the same clothing as the lowest-ranking soldiers. He let his men call him "Temujin," and so, even the lowest sheep herders called him "Temujin." He treated his soldiers like his own brothers, and, in front of him, the generals or the lowest-ranking soldiers were given the same individual human rights. He strictly forbade high-ranking soldiers from hitting the lower and each soldier could refuse a job given to him that was beyond his limit. The family members of the fallen soldiers had everything they needed, including daily necessities, and their children were well cared for and reared under good supervision.

Temujin never neglected his own training to build up his emotional power, to make sure his heart did not control his head. He was very cautious to not allow himself to fall deep into human emotions like pleasure, anger, love or sadness. He had a great dream, a fountain of passion, which was the energy source for his actions, and the outstanding wisdom and valor necessary to make it come true. He valued power, and pursued it diligently. He was a practical man who acknowledged that he could make his dream come true with that power.

CHAPTER FIFTY-FIVE

Fall of the Keraits

Temujin spent that summer at Baljuna. It was a long, painful summer. His soldiers, in many cases, had to drink muddy, smelly water and, in the mornings, they woke up with faces swollen from mosquito bites. Because of their insufficient food supply, Temujin had to go hunting in the faraway mountain area, risking exposure.

In early autumn, when the temperature began to drop, a man defected to Temujin; this man was meaningful to him. He was a young Kerait general, Chingai. He was not only an outstanding warrior, but also a man with brilliance and political sense. He valued Temujin highly for his leadership and philosophy and believed in his bright future, though he found him in temporarily unfavorable conditions. He wanted to fulfill his own dream through Temujin. He was a Nestorian Christian.

Temujin had the most recent, detailed information about the movements of the Keraits. Chingai said to Temujin, "Not long ago, Jamuka, Altan and Quchar made a plot to assassinate Wang-Khan, but failed. Wang-Khan tried to arrest them, but they had already escaped. They went to the Naimans, with their people. But I've heard that they lost the confidence of their own people."

Temujin knew his time had come. He immediately took action. He dispatched messengers to all the chieftains with whom he had been keeping close relations. At Temujin's call, the first one to arrive was Alchi, the Onggut. He came in with his 3,000 horse soldiers, under the permission of Ala Qus, the supreme ruler of the Ongguts. Followed by the Ongguts, were the Gorolas and the Ikires, with 2,000 horse soldiers each. In the past, they had been with Jamuka at Koyiten. However, when Jamuka's allied forces lost the battle, they surrendered to Temujin and became cooperative. Daritai, Temujin's uncle, also joined with his 2,000 troops. The others were a small number of Khitans, led by Yelu Ahai and his brother, Tuka, and some Muslim warriors. Now Temujin's troops were an international group.

Kasar, Temujin's brother, did not join the march to Baljuna, neither did Belgutei. Kasar was an ambitious man like his brother and wanted to have his own, independent power. While Temujin was busy calling for his allied troops, Kasar was visiting his in-law's hometown. His wife was the daughter of a chieftain of a tribe that belonged to Wang-Khan.

Kasar had just finished his breakfast with his wife and three sons, Yegu, Yesugge and Tuqu. Suddenly, 100 horse soldiers approached the yurt he was staying in with ground-shaking hoofbeats and noise. They were Kerait soldiers. Bewildered, Kasar opened the flap door and stepped out of the yurt. One of the soldiers, who seemed to be the captain, stepped forward and said to Kasar.

"Direct order from Wang-Khan, the lord! All of you, just as you are, have to follow me, right now!"

They were all heavily armed. Turning around, Kasar tried to step back into the yurt to pick up his scimitar, but it was too late. Several of them swiftly dismounted their horses and surrounded Kasar to hold his hands from both sides. Kasar and his family were dragged to Wang-Khan's ordu. Kasar faced Wang-Khan in his tent. Sitting on his soft sofa, Wang-Khan was enjoying a manicure by two young female slaves. Next to him, his son Senggum was sitting bent in his chair, with his two elbows on his lap, staring at Kasar as he entered. Ushered by the guard soldier, Kasar stood in front of Wang-Khan. Wang-Khan, after dismissing the two female slaves, offered a seat to Kasar.

"Hello, Kasar! It has been a while since I saw you last. How have you been?"

Wang-Khan ordered the slaves to bring tea. As the women slaves served the tea, Wang-Khan offered it to Kasar as he took a sip himself. Wang-Khan said to Kasar, while regarding him contemptuously, "I need your cooperation. I have heard a rumor that Temujin, though hiding somewhere, is trying to attempt a return. I need to find out if it is true. Can you do anything for me regarding this?"

As Kasar was keeping silent, because he did not know how to answer, Senggum intervened. He said, staring at Kasar, "We have vague information that Temujin is planning to strike back. However, we do not know his whereabouts and his present scale. We need more detailed information. My father wants not only the information, but also your help to remove him at the earliest possible time."

As Kasar continued his silence, Wang-Khan said, checking his nails one by one, which had been trimmed and polished by the women slaves, without even looking at him, "You've helped me a lot so far. I think I am going to approve you as the Kyat Mongol Khan. You do not need to serve your brother all your life. Am I right?"

Breaking his silence, Kasar opened his mouth and said gravely, "I have been looking for him myself, but to no avail. How can I find him in this vast land?"

At Kasar's reply, Senggum remarked, "We presume that he is hiding somewhere in the southern area. We sent messengers out to the Ongguts asking them if they knew his whereabouts, but they said they do not know. I think he should be somewhere around there, if you are looking for him."

Kasar sighed. Wang-Khan, as if he understood Kasar's mind, said to him in a pampering tone, "You'd be better keeping a relationship with me. Temujin cannot beat me. Even if he beats me, once he knows you helped me, he won't tolerate it."

After these words, Wang-Khan took a glance at him as if he was checking Kasar's response. Kasar nodded slowly. As Kasar agreed, Wang-Khan made a wide smile and said, "Smart decision! Later, if everything goes fine, you will be my second son."

Senggum said, "In the meantime, we will take good care of your family. Don't worry about that part, brother!"

Senggum was already using the word "brother" with him. When Senggum said that they would take good care of his family, he meant his family would be their hostages. Kasar knew that. Kasar also knew that a betrayer's female family members would become slaves and male family members would be kicked to death. That was the usual punishment at that time on the Mongolian Plateau. Kasar left Wang-Khan's tent.

Kasar set out on his journey to find Temujin with only three aides. Fifteen days were given to him. If he failed to contact Wang-Khan within fifteen days, his family members' safety could not be guaranteed. He traveled across deserts and plains. Ten days after he left Wang-Khan's ordu, he ran out of food. He had to hunt small animals in the desert and the plains for food. On the fourteenth day, he managed to get to Baljuna Lake. When Temujin saw Kasar, he hugged him and rejoiced in the reunion.

"Kasar, good to see you again. Why didn't you come earlier?"

Kasar told Temujin what had happened to him.

"Temujin, they took my family as hostages. They are in their hands now. If I don't contact them by midnight tomorrow, they will surely kill my three sons."

Temujin called an emergency meeting. Temujin said, in front of all the chieftains and generals, "If they are using my brother, we can make a reverse use of him. I will send out urgent messengers. However, the messengers should be new faces who are unknown to them. Of course, they should disguise themselves as Kasar's men."

Temujin picked two men. They should be completely trust-
worthy, fearless, strong, very skilled in handling weapons and,
most of all, eloquent. Temujin gave this job to Qaliudar of the
Jeurieds and Chaulqan of the Uriangqai. They left Temujin's
camp and rushed to Wang-Khan's ordu. Temujin also organized his troops and marched toward Wang-Khan at full speed.
The two messengers galloped all through the night and arrived
at Wang-Khan's ordu before noon the following day.

They were ushered into Wang-Khan's tent and one of them,
Qaliudar, gave the report, kneeling one knee.

"Urgent messages from Kasar! We have been sent by Kasar.
Our master has looked all around the southern area, but Temujin could not be found. According to the people around there,
about six months ago, a large group of people crossed the
border and ran away into the Chin territory. They insisted they
were Temujin and his followers. That is all he has discovered
and he is just waiting for your decision. He said he is ready to
serve you with all his mind and body."

Wang-Khan whispered to Senggum, who had been standing next to him for a while. Wang-Khan asked, looking at
Qaliudar, "Where is Kasar, now?"

Qaliudar answered, "He is staying at Arqal Geugi, near the
Kerulen riverside."

Wang-Khan, who was gazing at Qaliudar for a while with
eagle eyes, began to smile a bit and then said, "Fine! He is allowed to come under my protection."

Wang-Khan truly believed his words. Wang-Khan sent Iturgen, one of his generals, to Kasar as a guarantor for his word,

along with Qaliudar and Chaulqan. They headed for Arqal Geugi. To pass the time, they joked and giggled about women and many other things. Late in the afternoon, they arrived at Arqal Geugi. On the vast riverside of the Kerulen, a great number of Temujin's troops had gathered and their well-polished spears and javelins, along with their banners, were shining under the late afternoon sunlight. Knowing that he had been deceived, Iturgen turned his horse around and began to run back. Chaulqan immediately took an arrow from his quiver and shot at his horse. The arrow lodged in the rump of his horse, causing Iturgen to fall off. Qaliudar and Chaulqan, swiftly fell upon him, tied him up and dragged him to Temujin.

Temujin, who was fingering his golden baton, a symbol of the commander-in-chief, in his field chair, gazed at Iturgen for a while and then remarked, getting on his feet, "Take this man to Kasar! He is the one who should decide what should be done with this man."

After these words, Temujin left. Qaliudar and Chaulqan took him to Kasar, with several other soldiers. After hearing the whole story, Kasar drew his scimitar from his waist and cut off Iturgen's head, without hesitation. Iturgen's head rolled over on the ground a few times.

A surprise attack was Temujin's choice for Wang-Khan. After an early evening meal and short break, when it started to get dark, Temujin's troops began their march. Wang-Khan's ordu was on a hilly area of the Checher, downstream of the same Kerulen River. That evening, Wang-Khan was having a banquet with his generals. He was very relieved to hear the news that Temujin had disappeared somewhere.

The following day, before daybreak, Temujin had already completed his surrounding of Wang-Khan's ordu. At daybreak, Temujin's troops attacked Wang-Khan and his soldiers, who were drunk and in a deep sleep after the banquet. The battle was fierce and Wang-Khan's troops were strong enough to resist for three days and three nights. Tens of thousands of yurts were aflame, making the sky dark with smoke, even during the day. The streets were covered with dead bodies and the ground was sloppy from being soaked with human blood.

After three days and three nights, Qadak, the Kerait's commander-in-chief, gave the signal to surrender. That is how the Keraits, who had been considered the most powerful tribe on the Mongolian Plateau for a long period of time, were destroyed by Temujin and disappeared from the plateau.

CHAPTER FIFTY-SIX

The Last of
Wang-Khan

Temujin tried to find Wang-Khan and Senggum. They could not be found anywhere, not even among the stacked dead bodies. Temujin summoned Qadak, the surrendered commander-in-chief of the Keraits, and asked him, "Where are Wang-Khan and Senggum?"

Qadak answered, kneeling on one of his knees and lowering his head, "Temujin Khan, I helped them escape. I could not let them be captured by the enemy soldiers and killed with dishonor and humiliation. If you give me the penalty of death for that, I will accept it with no resistance. If you give me the chance to serve you, I promise to support you with all my heart and body, for the rest of my life."

Temujin regarded him silently for a while. He then opened his mouth heavily and said, "Your loyalty for your master is praiseworthy. I know the Kerait soldiers fought their best. I am considering giving you, and all other Kerait soldiers, a second chance. Do not change your mind."

Qadak showed his appreciation by lowering his head one more time. Unlike the Taichuts or the Tartars, Temujin gave an order for his soldiers not to kill or hurt the Keraits, unnecessarily. The casualties of war on Temujin's side were far less than Wang-Khan's and Kasar was able to have his family reunion.

Several days later, when everything was under control, Temujin put all the Kerait chieftains, generals and soldiers in an open place and shouted towards them:

Kerait brothers!

Have only one mind,
And have only one faith.

That is the only way you can win,
And you can survive on this land.

Those with clear minds,
Shall be embraced by heaven,
Yet those with cloudy minds,
Shall be refused.

Those with hot passion,
Shall be cared for by heaven,
Yet those with half-heartedness,
Shall be spat out.

Tens of thousands of ways are laid
In front of man,
Yet only one is heaven's way.

Kerait brothers!
Let's find heaven's way together.
And have our dream come true
On this endless land.

The Kerait soldiers began to shout in joy, and all the Kerait chieftains and generals pledged their allegiance to Temujin.

Temujin decided on a policy to amalgamate the two groups of people, the Mongols and the Keraits. Later, based on this policy, a great number of Kerait warriors were accepted into Temujin's troops and many royal princesses were married to Temujin himself or his descendants or the Kyat Mongol aristocrats. Chaul Beki was given to Juchi, as planned, and Ibaka, Jagambu's first daughter, became Temujin's third wife. Later, Bek Tutmish, the second daughter of Jagambu, became the first wife of Juchi, replacing Chaul Beki, who couldn't have any babies. At a later time, Sorqoqtani, Jagambu's third daughter, married Tolui, Temujin's third son.

At that time, the Mongol aristocrats were bound by levirate law, which meant they could not marry someone with the same blood, and yet they had a broad concept of individual marriage partners. Father and son could marry sisters of the same family, as long as they were of different blood and if a father or elder brother died, his son or younger brother could marry his widows. They had no limit on the number of wives, so they could have as many as wives they could afford.

Wang-Khan and his son Senggum had escaped, breaking through the encirclement on the second day of the battle, knowing that their defeat was imminent. A great number of Kerait soldiers were sacrificed to make their escape possible. They ran away in a southwestern direction. They galloped a whole day without eating anything and arrived at a place called Didig Saqal, on the Nekun riverside, which was the border with the Naimans.

They were thirsty, so they dismounted their horses and had a drink of water from the river. It was evening, and a red glow was on the western sky, and the declining sun was hanging on the western horizon. Many seasonal birds were flying over the river.

At that moment, seven or eight armed soldiers were galloping towards them from the west, along the riverside, with loud hoofbeats. At this sight, Senggum shouted at his father, Wang-Khan, hurriedly mounting his horse, "Father, the Naimans! Let's get out of here!"

Wang-Khan was fat and old, which prevented him from getting on his horse quickly, so he was surrounded and captured by the Naiman soldiers. Senggum had escaped and galloped at full speed toward the east, alone.

They were the Naiman soldiers. The Naimans were the sworn enemies of the Keraits for years.

The Naiman soldiers took him to Qori Subechi, the commander of the eastern border garrison. Qori Subechi, at that time, was staying in the garrison camp in the forest near the river. He stepped out of his tent when he heard some noise.

"What did you pick up?"

One of his soldiers answered.

"At the border, two men whom we presumed to be spies were drinking water. We lost one of them, but we have the other."

It was already getting dark, so Qori Subechi took a torch from a nearby soldier and flashed it on Wang-Khan's face. At that moment, Wang-Khan shouted at Qori Subechi.

"I am Wang-Khan of the Keraits! Don't treat me lightly!"

Surprised, Qori Subechi again flashed the torch in his face for confirmation. Unluckily for Wang-Khan, Qori Subechi had never seen him before. After a while, Qori Subechi moved the torch away from him and asked with a displeased look, "If you are Wang-Khan of the Keraits, can you prove it?"

Wang-Khan had changed his usual clothing for slave clothes to disguise himself while he escaped. And moreover, he threw away all his personal ornaments and jewelry. He had nothing to prove himself as the Keraits' Khan. The disguise that helped him safely escape had now turned on him. Qori Subechi, with an even more displeased look, handed the torch over to his soldier and spat, "Throw him away! He is either a spy or a lunatic."

He went back to his tent. The Naiman guard soldiers dragged Wang-Khan to a far-off, quiet place and cut off his head. They returned to their camp leaving his dead body there.

Elsewhere, Senggum galloped for a while in the field, which had already darkened. He could see a dim light coming from a faraway yurt in a remote area and headed for it. A middle-aged couple was living there. Senggum asked for help. Luckily, they were Keraits and recognized Senggum. They served him some leftovers of cooked mutton. The middle-aged man's name was Kokochu (but he was not the same person as Temujin's chief priest, Kokochu). He was a horse herder for the Keraits. But when the war broke out, all his horses had been retrieved by the troops, so they were just idling the days away.

The following morning, Senggum went out to the desert area with Kokochu to hunt for wild horses, which were occasionally found in the desert, and for provisions for his long journey. However, Kokochu was in no mood to help Senggum, a fugitive. It was not safe for him to help him, and besides, if he could take the information to Temujin, he would probably get a big reward. While Senggum was busy chasing the wild horse, he left there with his and Senggum's horses. When he arrived at his yurt, he told his wife to pull the yurt down quickly. After explaining his plan, he urged swift movements.

However, his wife scowled at him, "How can you do that? He is still your master, though he is a fugitive. Maybe you shouldn't help him and risk your life, but how can you leave him in the middle of the desert?"

Kokochu yelled at his wife, "Just do what I have said!"

His wife reluctantly pulled down the yurt and followed him. However, his wife couldn't free herself of the guilt of leaving Senggum alone in the desert.

She shouted at her husband, "At least leave him a cup so that he can use it for water!"

Unlike his father, Senggum was carrying a bag on his horse filled with necessary items, including golden cups. Kokochu gave a glance at his wife and turned his horse around, picking up one of the golden cups from the bag. When he arrived near the spot where Senggum was standing in exhaustion, he threw the cup towards him and said, "Take it!"

Kokochu and his wife arrived at Temujin's camp. Their information was invaluable. Now Temujin had the information of Wang-Khan and Senggum's whereabouts. They had convincing evidence: Senggum's belongings. Temujin met with them separately.

After hearing from both husband and wife, Temujin asked his staff, standing in a line around his chair, "This man, the horse herder Kokochu, has surely abandoned his master. Can we accept him as one of us?"

They all shook their heads, answering in the negative. Kokochu was dragged out and lost his head.

Temujin dispatched urgent messengers to the Naimans asking them to turn Wang-Khan over to him, and at the same time, sent out a chasing unit in pursuit of Senggum. Upon receiving

Temujin's messengers, Tayang Khan, the ruler of the Naimans, was astonished at the news and immediately dispatched his men to Qori Subechi to bring Wang-Khan to him. Since Wang-Khan had been cut into two pieces, Qori Subechi picked up his head from the field, put it into a wooden box and sent it to Tayang Khan.

Tayang Khan opened the box and picked up Wang-Khan's head by grabbing the hair, and made sure it was Wang-Khan's head. Wang-Khan's face was scratched and damaged by the desert fire ants.

Tayang Khan spat, throwing Wang-Khan's head on the ground.

"Old monster! Finally, you end up like this!"

He went back to his tent without leaving any instructions for Wang-Khan's head. Gurbesu, on the other hand, cleaned up Wang-Khan's head, wrapped it in a white wool cloth, and gave him an immediate, but short, funeral. Gurbesu put Wang-Khan's head on the arranged ceremonial table, and poured wine into a golden goblet placed in front of his head. She called in musicians to play the funeral music and let the Naiman princesses and royal women do the same thing. Many of the wives of the royal family of the Naimans were Kerait women.

Due to Kokochu's betrayal, Senggum stepped into the vast Gobi Desert, afraid that Temujin's troops would soon fall upon him. He was lucky to catch a wild horse. He crossed the Gobi Desert and stepped into the Tanguts' territory, the Shisha Kingdom. The Tanguts were thought to have originated from the Tibetans and were city dwellers. They were living in the walled city. Senggum was refused entrance to the city by the main-gate guard soldiers because he couldn't identify himself for security purposes. He turned around and headed for the Uighur territory. He stepped back into the desert. He had to run for small desert animals to fill his empty stomach. After great suffering, he made it to the Uighur territory. However, he wasn't lucky there. He was mistaken for a bandit by the border residents and was clubbed to death.

When Temujin's chasing unit arrived there, he had already been dead for several days. Temujin's soldiers cut off his head and brought it to Temujin. This was their fate, to end up this way.

CHAPTER FIFTY-SEVEN

Raise the Black Banner!

Another year had passed. It was early spring and yet the fields and the small and large hills of the Mongolian Plateau were still covered with snow. At this time of year, the sky above the plateau touched by the white horizon used to increase its blue tone, adding to its mysteriousness and awesomeness. The strong sunlight reflected from the snow was so pure and bright, it was powerful enough to make some viewers fall into hallucinations. The death-like stillness, icy coldness and strong hues provided a backdrop for some souls to have the illusion of traveling into an unknown, mysterious world.

After conquering the Keraits, Temujin's power increased dramatically. The only independent power left on the Mongolian Plateau who could stand against Temujin was the Naimans. Jamuka, Altan, Quchar, Toktoa Beki of the Merkids and all the other remnants of the defeated tribes like the Dorbens and the Saljuts were in the Naiman's territory. Temujin dispatched messengers to warn the Naiman king, Tayang Khan, not to accept them. Tayang Khan ignored Temujin's warning.

The Naimans were a group with a quasi-government system and a 50,000-strong cavalry. The Naiman generals and high-ranking officers warned their khan, "Be alert! Temujin will surely come to get us."

The Naiman king, Tayang Khan, was a man brought up in the court like a tender plant. He enjoyed falconing and playing polo instead of treading on the battlefields, and he enjoyed banquets and watching shows with singers and dancers rather than discussing tactics with his generals. He was a pleasure-seeker and a coward. His father, Inanch Khan, didn't make it clear before his death who would be his successor. Gurbesu, who had become regent by their custom, hand-picked him as the next khan because he was easy for her to handle. At that time, she was the one who grabbed and shook the Naimans.

Tayang Khan didn't have it in mind to go to war with Temujin; nonetheless, he gave a banquet in addition to a staff meeting under the pressure of the generals and high-ranking officers. About forty generals and high-ranking officers attended the banquet, held in the khan's tent, which was magnificent and luxuriously decorated. Tayang Khan and his wife, Gurbesu, formerly his stepmother, sat side by side in the seats covered with leopard skins and presided over the banquet. Like before, Jamuka was the only outsider who was invited to the meeting. Before the banquet, they completely blocked the area, allowing only a limited number of slaves to enter for service.

Tayang Khan opened his mouth first, "The eastern half of the plateau has fallen into Temujin's hands. Like there are not two suns in the sky, there cannot be two rulers on this land. One of them must perish. If you have any ideas as to how to remove Temujin, who is disturbing the peace on this land, don't hesitate to tell me."

After these words, Kuchlug, Tayang Khan's son, who was in his early twenties, shared his opinion. Unlike his father, Kuchlug was shrewd, crafty and had some courage, too.

"Most of Temujin's tribesmen, the Mongols, are here with Altan, Quchar and Jamuka. Even though Temujin has become more powerful since he conquered the Keraits, his main source of power is just a small group of Mongols with him. If we can remove those small groups, all the others might collapse and disperse themselves automatically."

After his words, Qori Subechi said in agreement, "Right! I've heard a rumor that Temujin is now admitting the former Kerait soldiers into his troops. However, nobody knows if they are really willing to be good fighters for him. I also think that if we could remove a handful of the Mongols, the problem would be solved."

Gurbesu intervened and uttered, "The Mongols are dirty. They are barbarians. They stink! They never wash their clothes. They are not even good as slaves. You will be nauseated if you try to drink the milk collected by their women's dirty hands. This is a good chance to remove them. Kill them all!" Gurbesu's humiliating remarks about the Mongols made some attendants laugh.

At this moment, Jamuka who had merely been listening to the others, opened his mouth and said in a gentle tone, "I know my anda, Temujin, very well. You should be careful with him; never underestimate him. At this time, if you try to remove him, you'd better have allies. If not, it might be difficult."

There was a stir among the attendants. It was quite shocking for them, because they believed the Naimans were invincible. Tayang Khan, after making sure he had all of the attendants' attention, opened his mouth slowly and said, "We have an opinion that we'd better have allies. What do you think?"

This time, Torbi Tashi remarked, "In any war, the more allies you have, the better. However, if you contact anybody thoughtlessly, you simply put yourself in danger of exposing your plan. We should be cautious. In my opinion, for an ally, Ala Qus of the Ongguts is worth contacting."

The Ongguts were the people most similar to the Naimans. The distant ancestors of the Ongguts were believed to be the Turks, the same as the Naimans and they both practiced the same religion, Nestorian Christianity.

Tayang Khan accepted Torbi Tashi's suggestion. They decided to dispatch a secret messenger to Ala Qus of the Ongguts and open a war with Temujin in early autumn.

Torbi Tashi of the Naimans made a visit to Ala Qus of the Ongguts as a secret messenger. The message from Tayang Khan to Ala Qus was this:

Greetings to the Onggut brothers,

In the name of the holy spirit!

I, Tayang Khan of the Naimans,
Am earnestly asking you,
Ala Qus of the Ongguts,
For help.

A handful of the Mongols are disturbing the peace
On the eastern side of the plateau.
My people and I have decided
To root out this evil before it is too late.

I plan to punish and destroy them
Early this coming autumn.
So, please be my right hand.

To remove them and restore the peace
On the plateau,
Would be the will of the holy spirit.

My Onggut brothers!
Please do not forsake
The will of the holy spirit.

After receiving the message, Ala Qus summoned all his chieftains and had an urgent meeting. They unanimously decided to reject the request. They thought Tayang Khan could never defeat Temujin, who had conquered the Keraits. Rather, they decided to send troops to Temujin to help when the war started, like they did before when Temujin went to war with Wang-Khan. Tayang Khan lost his diplomatic war. Ala Qus informed Torbi Tashi of their decision, "I am sorry to tell you that we have decided not to get involved in this war."

Ala Qus dispatched a secret messenger to Temujin after Torbi Tashi had left. Yoqunan, an Onggut secret messenger, galloped at full speed, crossing the plain covered with white snow towards the Temeen field, where Temujin was hunting. At that time, Temujin's ordu was in the Abjia Koteger river basin of the lower part of the Onon River, but he was out on the Temeen field hunting. After about 550 miles of galloping, Yoqunan met up with Temujin on the hunting ground. Upon hearing of the Naimans' movement, Temujin stopped hunting and called an urgent meeting on the hunting ground with the chieftains and generals who had joined the hunting there.

After confirming all the major staff members were present in a temporary field tent, Temujin opened his mouth, "Just now, I received a message that Tabuka of the Naimans has begun to make movements to attack us. What is the best way for us to handle this? If any of you have an opinion, let us know."

Some of the generals spoke out, and the majority of them were against the war in early spring because of the weakness of the horses. Their opinions were to postpone the war until autumn, when the horses would be full of energy and in good condition.

However, two men were against this. One of them was Temuge, Temujin's third, younger brother. People called him Ochigin Noyan. The Mongols called the youngest brother, "ochigin" in case there are more than two brothers in the same family. The title "noyan" meant grand duke and it was given to the khan's brothers or high-ranking noble men. Temuge was also a very ambitious man like his brothers. Temuge said, "If our horses are weak, theirs are weak, too. If we wait until autumn to make our horses strong, by that time, their horses will have become strong, too. So, what's the meaning there?"

Next, Belgutei said, supporting his opinion, "Even before this message, I remember I've heard many times that they are coming to take our bows and quivers. The Naiman nation is abundant in population and troops. We'd better do it before they are fully ready. Of course, we can beat them anytime, but what I mean is that we don't need to wait. I cannot tolerate their humiliation another minute!"

Many of the attendants nodded. To "take the bow and quiver away" from someone was an expression among the Mongols that meant to make them powerless and enslave them. Temujin nodded too. After confirming that their opinions were largely in accord to open the war right away, Temujin stated his opinion and declared, "Belgutei and Temuge are right. We'd better hit them before they are too ready. Raise the black banner! The war with the Naimans has begun!"

Temujin moved his base camp from Abjia Koteger to Keltegey Qada, near the Kalqa River, which were about 350 miles apart in the southeastern direction. That was the place where Temujin's former general, Quyilda, had died and been buried. Upon arriving, Temujin regrouped his troops. Temujin knew the war with the Naimans would be decisive for his future. Temujin organized his troops based on the decimal system. Ten warriors made an alban and ten albans made a jagun. Ten jaguns made a mingan and ten mingans made a tumen, which was 10,000 warriors.

Next, Temujin appointed six cherbies, staff officers or counselors, and seventy day guards and eighty night guards. The six cherbies were Dodai, Doqolqu, Ogele, Tolun, Bucharan and Soygetu. The day guards and night guards were mainly selected from the sons or brothers of the captains of 100 or 1,000, and they all had outstanding physiques, valor, military skills, appearances and loyalty.

Some qualified general warriors joined too. Temujin also set up the near guards, composed of 1,000 Bagatur, whose function was to become the vanguards in time of war and to escort him in time of peace. Temujin appointed Arqai as the captain of the near guards, and Ogele Cherbi and Qudus Qalchan as the captain and the assistant captain of the day and night guards.

Inside Temujin's war camp, the tuk, or black banner made of nine different horses' manes, was raised high. That meant the war had begun. The day before their departure, Temujin performed a ritual. He shouted at his warriors:

Raise the black banner high!
The war with the Naimans has begun.
Beat the drums of black cowskin, loudly!
We will proceed.
Hold the scimitars and spears tightly!
We will crush them.

The one who dies on the saddle,
Shall be remembered,
Far into the future.
The one who dies with his sword in his hand,
Shall have the death,
Like God.

Glory and pride are
What we are fighting for.
An ignoble existence is no better than
Death.
One thing is very clear for the fighting soul,
The victory!

Temujin began his march toward the Naimans. It was April 16, 1204, and the year of the rat in the Mongol chronicle.

War with the Naimans

Temujin marched towards the west along the Kerulen River. Temujin's troops were composed of three tumens and one near guard. Temujin's one tumen was only 6,000 warriors, instead of 10,000, due to the shortage of manpower. The total number of Temujin's troops was less than 20,000. On the other hand, the number of the Naiman troops was more than 50,000. On top of that, their allies, like Jamuka, Altan, Quchar, Quduka Beki of the Oyirads, Toktoa Beki of the Merkids and the remnants of the Dorbens and the Saljuts were 20,000 to 30,000 in number, and so the total number of enemies Temujin had to contend with was 70,000 to 80,000.

Temujin arrived at the Saari Plain, located at the center of the plateau, after several days of marching. They had marched almost 750 miles. Upon arriving at the Saari Plain, Temujin dispatched a scout unit led by Jebe and Qubilai. About twenty scout soldiers crossed the plain and arrived at Qangqarqan Mountain, located at the western end of the plain. However, the Naimans had already posted their sentry unit there. Having found Temujin's scout unit, they immediately sent out 200 cavalry to engage them. As the Naiman soldiers were coming down from the mountain, making clouds of dust, Jebe shouted, "The Naimans! Run!"

Temujin's scout soldiers turned around and ran back the way they had come. However, one of them was falling off his horse, slipping down from the saddle. Jebe hurriedly picked up that soldier and rode double on his horse. All twenty of Temujin's scouts returned safely; however, they didn't have the chance to retrieve the lost horse. The Naiman soldiers took the captured horse to their captain. The Naiman captain carefully examined the captured horse and said, nodding and smoothing his chin, "The Mongol horses are thin and weak!"

The Naiman captain immediately sent a report to Tayang Khan.

Temujin had a staff meeting and discussed fully the future plans and tactics. Temujin said, "One of our horses fell into the Naimans' hands. They must have noticed our horses are thin and weak. We have to consider a countermeasure to this. If you have any suggestions about what that could be, or for future plans, let us know."

After Temujin's words, Dodai Cherbi, a young warrior with brilliance and wits, got on his feet and said, "It is true that our horses are thin and weak. It is also true that the Naimans outnumber us. And more, our soldiers and horses are exhausted from traveling here. What we need is time. We need to exaggerate our numbers, to make them think we are not an easy target. In my opinion, at nighttime, we should put out many torches to make our numbers appear grander and, while they are hesitating, we can take a rest and feed our horses. And then, we can move to the next step."

Temujin laughed out loud, slapping his lap, "The toads swell themselves with air to scare their predators away. I think this idea fits our situation."

Temujin accepted Dodai's idea. A brilliant man acknowledges brilliant ideas. That night, Temujin's soldiers spread out in a wider area and each of them lit five torches to display. Soon, the Saari Plain was covered with an enormous number of torches. The Naiman sentries on the faraway Qangqarqan Mountain summit were astonished by the view. The image of 100,000 torches covering the great Saari Plain was powerful enough to strike terror into the enemies' hearts. It was like the feeling a man would have standing in front of an oncoming tidal wave. The Naiman captain immediately made a report. "The number of Temujin troops could be much bigger than expected. This presumption came from the number of torches they lit at night."

Temujin's tactic worked. Upon receiving the message, Tayang Khan, who had set up a base camp at the Qachir riverside, about 100 miles from Qangqarqan Mountain, dispatched urgent messengers to his son, Kuchlug, who was waiting for the attack order at a spot about thirty miles south of his father. "Temujin's horses might be weak, but their numbers are considered to be much higher than we thought. Instead of facing them at the present location, I think it would be better for us to retreat to the Altai Mountains purposely, forcing the enemy soldiers and horses to follow us and get tired. Then we will attack them. I think this could be the best plan at this time and if you have any other ideas, let me know immediately."

Upon receiving his father's message, Kuchlug, who was commanding much of the Naiman troops, jumped up from his chair and stamped his foot in anger. He lamented, "Ah! Unmanly Tayang Khan is ruining this country! Go and tell him that most of the Mongols are here with Jamuka and us. What is he out here for? He is just like a pregnant woman or a suckling calf."

At that time, on the Mongolian Plateau, pregnant women usually tried not to go far from the yurt, especially at nighttime, even for urination, because of their limited movement capabilities and the possible dangers in the darkness. Tayang Khan's messenger had returned and repeated Kuchlug's statement, word for word, to him. Upon hearing his own son's humiliating remarks, he raged, "What? A pregnant woman? A suckling calf? A spoiled brat! Let him fight all by himself!"

In truth, Tayang Khan, emotionally, was not ready to go into the battlefield, and had no intention of fighting. He was scared. He had not trained himself for a major battle. In this regard, the Naimans were very unlucky. Most of the Naiman generals were rejecting their khan's poor leadership. Qori Subechi, who was the actual second-in-command of the Naiman troops, was enraged with Tayang Khan's retreat plan. He stepped out and rebuked his khan in a loud voice.

"The late Inanch Khan never showed his back or the rump of his horse to the enemy! It is ridiculous that we are talking about retreat even before the battle begins! My lord Khan! Don't you understand this is the right time for us to get rid of the Mongols completely? Our soldiers have never suffered from low morale like this before! Let Gurbesu lead these troops!"

After these words, Qori Subechi took his quiver from his waist and threw it away. He cried out, "Oh, the Naimans! General Sabrak, where are you?"

He kicked open the door and went out. Tayang Khan, who had been humiliated twice, once by his own son and now by his own general, was frustrated and mad, but he couldn't push forward with his plan to retreat anymore. Finally, he gave the order for his troops to move forward.

"Fine! Everyone will die anyway. Let's go!"

Though he gave the order, he could not get over his fear of battle. He had never trained for this battle.

The Naiman troops crossed the Tamir and Orkhon rivers after leaving the Qachir riverside and approached the Chakir Mountain slopes, passing the eastern side of Mountain Naqu Qun.

Temujin's sentries stationed at the top of Chakir Mountain immediately made a report to Temujin of the Naimans' approach. Temujin received the urgent report that the Naiman troops were approaching while he was waiting in his war camp with his staff.

Temujin jumped up from his seat and shouted, "The time has come! This will be the decisive battle for them or for us! God is always with fighters! Victory is ours!"

Temujin issued an order to advance. All at once, huge cowskin drums began to beat in Temujin's war camp. Temujin's troops advanced with the Karaqana tactic. Karaqana was a short thorny desert bush, with thorns so sharp, strong and abundant that horses and cows couldn't use it for food. When they were advancing at a normal pace, the distance between each cavalry soldier was narrowed to increase defensive power.

Temujin entrusted his brother Temuge with leading the front group of his troops and Kasar with the center force, and he himself became the director. When Temujin's troops arrived at the midpoint between Chakir Mountain and Naqu Qun Mountain, they found the Naiman troops waiting in their battle array. As soon as they stood face to face with the Naimans, the drums began to beat all at once in Temujin's troops. Next, Temujin's cavalry began to spread out into a wider area in a very organized way. It was called the "water-spreading-out array," which was to prevent the large number of enemy troops from easily surrounding the smaller in number troops.

At this moment, Jamuka was with Tayang Khan. High on the hill, Jamuka carefully examined Temujin's troops' movements. Even being spread out into a wider area, Temujin's troops showed no signs of weakness or blind spots. All the troops were moving swiftly and systematically under one direct order line, just like the five fingers of one hand. Superior systemic organization and high-speed movements were the specific characteristics of Temujin's troops. After careful examination, Jamuka was surprised at their superiority and sensed that, regardless of numbers, the Naimans could never defeat Temujin's troops.

The two sides, upon facing each other, exchanged an enormous number of arrows for some time. Suddenly, from Temujin's side, with earsplitting sounds of beating nacaras, two separate groups of horse soldiers dashed towards the Naimans, from both the left and right sides. They galloped at full speed, protecting themselves from the showering arrows with their round leather shields. They were two light cavalries of 2,000 horse soldiers each, led by Jebe and Qubilai. They penetrated the Naimans' first defense line and went deep inside. They destroyed the Naiman's lines, hitting, thrashing and smashing the Naiman defenders with their battle-axes, lances and scimitars. It was called a wedge tactic, or chisel fight.

At the right moment, Temujin released his second attack group. They were two heavy cavalrics, each also of 2,000 heavily armed horse soldiers, led by Jelme and Subedai. They destroyed the Naimans' second and third lines of defense, sending them into chaos.

Having confirmed the Naiman's defense lines had been opened, Temujin sent the center force led by Kasar. They were the main force of destruction. The battle lasted almost a whole day. In the late afternoon, the picture of the winner and loser became clear. The countless dead bodies strewn across the field with their heads lost or their hearts cut open were mostly those of the Naimans. Tayang Khan himself was also wounded, hit by two arrows. Tayang Khan retreated to the top of Naqu Qun Mountain, carried on a litter. Panting, he asked Jamuka, who was standing next to him, "Who are those four men driving our soldiers into the corners, like a wolf does to sheep? I want to know their names."

Jamuka whispered in his ear.

"They are Temujin's four hunting dogs. Their names are Jebe, Qubilai, Jelme and Subedai. They are wind-riders and born killers."

Tayang Khan asked with labored breathing, "Who is the one behind them, crushing our troops like eggs?"

Jamuka answered, "He is Temujin's brother, Kasar. Once he picks up his bow and shoots an arrow, it can pass through twenty men, and he can shoot down an enemy from one side of the horizon to the other. He eats a whole sheep for each meal. He is a monster, not a human being."

Tayang Khan asked, "Who is the one directing all of them, moving around like an eagle in the sky?"

Jamuka answered, staring into his eyes, with his eyes half-shut, "He is my anda Temujin. He is greed itself. He doesn't even leave the foot skin of the goat. Any place he passes through, nothing will be left."

Among the five major livestock, horses, cows, camels, sheep and goats, the Mongols considered the goat least valuable, and the skin of the foot of the goat was the least valuable of all.

While Jamuka was talking to Tayang Khan on the litter, Qori Subechi came running and gave a report, panting.

"My lord, the escape route is ready! Your family members are waiting. Make your move, quick!"

However, there was no response from Tayang Khan. He was already dead. Jamuka got on his feet slowly, sighing. After confirming his death, Qori Subechi closed the eyes of Tayang Khan, who had died with his eyes wide open. Qori Subechi stared into space for a while. The sun was already close to the western horizon. He went down again and shouted at his soldiers, who building a defensive line in the middle of the mountainside.

"Our lord is already dead! Let's fight to the last man standing!"

After these words, Qori Subechi mounted his horse and went down to the base of the mountain, where Temujin's soldiers were waiting. A large number of Naiman soldiers followed him. Qori Subechi and his followers fought until the last man.

For this, Temujin remarked in admiration, "The Naiman soldiers are admirable. They are simply unlucky to have an incompetent leader."

That night, the remnants of the Naiman soldiers tried to escape from Naqu Qun Mountain. In the total darkness, without even moonlight, numerous Naiman soldiers fell over the cliffs and died. At the bottom of the cliffs, the Naiman soldiers' dead bodies and horses had stacked up. More soldiers died there than had successfully escaped.

The following morning, Temujin began to chase down the remnants of the defeated troops. Kuchlug, Tayang Khan's son, had built up a temporary defense line on the Tamil riverside with the regrouped defeated Naiman soldiers, but it was easily broken down. They continued to run away toward the west.

After 600 miles of chasing, Temujin annihilated the last resistant power in front of the Altai Mountains. The survivors of the Naimans, Jadarats, Qadagins, Saljuits, and Dorbens surrendered to Temujin. Jamuka, Toktoa Beki and Kuchlug had escaped. Kasar notified Temujin that Altan and Quchar were in captivity. Refusing to see them, Temujin sent them over to Alchidai to handle. Alchidai was Temujin's nephew. He took them out into the field and cut their ankles, knees, wrists and elbows, one by one, until they died. The rest of the job was done by the desert and plains scavengers.

Gurbesu, Tayang Khan's wife and stepmother, was dragged over to Temujin with the other concubines. Temujin eyed her for a while and asked her in a gentle voice, with a thin smile on his lips, "Are you Gurbesu, who said the Mongols stink and are dirty?"

Temujin gave her to his mother as a servant. Ouluun used her as a nursery servant in her orphanage. Gurbesu spent the rest of her life washing and cleaning the Mongol orphans. Thus, the Naimans, the last power on the Mongolian Plateau, suffered this dreadful fate.

CHAPTER FIFTY-NINE

Qulan, a Woman of Great Charm

In the fall of that same year, Temujin set out to mop up the remnants of the Merkids. Toktoa Beki of the Merkids had successfully escaped and a large part of the Merkids were still doing well. But a victory is not a victory when it is not complete. Temujin left Doloan Hill near the Kerulen River and marched towards the Qara Tala, the stronghold of the Merkids, located south of Lake Baikal. The defense line of the Merkids was easily broken down. Yet Toktoa Beki and his three sons, Qudu, Qal and Chilaun (a different person with the same name as Sokan Shira's son who was also Temujin's captain), successfully escaped again. Temujin's soldiers entered the Merkids' base camp. Plundering and killing were happening everywhere. Some of the Merkids escaped and some others surrendered. Since the Merkids were spread out in a wide area, it was not easy to annihilate them completely.

Dayir Usun, the chieftain of one of the three major tribes of the Merkids, decided to surrender to Temujin, because he was afraid that his tribe could be exterminated. He was one of the three leaders who had abducted Borte years ago. Dayir Usun, now an old man, set out on his journey to find Temujin's camp without any bodyguards, accompanied only by his seventeen-year-old daughter, Qulan. On the way, they met Nayaga, one of Temujin's captains. Dayir Usun and his daughter, Qulan, were shown the way to Nayaga by the soldiers.

"I am the chieftain of the Uuas Merkids, Dayir Usun. I want to surrender to Temujin Khan. Please take us to Temujin Khan. This is my daughter and her name is Qulan. I have brought her as proof of my truth. She is for Temujin Khan."

Nayaga eyed them carefully for a while and then said, "Temujin Khan is at a place that is about a half-day journey from here. It could be quite dangerous for you to continue your journey alone with only your daughter. In three days, I am supposed to return to the main camp. It would be much safer for you to travel with me, if you can wait three days."

Nayaga was right. Temujin's soldiers were everywhere and it was the norm for them to kill and rape the Merkids because it was war and war comes with a collapse of morals and rationality. War crimes are, in many cases, merely the retaliatory punishment for the losers. That is the history of wars of the past, present and, possibly, the infinite future.

Three days later, Nayaga took Dayir Usun and his daughter, Qulan, to Temujin. However, Temujin was enraged that such an important person, like Dayir Usun, had been detained in Nayaga's camp for three days.

"Why did he detain them in his camp for three days? Nayaga should be court-martialed."

Nayaga seemed doomed. However, surprisingly, it was Qulan, Dayir Usun's seventeen-year-old daughter, who stepped forward to defend Nayaga. Qulan was a woman with eyes imbued with intelligence and a clear voice.

"My lord, if it is a problem that Captain Nayaga kept us in his camp for three days, can you answer my questions?"

Temujin asked her, with his eyes wide open in surprise, "What is your question?"

Qulan asked, looking straight into his eyes, "If something happened to us on our way here, without direct protection from Captain Nayaga, it would have been a more serious problem. Am I right, my lord?"

Temujin answered in bewilderment, "Yes ... that is correct."

Qulan continued, "As you said, if Captain Nayaga brought us here the day we arrived, leaving his post, he would have been committing a different serious crime, desertion. Am I right, my lord?"

"Right ..."

Again, Qulan asked Temujin, looking straight into his eyes, "My lord, if your answer is 'yes' to both questions, the only choice Captain Nayaga had was to keep us safe until his return date and then bring us here with him."

Temujin didn't know how to answer, because she was quite right. Qulan continued, lowering her head, "My lord, my body is still just as clean as when I was born."

Temujin, ashamed of himself because she was reading his mind, murmured to himself, "What a woman! She is reading my mind like her own. She has wit and courage!"

Temujin's great concern was not only her father, but also the girl. That's why Temujin was suspicious about Nayaga.

Temujin closed his eyes and recalled one of the old bedtime stories he had heard from his mother when he was very young. A faithful fox. What a dangerous idea to make a hasty decision without definite evidence! How important it is not to make a single victim of false accusations, more so than making three people have a sense of gratitude. Temujin sat with Nayaga face to face and interviewed him.

"Who is the owner of all the war booty?"

Nayaga answered, "Of course, all the war booty belongs to the khan, my lord. All the captured women and horses belong to the khan also. I deserve the death penalty if my thinking is different from what I have said."

At that time, for the Mongols, their concept of property included people. Temujin asked, "If so, is it possible to kill or rape the captives without my permission?"

Nayaga answered, lowering his head, "Absolutely not, my lord; they cannot be forgiven."

Temujin guffawed, patting his shoulder and said, "If you think that way, you are quite correct. Never forget that!"

Temujin changed his decision. Nayaga was saved.

Temujin decreed the following:

Decree 1: Unnecessary killings are forbidden in the battle area.

Decree 2: Anyone who violates captive women shall be subject to the same accusation as a rapist in peacetime.

Decree 3: Anyone who violates the previous two decrees shall be punished with the death penalty.

Temujin accepted Dayir Usun's surrender. Because of this, many Merkids' lives were saved. Temujin kept Qulan close and favored her. Temujin was charmed by her wit and beauty. A woman's attractiveness is not based solely on her beauty. Qulan became Temujin's fourth wife.

Temujin continued to chase down the remaining Merkids who refused to surrender. Some of them escaped in the northwestern direction, making a strong fortress on top of Tayqal Qorka Mountain, while Toktoa Beki and his sons headed for the west to cross the Altai Mountains. Temujin gave 3,000 cavalry soldiers to Chimbai, Sokan Shira's son, to attack the fortress on Tayqal Qorka Mountain and he headed west to continue his chase of Toktoa Beki. After about 500 miles of tracking, Temujin arrived at the eastern border of the Altai Mountains. Winter was coming. The cold wind from Siberia began to blow with a snowstorm. Temujin stopped there, as it could be dangerous to try to cross the high mountains with large troops in the winter.

CHAPTER SIXTY

Last of Jamuka

The new year had come. Temujin spent the winter at the east side of the Altai Mountains. It was the place where the Altai Mountains stood like natural ramparts and thick forests of pine trees and fir trees under the mountains worked like a windbreak. Numerous peaks of the Altai Mountains, covered with snow, would reflect the strong morning sunlight, causing some viewers to be dazzled. At this time of year, the Mongol horses would break the ice and snow covering the ground with their tough hoofs to find their food. It would have been a peaceful scene, if not for the piercing cold.

When spring arrived, Temujin began to organize his line of battle. He had received information that the remnants of the Naimans, led by Kuchlug, and the Merkids, led by Toktoa, had made a new alliance for a counterattack.

Temujin crossed the Altai Mountains via the Arai Pass. After about 500 miles of marching in the northwestern direction, Temujin's troops arrived at Buqdurma, at the riverside of the Ertis River. There, they could see the coalition troops of the Naimans and the Merkids waiting for them, with their backs to the river.

Temujin immediately launched an attack. There was another fierce battle; however, within the period of a single meal, the coalition troops of the Naimans and the Merkids began to retreat. It was at this moment that Toktoa Beki, the ruler of the Merkids, was shot with an arrow and fell from his horse. His sons hurried back to save him, but he was already dead. Knowing that it was impossible to take their father's whole dead body, they cut through his neck and ran away with only his head. Many of the Naimans and the Merkids drowned in the Ertis River. Kuchlug and Toktoa Beki's three sons successfully escaped again. They crossed the river and ran away in all directions.

Temujin immediately organized a pursuit. Subedai was given 2,000 horse soldiers to chase down the three sons of Toktoa Beki, and Jebe was given 2,000 to chase down Kuchlug. Temujin gave advice to Subedai and Jebe:

Chase them to the end of the world!

If they become winged creatures and escape into the sky,
Become an eagle and seize them.

If they become marmots and hide in the ground,
Become an iron stick and find them.

If they become fish and hide underwater,
Become a net and catch them.

If you are running out of food, go hunting!
Game is everywhere, yet take no more than you need.
Otherwise, you will waste your time and energy.

Tighten the reins and check your saddle often.
Otherwise you will be chased by them.

Keep only your mission in your head.
Otherwise you will never accomplish your mission.

Remember that I am always with you.
Never forget you are under the protection of heaven.

Subedei, after six months of persistent chasing, finally anni-hilated Toktoa Beki's three sons, Qudu, Qal and Chilaun, along with their remaining power at the side of the Chuy River on the southeastern side of Balkhash Lake. Jebe, after nine months, also completely destroyed the remaining Naimans at Sarik Lake, close to the border of Kara Khitai. Kuchlug, all by himself, crossed the border of Kara Khitai and sought refuge there.

Jamuka, on the other hand, had slipped away from the battlefield when Qori Subechi's Naimans and Temujin's troops were in the final engagement. However, his people, the Ja-darats, refused to follow him anymore. They all agreed to surrender to Temujin. Being in terror for his own life, Jamuka escaped to the Tanglu Mountain area, close to Uvs Lake, with only about thirty of his close followers. He held out in the mountain area like a bandit for six months. However, as time went by, his followers couldn't tolerate such a life and slipped away from him, one by one, until finally, only five of them were left.

One day, Jamuka was eating barbecued wild ram with his men. By this time, his five followers had already reached an agreement to capture Jamuka and hand him over to Temujin. Jamuka, as usual, was eating his fill of the best part of the ram, leaving the rest, the less favored parts, to his men. The five enraged men fell upon him. One of them held his head firmly by grabbing his hair and the other four held his arms and feet, one each. After they tied him up firmly, he was put on horseback like baggage. As Jamuka was denouncing them at full volume, one of them gagged him with rope to silence him. Jamuka was dragged to Temujin. At that time, Temujin was staying by the Tula River. On the vast riverside, a great number of grey yurts were spread out in an organized way and the surface of the water of the Tula River was sparkling due to the reflection of the strong sunlight of high noon. Temujin was watching his soldiers' training in his rectangular sunshade tent, of which all four walls were rolled up. At that moment, Temujin's soldiers presented Jamuka to him with his hands tied behind his back. Temujin jumped up from his chair and squinted to see the man's face better. He was indeed Jamuka.

"Jamuka!"

Temujin walked up to him and looked at his face very carefully to make sure it was Jamuka.

Temujin shouted again, grabbing and shaking his shoulders, "Jamuka! It is really you! It has been quite a while."

It was a reunion after about eighteen years of separation. His hair was disheveled and his clothes were torn to ribbons. His face was distorted from exhaustion and shame, yet his two eyes were bright and sparkling like before, showing he still had his brilliance. Temujin ordered his men to untie him. Then he took him into the sunshade tent and let him take a seat. Soon, water and food were given to him. Temujin looked at him silently while he ate and drank.

Temujin moved his chair close to him and asked, "Who made you like this?"

Jamuka stopped eating and stared forward for a while. Then, without saying anything, he just pointed to one side with his chin and continued eating. In front of Temujin's shade tent, a great number of spectators were gathering having heard the news that Jamuka was in captivity, and soldiers had to use their spears to keep them from approaching. In one corner, where Jamuka had pointed with his chin, were five disarmed men who were Jamuka's former followers, waiting for Temujin's decision. They might have been expecting a great reward from Temujin. Instead, Temujin shouted at his soldiers.

"Arrest them!"

Upon Temujin's order, about twenty soldiers fell upon them, tying their hands back and forcing them to kneel down on the ground. Temujin got to his feet and walked up to them slowly. Temujin stared at them one by one and said, "You betrayed your master! Who will accept you if don't have loyalty to your own master?"

Temujin ordered his captain to cut their heads off, right on the spot. The line of Jamuka's five betrayers lost their heads by executioners at the same time. Jamuka stopped eating for a moment, while he was watching them lose their heads, and then continued eating. Some of Temujin's soldiers took the dead bodies away and some others covered the bloodstains with dirt.

Temujin said to Jamuka, sorrow in his eyes, "Jamuka, now we are together again. Remember? We swore to each other to die on the same day. Let's forget about the past. From now on, let's join our efforts and make the future."

At Temujin's words, Jamuka put a smile on his lips and responded, "Thank you, Temujin. However, you know that I have been your enemy for so long. I am done."

Temujin moved his chair closer to Jamuka and said, "Jamuka, you are my anda, whatever you say. Forget about the past. You have already provided me with meritorious service. I know it was you that sent me important information while I was engaged with Wang-Khan and I also know you didn't cooperate with the Naimans. That is more than enough to join me."

Temujin wanted to change his mind. Temujin had some good reasons. At that time, among the steppe people, to kill your own anda was taboo. It was considered even less acceptable than killing your own brother. Temujin also knew that he had been his enemy publicly, but, personally, he was his best friend. Temujin still had all the sweet memories of Jamuka in his early days.

Jamuka put his own hand on Temujin's and, while rubbing his hand, said, "Temujin, I understand you. You are still the only friend remaining in my mind. Our goals were the same, but we had differing opinions on how to reach that goal. That's all. Now, you have already unified the plateau. The world is waiting for you. You can do anything, all by yourself now. In this situation, if I remain alive, what use would it be to you? At night, I could bother you in your dreams and in the daytime, I could disturb your peace. I will be merely a louse in your collar or a spine in your sleeve."

After these words, Jamuka sighed lightly. He picked up a water cup on the table and relieved his thirst.

He continued, "I gave a lot of thought to the cause of my failure. I think it began when I was very young. My father died when I was so young that I don't even remember his face. And my mother was with me for some time, but later, she remarried and left me. I was all alone. I never knew my parents' love. I didn't have outstanding brothers, a good wife or loyal comrades, like you. I failed to earn another's love. That was probably because I never had the chance to learn how to love others. This is the real cause of my failure."

Temujin listened to him silently. There was a deep silence between them for a while. Jamuka continued, looking at Temujin with eyes filled with affection.

"Temujin, if I have only one wish left, that is to die without shedding blood. Bury me on the high hill. My soul will keep circling over the plain and will pray for you and your descendants to prosper on this land forever. Can I have my wish?"

The Mongols at that time believed that the soul exists in the blood. If someone died losing his blood, his soul would disperse into space and disappear. On the other hand, if someone died with his body and blood intact, his soul would live on.

Temujin closed his eyes with a sad look and nodded. They hugged each other for some time. Temujin got on his feet slowly and walked out of the tent with a heavy step. Temujin told about twenty of his generals and captains, who had been waiting outside the tent, "Keep his blood. Handle his dead body with care. Prepare for the best coffin."

After these words, Temujin left there. Alchidai, one of Temujin's captains, approached Jamuka and asked him carefully if he wanted some wine. It was offered to make it easier for Jamuka, yet he refused it. Since Alchidai and his five soldiers were hesitating, Jamuka guffawed and said to them, "I am ready! Why are you hesitating more than me? Go ahead and start!"

Alchidai went behind Jamuka and strangled him with a silk scarf. The rest of the soldiers stabilized his hands and feet. After a while, his body became still and his reddened face turned white and peaceful as Alchidai removed the scarf from his neck. Jamuka died with his eyes closed.

Temujin gave a grand funeral for Jamuka. Temujin ordered his men to wrap his dead body with silk cloth and put it into a coffin decorated with silver ornaments. He buried him on a high hill.

A man is lying here.

His will was like a rock
And his courage was incomparable.

He was a man of brilliance,
And an outstanding strategist.

He was the protector of traditions,
And the winner of friendship.

His name will be on a million people's lips,
And his traces will remain for a long time.

His name was Jamuka,
And he was the hero of the steppe.

Those were Temujin's words of condolence. Thus, Temujin removed his most powerful, dangerous rival and his best boyhood friend as well. Jamuka was a rare man with high intelligence, eloquence, diplomatic skill, intuitive power, keen insight, organizational ability and valor. Nevertheless, he lost to Temujin.

CHAPTER SIXTY-ONE

Birth of the Mongol Empire

I n the spring of 1206, on the plain near the upper part of the Onon River, a huge tent city was erected, larger than any of the past. About one-and-a-half million people with 400,000 yurts were gathered in one place. It was almost three-quarters of the total population of the plateau at the time. Though some minor tribes at the outskirts of the plateau had not yet been conquered, Temujin didn't wait. It was the convention for declaration of the birth of the new Mongol Empire and the enthronement ceremony for Kha-Khan, which meant Khan of Khans. It was called "khuriltai" in the Mongolian language and was a national meeting for important state events or for the declaration of war with other nations.

For about three months before the enthronement, Temujin laid the groundwork for the Empire. The first thing he did was unite all the tribes through a new system. The whole population was systemized like a military unit. Ninety-five aingans had been created, each composed of 1,000 cavalrymen. Eighty-eight "cofounders of the Empire" were declared and each one of them was appointed to be chief of one mingan. The eighty-eight men had been carefully chosen from a group who had notable meritorious achievements. Their previous positions or social statuses was completely ignored. Among them were Badai and Kishlik, who used to be slaves, Dekei, who was a sheepherder and Quchugul, a carpenter. One mingan was composed of men from many different tribes and, based on the unification policy, anyone who left his position or broke away from the troops was to be punished by the death penalty. Only a few limited groups of people were allowed to have their own troops; they were the 3,000 Ongguts who had helped Temujin on many important occasions, and the 2,000 Ikires. Also, Tooril, the son of Chakaunua, who died at the Dalan Baljut battle, was allowed to have his own troop after regrouping his people.

The commanders of the mingans had the right to rule the families of the soldiers, too, and their positions could be transferred to their descendants. Yet if they were not successful in their duty, at anytime they could be discharged. With the important units, two commanders were appointed to assure careful decisions and mutual restraint.

Temujin reinforced his security guards. The day guard and night guard were increased to 8,000 and 2,000, respectively, from 70 and 80, making 10,000 total. The guard soldiers were the elite of the elites, mainly young men, children or brothers of the commanders of the mingans, or someone recommended by others. They were high-ranking core members of Temujin's staff. The reason Temujin had picked children or brothers of high commanders was, in part, because they were the younger generation and hadn't been tainted with the dark side of the past and were therefore more adaptable to the new system, but also to reduce the possibility of rebellion by keeping them as hostages, just in case.

The Mongol troops established and organized by Temujin became the strongest and most powerful troops in human history.

Temujin issued draconian laws to clean up and correct the social degradation and chaos. Later, this code of law was called "Yassa" and some of the laws were:

- Adulterers shall be put to death regardless of marital status, reason or excuse.
- Anyone who steals other people's property, big or small, shall be put to death, if it was intentional.
- An intentional liar shall be put to death.
- Fake shaman or sorcerers who mislead people for dishonest reward shall be put to death.
- Anyone who declares bankruptcy three times or more shall be put to death.
- Anyone who commits sodomy shall be put to death.
- Anyone who contaminates drinking water with urination or anything unsanitary shall be put to death.
- If two people are fighting and someone supports one side simply because of personal motivation, the unfair supporter shall be put to death.
- Anyone who accepts stolen goods, regardless of whether or not they knew it was stolen, shall be put to death.
- False witnesses shall be put to death.

The Yassa helped the Mongols build up moral standards, clean up their society and regain their high spirits. As time went by, more and more laws and ordinances were added, and they worked as powerful social rules, regulations and guidance for daily life.

Temujin accepted the Naimans' administrative system, appointing Tata Tunga as the secretary-general; he held the same position in the Naiman government. Tata Tunga recommended the imperial seal system, which could be used for all the official and imperial laws, ordinances and orders. His recommendation was accepted and he became the Keeper of the Seal. Temujin created the supreme court, which handled all the criminal trials, and Shigi Khutuku was the first chief of that department. Shigi Khutuku was the Tartar orphan abandoned in the battlefield, rescued by Temujin, and then raised by Temujin's mother, Ouluun. Eventually, Ouluun accepted him as her foster-son.

Temujin accepted the Uighur writing system as the interim official alphabet to be used in all official documents and he allowed all the royal family members the opportunity to learn how to read and write. Temujin appointed Belgutei as the supreme darughachi, which was similar to the head of the government. Bogorchu became the number-one cofounder of the Mongol Empire and Mukali, who was young, but had already provided many distinguished services, became the symbol of the nation.

Temujin appointed himself Emperor of the Mongol Empire and the title "Genghis Khan" was given to him. This title meant "ruler of the world" or "origin of the power."

Temujin's enthronement ceremony was held at the upper part of the Onon River basin. At the northern end of the vast river basin, a huge altar had been built and at the northern side of the altar, a six-foot-tall bronze incense burner was arranged. The top floor of the altar was covered with red Bukhara carpets and to get to the top floor you had to ascend ninety-nine steps. Below the altar, the 100,000 newly organized Mongol cavalrymen were gathered and lined up in order with their banners in front of them. It was a balmy spring day, and the newly risen morning sun was pouring its strong sunlight over this historic site. The white banner, made with hair from the manes of nine white horses, was carried along the road by two cavalrymen to the rhythm of eighty-one drums being carried on eighty-one camels' backs. The Mongols called the banner "tuk." However, when their protective holy spirits were with it, it was called "sulde." This was designed by Temujin. The white one was used for peacetime and the black one for wartime. Later, this became the spiritual symbol of the Mongol troops when conquering the world.

After having the white sulde posted in front of the altar, Temujin, wearing his helmet and armor, rode a shiny white horse through the middle of the road leading to the alter and stopped in front of it. Having dismounted his horse, he climbed the ninety-nine stairs and when he arrived at the top floor, the awaiting nine celebrants handed the torch over to him. The chief of the celebrants was Kokochu, who had been appointed as the national priest by Temujin. The official name of Kokochu was Tab Tenggri, which meant the highest heaven.

After setting fire to the incense burner, Temujin prayed to the heaven, the earth, the sun and the moon. Tab Tenggri blessed him on behalf of heaven. Temujin declared the birth of the Mongol Empire.

All the high-ranking officials and the commanders of 1,000 cavalrymen or more kowtowed nine times toward Temujin after taking off their waist belts and putting them around their necks. The Mongolian-style kowtow was to touch their forehead to the ground, which meant complete obedience.

After this, Temujin changed from his military uniform into his traditional Mongolian del and uuden, or costume and cap, and attended the next ceremony. Inside the 2,000-person capacity tent, Temujin was greeted and congratulated by the high-ranking officials and generals. One by one, in the order of their ranking, they walked up to Temujin and shouted the same phrase after sipping the otok in the golden goblet, which was handed to them by the ceremony director.

"Genghis Khan! My lord!"

Now they had only one Khan and they were all Mongols regardless of the origin of their clan or tribe. The term Mongol, which had been used to categorize a small fraction of the people on the plateau, was now the official name of the newborn Empire. Temujin had united all the nomads on the plateau and built an Empire. He was thirty-nine years old.

After he became the Kha-Khan of the newborn Mongol Empire, he held the first official meeting. It lasted about a month. They talked and discussed many agenda items and made decisions. Genghis Khan had been empowered as the supreme ruler of the new Empire by this meeting.

"The Mongol Empire is a completely independent, sovereign nation and free to govern itself. All the people who are sharing the same will with us shall be accepted as comrades, regardless of their origin, tribe, race, language, religion, customs and historical background. Freedom of religion shall be guaranteed and everyone's traditional custom shall be respected. Anyone under the banner of the Mongol Empire should be equal and share the same rights, responsibilities and privileges."

That was the national ideal on which the Empire was created. They also talked about the direction of the Empire. To solidify their independence, they made the decision to remove all the powers that could get in the way of the Empire lasting 10,000 generations. They decided to conquer all the remaining tribes like the Oyirads, the Qori Tumads, the Uighurs and the Kirghizes. As for China, if they ignored the new Mongol Empire and were unwilling to accept their sovereignty, they decided to bring them under control as well.

They discussed many other things in detail. For example, the male citizens' obligatory military service started at age fifteen and continued, unless there were health problems, or if there were only one male offspring in a family, in which case they would be exempted from military service. The religious priests, the undertakers and the skillful artisans were also exempted from military service and state taxes.

Genghis Khan granted many favors to the cofounders of the Empire. They were granted not only material things, but also social privileges. For example, some of them were not to be prosecuted for nine crimes, unless it was for high treason to Genghis Khan or to the nation. These were very meaningful privileges in a new society ruled by draconian laws. Genghis Khan could now reward his comrades for all the hardships they had been through together and for their service.

The khuriltai, the Mongol Empire's official meeting, lasted for about a month and then came to an end. Right after that, they began a celebratory feast that lasted for another month. They had built a nation with Genghis Khan as the central figure and declared a national ideal. Yet the most important part of their decisions was the expansion policy. This became the nation's most important policy and the fundamental ideology in their world conquest.

CHAPTER SIXTY-TWO

Consolidation of the Empire

For about three years, Genghis Khan further consolidated his Empire. He was the leader of the spiritual revolution of the Mongolian people. He instilled in his subjects the concept of being the chosen people. For a very long time, the Chinese had been ruling, or influencing, the nomads on the Mongolian Plateau, treating them as barbarians or inferior groups of people. Genghis Khan considered it very important to remove the sense of inferiority that had been planted by others and to restore high self-esteem. Genghis Khan put it like this:

The everlasting blue heaven
Has allowed me
To rule this world.

All the land from the sunrise to the sunset,
Shall be under the rule of
The Mongols and their descendents.

The sedentary city dwellers are rotten.
Heaven will punish them,
And the world shall have a new order.

The Mongolians are the people
Who have been selected by heaven
To rule this world.

Since the social purification law, Yassa, had been enacted, violators had to face harsh punishments. Genghis believed the stability of the nation depended on the stability of each family of citizens. For several months after the birth of the nation, several dozen violators lost their heads each day. As time went by, the number gradually decreased, until finally, the Mongol society was changed dramatically. Even though valuable items were dropped on the street, nobody would pick them up and make them their own. No one was slandering or backbiting anyone blindly or recklessly. And the Mongols became the people who never told a lie, even in the face of death.

Genghis reinforced the function of the day and night guards. First, the number increased from 150 to 10,000, which included 8,000 day guards and 2,000 night guards. The night guards were empowered with many authorized functions and special duties in many areas. Their main job was to protect the khan, which meant they didn't join the war. They would do anything for the safety of the khan and their positions were considered much higher than others with the same rank. The chief of the night guard was Yeke Neurin.

The khan's ordu consisted of about ten yurts, and these were for the khan himself, each of his four wives, his children, a kitchen, official business affairs and visitors. These yurts were arranged in a circle, and about 400 yurts belonging to the night guards were arranged around the khan's ordu, also in a big circle.

After sunset, no one was allowed to step into the outside circle and anyone who violated this rule was arrested, regardless of their position. As for the khan's yurt, even the night guardsmen were not allowed to enter, so in the case of an urgent report, they had to shout from outside.

Some of the night guard members were dispatched to the other departments of the government, like the courts, the supply units, the armory and the khan's kitchen for observation or sometimes for actual assistance.

In the spring of 1207, Genghis Khan launched an operation to conquer all the remaining tribes on the outskirts of the Mongolian Plateau. He dispatched expeditionary forces instead of going himself. Three expeditionary troops were formed and three commanders were appointed, one for each troop. They were Juchi, the khan's twenty-one-year-old first son, and Boroqul and Qubilai, who were cofounders of the empire.

Genghis gave the following advice to Juchi, handing the commandership of 10,000 cavalrymen over to him: "The best way to win is to win without fighting. If possible, ask them to surrender. Try not to lose manpower. If they are resistant, completely destroy them and make them an example for others. Never forget that to beat the enemy, you must accept more risks than the enemy."

Genghis gave 5,000 cavalrymen each to Boroqul and Qubilai, with advice similar to what he had given Juchi.

Juchi's targets were the Oyirads, the Kirghizes and other small tribes whose main territories were the forest area at the northwestern side of the Mongolian Plateau. Boroqul was entrusted with the mission to conquer the Qori Tumads, whose dwelling place was the Siberian Forest at the northern part of Lake Baikal. And for Qubilai, the Qarluuds, whose territory was at the southern side of Lake Balkhash, were given to him.

Juchi set out on the expedition. His 10,000 troops moved forward with the black sulde, Genghis Khan's banner, in front of them. Several days later, they arrived at the southern side of Lake Baikal. Juchi's eyes gazed upon the grandeur of Lake Baikal, which was as big as an ocean and filled with uncanny mystery. One side of the lake was lined with cliffs and thick forests, and the nearby mountain peaks were covered with thin light-blue clouds. The dazzling afternoon sunlight was being reflected from the water surface and some icebergs were still floating, even though it was spring.

Juchi arrived at the Siksid, the stronghold of the Oyirads, who were the strongest forest tribe, after going around the southern side of the lake for two full days. The Oyirads were spread out in a wide area in the forest next to the lake and they were using cone-shaped tents. Before the attack, Juchi dispatched Buka, the vanguard and guide, to ask them to surrender. Quduka

Beki, the chief of the Oyirads, gave up any resistance when he received the report that Juchi, Genghis Khan's first son, had arrived with his troops. One time, he had fought against Temujin, joining Jamuka's coalition, and yet, once he saw the fate of Jamuka and the Naimans, he dropped the idea of resistance and decided to join the new Mongol Empire.

Quduka Beki presented Juchi with a pair of white horses and also a pair of white falcons, the symbol of surrender. After disarming the Oyirads' 10,000 troops, Juchi picked 2,000 of them for guides and vanguards and kept on marching to conquer the others. Quduka Beki accompanied Juchi as a guide and also as a hostage. Juchi conquered the other tribes one by one: the Buriyards, the Barkuns, the Urusuds, the Qabqanas and the Qangqas. Juchi always remembered what his father, Genghis Khan, had said: "Surrender does not mean simply giving up resistance. Those that have surrendered should join us and cooperate with us. If they don't accept this condition, do not accept their surrender and annihilate them. Otherwise, you will simply leave danger at your back. This is the safe path for the conqueror."

This advice for Juchi had been handed down from his ancestors, from generation to generation. Once the Mongol troops had passed through a certain area, one of two things could happen. These were either complete destruction of the area without any survivors, or an increased number of Mongolian soldiers, bolstered by the accessory troops who had been drafted from the surrendered people. Usually they became the guide troops or vanguards, and as the Mongol troops were moving forward, their numbers snowballed, and sometimes the number of the accessory troops was bigger than the number of Mongol troops themselves.

Juchi marched towards the west with Quduka Beki as his guide and arrived at the Kirghizes' territory.

The Kirghizes were valiant people with 10,000 troops; nevertheless, they decided to surrender after their tribal chieftains' meeting, acknowledging they couldn't stand against Genghis Khan, who had united the plateau. At one time, they were powerful enough to take a large area in central Asia. Three major chieftains of the Kirghizes, Yedi Inal, Al Diel and Orebeg Digin, showed up in front of Juchi with a pair of white horses, a pair of white falcons and a black sable fur, all symbols of surrender.

Juchi had also drafted 3,000 troops from the Kirghizes and continued to march further west, along with three surrendered chieftains and ten commanders of 1,000 as hostages. Juchi had conquered the Sibir, the Kesdyin, the Bayid, the Tuqas, the Tenleng, the Toles, the Tas and the Bajigid, one by one, over a period of several months. Juchi returned to his father's base camp with all the surrendered chieftains and thousands of soldiers, along with mountains of war booty. The khan was elated by Juchi's successful, safe return.

"He is worthy of being my first son. He accomplished his mission without losing a single soldier or a horse. He is very praiseworthy."

The khan entrusted all the land and people that Juchi conquered to Juchi himself. Based on the unification policy, Genghis

Khan made a marital relation to Quduka Beki. His daughter, Checheyigen, married Quduka Beki's first son, Inalchi.

Meanwhile, Qubilai, who headed southwest to conquer the Qarluuds, crossed the Altai Mountains and finally faced them south of Balkhash Lake. Arslan, the Qarluuds chief, surrendered to Qubilai, who had brought Genghis Khan's banner. He also knew that useless resistance would bring disaster upon him and his people. Qubilai accompanied him to the khan. Arslan, in front of Genghis Khan, kowtowed nine times in the Mongolian style. Upon seeing him, the khan was much impressed to find that he was a young man in his early twenties, with a smart appearance and good physique. Later, he became the khan's son-in-law.

Juchi and Qubilai were successful; however, Boroqul had a different experience. He advanced to the north to conquer the Qori Tumads whose primary residential area was the Siberian Forest north of Lake Baikal. Qori Tumads were living in a safe area, protected by the natural wall of the huge Siberian trees, which didn't allow horses or men to pass. It was the northernmost area where human beings could manage to live without breaking the normal pattern of social life.

The Qori Tumads were mainly hunters, and they lived in cone-shaped tents made of Siberian animal skins, mainly reindeer and wolves. In the winter, they sometimes used reindeer instead of horses. They took advantage of abundant, superior-quality iron ore in their territory to make high-quality weapons and consequently they had relatively strong troops, though small in numbers. Even though they were living in a remote area, they were well-off, bartering all kinds of animal skins, including tigers, mountain leopards, bears, deer, sables and foxes, for their necessities. Genghis Khan needed this area not only for political and geographical considerations, but also for the economic benefits of abundant natural resources, which his newborn empire desperately needed.

Boroqul and his 5,000 cavalrymen had detoured around Lake Baikal and gone deep inside the Siberian forest. The Qori Tumads' base campsite was on a highly elevated area, which was protected by several high mountains, cliffs and taiga, with only one passage in from the outside.

The Qori Tumads were ruled by their regent, Botoqui Tarkun, whose husband had died years ago. Botoqui was a shrewd woman and was also wild and fierce, like a wild Siberian leopard. Upon learning that Genghis Khan's expeditionary troops had left, she gathered all of her people on the open ground and shouted, "We have never been conquered and ruled by others! We will stand to die, rather than sit to live!"

She had her soldiers make many pitfalls, like the ones used for tigers, on the road to their base camp and they also set many strong nets (normally used for bears and boars) between the trees. She had many watch-stands made in the trees and put twenty-four-hour guards out.

Without knowing this, Boroqul, who was in front of his troops, stepped onto the road to the enemy's base camp. It was a relatively narrow road where only three or four horse soldiers could pass side by side, and both the right and left sides were walled with huge Siberian fir trees. Suddenly, Boroqul felt something was not quite right and sensed some kind of danger out there on the road. He stopped there and had two men examine the road. Two of his soldiers dismounted their horses and checked the road. One of them noticed that some part of the road was a little bit different from the other side. Upon receiving the report, Boroqul dismounted his horse and checked for himself. When he pushed his spear into the ground at that spot, he felt no resistance. He quickly realized it was a pitfall.

He shouted back to his troops, "Fall back!"

However, it was too late for him. No sooner had he shouted to his troops than a bunch of huge logs fell down with roaring sounds to block the road. At the same moment, Boroqul felt heavy ropes suddenly falling upon him. He was trapped in a net. He and two other soldiers, who were also caught in the net, were separated from their troops by the log barricade. Within a moment of that, a shower of arrows fell upon Boroqul's troops, resulting in a large number of casualties. They had to retreat. Boroqul, who could not move, couldn't do anything about the seven or eight enemy soldiers who were approaching him. They speared Boroqul's neck. He died instantly, along with his two other soldiers.

The Mongol troops retreated about fifty miles and built up their defense line. They dispatched an urgent messenger to the khan, to inform him of their commander's death.

"What? Boroqul was killed? Put out an emergency alert! I will go there myself!"

But Bogorchu and Mukali tried to stop him.

"My lord! They are a small group. You'd better not go yourself."

Genghis thought Bogorchu and Mukali were right. Genghis picked Dorbei Doksin among the commanders of 1,000 men because he was a fierce fighter and a native of the mountain and forest area. Doksin was his real name and Dorbei was his title, which meant "tough guy." He was given an additional 2,000 troops and a new commandership, as well. Genghis gave him advice, as well as an order:

"Take the rough road instead of the easy one. Danger might be hidden along the easy road. Get enough weapons and equipment for mountain and forest fighting. Hold tight with the soldiers' discipline. Spiritual armament is important. Pray for victory to the everlasting blue heaven."

Dorbei Doksin was a master of the mountain and forest battle. He prepared enough rope and other equipment for mountain climbing, and axes, big chisels and saws for opening the road in the forest. He reinforced his troops with short daggers and scimitars, which were more useful in a mountain and forest battle than long spears and lances.

When he arrived at the Qori Tumads' territory, he immediately took command of the 5,000 horse soldiers who had lost their commander. They scattered themselves over a wide area and advanced, avoiding the areas with possible enemy sentries. Doksin chose rough mountain roads used by wild rams and reindeer, instead of regular roads used by people and horses. They had to open the roads, cutting down the trees and branches. When they reached the point where their horses couldn't move forward anymore, the main troops and horses remained there. Doksin crossed the mountain with only the 2,000 soldiers he brought. First, the soldiers with mountain climbing experience went up to the top, and then dropped down ropes after tying them to big trees nearby, making it possible for other soldiers to climb up using the ropes. Doksin didn't spare the rods for the men who were hesitating to hold the ropes due to lack of experience or fear. Genghis told him to prepare at least ten rods. They conveyed all the necessary weapons and other items with the ropes.

After getting to the top, Doksin, with his 2,000 commandos, examined the area and the enemy's movements. Unlike the way they had traveled, the road from the mountaintop to the enemy's base campsite was an easy descent, with a lot of bushes and tall reeds. Their base camp town was on an amazingly large, flat land and there, thousands of cone-shaped tents were spread out in an organized way. It was late afternoon and a great number of Qori Tumads were out on the open ground with numerous camp fires around them. They were barbecuing, drinking and enjoying themselves. They appeared to be having a feast. They kept on shouting and laughing, watching two trained Siberian black bears dancing to the drumbeats.

Doksin and his commandos crawled as close to the site as possible, and fell upon them all at once. The feast site instantly became a hell. Being hit by the surprise attack, the

Qori Tumads didn't have a chance to organize themselves and resist. They fell into the attacker's hands. Only about ten defiant Qori Tumad young men lost their heads. After all the pitfalls were disclosed by the residents, the 5,000 awaiting troops entered the town. Doksin immediately dispatched an urgent messenger to Genghis Khan, telling him the Qori Tumads had been brought under control and asking for his next instructions. Doksin tried to find Boroqul's dead body, but failed. After being thrown into the forest, Boroqul's dead body had been eaten by wild animals, leaving only a few pieces of bone, his helmet and a torn uniform.

Genghis tried to turn them and make them join the empire voluntarily, considering that they were skillful blacksmiths. Genghis appointed Qorchi as the darughachi, or governor-general, for the Qori Tumads and their territory. Genghis whispered to Qorchi, sending him off to the territory,

"Qorchi Noyan! I want to keep my word that I gave you years ago. You can pick any women you want, up to thirty of them."

After saying this, Genghis winked at him.

However, the Qori Tumads revolted, as the occupation troops had been pulled out of the area, and they took Qorchi into their custody. Genghis took this seriously and dispatched an envoy, Quduka Beki, to find out what had happened there. However, they took him into custody also. At this, an enraged Genghis Khan dispatched Doksin again to annihilate them. The only survivors were the babies, toddlers, women and 100 of the best blacksmiths and leather workers.

Qorchi did get his thirty concubines, and Botoqui Tarkun, the wild woman of the Qori Tumads, was given to Quduka Beki. Genghis gave Boroqul, who was one of the cofounders of the empire, a state funeral and let his descendants inherit all his benefits, from generation to generation.

CHAPTER SIXTY-THREE

Dark Design
of Tab Tenggri

T he religion of the Mongols was traditional shamanism. The shamans ruled the spiritual world of the Mongols. The Mongols were influenced by the shamans from the very moment they were born. They prayed for the newborn baby to have a healthy, long life and divulged prophecy. They blessed the wedding couple and prayed for the bliss of the dead. They used to call the shamans first when they were sick, and when they were planning a journey, they visited the shamans for a prayer for their safe return. The shamans prayed for the soldiers before their departure to the battlefield and the soldiers could not relax at the battlefield without the shaman's prayer. They planned and managed all the ceremonies, rituals and ancestor memorial services.

The shamans had enormous power in their society and, in some cases, they were more powerful than the chieftains. If they had lost a lot of livestock due to an epidemic, and the shaman blamed it on the chieftain being cursed by evil spirits, the chieftain had to resign. Since they held such powers, in many cases, especially in the remote forest areas, the shamans themselves became the chieftains.

Tab Tenggri was the official state priest of the newborn Mongol Empire. He was the Qongqotan and the fourth of the seven sons of Munglik, who was one of the cofounders of the Empire. Munglik had been the loyal servant of Yesugei, the khan's father, for years and had since remained loyal to Temujin's family. One time he helped Temujin escape from Wang-Khan's dark plot. This was recognized as a meritorious service for the khan, so he was enlisted on the upper part of the cofounders of the empire list.

In addition, Munglik had a close relationship with Ouluun, the khan's mother, which the khan never ignored, but rather honored. The seven sons of Munglik were wielding enormous power within the newborn empire. Kokochu, whose official name was Tab Tenggri, held the most power. He knew the khan and his family inside and out. He also knew the khan was checking his brothers.

The newborn Mongol Empire began to have chronic complainers. Mostly they were the ones who had been enjoying high positions in their tribes but in the new empire couldn't achieve anything or had lost everything. Tab Tenggri was surprised to find, as he was contacting people through his duties, that there were so many complainers in the empire. A dark idea began to form in his mind. Many people, speaking nine different languages, gathered around him. He was no longer happy simply being a priest. He was thirsty for power. He emerged as a powerful rival to Genghis Khan in the Empire.

He embarked on his plan to reach the top. Since Genghis Khan held the military and administrative power, his first step was to weaken his military power by splitting it. He picked Kasar as the target for this purpose. Kasar, who had done a great deal of work in building the nation, was appointed as the second-in-command of the Mongol army, which was usually considered a meaningless position. On the other hand, Belgutei, the khan's half brother, was given the position of the supreme darughachi, which was a very important and powerful position. Another thing was that Kasar was given merely 4,000 men while Juchi, the khan's son, was entrusted with 9,000 men. Why did this happen?

At some unknown time, Kasar had fallen into discredit with the khan.

The seven brothers of the Qongqotan, with Teb Tenggri as their head, made a visit to Kasar. Kasar, without knowing the purpose of their visit, ushered them into his visitors' tent.

He served them tea and asked, "Reverend Tab Tenggri! What has brought you here?"

The seven brothers of the Qongqotan sat side by side around Kasar, making a half circle. They regarded him with contempt.

Tab Tenggri, who was six feet seven inches tall, like a human pole, had a tricky smile on his long face and said, "I am here with good news."

After he spoke, he picked up the Chinese porcelain, tea cup and sipped, secretly studying Kasar's face.

"What in the world is the good news?" Kasar asked bluntly.

Tab Tenggri replied, adding an element of dubiousness to his smile, "Some time ago, I received a message from God that your brother, Temujin, would unify the whole plateau. As you know, God's will has been fulfilled and has become a reality. I just received another message from God. It is that you will be the next khan, after your brother, and soon."

Kasar was astonished and jumped to his feet.

"What? I will be the next khan, after my brother?"

As Kasar stood up, all seven brothers of the Qongqotan got on their feet simultaneously.

Kasar shouted at them, "Get out of here! If not, I will arrest you!"

Saying this, Kasar put his hand on the handle of his scimitar at his waist. Six of the Qongqotan brothers fell upon him and held his arms from both sides. They had no fear of Kasar, who had been pushed out of the core power of the empire and was under the constant watch of Genghis Khan. Tab Tenggri slowly walked up to Kasar, who had lost control of his body. He took out his whip from his waist and then said, after whipping his face several times,

"You rat! I know you were a double spy for Wang-Khan, betraying your brother! Once your brother knows about that, you will surely lose your head. You'd better keep quiet about what I am doing from now on."

After they left, Kasar went to visit his brother, Genghis Khan, and told him about Tab Tenggri's visit. He told him about the fact that he had been whipped on his face by him, yet he couldn't tell the whole story in detail.

"Big brother! Get rid of Tab Tenggri! He is dangerous!"

However, the khan wasn't aware of Tab Tenggri's movements at that time and on top of that, he didn't trust Kasar's words.

"You are my brother. No living thing on this plateau can step on you. You said he whipped you. How could that happen? I don't think you are telling me the whole story. What is it?"

Genghis stopped asking Kasar because he kept silent. Genghis didn't do anything; instead, he just watched the development of events. Tab Tenggri began to spread a rumor within the Empire:

"Kasar will be the second khan of the Empire, soon! This is God's will!"

At last, the rumor reached the khan's ears. Acknowledging the seriousness and destructive nature of the rumor, he ordered his guard troops to arrest Kasar.

The news of Kasar's arrest was brought to Ouluun, the khan's mother, by Guchu and Kokochu (a different person from the Kokochu who was now known as Tab Tenggri). Guchu and Kokochu were the orphaned Merkid and Taichut boys abandoned in the battlefield. They had been picked up by Genghis and were entrusted to Ouluun. They were the close retainers of Ouluun and were both the commanders of 1,000 men.

Ouluun was shocked when she received the news and had her retainers get the two-wheeled wagon ready immediately. Ouluun rushed all through the night in the wagon pulled by a camel and at dawn, she arrived at the khan's ordu. As she was entering the tent, Genghis was surprised by her unexpected appearance. By that time, the khan was interrogating Kasar himself. Kasar's official helmet and belt, the symbols of the second-in-command of the Mongol army, had already been removed. The only person Genghis was afraid of was his mother. In Mongolian customs, the mother was the head of the family when the father passed away, regardless of the children's ages. The mother had the right to make the decisions where family affairs were concerned.

"Temujin! How can you do this to your own sibling? What has he done?"

She was filled with an overwhelming sense of outrage. As she was yelling at the khan, she untied Kasar's hands and recapped his helmet and belt for him. She sank down on the floor, cross-legged, overwhelmed by anger. She spoke in a harsh tone.

"I am still the head of this family! What in the world has he done wrong? If you have brilliance that came from heaven, he has talent as an archer. When your enemies tried to get you, his arrows laid them down. When they were revolting, his arrows made them quiet. You already have all this land and there are no more enemies for you. Is that why you don't need him anymore? No! You cannot do that! Never!"

The khan kept silent with his head hung at his mother's reprimand. Ouluun had loosened the upper part of her clothing, opening her top and exposing her two breasts. She continued.

"Take a look at my breasts! You grew up using the one on the right side and Kasar used the one on the left. If you are going to remove Kasar now, this wasn't necessary from the beginning."

After these words, she took out a well sharpened, small hand knife from her waist and cut her left breast. A stream of blood began to gush from the half-cut breast, and stained her lap red, continuing onto the carpet on the floor.

Stunned, Genghis sprung to his feet and shouted, taking the knife away from her, "Calm down, Mother! I promise I won't touch Kasar!"

The khan hurriedly stopped his mother. He immediately called in the doctors. After the emergency care, he had the serving women take good care of his mother.

Afterwards, Genghis didn't remove Kasar, just as he had promised his mother. However, Kasar lost his second-in-commandership of the Mongol army and his 4,000 men were reduced to 1,400. As his position and power within the empire fell, his closest follower, Jebke, disappeared and never returned because of his overwhelming fear. Afterwards, Ouluun's health deteriorated rapidly, and she died about six months later.

Tab Tenggri was successful in the very first step of his dark plan. Many people gathered around him. They were chronic complainers, newly joined opportunity seekers, admirers of his supernatural powers and simple followers. Tab Tenggri's ordu was crowded with these people. Ochigin Noyan, the youngest brother of Genghis Khan, noticed that many of his men had slipped out of his hands and joined Tab Tenggri. He was enraged. He dispatched Soqor, one of his loyal followers, to Tab Tenggri asking for the return of his people. Rather than returning his people, Tab Tenggri whipped Soqor and sent him back to Ochigin with his shoes taken off and his horse saddle on his back, as a gesture of mocking and humiliation. Ochigin was stunned. Enraged, he mounted his horse and dashed to Tab Tenggri's ordu.

Upon facing him, Ochigin upbraided Tab Tenggri and asked for the return of his people. The next thing he knew, the six brothers of Tab Tenggri had surrounded him.

Tab Tenggri said to Ochigin, staring into his eyes, "They came to me of their own free will. If they came to me of their own free will, how can you ask me to return them?"

Since Ochigin didn't know how to answer, he just kept silent.

Tab Tenggri continued, "Is that right? As long as they are here of their own free will, I cannot tell them to go, and more, you cannot ask me to return them. Am I right?"

Ochigin was browbeaten into answering yes, surrounded by seven giants.

"If you know you were wrong, get on your knees! You bastard!"

Ochigin was forced to kneel. Tab Tenggri snorted and left there, after watching Ochigin kneeling in fear.

Early the following morning, Ochigin made a visit to the khan. He couldn't get to sleep that night due to humiliation, which he had never experienced before. At daybreak, when the khan received a report of Ochigin's urgent visit from his night guard chief, he was still in his bed with Borte. Genghis got up and sat on the corner of his bed. Upon entering the tent, Ochigin knelt on the floor and shed tears of rage.

Genghis was stunned to see his younger brother crying like a child because he had never seen this before. A while later, Genghis opened his mouth, reluctantly, and asked him, "Temuge! What's happened? Tell me!"

Ochigin Noyan told the whole story. It was Borte who got mad before her husband. Getting up from her bed and after adjusting her nightwear, she sat next to her husband.

She said in an angry tone, "Who is Tab Tenggri? How dare he whip and humiliate the khan's brothers? Then, maybe someday, he will even whip my children. Who in the world is he?"

Acknowledging the serious nature of the problem, Genghis sought a solution immediately. The khan summoned Bogorchu and Mukali for discussion.

Mukali gave his opinion, "My lord, I think we'd better handle this problem with minimum exposure. If we open this up and make it big, it might be harmful to the newborn empire and might create a lot of innocent victims. If we remove the one or two leaders of this plot, the rest of them might collapse automatically."

Genghis thought there was some validity to what he said. Unity was one of the most important qualities of the newborn empire. Bogorchu shared the same opinion. Even the seven brothers of the Qongqotan wouldn't be a threat if Tab Tenggri was removed.

Genghis Khan called Ochigin Noyan.

"Summon three of the most powerful wrestlers in the empire. Tab Tenggri and his family members are to visit me this afternoon. Get ready for that moment."

In the afternoon, Munglik and his seven sons, including Tab Tenggri, made a visit to the khan. They were ushered into the khan's tent for visitors. No sooner had Tab Tenggri sat in his seat than Ochigin Noyan stepped into the tent, opening the flap door. He walked up to Tab Tenggri and seized him by the collar.

"You bastard! Yesterday, I was forced to kneel in front of you, but today will be different!"

Ochigin pulled him out of his seat roughly. This made Tab Tenggri's cone-shaped hat fall down on the ground. Picking up his son's hat, Munglik tried to stop them. Until that time, Munglik didn't know his son's plot and movements.

Genghis shouted at them.

"You two, get out of here! Any problems between you two should be handled between just the two of you!"

As Ochigin and Tab Tenggri stepped out of the tent, Genghis offered a seat to Munglik and filled his goblet with wine. Munglik's other six sons sat down in their seats as well.

When Tab Tenggri stepped out of the tent, he was immediately captured by three waiting wrestlers. The three wrestlers dragged him to a quiet place and pressed him down on the ground. While two of them were holding his hands and feet, the third one, sitting on his back, held his chin and pulled back strongly. With a dull cracking sound, Tab Tenggri's spine broke. He died right on that spot, with only a horrible, short scream.

Ochigin returned to the tent and gave a short report to the khan, ignoring Munglik and his other sons.

"Big brother, the wrestling is finished! I won! He was nothing!"

As Ochigin was stepping out of the tent after these words, Munglik quickly realized, with his sixth sense, that his son, Tab Tenggri, had been killed. He dropped to the ground on his knees and began to sob with his son's hat in his hand.

"Temujin, I have been serving your family since the earth was a mere handful of dust and the big river was a tiny stream. Please, do not touch my remaining six sons!"

Knowing that Tab Tenggri had been killed, and driven by their father's sobbing, the six sons of Munglik sprang to their feet and approached the khan. Upon being approached by six incensed giants, Genghis felt a moment of panic. Unlike Wang-Khan, Genghis Khan didn't keep in-tent guards.

"Stay where you are! If not, all of you will die, including your father!"

At the khan's shouting, they held their steps momentarily. At that moment, thirty of the day-guard soldiers rushed into the tent and brought them under their control with spears and scimitars. Munglik and his six sons were taken into custody.

Some Mongols were afraid of Tab Tenggri. Some of them even believed Tab Tenggri would come back to life, three days after his death, because he had shown so many supernatural powers during his lifetime. The khan issued an order to put his dead body in an empty tent for three days to prove that this belief was false. The grey tent in which Tab Tenggri's dead body had been laid was sealed off at all the entrances, even the ventilation hole. Ten guard soldiers were stationed there day and night to watch the tent. After three days, the tent was opened and his dead body was shown to the public. His body had already begun the decomposition process, making a foul odor. There was no miracle.

Genghis made a public announcement regarding Tab Tenggri's death and his wrongdoing.

"Tab Tenggri slandered the khan's brothers without any foundations and even touched them, so he has lost the affection of heaven. And so, at last, heaven took his soul away from his body."

Genghis took back the title of cofounder of the empire from Munglik as punishment. Munglik and his other six sons were left alone, based on the judgment that they were no longer a threat and because of the necessity of minimizing the incident. Nonetheless, Genghis admonished him severely.

"This happened mainly because of your negligence. You are the head of the family, and you didn't even know what your sons were doing. This is a case of treason and all your family members should have been massacred. However, in consideration of your previous sacrificial services for our family and this empire, I have decided not to accuse you anymore. Make no more mistakes regarding the educating and supervising of your sons."

Munglik thanked the khan greatly.

Genghis issued an order to arrest Jagambu, who had made a plan to mobilize his troops in accordance with Tab Tenggri's dark plan. Since Jagambu had run away with his close follow-ers the day Tab Tenggri was killed, Genghis dispatched Julche-dei to chase him down. Julchedei brought his head five days later. Genghis deposed his official third wife, Ibaka, Jagambu's daughter, and gave her to Julchedei. Later, Genghis appointed Usun, the Baarin, who was in his later years, but had a well-rounded personality, as the chief priest of the nation. This is how Genghis Khan handled Tab Tenggri's plot of treason, as well as a conflict between the head of the nation and the head of religion.

CHAPTER SIXTY-FOUR

Surrender of the Uighurs

They had the funeral for the khan's mother, Ouluun. They cut a huge, aromatic tree and made a cylindrical coffin out of it. First, the cylindrical log was split in half in the longitudinal direction, and then the insides of each half were carved out, making a shape and enough space to accommodate Ouluun's body. She had her face beautifully made up and she was wearing a luxurious silk dress and gown. On her waist, she was wearing an elaborately designed white leather belt and on her feet were a pair of boots made of doe leather. After they laid Ouluun's body in a comfortable position, they covered it with the other half of the log. They tied the coffin securely with four golden belts. Ouluun's coffin was guided by a woman shaman on a white horse, who was wearing luxurious garments and a hat decorated with colorful birds' feathers. Ouluun was buried beside Yesugei, her husband.

Someone prayed for her:

Here sleeps a noble woman.
We say goodbye to her,
In the midst of surging sorrow.

A fistful of days were given to mortals,
And their lives are shorter than
The glow of the firefly.

And yet, each of her days were
Glittering like jewels,
And shiny and bright like pearls.

As soft as an eagle's chest feather,
And as warm as spring sunlight,
Was her beautiful mind.

She will be with us forever,
Like an indelible shade,
In the hearts of all who miss her,
Sharing joy and sorrow,
Together.

Now, she is free from human bondage,
And has attained the everlasting freedom of heaven,
Like a phoenix.

Is there any other thing in the world,
More beautiful
Than rejoining a loved one.

Again, the new year had come. It was 1209 and the year of the snake in the Mongolian chronicle. The nation's political situation became much more stable. It was the time for the khan to look outside the plateau. The neighbors of the newly born Mongol Empire were the Chin Empire and the Shisha Kingdom to the south and the Kingdom of Uighur and the Kara Khitai of the Khitans to the southwest. Further west was the Khwarazm Empire ruled by Sultan Muhammad. All these countries were made nervous by the sudden emergence of the newly unified Mongol Empire, and among them the Chinese feared them the most.

At that time, China was divided into three nations. The Juchids, who ruled Manchuria, had grabbed the northern half of the Chinese continent, and the Southern Sung, the own ers of the heart of China and descendants of the mainstream dynasty, were ruling the southern half. To the northwest of the continent, as well as to the south of the Gobi Desert, was the Shisha Kingdom of the Tanguts, the descendants of the Tibetans.

The Juchids of the Chin were originally nomads and horse riders, yet once they conquered the northern half of the Chinese continent, they became sedentary city dwellers. They changed everything, including their political and social system, to the traditional Chinese style. The Mongols had been influenced by the rulers of northern China because, traditionally, they considered the Mongolian Plateau their territory. Sometimes the ruler of northern China appointed the king of the plateau and declared it their autonomous region. The Chinese rulers feared the Mongols' unification of the plateau and the growth of their power. They used to use a tactic called "barbarian for barbarian" to make them split and fight each other. If one tribe had become unexpectedly bigger and stronger and showed signs of absorbing others, they dispatched troops to destroy them or helped rival tribes weaken them. Sometimes they used the tactic "operation thinning," which meant sending the troops into the territory and killing all the boys they encountered. It was to reduce the future male population of the Mongols and to minimize future threats. Then why didn't they do anything while Genghis Khan was unifying the whole plateau? They were busy with constant conflicts with the Southern Sung, and they had never expected that he would be successful in such a short period of time.

Genghis Khan knew that he had to bring the Chin and the Shisha Kingdoms under his control to build a solid foundation for the newly born empire. They did not expect the Chin to approve of their newly born Mongol nation, but they thought they would dispatch their troops to break it up and cause them to revert to their earlier condition. On the other hand, the Tanguts of the Shisha Kingdom could not impose such an immediate threat to the Mongols, but they needed to be handled before the khan could go on to the Juchids of the Chin. Moreover, the Shisha were holding part of the Silk Road, and Genghis Khan needed it for financial security and as a road to the outside world.

Even though the unification of the Mongolian Plateau came under Genghis Khan's great leadership, they had been fighting and in conflict with each other for so long that there was a great risk of collapse unless they were given specific motivations to stand together. That was another reason Genghis Khan had to take his people out to the world.

Genghis knew that there was a proper order in which to do things. The Chin had 600,000 troops with an endless supply source, and the Shisha had 150,000 troops with superior financial support. Which one should be first? The weaker one, of course.

A couple of years earlier, in 1207, Genghis dispatched Yelu Ahai and his troops to launch a raid on the borderland of the Shisha. Yelu Ahai, the Khitan, gathered his people, made a successful raid, and returned with numerous livestock and war booty as well as some good information. It was a reconnaissance mission before a full-scale war.

In early 1207, Genghis Khan was ready. However, there was one more thing he had to deal with before he declared war with the Shisha. This was to conquer the Uighur Kingdom, which was bordered by the Mongol Empire and the Shisha Kingdom to the southwest. The khan's generals insisted on the use of armed force.

"My lord! One tumen would be enough for them."

Genghis stopped them.

"Let's wait a little bit. There's a good chance that they will come to me of their own will."

Genghis was right.

The Uighurs, at one time, ruled the Mongolian Plateau and some parts of central Asia. In the eighth century, a large area that covered north of Lake Baikal, south of the Yellow River and east and west of the Manchurian border and the Yenisey River, respectively, was under their rule. However, with the passage of time, their power had waned, so in the beginning of the thirteenth century, when Genghis Khan had unified the plateau, they were merely a small group in a tiny area at the southwestern corner of the Plateau. In the eleventh century, most of their homeland, the southwestern corner of the Mongolian Plateau, had been taken by the Tanguts, who built the Shisha Kingdom, leaving the Uighurs only a small area around the upper part of the Tarim River, to the north of the Taklamakan Desert. In the twelfth century, they were overrun by the new power, the Kara Khitai, and became their vassal state.

Idu qut was the title given to the king of the Uighurs. "Idu qut" meant "holy luck." However, Barchuq, the idu qut of the Uighurs, was not so lucky. His father, the former idu qut, left him a kingdom most of whose land had been lost to the Tanguts of the Shisha and whose autonomy had been lost to the Khitans of the Kara Khitai. Nonetheless, the Uighurs had the most highly developed culture around that area. From early times, they had held part of the Silk Road and absorbed both eastern and western cultures. They developed their own alphabet, gold and silver workmanship, handicrafts, textile techniques and manufacturing techniques for medicinal drugs.

Barchuq, who had become idu qut at age twenty, could not tolerate the interference of the Kara Khitans in ruling his own people. He not only had to pay enormous amounts of tribute to the Kara Khitans each year, but he was also forced to accept their supervision over his government. The shaukem, or national inspector, from the Kara Khitai, treated Barchuq like his own retainer. The shaukem from the Khitai set up his own office and inspected all the decisions made by the Uighur government. Without his approval, nothing could be done. Actually, he was the final decision maker, as well as the dictator of the Uighur Kingdom.

One day, Barchuq, a hot-blooded young man, had surrounded the town where the shaukem's office was located and issued an order to remove the shaukem. Being chased by Barchuq's soldiers, he went up to the top of the mosque tower through the spiral staircase. Bige Qut, one of Barchuq's generals, ran after him and caught him at the observatory. Bige Qut cut his neck right on the spot and picked up his head by grabbing his hair. He raised it high and showed it to the crowd gathered on the open ground below the tower. A great cheer went up from the crowd. After he swung it around a few times, he threw it down to the ground. The crowd on the ground kicked the shaukem's head around like a ball.

Barchuq had an urgent meeting with his high-ranking officials and elders.

"Now we are in a hostile relationship with the Khitans. It is very clear that they will send their troops to destroy us. If you have any suggestions regarding this, let me know."

One of the elders opened his mouth and said in a gloomy tone, "We don't have the troops to face them. They could destroy us. At this moment, the biggest question is how we can save our Uighur blood and make it continue to the next generation. There is only one way. We have to entrust ourselves to Genghis Khan, the newly emerged strong man on the plateau. He is the only one who can stop them."

Barchuq agreed. Most of those present at the meeting shared the same view. Barchuq immediately dispatched two envoys to Genghis Khan. Ad Kiraq and Darbai, Barchuq's two envoys, had an audience with Genghis Khan and handed Barchuq's personal letter to him. One of the civil officials read the letter written in Uighur characters:

> *When the clouds become clear,*
> *We can have warm sunlight.*
> *When the ice thaws,*
> *We can get the water of life.*
>
> *I, the idu qut of the Uighurs,*
> *Greatly rejoiced,*
> *When I heard the great name of*
> *Genghis Khan,*
> *Which is like the sun and the water of life.*
>
> *With the grace of Genghis Khan,*
> *And with your generous permission,*
> *I wish to be a ring of your golden girdle,*
> *And a shred of your crimson garment.*

I, the idu qut of the Uighurs,
With my heart and soul,
Kowtow in front of you,
In the desire of becoming your fifth son.

Genghis put a smile on his lips, smoothing his beard, when he heard the message in the letter, in the presence of several dozen of his high-ranking officials and generals. He was satisfied with the message.

Genghis said to the two envoys, "I will accept the true minds of the Uighur people. From now on, Idu Qut's enemy will be my enemy and Idu Qut's friend will be my friend. However, this decision will be held until Idu Qut's actual visit."

Genghis arranged for warm and cordial treatment of the two envoys.

Later, Idu Qut made a visit to the khan with his senior officials. He came with several dozen camels loaded with their specialty products like gold and silverware, silk products woven into brocade, damask and satin, precious stones and pearls. In front of Genghis, he kowtowed nine times in the Mongolian style. Genghis accepted his surrender and allowed them to govern themselves. Genghis valued and considered highly their well-developed culture and their specialty. Idu Qut and his people could continue to exist and they could keep their own culture. The Uighur Kingdom had been saved.

Afterwards, the Uighurs became very loyal to Genghis Khan and joined every war, though they were small in number. Genghis was very happy with Idu Qut, so he intended his daughter, Al Altun, to marry him. It didn't happen because she died of an illness before the wedding. Contrary to his name, Idu Qut was unlucky.

The Invincible Army

Just as he reformed his Mongol society, Genghis Khan made his troops invincible. Just as he issued the Yassa related to social reform, he also issued a Yassa for the establishment of strict military discipline. Tata Tunga, the secretary-general, always followed the khan like his shadow, wherever he went on foot. While he was observing or inspecting the people's condition or military units, if he gave any instructions, Tata Tunga immediately wrote them down in his notebook that he was always carrying. The cover of the notebook was blue, so later on it was called the "blue book." It was a collection of the khan's sayings, and most of them became social or military laws. Some of the military Yassa were:

- Besides Khan, anyone who declares supreme commandership and anyone who supports him shall be put to death.
- Anyone who refuses to follow a rightful order from his superior related to operations shall be put to death.

- All the commanders should make correct reports to the inspectors. Intentional false reporters shall be put to death.
- Anyone who steps into the tent of a commander of 1,000 soldiers or more shall be put to death.
- On the battlefield, after a charge order, anyone who intentionally falls behind shall be put to death. If two out of ten soldiers follow the charge order, it will be considered a rightful one.
- On the battlefield, if someone ahead of you drops a weapon or knapsack by mistake, you should pick it up and return it to him. Anyone who fails to do this shall be put to death.
- Anyone who provides food and clothing to a captive without permission shall be put to death.

Genghis Khan's martial law was draconian, yet at the same time, he issued laws pertaining to the rights of the soldiers. Some of them were:

- All soldiers have the right to refuse an order from their superior that is beyond the physical and mental limitations of a human being.
- Every soldier has the right to get help from his commander after a report or discussion about any difficulties in his family.

The Mongol soldiers had to keep all their weapons with them in perfect condition without missing a single item. They should be ready anytime, anywhere. They had frequent inspections and anyone who had any missing items had to face punishment. Even though there were some differences among them based on the units they belonged to, the weapons and personal belongings for each individual soldier were generally:

- Two bows, three quivers and more than sixty arrows, either for short, middle or long range
- One scimitar
- One spear with straight blade and hook
- Two daggers
- One battle-ax
- One leather shield
- A long rope for tying
- Two awls
- Two sheepskin bags for carrying water or milk, or for buoys when crossing a river.
- One military saucepan for cooking
- One metal helmet
- One set of leather armor and its accessories
- One pair of leather boots
- One combat uniform
- One pair of silk underwear

Any of these items could be replaced with new ones, when needed, after inspection. The silk underwear each soldier used was solely for protection. When a soldier was hit by an arrow, they could remove it more easily with less damage. Besides that, in the case of a poisoned arrow, it delayed its influence. On the battlefield, any wounded soldier could receive urgent care from the military doctors to minimize the loss of troops.

The soldiers were supplied with dried meat and dried milk for their combat rations, which were like bricks and, handled properly, lasted for several years without going bad. It was almost perfect food.

All the Mongol soldiers were cavalrymen or horse soldiers and they were given two or three horses each. They could switch to another one, when in need, to increase the total mobile power of the troops. Their speed was one of the greatest weapons of the Mongol troops. The Mongol soldiers could even sleep on their horses while they were moving. The Mongol troops had a very accurate concept of time. They used precisely calibrated sundials and sandglasses to minimize errors.

Genghis Khan created a speedy messenger system covering the whole empire. The messenger could take any horse nearby to switch with his tired one and nobody could stand in his way, not even the noyan, or the grand duke. He used specially designed saddles and apparatus that helped him avoid falling from his horse when he was sleepy. He hung a unique bell on his horse's neck to tell everybody that he was a special messenger. With this system, over a distance that normally took more than three weeks to travel, the messengers could make it within a few days.

Genghis Khan reformed Mongol society. One reform was the equal rights of men and women. When the Mongol troops were engaged in a long-range battle, their families moved together with their troops. This was probably a holdover from their original lifestyle, and yet this was generally considered a great advantage for them. The Mongol soldiers were emotionally stable with their families.

While the Mongol women enjoyed equal rights, they were willing to accept their liabilities, too. They took good care of their husbands' weapons, armor, battle boots and combat rations. Sometimes, they joined the battle. In that case, after the battle, they picked up the weapons and armor and performed confirmatory killings of the enemy soldiers. In later times, women's wrestling championship tournaments became a popular event.

The Mongol horses were strong. At that time, the horses were weapons themselves. Mongol horses were smaller than Arabian horses, yet they had more endurance and stamina. They had larger heads and wider nostrils, which meant they could take in more oxygen while they were running. Mongol horses were the only breed that could go without eating for several days and could eat snow instead of drinking water. In addition, they could dig up the frozen ground with their tough hooves to find food. They were tough like the Mongols, probably as a result of the harsh environment that they had endured for so long.

In peacetime, Mongol soldiers had to join the group hunting. Hunting was a traditional game of the Mongols, yet Genghis Khan used it as military training. The group hunt usually took two to three months, and hunting season started around the end of October. Several thousand or sometimes tens of thousands joined the hunting games as a unit.

About a month before the hunting event, scout teams were sent out for preliminary reconnaissance. After careful research, they reported to the khan what they had found, including the possible best location and the kinds of game. Based on this information, the khan decided the number of units and the number of soldiers in each unit.

When the hunting started, the participants surrounded a certain area and gradually closed the circle. Each of the segments of the circle had its own director, and they supervised and managed their soldiers. If they lost a large game through a broken circle, it was a terrible dishonor for the director of that segment, usually noyans. A soldier, or a group of soldiers, of that segment could face severe punishment in the case of negligence.

On the final day, the circle usually became two or three folds, and within the circle, all kinds of wild animals like tigers, leopards, wolves, bears and boars would be roaring and growling while deer and gorals were jumping around. Usually it was the khan who drove his horse into the circle and made the very first kill. Upon picking the target, he would then send an arrow to strike a deadly blow. When the fierce animal fell down with a piercing shriek, the khan would meet with a storm of applause from his soldiers. After that, chances were given equally to every soldier who wanted to show his courage in front of his superiors. In many cases, the Mongol soldiers matched the beasts with only a dagger. Most of them were successful and would hear the applause from their peers and superiors; however, sometimes they were torn into pieces by angry beasts.

When the last moment was approaching, the game was stacked up like a mountain. By their rule, they let baby animals and the impregnated ones go. The hunter's name would be on the hunted game and their skins, hooves, horns, and antlers were given to him as a gift, and the meat was shared equally with everybody. The Mongol soldiers learned the importance of group movement and cooperation, while at the same time, they gained camouflage skills and infiltration techniques. All this was naturally applied to actual combat and battles.

Genghis Khan was well aware of the importance of espionage and psychological warfare. He set up a special unit specializing in intelligence and espionage, and appointed Jafa, who was the Islamic caravanner, and Yelu Ahai, the Khitan, as the chiefs. Genghis usually put two commanders in the same unit if its function was considered important. Each commander had his own manpower and his own system. This was for mutual control, competition and to assure more accurate information.

Jafa disguised himself as a caravanner and made a very precise map of the area from the Mongolian Plateau to Zhongdu, the capital city of the Chin, for military purposes. He took advantage of his acquaintanceships with some of the high-ranking officers in the Chin court to get access to the major members of the court and successfully collect personal information about their individual characters and personal lives.

Yelu Ahai was originally a Chin military officer whose ancestors were the royal families of the Khitans, who had been conquered by the Juchids of the Chin. He had been accredited as an ambassador to Wang-Khan's court. He surrendered and vowed his loyalty to Genghis Khan just before the collapse of the Keraits. Officially, he was the Chin's ambassador to Wang-Khan's court, but actually, he was a spy for the Chin and he regularly had to come and go between the plateau and the city of Zhongdu. Since he was appointed the chief spy for the Chin Empire and the Shisha Kingdom by Genghis Khan, he actually became a double agent.

Based on his outstanding activity, Genghis could get accurate information about the Chin emperor and his top-ranking officers, including their philosophies, personalities and hobbies.

The Juchids, the rulers of the northern half of the Chinese continent, were originally from Liodong, or Manchuria, and were half nomads. Nevertheless, once they became the rulers of the northern half of the continent, they changed. They built up cities and walls and closed their minds. The nomads' nature, an open-minded sharing of all the joys and hardships among their people, had left their minds. They allowed themselves to fall into a traditional crooked Chinese philosophy of the ruling class, which maximized their glory, wealth and pleasure at the sacrifice of their own people.

Therefore, the lifestyle of the ruling class living inside the city walls was luxury itself. The streets of Zhongdu were busy and crowded with stores carrying luxurious, rare and valuable goods and merchandise from all over the world. First-class carpets from Persia, ivory products from India, porcelain products and ginseng from Korea and pearls and bamboo products from Japan were the norm. Theaters for opera, dancing and circus teams were everywhere. They also had banks, where they could change foreign money for the Chin currency or gold.

On the other hand, the people living outside the wall had miserable lives. Mostly they were farmers and low-class workers, and though they were the majority of the population, their living standards were no better than those of the animals. In addition, they had to pay high taxes. When they could not pay the taxes on time, first they lost their wives. Next they lost their children and finally, if they still could not pay, they lost their heads. The number of women and children who were taken away from their homes reached tens of thousands each year.

The Juchids who had refused to move to central China and remained in Liodong resented their changed fellow tribesmen. Significant numbers of Chin generals and officials surrendered to Genghis Khan, though they were mostly the Khitans, and they brought valuable information with them.

Before the wars against the Shisha Kingdom and the Chin Empire, Genghis had to develop some kind of device to attack the walls and fortresses since previously he had only fought nomads, not city dwellers. Genghis had set up a research center for this purpose and they developed the catapult, the mangonel and the ladder carrier. The catapult and mangonel were two kinds of stone throwers that allowed them to shoot heavy rocks at the walls and fortresses to break them down. The ladder carrier was a framed structure to carry soldiers safely to the top of the castle walls or ramparts. Since the Mongols had never built up buildings, they faced some difficulties at first. However, soon they made highly efficient products with the help of Chinese and Persian construction technicians among the captives.

The khan also set up a military school, or training center, to train his soldiers and familiarize them with these new products. The training focused on how to assemble and disassemble these machines in the shortest possible time and how to use them in the most accurate way.

In later times, the Mongols worked out a way to use gunpowder, invented by the Chinese, on the battlefield as an actual weapon. At that time, the Chinese used to put the powder into bamboo cylinders and use them as explosives. The explosives had some impact on the psychological side of war, but did not have much actual destructive force. The Mongols replaced the bamboo cylinder with a bronze one to create a deadly force. The first cannon was invented and introduced to the human world. The Mongol soldiers disassembled all the catapults, mangonels and ladder carriers when they were moving and reassembled them when in need. The Mongols invented grenades later on too. In later times, people acknowledged Genghis Khan as the founder of the artillery unit.

Genghis also set up an engineering unit. They removed obstacles on the roads or made new roads and put floating bridges over the rivers for the troops. Genghis Khan's engineering unit could install a floating bridge, even on the widest river, in only half a day. To build a bridge, first, a veteran swimmer crossed the river with the ropes. Next, with a system of ropes and pulleys, they sent the leather bags filled with air to the other side of the river. On the overlapped air bags, they placed wide and thick boards and then secured them. Even horses and cows, with a safe distance between them, could cross the river safely.

People later described this highly efficient engineering unit like this: "When the Mongol troops passed, the mountains became flat and the rivers changed their direction."

Genghis Khan's tactics and strategies were perfect. In any battle or any war, he formulated the best possible operations based on the condition of his troops and the enemy's, geographical considerations, timing and weather. As far as military tactics and strategies were concerned, his head was filled with limitless and infinite ideas. He understood the fundamentals of physical force. His brain always promptly figured out the amount and direction of the force he needed to destroy the enemy. Sometimes, the Mongol troops moved over a wide area that could be several hundred square miles, and then suddenly, they came together in an instant and destroyed the enemy. This was the combined force of Genghis Khan's military sense and accurate, dynamic calculations with the mobile power of his troops. No other troops, even with the best weapons and armor, could stand against this force.

Genghis Khan was the perfect warrior and, just as the Persian historian Juvaini said, the Mongol troops were the most powerful in the history of humankind. What was the basis of this powerful force, born in the Mongolian Plateau, and what motivated them to come out into the world?

CHAPTER SIXTY-SIX

Break-up with Chin

I t was March, spring, yet patches of snow still covered the plains of the Mongolian Plateau. They have long winters on the plateau. The plains of the plateau used to be surrounded by eerie silence just before the arrival of the sand-storms. At this time of the year, there were no migratory birds, either. Unless you have eyes that can catch the tiny movements of the sun that radiate dazzling sunlight over the plain, you will fall into the illusion that you are in a world of stillness, even in time.

Late in the morning, on the southern horizon, which was forming a beautiful white curve with the cobalt-blue sky over it, a small dot appeared. As if to prove the world was still alive and moving, the dot became bigger and bigger as time went by. The dot eventually formed into an image of a man on his horse. The sound of the horse's hooves gradually in-creased in volume and echoed through the space of stillness like a wave. The Mongol soldier in his helmet and armor had beads of sweat covering his forehead and the black skin of his horse was glossy with sweat. On his back was tied a small pole with a constantly flapping rectangular flag showing he was an urgent messenger. At the same time, a small metal bell, the second symbol of his duty, which was hanging around his horse's neck, was making pleasant sounds in harmony with the clatter of hooves. He was an urgent messenger and until he arrived at his destination, the khan's ordu, nobody could stop him.

At that moment, Genghis Khan was presiding over a morning meeting in his tent with about thirty of his high-ranking officers and generals. As the southern side flap door was opened, Alqai, one of the eight day-guard captains, stepped inside, walked up to the khan and gave him a report in a low tone. The meeting had been interrupted.

"My lord. An urgent messenger has arrived from the second border garrison."

Genghis Khan asked him, "What is the report?"

Alqai, stooping down, said in a lower tone, "An envoy from the Chin has arrived at the second border garrison and is waiting in their captain's tent."

The khan summoned Yelu Ahai, who arrived immediately upon the order. Yelu Ahai was one of the two spy chiefs.

"I just heard that the Chin envoy has arrived at the second border garrison and is waiting. What could that be? Do you have any idea?"

The Chin did not send envoys on a regular basis, only on special occasions. The Chin considered the Mongolian Plateau their territory. At one time, the Chin emperor had enthroned Wang-Khan as the king of the Mongolian Plateau. Wang-Khan received the title for the emperor's personal and practical reasons. Now, Wang-Khan was dead and his Kerait nation had disappeared, which meant there was no more king who needed approval from the Chin emperor. There was only Genghis Khan, who had united the whole plateau.

Yelu Ahai gave an answer in a low voice.

"Maybe they have a new emperor. The Chin emperor, Zhaozong, has been sick for about six months now. But, I don't know who became emperor, because it has been a while since I was there."

Genghis gave this a little thought and then gave an order to Alqai, who was waiting next to him.

"I will see the envoys. Get the horse ready!"

Genghis headed for the second border garrison, which was about 150 miles southeast of his ordu. The second border garrison consisted of 800 soldiers with the duty of patrolling the border area between the southeastern corner of the plateau and the Gobi Desert. The khan was accompanied by Yelu Ahai, Alqai and 300 day-guard soldiers. About three hours later, they arrived at the second border garrison camp. When the khan arrived at the entrance of the camp, he was greeted by Tuge, who was the captain of the garrison.

"Where's the envoy?"

To his question, Tuge answered, "They are waiting in my tent, my lord."

When Genghis Khan arrived at the tent, he saw the Chin envoy with his two assistant envoys. About twenty official entourage members were waiting outside the tent in their official uniforms and headgear, which were all golden-colored, the official color of Chin. On the open ground in front of the tent was a red carpet beneath a short, rectangular purple table. On the table was a rolled letter wrapped with golden silk cloth. It seemed they were ready.

As Genghis dismounted his horse and walked up to them, the three envoys bowed to him deeply and one of them made a half-step forward and said, "We brought the emperor's royal letter for the Mongol Khan! Please, receive it, after bowing thrice!"

Originally, Genghis Khan was supposed to kneel down and touch his forehead on the ground three times. Staring at him, the khan said to the envoy in a loud voice, while standing, "Go ahead and read! I came here to listen to the message."

As Genghis Khan was refusing to kneel and bow, the Chin envoy had no choice but to open and read the letter. Yelu Ahai, standing next to Genghis Khan, interpreted the message into Mongolian, word for word.

The message was that since the new emperor of the Chin had ascended to the throne, the Mongol Khan had to vow allegiance to him and had to be present at the royal court once a year.

That meant Genghis Khan must make a visit at the beginning of each and every year to Zhongdu, the Chin capital, to show that his loyalty had not changed. Having heard this humiliating message, instead of getting angry, Genghis asked the envoy in conversational tone, "Who is your new emperor?"

The envoy answered, as he was stooping, "The king, Weishao. Wanyen-Youngji is the new emperor now."

Genghis gave a little thought and then said to himself, "King Weishao is the one known to be stupid! How could he become an emperor of a nation?"

Genghis clicked his tongue. Actually, King Weishao was considered by many a silly and timid person.

The khan told the envoys in a loud voice, "Listen to me! The Mongol nation is now completely independent! The Mongol khan will never bow to anybody! Tell your emperor!"

Genghis spat these words and mounted his horse. He stared at the south once and spurred his horse. He galloped back, and Yelu Ahai, Alqai and his 300 day-guard soldiers followed him.

The Chin envoys could do nothing but watch Genghis Khan and his followers disappear into the distance.

The Chin emperor, Weishao, a fat man in his forties, was enraged when he heard the bad news. Upon realizing that Yelu Ahai, the ambassador to the Mongol nation, had defected, he issued an order to put about ten of his family members in prison. Yelu Ahai's wife and his children remained in Zhongdu since he was not allowed to take his family with him by order of the Chin emperor. They were hostages to the Chin.

Yelu Ahai knew the fate of the Khitans in Chin. The Khitans, who had been conquered by the Juchids of Chin, could make it in their society, but there were limits. They were always second-class citizens, and all the dangerous, dirty jobs were left to them. Being sick of this, Yelu Ahai secretly defected to Genghis Khan and became one of the Baljuntus. However, he had to bring his brother Yelu Tuqa as a hostage to Genghis Khan, voluntarily, because he had to come and go between the Mongolian Plateau and Zhongdu two to three times per year on official duty. It was the minimum required condition that would satisfactorily gain the khan's confidence. Later, Yelu Tuqa became a day-guard member. Yelu Ahai was a double agent. Genghis knew that. Since he was a double agent, did he have two minds, too?

About fifteen days after the Chin envoys' visit, Genghis noticed in the official meeting that Yelu Ahai's face was clouded. After the meeting, Genghis met him individually.

"General Yelu, you don't look well. Do you have a problem?"

He sighed and replied in a despondent tone, "They put my wife and children in prison."

The khan seemed shocked.

"What?"

The khan's eyes showed mixed feelings of anger and sadness. Without any words, the khan just gazed at his eyes for a while, as if dumbstruck. Yelu Ahai kept on sighing, as if he did not know how to handle his despair. Genghis patted his back in a gesture of sympathy.

"Don't take it too hard. We'll try every possible way to save them."

They walked together, side by side, talking over the possible plans.

Early the following morning, a large group of caravanners left the Mongolian Plateau. There were 200 Khitans and Persians, all of them with big and powerful physiques. They galloped without a single pause, and arrived at the Onggut territory, north of the Great Wall, that afternoon. One hundred camels and appropriate luggage were waiting for them, readied by Ala Qus, the chief of the Ongguts, who had already received the urgent message. They took the camels and luggage, disguising themselves as a real caravan.

With the help of Ala Qus, they crossed the Great Wall and rushed to Zhongdu. They arrived at Zhongdu four days after they had left the plateau and all 200 men successfully infiltrated the city. They were commandos on a mission to attack the prison retaining Yelu Ahai's family members and rescue them. However, they were unlucky. Though they had rushed at maximum speed, they were one step too late. The day before their arrival, all ten of Yelu Ahai's family members were massacred on the open ground in front of the prison, under the eyes of thousands of spectators, on the charge of being the family of a betrayer.

The rescue operation had been framed by Yelu Ahai himself, based on the fact that the prison was guarded by only 200 soldiers and located at the southwestern corner of the city, which was an isolated area with infrequent traffic. After saving his family from the prison, they were to escape in disguise from the city with the help of Genghis Khan's enormous spy system in Zhongdu. Originally, it was estimated they had a 50 percent chance.

The khan knew it was hard to find words to console Yelu Ahai.

"Among them was my four-year-old son. I heard they pressed his chest down with their feet until he died."

Yclu Ahai sobbed in sorrow as he was saying this.

CHAPTER SIXTY-SEVEN

Attack on the
Shisha Kingdom

The Shisha Kingdom was founded by the Tanguts, the descendants of the Tibetans, and was located at the northwestern corner of the Asian continent south of the Gobi Desert. It were composed of Tanguts and some Uighurs and Han Chinese as minorities. Most of the inhabitants were engaged in foreign trade, animal husbandry and farming, and their main religion was Buddhism. They were very independent people, and they made and used their own unique writing system, modified from the Chinese.

In 1038, Li Wonho, the founder of the Shisha Kingdom, had taken control of a part of the Silk Road, driving the Uighurs, who were the former occupiers of that region, out. Having become stronger since then, they began to conquer nearby cities one by one, including Dun Huang. They had 150,000 strong troops supported by the economic power to protect their main source of income, the Silk Road. Since their economy depended heavily on the international trade business and taxes from the caravans, they kept a keen ear on international politics and changes in the situation.

In the year 1207, as the Khitan troops led by Yelu Ahai, under the permission of Genghis Khan, invaded and plundered their territories, there was a coup in their court.

"How can the Mongols wage a war against us without any justification?" asked one of the senior officials who belonged to the moderate party in their royal meeting. General Weiming Linggong, a hardliner among them, countered. He had a vision and was a man of resources.

"Did we take the Uighurs' land on any moral justification? It is very clear that the Uighurs will surrender to the Mongols. In that case, they might come to us asking for the return of their old territory with their new friends, the Mongols. Anybody can go into war, if they need to, without any moral obligation."

Another senior official, a moderate, opened his mouth and said, "Even though the Mongols are coming to us, we have our own ally, the Chin, and we can ask them for help. How can the Mongols think of standing against a nation with 600,000 troops?"

The Shisha Kingdom had had a mutual defense treaty with the Chin since 1165, and it was still in effect at that time. Weiming Linggon jumped to his feet, pounding the table with his fist. He argued in a loud voice, staring at the official who had just said that.

"The mutual defense treaty is good only when it is beneficial to both parties! The chances are less than half that they would send their troops to help us! Do not trust anybody! We have to take care of ourselves!"

They disputed. Since their king, Li Chunyu, took the side of the moderates, Weiming Linggon and Kao Liang Hui, along with other hardliners, plotted and carried out a coup. They deposed Li Chunyu and backed Li Anqan, who was also a hardliner, as their new king. The citizens of the Shisha Kingdom accepted this and cooperated with them because they understood their motivation was for their own protection.

Li Anqan, the new king of the Shisha, had the Wolohai fortress, which was the gateway from the Mongolian Plateau to Chunghing, the capital city of the Shisha, repaired and reinforced to be impregnable. He also reinforced the city walls of Chunghing and hired 20,000 new mercenaries, increasing his defense troops from 150,000 to 170,000. It was the year 1208.

In May 1209, Genghis Khan advanced towards the Shisha Kingdom. He sent about 60,000 troops. The Mongol troops crossed the Gobi Desert. They marched day and night across about 200 miles of desert road. They marched slowly yet steadily, making huge plumes of golden dust on the rough desert road with scenery of dunes, faraway horizons and occasional short, dried out bushes in the ground of sand and mud. The front group, Jebe's cavalry, was holding Genghis Khan's banner made of nine horses' manes high, and its dark silhouette made by the desert's strong sunlight was fluttering, dancing. At night, the desert moon in the dark sky was pouring its bright moonbeams on the heads and shoulders of the soldiers and horses, making long moon shadows on the sandy field. Their well-sharpened and polished spear blades were flashing under the moonlight, giving off a chilly image. Their long line stretched from the northern to the southern horizons, and their horses' hooves continuously shook the ground, making a deep rumble. It was majestic scenery. They were full of passion, dreams of the outside world, confidence in victory and glory. They were full of spirit.

After about 650 miles of marching, on the fourtth morning after they had left the plateau, they arrived at a spot where they could see a huge fortress built on elevated ground. On both sides of the fort, high ramparts of red brick, built Chinese style, were stretching out to a wider area, encircling the whole city, and chains of high hills with thick forest also encircled the outside of the city like a second rampart. It was Wolohai, the northernmost city of the Shisha, with a perfect fortress.

Genghis stopped there and reorganized his troops. Genghis went up to a nearby hill and looked at the fortress and ramparts. The ramparts of strong mud bricks were reflecting pure red under the morning sun.

"Why didn't they cut off all the trees on the hills around the city?" the khan thought to himself, eyeing the high hills and mountains with thick forests near the rampart. The forest around the rampart could get in the way of their protection rather than provide it. The Shisha troops didn't show any sign of movement, though the Mongol troops had arrived. It seemed that they were using the defense-only tactic.

The khan called a staff meeting. First, Yelu Ahai explained the situation and the arrangement of the fortress and the city on the map.

Genghis asked, "How far is it from the fortress to the Yellow River?"

Yelu Ahai answered, "It is thirty li by the Chinese measurement system."

It was about seventy-five miles.

Genghis gave this a little thought. It was clear that the reason the Tanguts didn't cut down the trees was to retain their source of water. They were using the mountain streams as their source of drinking water. Genghis asked his staff for opinions. Many of them insisted on a direct attack on the fortress and ramparts with the equipment they brought, since the soldiers had already invested a lot of time in training for that.

Genghis concluded, "We will attack them with fire. If we launch a direct attack from the beginning, we will lose many soldiers. We have to pull them out of their fortress."

Genghis moved his left wing to block the route from the Yellow River to the fortress and, at the same time, sent 3,000 Uighur troops to take over the mountain streams in the forest near the rampart. Genghis presumed that since the Wolohai fortress and city were built on elevated ground, it would be hard for them to get water, and all the houses in the city would be made of wood, because it was in a wooded area.

The Wolohai fortress was originally a city of 20,000 civilians with 5,000 garrison border troops. About a year prior, the Shisha prince, Li Tsun Hsiang, and General Kao Liang Hui had moved in with their 50,000 regular troops. They evacuated the civilians to other cities and took over all their houses for their troops. They were using them as barracks. They knew that the fortress Wolohai was at a high elevation, which was good for protection, but difficult to get water to. They dug wells in several areas, but to no avail.

The impregnable Wolohai fortress revealed its weakness, the water problem. The amount of water needed for 50,000 soldiers and 50,000 horses was enormous. About fifteen days later, they faced real trouble. The Mongol troops who occupied the high hills and mountains near the rampart began to shoot giant arrows into the city. Their giant bows were made of huge, resilient iron rods and were designed to be carried on a two-wheeled cart and pulled by a horse. When shooting, two to four soldiers had to combine their strength to draw the bow to shoot the giant arrow, the size of a regular spear. They tied a cloth soaked with oil firmly at the tip of the arrow, lit it on fire and shot at the fortress. These huge metal arrows traveled far beyond the shooting range of regular arrows and lodged in the wooden walls and columns of the houses within the fortress. In a moment, numerous houses were wrapped in flames, making thick smoke. They did not have water to put out the fire. The terrified horses began to neigh and jump around.

Kao Liang Hui issued an order to his 50,000 soldiers.

"Open the gate! We will fight to the last man!"

After tightening his helmet cord, he mounted his horse.

At last, the gate of the fortress was open, and a great number of the Shisha troops poured out of the fortress. Genghis Khan's main troops were waiting for them in the field, in five lines. As 50,000 Shisha troops were dashing out, Genghis, watching this from a small hill, gave an order to his adjutant officer to raise the blue flag. At this signal, the Mongol archers in the first line began to shoot to the accompaniment of loud tin drumbeats. The front runners of the Shisha cavalrymen fell down from their horses in a multitude, like autumn leaves. Upon completion of their job, the archers retreated backward through the pathway made in the middle of the other four lines. After this, the second line, 10,000 of the light cavalry, dashed toward the incoming enemies. Their main weapons were short-range bows and arrows and javelins. They dashed toward the enemies even as they were shooting the arrows. Only Mongol soldiers could shoot arrows while they were galloping at full speed. They were so quick, none of them fell from their horses until they completed their retreat. Now, it was the third line's turn. The third line was also light cavalry and their main weapons were javelins. Each of them had four or five javelins and they shot down approaching enemies one by one. Their main task was to put the enemy battle line into disorder; yet more than half of the Shisha troops had been destroyed by this time. Following this, a red flag was raised high among the deafening sounds of the drumbeats of the nacaras. The fourth line, the heavily armed cavalry, dashed toward the enemies. They were protected by heavy armor and metal helmets, and even their horses were wearing armor. They were the main destructive power. They used the long spears with hooks, scimitars, battle-axes, maces and man-to-man combat.

Soon, the number of the Shisha troops was reduced by half. The battlefield was covered with dead bodies, mostly the Tanguts. Kao Liang Hui retreated back into the fortress with his remaining troops. Genghis Khan ordered his troops to take the fortress. The Mongol soldiers went over the fortress walls with the ladder carrier. The ladder carrier moved on four wheels and was as tall as the enemy rampart. The front, left and right sides of the ladder were covered by wooden walls to protect the soldiers while they were moving the structure or using the ladder.

The gate of the fortress had been opened by the Mongol commandos and the Mongol cavalrymen poured in. There was another big massacre inside the fortress and Kao Liang Hui was torn to pieces by the Mongol soldiers. The Shisha prince, Li Tsun Hsiang, surrendered with his remaining 15,000 soldiers. The Wolohai Fortress had fallen to the Mongols. The door to Chunghing, the Shisha capital, had been opened.

Surrender of the Shisha Kingdom

Genghis Khan took a three-day break at Wolohai, then again began marching toward the south. It was about 120 miles from Wolohai to Chunghing, the capital city of the Shisha. Chunghing was a big city on the banks of the Yellow River. The city was protected by high ramparts and most of the houses within the city were built in the Chinese style. The majority of the citizens were Tibetan Buddhists, so there were many Buddhist temples within the city. The tall pagodas built on every corner of the city could be seen from far away. The streets within the city were wide, and the houses were well built and neatly arranged. This city was a stopover for caravans traveling between Chang-An in China and Samarqand or Baghdad, so shops, stores and inns for the caravans closely lined the streets. They built a canal through the city and received daily necessities, such as vegetables, fruits and meats, from outside the city through this passage. Every day, alongside and around the canal, it was crowded with sellers and buyers of merchandise from dawn until noon, the official hours of the market. At the entrance and exit of the canal, they installed gates made of thick iron bars that could be freely raised and lowered to control the traffic. These bar gates were opened at dawn and closed at dusk like all other gates.

The Mongol troops, who had left Wolohai at daybreak, arrived at noon at a spot where they could see a few high hills covered with thick forest. It was about thirty miles from the city. Genghis Khan stopped there and had a staff meeting.

Genghis asked, "Who is Weiming?"

Yelu Ahai answered, "He is considered to be the best general among them. He has won many victories in small and large battles with the neighboring nations. He is said to be somewhat hot-tempered and reckless."

The khan, after discussing with his staff generals, gave his conclusion.

"Presumably, Weiming might have hidden his big troops in those hills. We will trick them."

The Mongol troops marched on. As the Mongol vanguards stepped onto the road between the hills, a shower of arrows fell upon them from both sides of the hills. As the vanguards kept on marching, covering their bodies with large shields, a great number of Shisha soldiers came pouring out of the woods. The Mongol vanguards turned around and began to retreat. Encouraged by this, the Shisha general, Weiming, ordered an all-out attack. Even after about five miles of chasing, they could not catch up with the retreating Mongol vanguards.

The Mongol cavalry soldiers surpassed the Tanguts in horse-riding skills.

At this moment, from the woods on both the left and right sides of the retreating passage came loud battle cries. They were the Mongol left- and right-wing troops, ambushing the enemy. Weiming, who was leading his troops at the head, regretted and lamented. However, it was too late.

"Alas! I fell into their trap!"

A great many Shisha soldiers fell from their horses, pierced by the arrows showering down on them from the woods on the left and right sides of the road. At the same moment, the retreating Mongol vanguards turned around and launched a counterattack, backed by the Mongol center force. The large number of Shisha troops, 100,000 of them, had been cut in half by the Mongol left and right wings, like a snake being cut into two pieces. Across the field and on the hills, the dead bodies of the Tanguts were strewn. They suffered a great loss. Only half of them made their way back to the city, and Weiming, the commander-in-chief of the Shisha troops, was taken captive at the hands of the Mongol soldiers. The Mongol troops continued marching and surrounded the suburbs of Chunghing. Genghis Khan looked around outside the city. The city rampart built with red bricks appeared to be incomparable in its size and sturdiness. Genghis admired it, but thought, "To take this fortified city, we will suffer a great loss of soldiers. I must find an alternative way."

At this moment, in the city, an urgent meeting was being held by the Shisha king, Li Anqan, in the presence of high senior officers and his generals. Li Anqan said in a gloomy tone, "The

Mongols have surrounded the city. What shall we do? Let me know what you have in mind."

A heavy silence hung among them for a while. Nobody was willing to open his mouth lightly. They could not find an easy way, after the collapse of their 100,000 troops and their entrusted general Weiming Linggong being held captive by the Mongols.

After a long silence, a senior general got on his feet and said, "All we can do right now is close the gate firmly and muster ourselves for defense. We still have 70,000 troops in the city and we have stored enough provisions for one year. We have a very strong and well-built rampart. Even the Mongols might not be able to come over it easily. Also, we'd better send out an urgent messenger to the Chin for help, since we have a mutual defense treaty with them."

Li Anqan accepted his suggestion.

At midnight of the same day, a barge slipped out of the city silently, passing through the opened iron gate between the canal and the Yellow River. The eastern side of the city, across from the Yellow River, had not been occupied by the Mongol troops. Two messenger soldiers and their two horses were on the barge and a ferryman was leading them. In the total darkness, without even the dim moonlight, the experienced ferryman safely took them over to the other side of the river. Upon landing, the two messengers immediately got on their horses and galloped towards the east at full speed. Their destination was the city of Zhongdu, the Chin capital. With very little pause or sleep, they galloped across 700 miles and, three days later, arrived at Zhongdu. They successfully completed their mission, handing the letter from the Shisha king over to the Chin emperor.

The Chin emperor, Weishao, called a meeting. It was almost six months since he had become the emperor after his predecessor, Zhaozong, had died. First, the Chin emperor had his clerical staff read the letter from the Shisha king. After listening to the message in the letter, the Chin emperor looked over the whole assembly of attendants, about 100 of his high-ranking officials and generals, and said, "As you all heard, the Mongols have besieged Chunghing, the Shisha capital. The Shisha king is asking for rescue troops, based on the mutual defense treaty, which was agreed upon by my predecessor. I want to hear what you think about this."

Hushahu, known as the "Great General," got on his feet. Hushahu was an outstanding man who had both valor and resourcefulness. He gained a series of victories in the war with the Southern Sung, which made him very popular among his people.

This ambitious man with a big appetite said, "There's an old saying that 'if you lose your lips, your teeth will suffer.' If Shisha falls, the Mongols will surely come to us. We had better send our troops to help them. That's how we can help ourselves."

Some other attendants shared the same opinion with him. However, Weishao, the emperor, was a narrow-minded man with poor vision. He did not accept Hushahu's advice.

"The Tanguts of Shisha and the Mongols are both enemies. I think it would be profitable for us if they fight each other. Leave the dogs to fight each other."

There were no rescue troops sent by the Chin. Thus, the mutual defense treaty, which was enacted in 1163, was invalidated by the Chin emperor's ignorance.

Having received information through his spy network in Zhongdu that the Chin were not dispatching rescue troops, Genghis set up the second phase of his plan, a long war. Without relieving his encirclement, he blocked all the supply lines to the city of Chunghing from the outside. Three months passed. In the meantime, there was no full-scale battle, just a few minor skirmishes. Some Mongol soldiers ridiculed the Tanguts by showing their superb horse-riding skills when they got bored. They galloped close alongside the rampart, hanging off the sides of their horses, after covering the side facing the enemy with armor. At other times, some of them even did handstands on their running horses when they were at a safe distance.

As autumn was drawing near, Genghis had to try a different tactic. Genghis realized that they had enough food for the prolonged war, since they showed no sign of trouble after three months of blocking the road. Genghis ordered Yelu Ahai to interrogate the prisoners. First, Yelu Ahai tried Weiming Linggong and the prince, Li Tsun Hsiang.

Yelu Ahai asked Weiming, "What is the amount of stored provisions inside the city?"

However, there was no response from Weiming, who was sitting on the ground, cross-legged. It was hardly expected that someone like Weiming would reveal their top secret on any account. As Yelu Ahai was repeating the same question, Weiming responded with an unyielding attitude.

"I am a defeated soldier. Go ahead and cut my head off! That is what I want!"

An awkward silence hung between them for a while. Yelu Ahai opened his mouth slowly and said again, "General Weiming, you'd better surrender. My lord, Genghis Khan, accepts anybody who surrenders from his heart. You will be his friend. But, if you keep on resisting, you and your people will be annihilated completely."

After these words, Yelu Ahai took him to the huge hollow, where 20,000 Shisha captives were packed in. The hollow was naturally made, but was enlarged by human hands to make it big enough to accommodate 20,000 captives. The hollow was so deep, it was impossible for them to climb up to the ground level without the help of a ladder or rope. A Mongol guard soldier on the ground level threw several pieces of beef jerky into the hollow and thousands of them swarmed to catch it.

"Look! We do not have enough food to feed 20,000 captives. Several dozen of them die each day. Their fellow soldiers in the city will never know of their suffering. There is nothing we can do about this. Remember, they are the ones who surrendered to live."

Until that moment, Weiming did not know the situation of his former soldiers, because he and the Shisha prince, Li Tsun Hsiang, were allowed to stay in separate tents with special foods and services, even though they were prisoners.

Genghis found that they had enough provisions for 300,000 city residents and the 70,000 remaining soldiers for at least one year. At the same time, he found that most of the provisions were stored in basements, in the form of rice, wheat and dried beans. Genghis set up a new strategy based on the knowledge that most houses in the city were made of bricks and mud and they had more than enough water because of the canal.

"We will attack them with water!"

Genghis ordered his engineering corps to build a dam on the Yellow River. The engineering corps began to build a dam just below the city. They used the Tangut prisoners to carry the rocks and mud. The dam-building construction started in early fall and lasted more than three months. As the dam construction was approaching completion, the water began to fill the city. The canal was overflowing. The water began to flow into the basements. The city was put under a state of emergency. A great number of soldiers and residents were put into action to move countless bags of grain to higher places; nevertheless, they had already lost more than half of their supplies. Moreover, the warehouses, filled with millions of rolls of silk and hundreds of thousands of carpets, were flooded. Those were the items that were on top of their priority list. If those items were ruined, their economy would be ruined along with them. The water level in the city rose higher, up to the level of an adult's knee. They couldn't even make a fire for cooking. The residents became restless and agitated. The talk of surrender among them was on the rise.

At this time, something came up: the dam collapsed. The Mongol engineering corps did not have enough experience building dams. They also did not have enough qualified engineers. The big waves of the Yellow River began to sweep over the Mongol campsite. The Mongols immediately pulled down the tents, picked up their weapons, equipment, and food, then escaped to higher ground. Genghis keenly felt the necessity of scientific technology and related specialties to win the war, in addition to excellent generals, brilliant strategists, valorous soldiers and superior-quality weapons. After this, Genghis always kept the technicians, engineers and specialists in a particular area wherever he went. He not only saved them but also treated them very well, so as to win them over to his side.

While they were busy escaping, Yelu Ahai hurriedly rushed to the khan and reported, "My lord, the hollow has been flooded. What shall we do with the prisoners?"

The khan's answer was quick and clear, "Save them!"

The operation to save the 20,000 Tangut prisoners began. The Mongols saved most of them using ladders and ropes. A few days later, the Yellow River went back to its original level, leaving numerous small and large pools and even a new lake. This was the moment when Weiming Linggon of the Shisha voluntarily showed up in front of Genghis Khan. He kowtowed nine times toward the khan, which he had refused to do up to that point.

He opened his mouth and said gravely, "If you give me a chance, I will try to persuade the Shisha king to surrender."

Upon these words, Yelu Ahai, who was standing next to Genghis, whispered in his ear, "My lord, can we trust him?"

Genghis offered him a seat and let him be served with some warm tea.

"General Weiming, from now on, you are my friend. Try your best not to make your words in vain."

Weiming, as he promised, successfully persuaded the Shisha king, Li Anqan to surrender. He acknowledged that Genghis Khan would not go back without Shisha's surrender and it was the only way to save Prince Li Tsun Hsiang, 20,000 prisoners and the Shisha economy. Actually, since their main source of income was the profits from the commercial activities and taxes from the caravans, their economy was already seriously damaged by the prolonged war. After about two months of negotiations, a white flag finally appeared on the main gate of the city.

The official ceremony of surrender was held on the large open ground in front of the main gate of the city. As the huge main gate was being opened, an event unseen in the last eight months, the Shisha King, Li Anqan, showed up with a pair of rare white camels and a pair of white falcons, symbols of surrender. Li Anqan was wearing the official costume and headgear, the light-golden silk garment with luxurious designs and the short, purplish, cylinder-shaped cap. He was followed by about twenty of his high-ranking officials and next to him was his seventeen-year-old daughter, Chaqa.

The Shisha king was ushered into Genghis Khan's official tent. About 200 of the Mongol generals and important people were standing in the tent in two lines, with the east and west walls of the tent to their backs, and a red carpet was spread out neatly from the southern entrance to the khan's seat at the northern end. As the Shisha king stepped into the tent, Genghis stood up from his seat. The Shisha king walked slowly on the carpet and bowed when he arrived in front of Genghis Khan. He didn't need to kowtow based on previous negotiation. In return, Genghis also bowed toward him and offered him a seat on his right side. Having a seat, the Shisha king opened his mouth and said in a gentle tone,

"We, the Tanguts, have been hearing of your great and awe-inspiring name. Now you have made your appearance in person, and we, the Tanguts, with your permission, promise to be your right hand, with our best."

Yelu Ahai, who was sitting behind Genghis Khan and the Shisha king, interpreted his words and told Genghis in Mongolian. Yelu Ahai was fluent in the Tangut language.

Genghis said to the Shisha king with a smile on his face, "Thank you very much for your sincere words. From this moment on, the Mongol Empire and the Shisha Kingdom will be mutual friends, sharing the same destiny."

The Shisha king, Li Anqan, continued, "We, the Tanguts, unlike the Mongols, are sedentary people. We build houses and stay there. We have houses and ramparts to keep. We cannot join the battle quickly and we cannot make and carry out strategic plans swiftly. Instead, we will supply enough camels, which can be used both for transportation and as a source of food. At the same time, we will also supply woolen goods and silks."

Upon hearing these words, the smile disappeared from Genghis Khan's face. It was against the number-one condition of surrender, which Genghis had strongly demanded. That was, at any time, on demand, the Shisha king must mobilize and send troops to Genghis Khan to support him, and it had already been agreed to. What the Shisha king said was that their economic support was possible, but not their military support.

Staring into his eyes, Genghis Khan said clearly, "Without the promise of military support, this treaty won't be accomplished."

As Yelu Ahai said this to the Shisha King, he lowered his head and agreed to accept that condition. The document for the peace treaty, actually an instrument of surrender of the Shisha king to Genghis Khan, was made. It was written in two languages, and both of their national seals were stamped on it. The instrument had been made by Tata Tunga and they made two for each nation. By this time, the Mongols already had their own writing system, developed from the Uighurs', which had been developed by Shigi Qutuku by the order of Genghis Khan. The Tanguts also had their own alphabet, modified from the Chinese scripts. The Shisha king and his kingdom remained in existence with their own autonomy.

After the peace treaty, the Shisha prince, Li Tsun Hsiang, and 20,000 of their prisoners were released. And Chaqa, the seventeen-year-old daughter of the Shisha king, joined Genghis as his fifth wife. In addition, 2,000 camels and mountains of silk and woolen goods, along with numerous other gifts were given to Genghis Khan. It was January 1210.

CHAPTER SIXTY-NINE

War with the Chin

In March 1211, a khuriltai was held on the Kerulen Riverside on the Mongolian Plateau. A huge tent, which could accommodate more than 2,000 people, was erected. All the high-ranking officers, generals in the Empire and Barchuq, the idu qut of the Uighurs, and Arslan, the king of the Qarluuds, gathered together. Through this khuriltai, they officially approved the Uighurs and the Qarluuds as vassal kingdoms, and at the same time, more importantly, they unanimously approved the war with the Chin Empire.

The Mongols were ready. Genghis Khan had been preparing for this war over the last two years. The war with the Chin would have a profound impact on the future of the newly born Mongol Empire. If the Mongols won, they might be able to establish a solid foundation for the new Empire, if they lost, their dream would vanish. Genghis estimated that the war with the Chin would take about five years. At that time, Chin was at the height of its power and influence. After they won the war with the Southern Sung, they took over the heart of the Chinese continent and all the major cities.

Even on a giant rock, there is always a crevice you can put a chisel into. That was what Genghis believed. Genghis already had an almost perfect plan.

Before departure, Genghis went up to the Burkan Mountain. He set up a tent there, in which he planned to stay all by himself. The Burkan Mountain, which was unchanged and still had its grandeur and majestic features, seemed to be covered with holiness. The lofty peak of the mountain was shrouded in mist and was connected to the purple sky.

Genghis fasted and prayed for three days and three nights. For three days, he had nothing but water. On top of the mountain, where he could hear only the sound of the wind passing through the pine needles like waves, he spent three days praying and meditating. The outcome of the war with the Chin would determine the fate of himself and his people. He slept only five hours during the three days, with a few drinks of water from a sheepskin bag he had brought. The mountain summit in May was still cold, yet numerous beads of sweat were standing out on his forehead. He shouted toward the sky with his belt around his neck:

Tenggri, god of the everlasting blue sky!
Allow me the power.
Let me have revenge for Ambakai Khan and Okin Barak.

Allow me to punish the Juchids,
Who gave my forefathers
Never-ending humiliation and agony.

Allow me to punish the Juchids,
Who kept on breaking our wings,
And gave us never-ending disunity and conflict.

Allow me to punish the Juchids,
Who are going to put an
Everlasting bridle on our children.

Destroy the world with no souls,
Which is full of falsehoods and selfishness.
Allow me to be your right hand,
To create a new world with new order.

Allow me the victory!
So the sacred name of the Mongols,
Should not be trod on,
Anymore.

On the fourth morning, Genghis descended the Burkan Mountain. About 200,000 Mongols were waiting for him on the field at the foot of the mountain. They had participated in Genghis's three-day fasting and prayer. Previously, they had built two temporary camp towns, one for men and one for women.

Genghis walked up to them and shouted, "Heaven allowed me victory! Victory is ours!"

The 200,000 Mongols began to chant in a loud voice, pounding their fists in the air.

"Tenggri! Tenggri! Tenggri!"

Their shouts echoed into the mysterious blue sky, the depth of which was unknown and filled with desert air.

Genghis Khan headed south toward the Chin with his troops, which had been divided into three groups. It was in the middle of May, two months after the khuriltai. He took a total of 65,000 horse soldiers. That was the maximum number he could take.

The number of enemy troops he had to deal with was 120,000 horse soldiers, plus a half-million foot soldiers, making a total of 620,000. It was almost ten times more than his own troops. In the eyes of the third party, he must be gambling. Genghis left 20,000 troops in the Mongol mainland to handle a possible rebellion and appointed Taquchar, the Onggut, as the commander.

The war with the Chin was anticipated to last about four to five years, so the married soldiers were allowed to have their family members accompany them. Because they did not build houses, but used portable yurts, their lifestyle made this possible. It gave them emotional and psychological benefits, which made them feel much more comfortable with the long-term expedition. However, not every family member was allowed to go with them. Before departure, all the applicants had to pass a screening and anyone who was considered inappropriate for the long-term expedition was denied, including those who were too young, too old or handicapped. They had a good system in their homeland of taking care of their remaining family members.

Genghis was taking two of his wives with him, Yesugen and Qulan. Previously, Genghis had deposed his third wife, Ibaka, because of her father's rebellion, and put Yesugen, his second wife, also Yesui's sister, as his third wife in her place. Genghis let his four sons, Juchi, Chagatai, Ogodei and Tolui, take part in the war also. Although seventeen-year-old Tolui was not allowed to command an independent unit, he was to accompany his father and learn the art of war.

Genghis had never neglected to educate, teach, advise and train his four sons. Whenever time allowed, he sat with his four sons and told them all the stories he had heard from his parents and all the other elders when he was a child, about their actual experiences and philosophies.

One time, he was sitting with his four sons, in front of a big tortoise that a Muslim merchant had left as a gift. Genghis said to his four sons, "Look at this tortoise! He is endowed with natural protection. While he is in the shell, his safety is guaranteed. However, when he is in his shell, he cannot move. The Chinese are like this. They built castles, ramparts and high city walls to safely live in, but because of that, they cannot move out of their world at all for thousands of years."

After these words, Genghis Khan asked a question of his four sons, "There is an animal that eats this creature that is protected by a rock-hard shell. What creature could that be?"

Since nobody gave an answer to that question, Genghis said, with a smile on his lips, "A tiger. Do you know how a tiger eats this tortoise?"

Again, as there were still no answers, Genghis told them, "They just bite hard on it to crush the shell. Their teeth and jaw bones are strong enough to do that."

After these words, Genghis let out a loud guffaw.

A while later, Genghis looked around at his four sons and asked again, in a serious manner, "Chinese eat tortoises. Do you know how they kill them before cooking?"

Since they had never seen such a thing, they could not give an answer. Juchi speculated an answer, "They can just put it in boiling water, is that right?"

Genghis answered in the negative, "Chinese don't like that cooking method. They take out their blood before cooking."

Genghis Khan told one of his nearby servants to bring a piece of meat and a metal stick with a small hook at the tip of it. When the meat and hook were ready, Genghis cut the meat into small pieces and put one of them onto the hook. He put the meat close to the mouth of the protected creature and waited. Being enticed by the smell of the meat, it immediately took the bait. As he pulled out the stick with the hook, its neck was stretched out almost the span of a hand.

Genghis continued, "They put it like this on the chopping board and cut the neck."

One time, Genghis Khan asked his four sons, "What is man pursuing in the end?"

Ogodei, the third son, answered, "One time you told us it is freedom."

Genghis Khan replied, "Right! Men pursue freedom. However, even though freedom can give them a feeling of comfort in their minds and souls, it cannot conquer the feeling of emptiness. They are constantly looking for something with which they can conquer the feeling of emptiness. Some people indulge themselves in religion and some others give their lives to their children. Some people even give up the freedom they had been striving for for this. This is what leaders have to do, to find something for them. If you can find it for them, they will follow you to the end of the world."

The Mongol troops stepped into the desert. The soil mixture of sand and mud stretched endlessly to the faraway horizon. From there, the Mongols began to fan out. The first army, led by Jebe, turned in the western direction, and the third army, led by Genghis Khan's three sons, turned to the east. This was to confuse the enemy and to split the enemy defense line.

Genghis Khan's second army, the main group, arrived at the northern side of the Great Wall in early June after marching 450 miles across the Gobi Desert. It was the Ongguts' territory. Ala Qus, the chief of the Ongguts, came out to see Genghis. Genghis and Ala Qus were already relatives by marriage. Genghis had four sons and five daughters with Borte, his first wife, and one of his daughters, Alaqa, married Taquchar, the first-born son of Ala Qus.

"I welcome you, Genghis Khan! It is a great pleasure to see you again."

With his several dozen generals, Ala Qus showed his hospitality. Side by side they drove their horses to look around the Great Wall. The Great Wall, built with red bricks, was winding over the hills and mountaintops, stretching endlessly and shining blood-red, reflecting the afternoon sunlight. Genghis was filled with admiration for the scale of the structure; he also was full of contempt for the builders.

How many of them had to be sacrificed for this? And how long? Didn't they know the real protective wall should be built inside their minds?

The director, manager and supervisor of the Great Wall were the Ongguts. Ala Qus, the head of the Ongguts, not only opened all the gates of the Great Wall for Genghis Khan, but also supported him with 10,000 of his own troops as volunteers. Jebe's first army and Genghis Khan's three sons' third army had no problem crossing the Great Wall. Genghis Khan discussed all the possible consequences of the war with Ala Qus. Ala Qus promised full support to Genghis Khan.

Genghis Khan continued to advance toward the south, looking at the vast Chinese territory. The three armies were keeping in close contact, using speedy messengers every day. Even though the Mongol troops were moving in three separate groups, because of this messenger system, they were moving like one body, and when in need, they could come together in an amazingly short time.

Genghis went over the framework of the war plan and strategies with the high-ranking generals and commanders. Each commander was allowed to operate his own plans and tactics within the boundaries of the main outline.

Genghis Khan's main troops advanced farther south after attacking and taking the Chin's northernmost city of Fucho, and then swept over the area, also taking Kalgan and Xiandefu. All the cities close to the border had relatively low city walls and their garrisons were mainly filled with foot soldiers, so they could not match the Mongol troops of horse soldiers. Genghis made a movement farther south, with his two spy chiefs, Yelu Ahai and Jafa.

Several days after crossing the Great Wall, Genghis arrived at the foot of the huge mountains.

Genghis asked Yelu Ahai, who was driving his horse next to him, "Do you know of any mountain passes we can use to cross the mountains?"

Yelu Ahai replied, "Yes, we have the Yehuling Pass."

Genghis looked around the Yehuling Pass, which meant "wild fox" pass. Between the high mountains covered with thick forests there was a route through which a large number of troops could pass, though it was narrow. Genghis issued an order to his generals.

"We will stay here and wait for the time being."

Genghis Khan's strategies and tactics were unique, and therefore almost impossible for the enemies to guess. They could never predict where and when he would come. Genghis Khan's strategies and tactics were always different, just like a master chef creates a thousand different kinds of dishes with only the materials given to him. Genghis Khan used to advise his generals: "To win the battle, you should be willing to take more risks than your enemies do."

Jebe's first army was sweeping over the towns and cities in Shansi Province. Genghis dispatched a messenger to tell Jebe to attack Xijing. Xijing was located about 200 miles northwest of Zhongdu, the Chin capital, and was in the center of Shansi Province. Its population was about 200,000 and a garrison of 50,000 troops was defending the city. By the order of Genghis Khan, Jebe's first army attacked the city every day. However, it never fell to the attackers due to the protection of the high, tough city wall.

About fifteen days later, at midnight, two Chin horse soldiers were rushing out of the city through the half-open gate and galloped at full speed toward the south after breaking through the encirclement.

They were urgent messengers, sent by General Hushahu, the commander-in-chief of Xijing. The Chin emperor, Weishao, had an urgent meeting after he received the message. Until that time, he did not know the movements of the Mongols. Previously, conflicts and minor troubles were the norm at the border area, so Weishao did not pay much attention to that report. Yet many of his officials and generals, who had felt that something was different in this case, strongly pushed him into taking action. At last, the Chin emperor issued an order to Jujin, the "great general," to take care of the problem, allowing him 100,000 troops.

Jujin, the Chin general, headed for the north toward Xijing with his 100,000 troops. The Chin troops of 100,000 men began to cross over the Yehuling Pass. Not knowing Genghis Khan's three army groups were waiting in ambush, they began to cross the pass in a long line. When half of their troops had crossed the pass, they were attacked by the Mongols. Cut in half, without time to reorganize themselves, the Chin troops met with a crushing defeat. About 70,000 dead Chin soldiers were strewn across the Shansi field within a mere half day. This was the biggest victory the Mongols had achieved up to that point. The Mongol soldiers shouted in jubilation, raising the head of the enemy general, Jujin, which had been cut off and put on the tip of a spear. Genghis had Jebe's first army advance farther south to open the road to Zhongdu and also had his three sons attack and occupy the cities in the Province of Hopei.

Jebe's first army continued to advance to the south and attacked the Juyung Kuan, the first gate to Zhongdu. The Juyung Kuan, the impregnable fortress, was seated on top of a high hill and guarded by 30,000 garrison troops. Jebe's first army of 15,000 troops attacked the fortress every day. The Mongols shot rocks weighing about 150 pounds with the catapults they had brought. However, the rocks could not reach the fortress because of the lack of power.

Jebe decided to try a different tactic: a fake retreat. The Mongol troops left all the equipment there and retreated. Having watched the Mongol troops disappear into the horizon, the Chin troops opened the gate and came out to take all of the equipment and luggage. While they were busy moving them into the fortress, suddenly the Mongol troops came back. They did not even have time to go back to the fortress and close the gate. Speed was one of the greatest weapons of the Mongols. They didn't allow their enemies to make an accurate estimate of time. The impregnable fortress, Juyung Kuan, fell to the

Mongols after complete destruction of the 30,000 Chin garrison troops.

Upon receiving the report that the Juyung Kuan had been taken, Genghis Khan issued an order to Yelu Ahai, who was with Jebe, to launch an attack on the horse ranch owned by the Chin royal family, located near the city of Zhongdu. Yelu Ahai, with his 2,000 troops, attacked the ranch, making 50,000 horses scatter in all directions. They also took several thousand of them. The Chin troops fell into a difficult situation trying to retrieve the horses, which would take several months. The road to Zhongdu had been opened.

CHAPTER SEVENTY

The Split of Chin

Zhongdu was the biggest city in the world at the time. The city of one million people was protected by a forty-foot-high rampart made of tough bricks. The width of the rampart at the bottom was fifty feet and at the top it was forty feet, which was wide enough for four cavalrymen to run on the rampart road side by side. Below the rampart were three moats that blocked an enemy approach, and the total length of the rampart was twenty-six miles. Nine hundred watchtowers were installed on the rampart, and its twelve gates, all made of thick metal, were impossible to break down with any equipment known at that time.

The city of Zhongdu was the capital city of many empires. Before the Chin Empire, it was also the capital city of the Lio Empire of the Khitans, when they named it Yenking, and, at later times, it was called Peking or Beijing.

Some of Genghis Khan's generals insisted on a direct attack on the city of Zhongdu. However, Genghis explained to them, "China is a country with a huge amount of land and an enormous population. Before we advance to Zhongdu, we have to take the Xijing and Hopei provinces first. If not, we could be surrounded by them."

At this moment, an urgent messenger sent by Jebe arrived in Juyung Kuan. The message was that the peace negotiation team from the Chin had arrived there and was waiting for the khan's answer. Genghis decided to see them.

The Chin negotiation team included a chief envoy and two assistant envoys, and one of the assistant envoys was a Khitan named Simo Mingan. He was an acquaintance of Genghis's. The Chin side specially picked Simo Mingan as one of the envoys because of his fluency in Mongolian and his acquaintanceship with Genghis Khan. In the past, Simo Mingan had met with Genghis several times in Wang-Khan's court. Yet this time, he was actually a spy. He was told to collect all possible information related to the Mongols' movements.

The negotiation did not work out. There were too many differences between them. One day before their return, Yelu Ahai, who had guided them from the Juyung Kuan to Genghis Khan's campsite, came to him and said, "My lord, Simo Mingan wants to see you privately. What do you think?"

Genghis accepted. Upon the arrival of Simo Mingan, Genghis Khan's guard soldiers tried to take off his clothing. Historically, the Chinese frequently used tricks to have their assassins approach the enemy chief disguised as a special envoy or defector. Because of this, they usually had them take off all their clothing and gave them new clothes to wear before their audience.

"Leave him alone! If I do not trust him, he will not trust me, either."

Genghis welcomed him, raising his two arms highly, and shook hands with him.

"Welcome! General Simo! How is everything with you?"

Genghis offered him hot tea. Simo Mingan, a man in his late forties, honestly confessed that he was the Chin's spy.

At this, Genghis replied with a smile on his lips, "I already knew that."

He spoke his mind that he wanted to surrender to Genghis Khan. The Khitans, who had been conquered by the Juchids of the Chin, were second-class citizens in the Chin society. They could not get the highest, most important positions and all the difficult and dirty jobs were theirs. One group of them gave up everything and took the world as it was, and yet, there was another group who were constantly trying to free themselves from the oppression of the Juchids. Simo Mingan belonged to the latter.

Originally, Mongolian and Khitan were the same language. However, with the passing of time, their languages had changed, little by little, and at the time of Genghis Khan they couldn't communicate at all without interpreters.

"This war is not only for the Mongols, but also for the Khitans to free themselves from the grip of the Chin," Genghis explained.

Genghis received valuable information from him. Besides the fact that they had enough provisions in the city of Zhongdu to last a year for a million people, he found that the Khitans in

Liodong Province had the willingness to fight against the Chin, with the help of Genghis Khan.

"I promise the Khitans their own autonomous government and land," Genghis told Simo Mingan.

Simo Mingan did not go back to Zhongdu. Upon realizing Simo Mingan's betrayal, the Chin emperor issued an order that all his family members should be beheaded. They took about forty of his family members into the market place and cut their heads off on the charge of being the family of a betrayer.

Simo Mingan shed tears when he heard this bad news.

"The Khitan people are bigger than my family." Saying this, he repressed his tears. Genghis tried to console him.

At the same time, bad news was continually coming from the third army of 15,000 cavalrymen, who were attacking Hopei Province. The report was that they could take the small cities and towns, but failed to take the big ones due to strong ramparts protecting the cities. They said it was impossible to cross over the ramparts with the equipment they had. The war came to a lull. Genghis felt the urgent necessity to make improvements on the equipment.

In March 1212, Genghis worked out a new strategy. He sent out Yelu Ahai and Simo Mingan on a secret mission to contact Yelu Luko, who was the descendant of the Khitan royal family of the past Lio Empire and a spiritual leader for many Khitans. They successfully contacted him and made a secret agreement to work together in rebuilding the Khitan realm. Genghis Khan dispatched Jebe with 20,000 cavalrymen to help them. Jebe's

20,000 cavalrymen and the Khitan militia worked together and successfully took over the city of Lioyang, which was the former capital of the Lio Empire, and the nearby large territory. Genghis Khan approved of the newly born Khitan Kingdom and allowed them autonomy.

Genghis Khan kept his promise to Simo Mingan. Yelu Luko, the new king of the newly born Khitan Kingdom, remained loyal to Genghis Khan out of true appreciation for eight years, until he died.

In May, Genghis launched an attack on the city of Xijing with his main troops. They used much-improved equipment to attack the fortress and rampart, but they still could not take it easily. The battle lasted about a month. At this time, something came up. Genghis, who had been urging his men at the front line, was shot by an arrow from the city fortress. The arrow lodged in his right shoulder, breaking the clavicle. A Uighur military doctor performed emergency surgery.

"Everything will be all right, my lord. However, you will need at least several months before you can use your shoulder freely like before," the Uighur military doctor said.

The Mongol troops retreated from all battle lines, due to Genghis Khan's wound. Genghis crossed back over the Great Wall and set up interim headquarters near Dalan Lake, in the Onggut territory. He stayed there until the spring of 1213, taking a rest, and gave an order to his engineering unit to develop new equipment for the high-walled cities in the meantime.

In the spring of 1213, Genghis Khan crossed the Great Wall again. The Mongols advanced unchallenged, taking the cities one by one with their newly developed equipment, including the ones they could not take before. One of the newly developed machines for crossing ramparts was a huge ladder vehicle, which was pulled by sixty oxen. The Mongols, in preparation for attacking a big fortress or city, attacked the nearby small cities first, isolating the large city, and only then would they proceed. During these battles, if the people in the small cities surrendered, they were saved. If not, they were all massacred. It was part of the psychological warfare to terrorize the enemy. The people in the cities, once they learned that the Mongols were coming, were terrified and lost the will to fight.

It was inevitable for the Mongols, who had to deal with an enemy with a much larger population in a vast land. After taking the cities of Hsuan Hua, Pau An, and Huai Lai, the Mongols destroyed the Chin garrison of 100,000 troops near Nan Chow. Genghis Khan advanced to Lung Hu Tai, the town near the capital city. However, at this time, something else came up: the Ongguts rebelled.

From the beginning, the Ongguts had been divided into two groups. One group was pro-Mongol, and the other was pro-Chin. The chief of the former group was Ala Qus, the present chieftain, and the head of the latter was Kelmish, his nephew.

Kelmish was the official heir to the chieftainship. He was unhappy with Ala Qus, who was cooperating with the Mongols one-sidedly, opening the gate of the Great Wall and keeping all the war booty for them. He began to agitate his people: "There's no guarantee the Mongols will win this war! If they lose, the Chin will retaliate against us. We'd better keep neutral."

He attacked Ala Qus's tent with his twenty followers, and put a spear through the chest of his uncle, Ala Qus. He declared himself the new chieftain and seized enormous amounts of war booty that Genghis Khan had entrusted to Ala Qus. Genghis took this very seriously, because the Onggut territory was his military supply warehouse and complex. He immediately called off all battle plans, dispatching Subedei as the commander of the suppression troops. Subedei, with his 5,000 troops, easily subjugated the rebels. A large part of the suppression troops were the Ongguts. After arresting about 2,000 rebels and their families, Subedei asked Genghis for their punishments. Taking into consideration their relations with the Ongguts, Genghis ordered him to execute only Kelmish and his close followers with their family members, making about 200 in total.

Hushahu, the garrison commander of Xijing, the largest city in the western region of Chin, was unhappy. Even though he was a very popular general who had won many battles with the Sung, he was sent to Xijing, the city of second or third importance to the Chin. The Chin emperor, Weishao, was jealous and uncomfortable with his rising popularity. Historically, the Chinese emperors used to send the generals with rising popularity out to remote areas to prevent possible rebellions. The combined motivations of the unhappy feelings of a victim of unjust treatment by his emperor and an uncontrollable desire for power made

Hushahu return to Zhongdu, abandoning Xijing. He left only 10,000 troops in Xijing, under the leadership of one of his lowest ranking men, and headed to Zhongdu with his 40,000 regular troops. He successfully entered the city, tricking and killing the garrison commander, and surrounded the palace. He carried out a coup. He captured and killed Emperor Weishao, along with his wives, concubines and children, about 300 people in total. He became the regent and emerged as the new ruler of the Chin Empire. He picked Prince Udabu, the cousin of Weishao, to be the new emperor, with the title of Xuanzong.

The puppet emperor, Xuanzong, was not happy, because he knew he had no power. Hushahu, the regent and dictator, began to take action to remove his political rivals. The first one was general Shuhu Gaoqi. He appointed him chief of the field troops to fight against the Mongols. In those days, the rulers or dictators used to send their political enemies out to the battlefield when they had a very slim chance of winning, to remove them.

Shuhu Gaoqi went out to the field, but soon, he decided to return. Once he lost the battle, it was clear that he would be removed by Hushahu. Entering the city with his troops, he surrounded Hushahu's house. His soldiers destroyed everything in their way, killing all of his family members. Hushahu tried to escape in his pajamas, crossing over the back wall. He was too late. A lance thrown by Shuhu Gaoqi lodged in his back and he fell down.

"You, bastard!" said Shuhu Gaoqi, gripping Hushahu's hair with his left hand, lifting his head, and then cutting his neck with the sword in his right hand. His twenty-one days of power ended like this. Shuhu Gaoqi presented his head to Xuanzong, the new emperor, which made him rather happy. In return, he appointed Shuhu Gaoqi as the commander-in-chief of the Zhongdu garrison. Shuhu Gaoqi told Xuanzong,

"It is impossible to face the Mongols in the field. However, if we concentrate on the defense of Zhongdu, they will never be able to cross the rampart."

Shuhu Gaoqi reinforced the defense system of Zhongdu. It was September 1213.

Negotiation with the Chin

After the coup and the political change in the government of the Chin, the Mongols swept over the land above the Yellow River for six months. Genghis divided his troops into five groups and then he sent them take Shansi, Hopei, Shantung and the southern Manchurian areas. The first, second and third armies were given to Genghis Khan's three sons, Juchi, Chagatai and Ogodei, respectively, and the fourth army was left to his two brothers, Kasar and Temuge, known as Ochigin Noyan. Genghis kept his promise to his mother to leave Kasar unharmed, and at a later time, he allowed him to earn back some of his positions. Genghis, with his fourth son, Tolui, and the fifth army, advanced toward Shantung Province.

During this period of time, the Mongol troops took over, or destroyed, ninety small and large cities in this region. The people of resistant cities were massacred completely, and the houses, buildings and ramparts were leveled. The northern part of the Chinese continent was stained with blood and covered with the dead bodies of the Juchids. If a city surrendered, a Khitan or a Han Chinese was appointed as the head and all the residents had to cooperate with the Mongols in their next battle.

Kasar, who had advanced towards southern Manchuria, taking over all the cities in that region, stepped into the territory of the Koryo, or Korea, crossing the Yalu River. He sent out the envoy to the Koryo government, asking if they would cooperate with them in removing the remnants of the Chin troops hiding in their territory with additional troops and food support. Realizing that they could not stand against the Mongol troops, the Koryo government agreed to cooperate. With the support of food and road guides, Kasar destroyed the Chin hiding in Korea and returned, crossing back over the Yalu River.

Thus, Genghis conquered almost all of the northern part of the Chinese lands and collected an enormous amount of war booty. He appointed Lu Bailin, the surrendered Han Chinese, as the head of the fallen city of Xijing, the former western capital of the Chin. Now Zhongdu, the capital city of the Chin, was like an island in the ocean.

In April 1214, all five armies of the Mongols gathered on the field near the city of Zhongdu. It was called the Sira Keer by the Mongols, which meant the "golden field," and it was covered endlessly with grass that reflected a bright, golden color in the afternoon. From there, they could see the vague image of the grand city of Zhongdu. While they were there, Genghis gave his soldiers and horses some time to rest.

The Mongols commenced an attack, first with the catapults, targeting four fortresses near the city. They shot rocks of 50 to

150 pounds toward the fortresses. The catapults worked on a similar principle to the bow. With the catapults, they used a huge, resilient, thin sheet-metal rod instead of a wooden frame like that of the bow. To shoot the rocks, about ten soldiers had to pull the thick rope, tying both ends of the metal rod to the wooden lever that was connected to a bag holding the rock. The rocks could reach up to 100 yards, based on their size.

The ladder carrier was designed to carry the soldiers safely up to the top of the rampart. Viewed from the side, it resembled a right triangle, and the front, meeting the bottom at a right angle, was covered with a protective wooden plate. The inclined part, the hypotenuse, was the ladder area. This type of structure usually had four to six huge wooden wheels, and could either be pulled or pushed.

The rocks shot by the Mongol soldiers sailed in the right direction and destroyed the fortress walls built with logs and mud. Next, the Mongol soldiers went over the walls with the ladder carriers. Within a few days, all four fortresses fell into the Mongols' hands. After this, Genghis ordered a direct attack on the city of Zhongdu. However, the rampart of Zhongdu was so strong that the rocks shot by the catapults did not damage it at all. In addition, the three layers of moats did not allow the ladder carriers access to the wall. The Mongol troops made two attempts, but both failed. They could not cross over the wall, and they could not destroy it.

Genghis Khan held back the third attack. The continual attacks with a slim chance of success would merely increase the number of casualties, and his soldiers, who were in an unfamiliar climate, began to show signs of unknown epidemics. The weather was becoming hot.

Genghis decided to open negotiations with them. Four special envoys were dispatched into the city of Zhongdu. The envoys consisted of two Mongols, one Khitan and a Muslim Persian, Jafa, who had good inside knowledge of the Chin. They were carrying the personal message of Genghis Khan:

> *With the help of heaven,*
> *And the guidance of God,*
> *All the land above the Yellow River,*
> *Has come under my rule.*
> *If I take your last stand,*
> *I do not know what heaven will tell me.*
> *I plan to pull my troops back.*
> *But you must find a way*
> *To appease my generals,*
> *Who will never step back,*
> *Without complete destruction*
> *Of your city.*

Along with this personal message, Genghis Khan imposed four conditions:

1: The land above the Yellow River shall be under Mongol rule.
2: Approve the full sovereignty of the new Khitan Kingdom in Liaodong Province.

3: Pay the reparations.

4: Send an acceptable hostage.

Upon receiving the message, the Chin emperor, Xuanzong, had a meeting with his senior officials and generals. Wanyen Fuxing, the premier, got on his feet and said, "Everything has its own time. Now is the time for the Mongols. Heaven and earth are on their side. They destroyed our powerful troops and took over the Juyung Kuan, which is like the lifeline for Zhongdu. If we continue this war, the future of our empire will be very uncertain. At this moment, the best way is to appease them, turn them away, and at a later time, we will make a better plan for them."

The Chin emperor, Xuanzong, accepted his opinion. In May 1214, the agreement was made. The Chin emperor accepted Genghis Khan's four conditions, sending his eighteen-year-old daughter, princess Chikuo, as Genghis Khan's new bride. The princess Chikuo came with her dowry of 3,000 fine horses and an enormous amount of silk and valuable treasures. At the same time, similar amounts of silks and treasures were given to the Mongol generals. It was known that they could not take all of the given treasure with them, because it was simply too much for them to carry. Princess Chikuo also came with 500 boys and girls, ages nine to twelve, to be her personal servants.

Genghis left Zhongdu. As he was crossing over the Great Wall, Genghis released Wanyen Fuxing, who had accompanied them as a hostage. Genghis did not go back to his hometown;

instead he stationed himself near Lake Dalan, which was in the Onggut territory.

Princess Chikuo was weeping. She became Genghis Khan's official fifth wife. It was the first night for the married couple. Inside Genghis Khan's tent, which was decorated for the newly married couple, the lights from the Chinese beeswax candles were dimming. The bed was laid with silk bedding and pillows. The floor was covered with high-quality red carpets from Bukhara. In the corner of the tent there was a luxurious Chinese tea table, set with a large silver plate with a neatly arranged silver tea set. Just next to it was another table with two silver plates with some tropical fruits and light foods on each. Both plates were covered with silver lids, to keep the smells from clouding the tent.

Genghis, sitting on the bed, was looking at the princess weeping as she sat next to him on the bed. Genghis Khan, a forty-seven-year-old man, now had an eighteen-year-old new bride. The princess, in traditional costume, was giving off the faint fragrance of roses.

"Princess, now you are my wife. I already have four wives, but in our Mongolian custom, the fifth wife has the same rights and standing as the first one. The only difference is the children from the first wife can inherit the positions and property from their father. I did not make that rule. It is a long-standing tradition, handed down from generation to generation. I understand how you feel, leaving your hometown to live in a foreign land."

Genghis tried to comfort her, but he was not successful.

He continued, "The relationship between you and me is just as a man and a woman. Once you became my wife, it had no more to do with the relations of two countries. Whatever happens between the two countries, the husband and wife relationship we share will never be severed."

At these words, Princess Chikuo raised her chin and said, looking at Genghis, "My lord, I am not crying because of that. I am not the real daughter of Emperor Xuanzong, I am just an adopted one."

Genghis Khan kept silent for a moment. Then, he let out a loud guffaw. He said, smoothing her back, "I already knew that. I know you are the daughter of the former emperor, Weishao, not of the present one, Xuanzong. Now do you feel better?"

When Hushahu revolted, he killed all the male family members and descendants of Weishao, leaving only the females alive. The new emperor, Xuanzong, took pity on them and adopted some of them as his daughters. Princess Chikuo stopped weeping. It was another long night for Genghis.

CHAPTER SEVENTY-TWO

Fall of Zhongdu

After the Mongols' departure, the Chin immediately embarked on reconstruction. They repaired the city rampart and rebuilt and reinforced the Juyung Kuan, the main gate from the north to the city of Zhongdu, as well as the most important fortress for defense. The Chin emperor, Xuanzong, thought he had won the negotiations with Genghis Khan. Of course, huge amounts of property and treasure had to be given as reparation, yet it was just a fraction of what he had in his warehouse. In addition, Princess Chikuo was not his real daughter, but an adopted one. Unluckily for his people, he was no better a ruler than his predecessor, Weishao.

He summoned the premier, Wanyen Fuxing, and said, "I think I am going to transfer the capital. Don't you think Zhongdu is too close to the Mongols?"

Stunned, Wanyen Fuxing replied, "Your Majesty, that is out of the question! We do not have another city like this in our territory that has a perfect defense system. If we transfer, it would be like we are giving up the land above the Yellow River."

However, Xuanzong insisted on transferring the capital, based on his shallow idea.

"The city of Kaifeng is my preference. It is located below the Yellow River, so it would be a safer place against the Mongols, who do not fight well on the water."

Kaifeng was the city below the Yellow River, but its overall defenses were far less than that of Zhongdu. A cloud passed over Wanyen Fuxing's face.

He said earnestly, "Your Majesty, I have to remind you that the Mongols are to the north, but the Sung are in the south. They are both our enemies. Our original homeland is in the north, not the south. What are you going to do with the demoralization of our people to the north of the Yellow River?"

Xuanzong replied lightly, "I am going to leave my son, Prince Shu Tzung, here."

Xuanzong did not change his mind. He surely thought more of himself than the whole nation. He did not understand that narrow-minded selfishness could be his worst enemy.

Xuanzong held an imperial meeting and declared the transfer of the capital city. Many generals were astonished and enraged with the decision.

"This is not a smart decision! It is a cowardly act, trying to get away from the enemy instead of facing them. This is the very first step of the self-destruction of the Chin Empire!"

They uttered a cry. None of their protesting mattered; the Chin emperor confirmed his decision. At the same time, he issued an order to attack the newly formed Khitan Kingdom, which he had been forced to approve by Genghis Khan. This plan was accepted by most generals; however, it was rejected by the ones of Khitan origin. Since Genghis Khan had declared the liberation of the Khitans before the war, a good many of the Khitans turned to him. Still, the majority remained unchanged and were loyal to the Chin.

"They are all bastards! Unless we get our own independence, all by ourselves, we cannot expect any change."

That was what they thought. As for the decision to transfer the capital, they were against it, but from a different motivation. All the dirty jobs were theirs, and so the task of defending the city, until the last man, would be theirs.

In July 1214, the capital city of the Chin was transferred to Kaifeng, in Honan Province. It was about two months after the peace treaty. At the same time, the Chin dispatched 50,000 troops to attack the newborn Khitan Kingdom. Upon receiving this news, Genghis was enraged. This was the main reason why he stayed in the Onggut territory, which was only halfway to his homeland.

It had been almost three years since he had left his homeland. He could not ignore the possibility of problems due to his long absence. He had already received information about some troubles in the area between the Kara Khitai and the Shisha and even in his homeland. Genghis had to make a quick decision. Time was not on his side.

Genghis again crossed the Great Wall. He divided his troops into three groups and ordered the left wing to stop the Chin's 50,000 troops and take over the northern and middle part of Manchuria, which had remained untouched to that point.

Mukali, the commander of the left wing, easily defeated the Chin's 50,000 expedition troops and attacked and took over thirty-two new cities in that area, making it a secure occupation. The city of Taning, the northern capital of the Chin Empire, as well as their last stronghold in that area, surrendered after being surrounded and attacked by the troops of Kasar, Julchedai, Alchi and Tolun. That area was the original homeland of the Juchids, the builders of the Chin Empire. The Juchids mourned, hearing the news that they had lost their homeland.

On the other hand, Genghis headed for Tung Kuan, where the Chin's main forces were stationed, and at the same time, he had Jebe attack the Juyung Kuan, the fortress that had been repaired and reinforced. At Tung Kuan, the last stand of the Chin Empire, 100,000 of the Chin's suicide troops were waiting. The three Chin generals, whose names were known only in the Mongolian pronunciation of Ile, Qada and Hobogetur, made heroic resolves to fight to the end. They were still completely destroyed by the troops led by Juchi, Genghis Khan's first son, and Chugu Gurigen, Genghis Khan's son-in-law.

Jebe, who was dispatched to retake the Juyung Kuan fortress, realized that a direct attack was impossible. He discussed this with Jafa, who was familiar with that area, and successfully found a secret mountain pass to reach the fortress. He led 2,000 commandos and made a surprise attack. The 5,000 Chin troops were destroyed.

The city of Zhongdu was surrounded again, but just the day before the arrival of the Mongol troops, the Chin emperor secretly took his son, Prince Shu Tsung, out of the city and brought him to Kaifeng, the Chin's new capital and the place where he was staying. Wanyen Fuxing, the loyal and faithful vassal of the Chin, helped him escape.

Wanyen Fuxing, who had made a firm resolve to defend the city until his last breath, reinforced the defense line, and still the city was falling into uncontrollable chaos. One million citizens of Zhongdu were enraged at the news that Prince Shu Tsung was no longer with them. They felt that they had been betrayed by their own ruler. They tried to escape the city, if possible, and began to plunder and loot each other's properties. Wanyen Fuxing had his troops stop the escapees and behead the plunderers and looters, hanging their heads on the city wall as a warning.

Genghis Khan clicked his tongue, looking at the city of Zhongdu from afar. "Why doesn't the Chin emperor know that their defense powers are in their minds, not on the high wall? What an idiot!"

Genghis Khan left there after giving Mukali, who had come back after the successful conquest of the middle and northern parts of Manchuria, an order to take over Zhongdu.

"The fall of Zhongdu is inevitable and only a matter of time. They will collapse by themselves. Wait until that moment, then you will not lose any of your soldiers. I do not even need to be here."

Genghis Khan moved back to the place close to the Great Wall.

Zhongdu gradually turned into a city of death. The hungry citizens attacked the food storehouses, only to find them empty. The Chin emperor had taken most of the provisions with him when he was transferring the capital, and the rest had been used up by the soldiers since. Upon receiving an urgent request, the Chin emperor dispatched 10,000 troops with 100,000 bags of rice, but they were stopped by the Mongol troops.

After the turn of the year, around March, the hungry citizens began to eat human flesh. The last moment was near. By May, the city of Zhongdu was completely defenseless.

Wanyen Fuxing gathered his men and said, "We will fight to the last man, instead of surrendering. Get ready for the last battle."

However, nobody listened to him. The hungry soldiers looted the last remaining food and speared anyone who tried to stop them. Some of them opened the gates and began to run away. Realizing resistance was no longer possible, Wanyen Fuxing summoned his doctor.

"Is there any medication I can take to quickly end my life?"

Without saying anything, the doctor put a tiny leather bag on his table. Wanyen Fuxing put the blue powder from the bag into his wine cup and drank it one gulp. Soon his body went into severe convulsions and his face turned dark blue. At last, as his eyes started rolling up, he became quiet.

Mukali sent Samuk, who was known as a tough character, and Simo Mingan into the city. The 5,000 Mongol troops entered the city after minor resistance from a handful of remaining garrisons. Some of them began to shoot fire-arrows at the houses, and the other group began the massacre. It was evening time and the dark smoke from the burning houses was blocking the sky, which just had begun to show the evening glow. The city of Zhongdu was changing into a living hell, with screams and cries of the dying people and the beating sound of the horse's hooves. The dead bodies began to pile up everywhere, and the blood from them flowed into the street gutters, making streams. Some of the citizens went up to the rampart and threw themselves down to the ground. Most of them were girls and women. Underneath the rampart, which was more than forty feet tall, were moats made of stone. They were instantly killed, hitting their heads on the stone. The rampart wall of Zhongdu city, a total of twenty-six miles long, was embroidered with the fluttering white, red and yellow skirts of falling girls and women. A total of 60,000 girls and women killed themselves in this way.

Several days later, the streets of Zhongdu were covered with the fatty tissue from human bodies, making them very slippery and difficult to walk across. All the houses in the city had been burnt down, including the palace. Mountains of dead bodies had been piled up outside the city. Destruction and plundering lasted for a month.

Genghis Khan dispatched three men, Shigi Khutuku, Onggur and Alqai, to take over the treasures in the Chin royal family's treasure storehouses. The treasure storehouses were opened. They found mountains of treasure that the Chin emperor did not take with him when he moved to Kaifeng. There were silks; all kinds of woven fabrics like satin and damask; helmets and armor decorated with gold; swords and daggers decorated with precious stones; wooden chairs with golden armrests; big treasure chests filled with pearls, emeralds and sapphires; luxurious furniture and big full-length mirrors decorated with pearls; all kinds of perfumes in bottles; decorative ivory products; and more. The three men were stunned by the scale and amount of the treasure. They could not close their mouths. At last, two of them, Onggur and Alqai, lost their heads. They began to take treasure for their own, with the help of their own soldiers.

Watching this, Shigi Khutuku held their hands and tried to stop them. "All these things are the khan's property! You cannot take these!"

However, they did not listen. Later, having heard about this, Genghis Khan was enraged. The two men were strongly rebuked and all the items were taken back. They avoided physical punishment, yet their wrongdoings were put into their official military records.

The line of Chin captives walking towards the Mongol mainland was endless. About 200,000 captives were taken to the Onggut territory. Once there, they were put through a screening process. Among them, technicians, artisans, engineers and government officials were selected first. Next, anybody who was considered to be useful to the empire was selected. The rest of them were released or executed, depending on whether they were compliant or resistant.

Genghis Khan looked around the lines of tens of thousands of captives. While he was driving his horse slowly, an image of a unique man came into his sight. Most notably, he was quite tall. The man was in the Chin's official uniform and looked to be at least six feet six inches tall.

He had a long beard that hung down to his navel. Below his wide forehead, two large eyes were sparkling, imbued with brilliance, and his firmly closed mouth showed his strong will and decisiveness. Genghis Khan quickly noticed that he was an outstanding man. He asked some questions of the man with the long beard, stooping down from his horse.

"What is your name?"

The tall man answered with a unique clear and sonorous voice, "My name is Yelu Chutze, sir."

Genghis Khan said, "Oh! Your name, 'Yelu,' tells me that you are a descendant of the Khitan royal family. Then I could be your benefactor who destroyed your ancestral enemy, the Juchids of the Chin."

At this, he answered without hesitation, "That is not right, sir. My father and grandfather were both government officials for the Chin. I was also a salaried government official, so I am just a subject of the Chin."

Genghis Khan was a little surprised at that answer. He looked at the man for a while. At last, a smile arrived on his lips, as if he were happy with his answer.

"Are you willing to work for me?"

This time also, he answered without hesitation.

"I am just one of your captives. You are the decision maker, sir."

Genghis took that answer as a "yes." Genghis said to him, with a smile on his face, "From now on, I will call you 'Nice Beard.' That will be your nickname."

Genghis watched him carefully from then on. Yelu Chutze, a young Khitan of twenty-six years of age, turned out to be an extraordinary man, as Genghis had assumed. He was brilliant in many areas, including astronomy, geometry, history, religion, mathematics and statistics, law, public administration, military science and even medicine. Later, he became the top-ranking official of the nation and supported Genghis Khan in building his empire.

Genghis Khan stayed in China for about one more year, consolidating his foundation there. He put darughachis in many different areas and built up the ruling system.

One time, he discussed with his officials and generals the overall plans for the newly conquered northern Chinese land.

Julchedei gave his opinion.

"The best way is to remove the whole population of those areas, step by step, and let the Mongols immigrate there, making it our horse pastures and grazing lands. After all, their descendants will be the enemies of our descendants."

At this opinion, Genghis Khan's eyes sprang open.

"Remove all the people there and make it our horse grazing land?"

Next, Genghis turned his eyes to Yelu Chutze and asked him, "What is the population of the Juchids and the Han Chinese in the land above the Yellow River?"

Yelu Chutze gave it a little thought and answered, "According to the statistics compiled about ten years ago, their population was fifty million. The actual number could be much higher because they had the tendency to report a reduced number for their families to lower their taxes."

Genghis asked him, "Do you agree with Julchedei?"

Again, he gave it a little thought and then answered, "Among all properties, humans are the most valuable. Man surpasses land or material property. The same thing goes for both individuals and nations. Instead of complete annihilation, if they were to be governed by a good system, they would be a source of power to produce enormous riches, rather than remaining as the enemy."

Genghis shared the same opinion with Yelu Chutze.

In the year 1216, Genghis Khan left China. He left 23,000 Mongol troops and 40,000 accessory troops of the Khitans to Mukali with the mission of continual operations against the Chin. He gathered all the soldiers in one place.

"Mukali is one of my most trusted generals. All the orders coming from him are the same as mine. Anyone who disobeys him will be disobeying me. Even though I am not with you, do your best and complete the missions with him."

Genghis Khan appointed him the commander-in-chief of the Mongol troops stationed in China and one year later made him the governor of northern China. Genghis Khan returned to the Kerulen riverside and never stepped on Chinese soil again.

The Trade Agreement with the Khwarazm Empire

There was a Khwarazm Empire. Originally, Khwarazm was the name of a small region west of the Aral Sea. A man named Qutbeddin Muhammad, a native of Khwarazm, seized this area with his Turkish mercenaries. His son Ala Addin Muhammad II, conquered Khurasan (later called Iran), the Persian territory, also using Turkish mercenaries. Later he declared himself the "Chosen Prince of Allah" and began to conquer the nearby area with the Koran in one hand and a sword in the other. By the time he conquered Transoxania, the richest kingdom in the area, Khwarazm was already a great empire.

His territory extended as far as the Aral Sea to the north, the Persian Gulf to the south, the Zagros Mountains to the west and the Pamir Heights to the east, covering most of central Asia. The neighboring nations of this new empire were caliphates, considered to be direct descendant of Persia, with the capital city in Baghdad, India to the south with the border at the Indus River, and Kara Khitai to the east. When he conquered the city of Samarqand, the commercial and political center of central Asia, the people feared him, calling him the "second Alexander." The Khwarazm Empire was a new superpower and Ala Addin Muhammad II was the newly arisen conqueror.

The Kerulen riverside was still beautiful and peaceful to Genghis Khan, who had returned after five years of absence. The Kerulen River, flowing with clean, sparkling water, was winding along the enormous steppe, hiding its tail in the faraway horizon. Along the Kerulen River, which was a lifeline for the nomads, countless yurts were spread out, making a large city. It was hard for the nomads to live together in one place because of the limited supply of grass, which was the food for their livestock, the original source of their food, clothing, shelter and transportation. In a normal situation, they were supposed to spread out in a large area, making small and large ordus. In the past, the basic unit of an ordu was a tribe; however, after the emergence of the new Mongol Empire, an ordu meant a group led by a prince or a noyans. Genghis Khan's ordu along the Kerulen River was now a huge group. The captive Chin alone numbered more than 200,000. They were scholars, administrators, artisans, technicians, engineers and servants. The numerous Muslim caravans and merchants who continued to come and go from this huge group stayed in their own sector, restricted to one corner of the city, with permission and registration. Now that the Mongol nation was a rich country with numerous slaves and an enormous amount of war booty, the money-wise merchants would never leave this large, newly emerged market. They were from many different parts of the world, including Persia and India. The captive Chinese artisans, craftsmen and technicians began to make different kinds of products based on their specialties. They made gold and silver products, ivory products, luxurious furniture and all kinds of clothing and leather products from Siberian furs and hides.

In the autumn of 1216, three envoys from the far west arrived at Genghis Khan's ordu. They were a goodwill mission sent by Ala Addin Muhammad II of the Khwarazm Empire. Genghis met them at the tent for official visitors, which could accommodate 200 people. It was an official reception, so most of the high-ranking officials and the noyans of the empire attended. Sitting due north was Genghis Khan, wearing his del and yuden, the traditional Mongolian costume and cap, and next to him was his first wife, Borte, also in her traditional costume including a cylinder-shaped headgear called a bog-taq. Next to Genghis Khan, to his right, were standing all the high-ranking officials and noyans of the Empire and to his left, also standing, were his second, third, fourth and fifth wives and their children. The three envoys were wearing turbans and milky official uniforms luxuriously decorated with golden threads. At the front center of their turbans, large blue or red jewels were embedded, and these were decorated with gold at the margins and just above them were two long, colorful peacock feathers, presumably for decoration.

"Greetings, in the name of Allah!"

The envoy's greetings, filled with all sorts of flowery words, started like this and lasted for a while. After that, they presented the gifts from their sultan, Ala Addin Muhammad II, consisting of a big silver chest filled with all kinds of jewelry and many bottles of perfume.

"I welcome you in the name of the Mongol Empire, and appreciate all the kind words and gifts."

Genghis Khan accepted the gifts happily. The official interpreter for the occasion was Yalavachi. Yalavachi was originally a caravanner from Khwarazm but had joined Genghis Khan many years earlier, and later, was appointed as the spy chief of the Khwarazm area.

That evening, at the welcome banquet for the envoys, he whispered in Genghis Khan's ear, "My lord, they are spies. I think you'd better be careful of what you are saying."

That was true. They came in the name of a goodwill mission, but they were assigned to find out the truth about the Mongol conquest of northern China, the size of the Mongol troops and the future plans of Genghis Khan. That was their main job and the purpose of their visit.

"I thought so, too. However, as long as they are here in the name of a goodwill mission, what can be done?"

Genghis suggested free trade between the two nations. Genghis summoned Tata Tunga, who was the secretary-general, and ordered him to write a letter with these contents:

> *I am the ruler of the land with the rising sun,*
> *And you are the ruler of the land with the setting sun.*

I am suggesting a free trade agreement,
For our friendship and mutual peace.
Based on this agreement,
Merchants and caravans from both sides,
Will travel freely between the two nations,
To buy and sell the daily necessities and specialties.
Thus, this agreement will promote mutual economic
    development,
And eventually will contribute
To the developments of the human world.
That is what I believe.

In exchange for their visit, Genghis Khan sent his own trade mission representing the Mongol Empire to accompany the returning Khwarazm mission. The three members of the Mongol trade mission were carrying Genghis Khan's personal letter, along with gifts including artwork of gold and silver, decorative items of jade, ivory products and a cloak made of the fur of a white camel, which was a very rare breed. They arrived in Samarqand, the capital city of Khwarazm, and successfully made the trade agreement with the sultan, Ala Addin Muhammad II. The Mongol trade mission came back after five months, including their fifteen-day stay in Samarqand, having traveled 4,500 miles round trip.

Yalavachi, one of the members of the mission, gave his report to Genghis Khan.

"The size of their troops could be about 400,000. Ala Addin Muhammad II is not a popular ruler among them. A few years ago, there was a revolt against his suppressive policies and high taxes. His original plan might have been to conquer the Kara Khitai and open his own direct trade line to the city of Zhongdu. He seemed to be very sorry that Zhongdu has come under your rule. I found out that he was the one who had helped Kuchlug and his Naiman stragglers take over the Kara Khitai."

Having heard his report, Genghis sat back in his chair, making a low moan of unhappiness. When he returned from the conquest of northern China, the first news he heard was that the Kara Khitai troops, led by Kuchlug, had invaded the Uighur territory, killing and looting, and the remnants of the Merkids, whom they believed no longer existed, gathered at the Tien Shan Mountains to strike back.

After sending Yalavachi off, Genghis Khan walked out of his tent and looked at the Kerulen riverside shining in the angled afternoon sunlight. In the huge basin around the winding Kerulen River, countless numbers of dome-shaped felt tents were spread out in an orderly manner, reflecting the dazzling orange of the afternoon sunlight like topaz. It was a harmonious arrangement of colors in the sky, which, as the sun was going down, began to turn into a mysterious ruby red.

> *What can be found, after a man crosses over the*
> *mountain?*
> *Another mountain to be crossed over.*
> *What can be found, after a man defeats his enemy?*
> *Another enemy to defeat.*

It is the man who starts,
But it is God who ends.
This world is the joint work of
The men and God, after all.

Genghis Khan decided to conquer the Kara Khitai.

Footsteps of Kuchlug

Kara Khitai was the nation built by the descendants of the royal family of the Liо Empire, which had been destroyed by the Juchids, the founders of the Chin Empire. Yelu Tashi, a royal member of the fallen Lio Empire, and his Khitan followers, had sought safety in flight toward the west, away from their enemies. They crossed over the mountains and deserts and settled down at a place near the Tarim Basin, between Lake Balkhash and the Pamir Heights. They picked the area in the upper part of the River Chu as their base and named it Balasagun. Once there, they declared the birth of a new nation named Kara Khitai, with the capital city of Balasagun. They began to conquer nearby tribes and small nations, expanding their territory, and so, by the middle of the twelfth century, they were already a great power in this region.

After pushing away the nearby kingdoms of the Uighurs and Qarluuds, they extended their power to Samarqand. The ruler of Samarqand had to pay tributes to Guru Khan, the ruler of the Kara Khitai, each and every year. Since their ancestors ruled northern China for a long time, their systems were much like those of the Chinese. The royal family's last name was Chinese and their main religion was Buddhism. However, at the end of the twelfth century, they were a multiracial, multi-ethnic group, with the conquered Islamic Turks and Tajiks in the majority.

In the past, when the Naimans had been destroyed by Genghis Khan in 1204, Kuchlug, the son of the Naiman ruler at the time, Tayang Khan, tried a counterattack after gathering his remaining people. However, when he was defeated again by Jebe's troops, he had to run away to the Kara Khitai with only a few of his remaining followers. When they were roaming the fields without horses, a bunch of cavalrymen approached them from the south. They were the border guards of the Kara Khitai. Soon, forty of the Kara Khitai cavalrymen surrounded Kuchlug's group of six.

"I am Kuchlug, the son of the Naimans' Tayang Khan! Take me to your ruler!" Kuchlug shouted at them.

The guard soldiers took him to their captain and later, the captain took him to Balasagun, their capital city. Yelu Che-luku, the Guru Khan of the Kara Khitai, allowed him political exile. He could lead a comfortable life under the protection of Guru Khan. Occasionally, he was invited to Guru Khan's banquets. One day, he met Qunqu, the nineteen-year-old daughter of Guru Khan, at the banquet. Qunqu immediately lost her heart to him; he was handsome, eloquent and courteous. Gurbesu, Qunqu's mother, also favored him. However, he was a wolf in sheep's clothing. Guru Khan, old and feeble, did not have a good eye for character. He allowed his daughter to marry him. Then, Kuchlug, the son-in-law of Guru Khan began to reveal his true character. Soon, he had the Kara Khitai court in his grasp.

At this time, the Khwarazm Empire was rising. As the sultan of the Khwarazm attacked and seized the city of Samarqand, Guru Khan was forced to dispatch his troops to take it back.

Kuchlug came to Guru Khan and said, "My lord, help me collect my Naiman people. They are spread all over the plains and desert. If I can add them to your troops, you will surely defeat the sultan's troops. I pledge my loyalty to you and I will not break my neck by disobeying you."

Guru Khan made his second mistake. He allowed him to collect his Naiman remnants. Thereafter, for a few months, he gathered all the Naimans from the Qayaligh and the Beshbaligh regions, their most populated areas, and brought them into the Kara Khitai territory. He organized them into his personal troops, making himself the head of them. They were armed and equipped with weapons and armor from the Kara Khitai armory.

Kuchlug, the master of 20,000 personal troops, dispatched a secret messenger to Sultan Muhammad of Khwarazm, instead of marching against them. "I will attack the Kara Khitai from the east, so I want you to attack from the west. If your Khwarazm troops defeat the Guru Khan's troops, the present Kara Khitai territory of Almaligh and Kashgar will be yours. If I defeat them, the east side of the Syr River will be mine."

Upon receiving this message, Sultan Muhammad regarded the three envoys contemptuously, smoothing his long white beard. He thought, "This man is a real snake! How can he betray someone who has done him so many great favors? This bastard will surely be killed by my hand someday. However, at this moment, he is very useful."

Sultan Muhammad sprang to his feet and shouted toward Kuchlug's three envoys.

"Go and tell your master! The agreement has been made and confirmed! I will start the campaign exactly thirty days from today!"

Exactly thirty days after, Sultan Muhammad and his Khwarazm troops launched an attack on the Kara Khitai from the west. At the same time, Kuchlug's troops marched towards Balasagun from the other side. Realizing his son-in-law's betrayal, Guru Khan was enraged, but it was too late. He was doomed. Attacked from both sides, Guru Khan had to divide his troops into two parts. The Guru Khan's troops defeated Kuchlug's troops from the east but were not very successful on the western front. Guru Khan, who had led his troops in the western front, suffered a crushing defeat to the sultan's troops. He retreated several hundred miles back with his remaining troops and set up a base camp near his capital city, Balasagun.

In the middle of the night, everyone fell asleep, exhausted, and a group of surprise attackers fell upon them. They were part of Kuchlug's troops. Having heard the news that the Guru Khan's troops had been defeated, Kuchlug gathered his remaining troops and launched a surprise attack. The Kara Khitai troops lost and Guru Khan was taken captive.

"Take good care of my father-in-law," Kuchlug told his men. However, Guru Khan was ushered to the prison. Later, he was released from prison, but was confined to his house. Several months later, he died of an illness caused by the anger he could never control. His first wife, Gurbcsu, poisoned herself, and Qunqu, Guru Khan's daughter, left to become a nun. Some people presumed later that she had gone to the Shisha Kingdom. Kuchlug took all of Guru Khan's concubines.

Kuchlug, who had the Kara Khitai in his grasp, began to oppress the Muslims. By that time, he had converted to Buddhism from Nestorian Christianity. Before his conversion, he had frequently been in contact with Buddhists and was also greatly influenced by the Khitai, who were mostly Buddhists, and his former wife, Qunqu, an ardent Buddhist.

He issued an order to close all the temples except the Buddhist ones, and prohibited all religious activities except those of the Buddhists. At that time, in Kara Khitai, the number of Buddhists and Muslims were split evenly and yet the Muslims had many more temples.

Due to his policy, ignorance of religious freedom, a revolt broke out in the Khotan, the area with the highest Islamic population. Instead of settling the problem by force, Kuchlug had his soldiers set a fire in the cornfield, the staple source of food for the people of Khotan, every year. After three years, suffering from the lack of food, the people of Khotan submitted themselves. After taking over Khotan without shedding even a single drop of blood, Kuchlug ordered all the divinity schools teaching Islam to close. At the same time, he gathered all the Islamic imams in one place. There were almost 3,000 of them.

Kuchlug shouted toward the imams, "If any one of you can debate with me about religious beliefs and think you can defeat me, step forward!"

At this, Ala Addin Muhammad, the imam of Madrasa, the largest Islamic school, stepped forward.

"Where is your God?"

Kuchlug asked this first question to the imam of Madrasa, as they faced each other with a table in between them.

"Allah is everywhere."

At this answer, Kuchlug regarded him with contempt and argued in a high-pitched tone,

"Liar! You believe your God is in the black stone. Is that right?"

The Imam answered in a gentle voice, "It is only a symbol. Allah is everywhere."

Kuchlug asked, "What are you pursuing in the end?"

The Imam answered, still in a polite and gentle voice, "Allah taught us through the Koran that this world is just a road for travelers."

"Then where is your destination?"

"Not in this world. It is in another world."

At this answer, Kuchlug pounded the table with his fist and shouted, "That is fraud! God, who is ignoring this world, doesn't need to exist."

The Imam continued still in a quiet and gentle voice.

"Allah surely exists."

Kuchlug said to him, staring at him contemptuously, "If so, prove it!"

"It is impossible. It is only possible inside your mind."

Kuchlug stood up from his seat and said, "You have lost! If you cannot prove it, it does not exist. You are nothing but a liar and a fraud! You are merely a madman because of something that does not exist. One time, I tried hard to find God, only to find that there's no such thing in the world."

Kuchlug said to the Imam, staring and pointing at his face with his finger, "You will be nailed to a cross, three days from now. Pray to your god!"

After these words, he left. Kuchlug's soldiers stripped him completely naked and shackled him on his ankles. They did not give him water or food for three days. He was crucified in front of his school.

After that, Kuchlug sent his 20,000 Naiman followers into about 30,000 Muslim households to live, one in each, out of fear of a second revolt. Those who had to lie with someone whom they had never wanted or desired suffered greatly. They bossed people around in their assigned households and routinely hunted for the hidden Korans in each house, gathering them and burning them on the open ground.

The Muslims impatiently waited for change.

Genghis Khan Conquers the Kara Khitai

In the spring of 1218, Genghis Khan dispatched Jebe with 20,000 troops to conquer the Kara Khitai. Genghis Khan was well aware of what was happening in Kara Khitai. At the same time, he gave 20,000 troops to Juchi and Subedei to annihilate the remnants of the Merkids gathered near the Tien Shan Mountains, north of Kara Khitai. Genghis gave some instructions to Jebe before he left.

"As soon as you step into the Kara Khitai territory, open all the Islamic temples and publicly announce that the Mongol Empire will secure the freedom of religion."

Jebe's troops entered the Kara Khitai territory with Genghis Khan's banner in front of them. In some areas, Jebe's troops faced minor resistance, but they were easily subdued. As for Genghis Khan's order, Jebe immediately opened all the Islamic temples and announced the freedom of religion.

The savior of the Muslims had arrived! The Mongol troops were welcomed everywhere as the liberation army. The Muslims welcomed Jebe with bread and salt, the symbols of welcome, in their hands.

At that time, Kuchlug was in Kashgar. He tried to mobilize the troops, but the people in Kashgar did not listen to him. They were influenced by the pacification unit sent by Jebe. The members of Jebe's pacification unit entered the area disguised as travelers and made it known that Genghis Khan had approved the freedom of religion and anyone who supported or joined him would be accepted as a comrade and be given the same opportunities, regardless of their race, religion, language, native place or ancestral background. The people in Kashgar and Khotan revolted against Kuchlug even before the arrival of Jebe's troops. Since they had not been allowed to possess weapons, they picked up farming equipment or heavy sticks and killed the Naimans in every household and every corner of their region. The revolt, which started in the early afternoon, lasted until late in the night. With torches in their hands, they hunted everywhere, killing them one by one. The dead bodies of the Naiman remnants were everywhere in Kashgar and Khotan. Kuchlug's main forces collapsed in an instant.

Kuchlug ran away toward the Pamir Heights with only about ten followers. Jebe immediately organized pursuit. Five groups of chasing units, 400 men each, making 2,000 in total, left for every possible direction that Kuchlug could use to escape. The chasing units were given one month's provisions. Jebe's third chasing unit, which had headed for the Himalaya Mountains through the Pamir Heights, found a trace of Kuchlug. They kept on tracking the enemy, crossing over the Himalaya Mountains. Below their feet, clouds were floating like a sea and the dim image of the distant Punjab plain came into sight through an opening in the clouds. It might be impossible to track them down once Kuchlug and his men entered the Punjab region. Jebe's third chasing unit followed the road to the Punjab region from the mountaintop, but found it impossible to keep on moving with horses because the mountains were so steep. They set up camp there and kept on chasing after selecting a special unit of eighty chasers.

In the meantime, Kuchlug and his men had crossed over the mountains and arrived near Badakhshan, a big town in the middle part of the mountain. They stepped into a ravine called Sariq Qol. The Sariq Qol, which meant yellow ravine, was 10,000 feet high and made of steep rock walls. It was said that once they fell from it, their bodies would be torn into pieces before they could even reach the bottom. Kuchlug made a mistake as he stepped into this ravine. He took the road with no way out. At that moment, the chasing unit caught sight of them.

Since the chasing unit members were not familiar with the area and the road was too rough and dangerous, they decided to get help from the natives. Luckily, they found a group of Badakhshan hunters at a place nearby.

"We are Genghis Khan's troops. We are chasing Kuchlug. Please be our guides. Your merits will be reported to the khan."

The Badakhshan hunters agreed. Once they had guides, the chasing unit captured Kuchlug successfully, safely avoiding the death traps hidden everywhere. Considering that it could be difficult to take him all the way back to base camp alive, they cut off Kuchlug's head and returned with it.

Jebe sent Kuchlug's head to Genghis Khan, along with the war trophy of 1,000 horses with white muzzles, a symbol of good luck for the Mongols. Genghis Khan appointed Yelu Ahai viceroy of Kara Khitai, and rewarded the Badakhshan hunters and residents with a large amount of gold, silver and money. Jebe completed the conquest of Kara Khitai in one month.

Elsewhere, Juchi and Subedei, with their 20,000 troops, headed for the Tien Shan Mountains, the base for the remaining Merkids. Takuchar, who was the commander of the defense forces of the Mongol mainland while Genghis Khan was out for the conquest of northern China, accompanied them. The commander-in-chief of this operation was Juchi. The Merkid remnants would occasionally attack the Mongol mainland during Genghis Khan's absence. They attacked the border towns, killing the residents and looting the livestock and other property. If Takuchar, then commander of the Mongol troops, counterattacked and chased them, they simply ran away and dispersed into the vast mountains instead of facing the Mongol troops. Some time later, they would regroup and attack again. They repeated this over and over again. This was guerrilla warfare.

Takuchar interrogated the captives a few times, but they did not even know who their commander was. They only knew their captain who gave them orders directly. Normally, they did not stay in one place. Instead, they dispersed across a wide area, and stayed like that. That was why it was almost impossible to root them out.

When Genghis received this report from Takuchar after he had returned from China, he worked out a countermeasure. Genghis Khan gave an operation order to Juchi, Subedei and Takuchar before their departure:

"Based on all the information, their active members are less than 10,000. However, they are dispersed over a wide area, so we need double the manpower to destroy them completely. Use the same tactic that we use in hunting."

For this reason, Genghis Khan needed 20,000 troops to clear out 10,000 enemies. Juchi and Subedei's 20,000 troops advanced towards the Tien Shan Mountains and encircled all the mountains. Then, they gradually closed the encirclement. The Mongol soldiers did not allow a single escapee, just as they did not allow a single animal to break through the hunting encirclement. On the last day of closing the encirclement, the Mongol troops annihilated the Merkid guerrillas, who were pushed into one spot. Genghis Khan's order was not to allow a single enemy survivor. The dead bodies of the Merkid guerrillas were strewn across the valley and the mountainsides. The Mongol soldiers checked all the dead bodies of the guerrillas, one by one, and performed confirmatory killings if they seemed to still be alive or pretending to be dead.

At this moment, one Merkid guerrilla got up from the dead bodies and picked up a nearby horse, mounted it and began to run away with lightning speed. His movement was so swift, even the nearby Mongol soldiers could not stop him.

Juchi immediately dispatched a chasing team. About twenty of the Mongol soldiers began to chase him. The escapee, while he was galloping at full speed, took one arrow from the quiver on his back, and fixed it to his bow from his waist. Next, he turned the upper part of his body around and shot it. One chasing soldier in the front fell down on the ground with a short scream. Soon, another one fell down and another and another. A total of five of the chasers had been shot and fell to the ground. Finally, they were able to capture him alive because his horse had been shot in the rump and dropped him to the ground by rearing on its hind legs.

CHAPTER SEVENTY-SIX

Tragedy in Otral

In the fall of 1218, a large-scale caravan left the Mongolian Plateau. Their destination was Samarqand, the capital city of Khwarazm. They were 150 Muslim merchants and 300 laborers, making a total of 450 travelers with 500 camels fully loaded with high-quality Chinese silks, gold and silver artifacts, ivory products, jade and jewels and high-quality Siberian furs. The owner of the caravan was a group of aristocrats from the Mongol Empire. They were also carrying a huge amount of Khwarazmian gold coins to use to buy metal helmets, chain tunics, glass products, chemical products and perfumes from Baghdad and Bukhara. It was the first caravan since the free trade agreement between the two nations.

They crossed the deserts and went over the mountains, making a long line. After traveling over 1,000 miles, passing through the former Kara Khitai, now the new domain of the Mongol Empire, they arrived at Otral, the easternmost city, and the entrance gate, of Khwarazm. The garrison chief, who was also the governor, of this border city was Inalchuq, who was the nephew on his mother's side of the sultan Muhammad and had strong power in the Khwarazm Empire. The people

of Otral treated him with respect, calling him "Ghayir Khan."
He was a wild, merciless, tough and greedy man.

The Mongol caravan set up camp in a large open area near
the poplar forest outside the city. They had to wait until they
had permission from the garrison chief to pass through the
city. One day later, they were told that the people could come
and go, but not the animals and packages, and for permission
for both, they had to wait longer.

In the meantime, some of the caravan members went into the
city and began to contact people, buying daily necessities.

Among the caravan members was an Indian man named
Raju. He was an acquaintance of the governor, Inalchuq. One
day, Raju had a chance to sit together with Inalchuq. Inalchuq
asked him why he was working for the Mongols.

He answered, "Genghis Khan is a great man. He conquered
northern China and Kara Khitai. He accepts anybody who
follows his line. He has an open policy. Anybody can be his
friend, regardless of his origin."

Inalchuq was annoyed by his words. The leaders of Khwarazm were very disappointed and unhappy with the fact that
Kara Khitai had been occupied by Genghis Khan before they
could do it and they had already begun to consider Genghis
Khan their next enemy. Kara Khitai was the important part of
the Silk Road.

Inalchuq sprang to his feet and shouted towards his guards,
"Arrest this man! He must be a Mongol spy!"

Next, two other Muslim merchants who were making similar
comments in the marketplace, were arrested on a charge of the

same crime, espionage. Soon after, all 450 caravan members and all their packages were taken into custody or seized by the soldiers sent by Inalchuq. Inalchuq also dispatched an urgent messenger to Samarqand, reporting to Sultan Muhammad that he had found Mongol spies among the caravan members and requested the sultan's decision for the next step.

Sultan Muhammad had a meeting with his senior officials and generals and said, "The Mongols are now our enemies. They took Kara Khitai before us. Soon, we must open a war to take this important trade route back from them."

That was their conclusion. The messenger returned to the city of Otral with Sultan Muhammad's answer and handed it over to Inalchuq. "Get rid of three spies."

That was the answer. Inalchuq was not happy with the answer. In spite of the fact that he had been ordered to release all the other caravan members and return the packages to the owners, he killed all of them and kept all the packages as his own. He had his soldiers dig a huge pit and buried the 300 laborers alive. The rest of the 150 Muslim merchants were hanged upside down in the trees and were killed by arrows. Most of them did not even know why they had to die.

There was one survivor among the caravan members. After watching all the inhumane cruelty that happened in Otral, he returned to the plateau and reported to Genghis Khan on every detail.

"What, all the caravan members were murdered? All the packages were seized?"

Genghis Khan jumped to his feet when he heard this terrible news. He was stunned and unable to close his mouth. He stood there for a while just gazing into space. His face was distorted by rage and his eyes flashed extreme anger. His neck vein was swollen and his cheeks flushed with shame. He remained like that for a moment. Soon, he uttered to himself, clenching his teeth and fists, "War! They want war!"

This was the beginning of a war that has been marked as having the most unimaginably brutal and largest-scale massacre of any others known to the human world.

Genghis Khan dispatched his urgent messengers to Samarqand, the capital city of Khwarazm, in consideration of the importance of the incident. The three messengers were carrying Genghis Khan's personal letter. It said that Genghis Khan wanted the transfer of the criminal, Inalchuq, the garrison chief of Otral, for punishment. The three messengers galloped day and night, bypassing the city of Otral, and arrived at Samarqand seven days later. They were ushered to Sultan Muhammad II, ruler of Khwarazm. Sultan Muhammad regarded the three messengers with contempt from his golden chair. He crumpled the letter up into a ball and handed it over to his man standing next to him. Next, he slowly raised his big, weighty body from his seat. He walked several steps down to the three messengers who were kneeling on one knee and waiting for his answer. He pushed the three messengers down on the ground on their faces or shoulders with his foot, one by one.

"Dogs of the Mongols!"

As he spat these words, he shouted towards the three messengers, "How dare a man called Genghis Khan ask me to hand over my subjects!"

He turned around and walked away to his living place without any further remarks. One of his twenty men, possibly an aide captain, who was standing beside him, immediately followed him and asked him something. Sultan Muhammad talked to him for a while and then disappeared. The aide captain returned to his position and gave an order to about forty guard soldiers in the reception hall to arrest the three messengers. The Khwarazm soldiers tied their hands back and took them out. The three messengers were dragged out to the execution ground about five miles from the city, passing through the huge and weighty main city gate. It was early evening, so dusk was falling on the field and nearby hills. Several crows were making noises, circling high in the sky, as if they already smelled human blood.

They lit the torches. One of the Khwarazm soldiers, seemingly the captain, approached the three messengers and asked, "Who is the head of your group?"

Genghis Khan's messenger group consisted of one envoy and two assistant envoys. The envoy was a Turkish Muslim, Alik. As he stepped forward, the captain unbound his turban, grasped his hair, and dragged him several more steps. There were numerous cylinder-shaped logs lined up, secured to the ground, designed and shaped to cut human necks. The captain pulled his hair down, making Alik's neck touch the top side of the nearby log, and gave a signal to the soldier standing next to him, nodding his head. At this moment, one of the assistant envoys, Yalavachi, shouted at them:

"No! You cannot do this. We are envoys. Envoys must not be killed!"

Ignoring his protest, the Khwarazm soldier cut off Alik's head with his huge, half-moon shaped axe. With a thudding sound, Alik's separated head hit the ground and rolled over a few times, and blood spurted from his severed neck. A couple of other soldiers held the feet of his headless, dead body, one each, and dragged him to a nearby pit and threw him in it. When the pit was full, they covered it with soil.

Even though it was nighttime, numerous crows were making loud noises. Yalavachi cried out, "You know nothing about Genghis Khan! You will surely pay for this!"

The captain came back to the two assistant envoys. He glared at sobbing Yalavachi and the other, one after another, and gave an order to his nearby men.

"Burn their beards away and give them horses to return."

At this, one of his men said, "Sultan said, 'cut their beards.'"

The captain glanced at him and spat, "Just burn them! It is much easier!"

After this remark, the captain left. His soldiers held the two messengers' hands, on both sides, and another one stabilized their heads by grasping their hair. Then, one of them began to burn their beards with his torch. The bad smell of burning human hair filled the air. The Khwarazm soldiers left there, leaving two moaning messengers.

When Genghis Khan received Alik's head, tears gathered in his eyes. Even between two hostile nations, generally recognized international norms did not allow the killing of messengers and envoys for any reason whatsoever. For the Muslims, the beard was regarded as a symbol of dignity and the act of cutting their beard was considered a big humiliation, like cutting off a women's hair.

"Khwarazm is not a nation! They are just a gang of bandits!" Genghis Khan got on his feet and declared in front of about 100 of his officials and generals, who were also standing with grave and sad looks,

"History should remember! I am not an instigator of this calamity. From now on, whatever falls upon them, it is their own making and my hands will not be stained with their blood."

Genghis Khan Decides on War with Khwarazm

In January of 1219, they had a large-scale khuriltai on the Kerulen riverside. All the noyans, generals and high-ranking officers of the Mongol Empire gathered together. They unanimously approved the war with Khwarazm. They were ready. They had already completed construction of 3,000 bow machines, which they used to shoot lances like arrows, 300 catapults, 700 naphtha flamethrowers and 4,000 ladder carriers. In the meantime, an accurate military map of the Khwarazm Empire had been completed, thanks to the activities of Genghis Khan's espionage network, as had a collection of all the information about the population and the size of the troops in each area.

Khwarazm was the newly emerged superpower. Their land was vast and their population was more than one could imagine. Sultan Muhammad had 400,000 troops in the Transoxania region alone. The upcoming war with Khwarazm would be a decisive one for the Mongol Empire. It was clear that the scale of the war would be different from the ones the Mongols had experienced previously. Genghis had already made a great plan for the conquest of the western land.

At that time, the Islamic world was divided into three groups. One was Sunni, based in Baghdad and ruled by a caliph, and another was Shia, which Sultan Muhammad belonged to. The last one was Ismaili, which was a separate, independent branch of Shia. They were also called Assassins since they were the terrorists, hiding deep inside the mountains of northern Persia and Syria. They were fighting with one another.

Farther west, there was the Christian world ruled by the Pope. Their crusaders were involved in an endless war with the Islamic world.

What was Genghis Khan's great plan for the conquest of the western land? Nobody knew it. One thing was clear, though: he was a man who knew how to change a crisis into an opportunity.

Before departing, Genghis decided to carry out two things he had been holding off on for a while. One thing was to decide his successor and the other was to summon a man named Chang-Chun. Up to that point, Genghis had been watching his four sons carefully. It was not an easy decision. However, since the war with Khwarazm was approaching, which could take years and would be the largest war ever experienced, people around him began to mention this issue. One of those people was his second wife, Yesui. One day, when she was with Genghis Khan alone, she brought it up.

"My lord, make your decision. Any living thing born in this world is mortal. A herd of horses without the herdsman would scatter into the field, and houses without a pillar would collapse. Think about the nation you founded and all the people who are following you."

Genghis thought Yesui was quite right. Genghis was now fifty-two years old. He was still a fighter, but the upcoming war with Khwarazm was a mystery.

"You are right. I myself do not understand why I have been unaware of my own death. I have been very forgetful on that issue so far."

Genghis let out a loud guffaw, while smoothing his beard.

Several days later, Genghis Khan's four sons were all called for a meeting. All the royal family members, all the senior officials and the generals were gathered in one place. They were the witnesses. Choosing his successor was not an easy job for him. As long as he was alive, everything would be fine, Whoever he picked as his successor, everything would be fine while he was still alive. However, problems from the wrong decision would come in later times, after his death. His successor should be the one who could be accepted by everyone, from their hearts.

The original Mongol custom dictated that the firstborn son inherited the right to perform the ancestral memorial ceremony and was the last one to get the property. However, that was for a regular family, not for the emperor's family. They did not have any traditions yet. In the past, at the time of the primitive Mongol nation, they elected their khan. However, at the time of Genghis Khan, their concept and system had changed to an absolute monarchy. All the power was coming from only one man and all the land and the people belonged to one person, the kha-khan. The Mongols supported the absolute monarchy system from their hearts. In the past, they were divided into hundreds of tribes and were fighting with one another. They might have enjoyed their own respective independence, but they realized that such disunion weakened their power in a terrible way and led them into chaos and miserable societies.

Juchi, the firstborn son, had trodden the battlefields with his father numerous times and was helpful in building the empire. Genghis Khan valued him as a great hunter. "Great hunter" meant more than just a hunter. However, he was not perfect as the possible successor because he had been the target of debate on the legitimacy of his lineage.

The second son, Chagatai, had a sharp and delicate personality, and put strict rules and regulations even upon himself. He was known to give harsh punishments to subordinates who broke the codes. He was valued by Genghis as the "Protector of Yassa." Yet Genghis Khan thought he was narrow-minded.

The third son, Ogodei, was brilliant. He had a generous and well-rounded character. His good judgment and decisiveness were his other strong points. He designed and improved many of the offensive weapons and equipment, like catapults and ladder carriers. He invented the naphtha flamethrower, which allowed them to shoot huge flaming balls of cotton soaked with highly flammable naphtha. On the other hand, he was a pleasure seeker and a heavy drinker.

The fourth son, Tolui, was most like a warrior among his brothers. He was a superb soldier and a brilliant strategist. He had valor and was skillful in using all kinds of weaponry. However, he was considered too cruel and brutal.

Who should be the next kha-khan? Genghis said to Juchi, as he was looking at him, "Juchi, you are my first son. You are entitled to speak first. Tell me what you have on your mind."

There seemed to be a good reason that Genghis Khan picked Juchi as the first speaker. As Juchi stood up from his seat, all the eyes of the royal family members, the noyans, and the senior officials and generals, about 200 people in total, fell upon him. Just as he opened his mouth and tried to say something, someone shouted from the corner:

"He was asked to be the first speaker. Does that mean he will be the successor? No! Never! If he becomes the khan, how can we bow to him and obey the Merkid bastard!"

After this statement, there was a sudden, deep silence and a feeling of tension filled the air. The speaker was Genghis Khan's second son, Chagatai. From an early age, they never got along. Why was that? Probably because of mixed emotions of self-protection and jealousy. It was like an eagle's chick pushing down the other, unhatched eggs from the nest or the newborn praying mantises eating each other to grow up. Juchi had achieved many praiseworthy accomplishments following his father so far, but Chagatai had not.

Upon Chagatai's remark, Borte, who was sitting next to Genghis, got on her feet and left. Two of her maids followed her immediately. There was quite a stir in the meeting hall.

Juchi slowly walked up to Chagatai and stood in front of him. For a moment, he stared at him and then said to him in an angry tone, "You rat! How can you say that? I have never been discriminated against, even by my father! What can you do better than me? Are you a better archer or a better wrestler than me? You are not a match for me!"

The two began to fight by grabbing each other's collars. As they were pushing and pulling, intolerant Bogorchu and Mukali, who was there on a brief visit from China for the meeting, tried to stop them. Bogorchu and Mukali held Juchi and Chagatai's arms, respectively, and pulled them apart. Genghis Khan watched this without saying anything. They kept on swearing at each other, even after they were apart. They were in a similar age group. At that time, Juchi was thirty-three years old, Chagatai thirty-one, Ogodei thirty and Tolui was twenty-six.

After an awkward moment, Koko Chos, in one corner, got up from his seat and opened his mouth. He was the personal tutor for Chagatai. In earlier times, when Genghis assigned him to be the personal tutor for Chagatai, he told Koko Chos this:

"Chagatai is a very difficult child. He is very delicate and pays too much attention to small things. Usually those kinds of people fail to see the whole picture of life. One needs two eyes, one for the small things and the other one for the larger ones. Stay with him, day and night, and help him to develop an eye for the larger things." It was certain that Genghis Khan was worrying about Chagatai's narrow-mindedness.

Koko Chos said, looking at Chagatai, "Chagatai, I always said that your father Khan wanted you to have an eye for the larger world. That means your father has high expectations for you. This is an occasion for deciding the next generation's leader of the great Mongol Empire, not just for the heir of a family. That is why we are all invited. Your father already confirmed his first son, Juchi's, legitimacy at the time he was born. In light of that, how can you still talk about that? If you think you are the right person to be the next generation's leader and all the others in this room agree with you, you will be the one."

After Koko Chos, Chagatai got on his feet and said, "First of all, I want to give my sincere apologies to my father Khan and everyone in this room. Moments ago, Juchi said he could defeat me in every aspect, but I do not accept that. He and I have never had such competitions before. I think the best one to be the next leader is Ogodei. He is honest. If he becomes khan in the future, I promise I will do my best to support him."

At Chagatai's remarks, Genghis said to Juchi,

"Juchi, what do you think? Speak up."

Juchi got up from his seat with a grim look and said, "I have no objection to Ogodei's succession. I also promise to support him when he becomes khan."

After his short remarks, he sat down right away. This time, Genghis said to Ogodei, who had been recommended as the successor by his two elder brothers, "What do you think? Let me know your opinion."

He hesitated a second, but got up and said, "If my father Khan asks me to say something, what else can I say but that

I will do my best? I think whoever becomes the next khan should sacrifice himself for this nation, which father Khan has founded, with the plan of eternity and the glory of the Mongols."

Genghis was satisfied with that answer. This time, Tolui was asked to say his words. Tolui answered, "I also agree that my third elder brother, Ogodei, should become the successor. If he becomes the khan, I will do long marches and short battles. At the same time, I promise I will be a truthful guardian of my father's decision and my brothers' promises."

After him, Genghis Khan looked over the whole assembly of the attendants, from his seat, and said in a solemn tone, "You have to keep what you have said. In the past, Altan and Quchar made a similar promise. However, they did not keep their word. Remember what happened to them? Ogodei is right, anyone who becomes khan, should sacrifice himself for the eternity of this nation and the glory of the Mongols. The land is large and rivers are everywhere. In the future, the Mongol nation might not be able to be ruled by one leader. You and your descendants will have your own land and people to be ruled. This is the will of heaven, as well as my well. Do not forget the story of five arrows and the fable of the two-headed snake that I have told you many times."

Genghis Khan decided Ogodei would be his successor. He valued highly his well-rounded character. His judgment was that for the next generation, such a person might be needed.

Chang-Chun was one of the men Genghis Khan wanted to meet. Genghis Khan heard of him while he was on his way to conquer northern China. Chang-Chun was named as the sage of those days in China. One time, even Yelu Chutze mentioned him, and Khan's Chinese doctor, Liu Wen, had strongly recommended seeing him.

Yelu Chutze told Genghis this, "He is the number one man of Taoism. Taoism is the science studying the origin of nature and the relationship between nature and man. They have been working on this for a long time, so there is probably something valuable in it."

As his name Chang-Chun signifies the long spring day, he was known as someone who had found the key to open the mystery of nature and the secret of health and longevity. Genghis Khan was not the type of person who listened to rumors; nonetheless, he decided to see him, because he thought the great ruler needed the help of a great philosopher. Genghis Khan extended an invitation, instead of issuing a royal summons, to him. He was living in a monastery in the Shantung region of China, and all the necessary duties and work were assigned to Chingai, the darughachi of northern China, and Liu Wen, the khan's Chinese doctor. Since Genghis Khan went to war with Khwarazm just after sending the invitation to him, Chang-Chun had to travel 4,500 miles for two years, and finally met him in the war camp in the Hindu Kush.

CHAPTER SEVENTY-EIGHT

March Against Khwarazm

In the summer of 1219, a large number of Mongol troops began to gather on the Irtish riverside, on the east side of Lake Balkhash. In the wide area of the riverside, countless military tents were built and 200,000 horses were spread over the field. By July, 150,000 troops had gathered, including the 30,000 accessory troops from the Uighur kingdom and the Kara Khitai. That was the maximum number of troops Genghis Khan could bring together, but it was not even half the number of the enemy defense force of 400,000. Genghis dispatched an urgent messenger to a vassal nation, the Shisha Kingdom, to make up the deficiency. However, the Shisha Kingdom refused his request, breaking the number-one condition of the surrender agreement, that they would be Genghis Khan's right hand in case of war. The reply, which arrived five days later, was this: "How can the man who does not have enough troops to punish his own enemy call himself the kha-khan?"

When Genghis Khan heard this through the interpreter, he was enraged. It was a great humiliation to Genghis Khan.

However, the present enemy was Khwarazm. Genghis Khan did not have any choice other than to postpone the Shisha's punishment until after the war with Khwarazm.

Genghis Khan divided his troops into four groups. The first army group of 50,000 troops was for him and the second army of 50,000 was for both Chagatai and Ogodei. The commanders of the third army of 30,000 and the fourth army of 20,000 were Juchi and Jebe, respectively. Genghis Khan assigned the mission of defending the Mongol mainland during his absence to his younger brother, Temuge, the Ochigin Noyan.

In July 1219, the Mongol troops commenced their marching. Jebe's fourth army was first. Jebe's fourth army started their marching not from the Mongol base camp by the Irtish riverside, but from the Kashgar region, which was further south. Actually, Jebe's fourth army was a separate, detached force. It was the first part of Genghis Khan's strategy to confuse the enemy.

There was a small sea, called Aral, between Lake Balkhash and the Caspian Sea. Two rivers flow northward to the Aral Sea, one from the southeastern direction, originating near the Pamir Heights, called the Syr River, and the other one from the southwestern direction, called the Amu River. The region between these two rivers was called the Transoxiana and the region west of the Amu River was called the Khurasan.

At the northern most part of the Transoxiana, or the area just below the Aral Sea, was the Kyzil Kum Desert, which was harsh and uninhabitable. However, the vast area south of the desert and between the two high elevated areas, the Pamir Heights and the Hindu Kush, was a land with rich, fertile soil and a mild climate, which was perfect for human inhabitation. In this vast area, numerous large and small cities were scattered, including Samarqand, the capital city of Khwarazm, Bukhara and Urgenchi. Along the Syr River were important cities like Otral, the northernmost city, Fenaket, Jand and Khojent.

Jebe's fourth army crossed over the Tien Shan Mountains. The stiff mountains of Tien Shan were densely filled with giant trees, so the Mongol soldiers had to open the road by cutting down the trees. As they crossed over the mountains, the great basin of Fergana showed up in front of them. It was an area of vast fields and some low hills, which were covered with reeds the height of a human knee or waist. From there, it was Khwarazm territory. The Syr River and the city of Khojent, which were commercial and strategic points, were not far from there. The city of Khojent was like the east gate of Samarqand, due to its location and proximity. Jebe's fourth army was about to attack this city.

What was the sultan Muhammad's defense strategy against the Mongol attackers? First, he chose the Syr River as the first defense line. He increased the defensive power of the cities along the river by increasing the number of troops. At the same time, he put his strongest troops in the major cities like Samarqand and Bukhara. Sultan Muhammad's strategy was mainly for defense and his troops were divided and posted into many different areas. The Persians called him the living son of Allah and the second Alexander. Would he win the victory over Genghis Khan? Nobody knew.

By the time Jebe's fourth army was advancing toward the city of Khojent, Genghis Khan's main force had crossed the river Chu and was going around the southern boundaries of the Aku Kum Desert. At the point where the desert ended, the Mongol troops of the first, second and third armies began to fan out. The second army, led by Chagatai and Ogodei, headed for Otral, while Juchi's third army turned to the south and advanced toward the city of Jand. Where was Genghis Khan's first army? They were moving to the north and then they suddenly disappeared. They were the ghost troops. Their movements had been made in complete darkness and at an unimaginable speed.

The city of Otral was being guarded by Inalchuq, known as Ghayir Khan, and his 50,000 troops. Before the Mongol troops' arrival, Sultan Muhammad sent out one of his generals, Qaracha, with an additional 10,000 troops to reinforce the defense, so the total number of the garrisons of the city became 60,000. Chagatai and Ogodei's second army of 50,000 troops surrounded the city. Inalchuq had already made up his mind to fight to the last man, because he was the one who had caused the problems; in case they lost, the Mongols would not keep him alive. He had been repairing and reinforcing the rampart and citadel inside the city. He already had enough provisions, which his 60,000 troops could use for at least one year, and also enough of all kinds of weapons. He beheaded about thirty citizens who tried to run away in fear of the approaching Mongol troops, and hanged them on the rampart wall as a warning.

Upon arrival, Chagatai and Ogodei prepared for the attack after looking around outside the city. Otral was protected by a rampart built of strong bricks made of mud and tough reed stalks, and around the rampart was a moat. Chagatai and Ogodei issued an order to commence the attack. The Mongol soldiers began to shoot rocks onto the rampart using the catapults and numerous huge flaming, naphtha balls of cotton flew into the city. The Khwarazm garrison soldiers counterattacked with long-range arrows and showered arrows onto the approaching Mongol soldiers. They were also equipped with devices and weapons such as rocks and boiling oil, in case the Mongol soldiers climbed the rampart wall using the ladder carriers. The rampart wall was so strong that the Mongol soldiers could not break it down easily. It could be a long war.

Meanwhile, Juchi, who had marched down to the south along the Syr River, gave 5,000 troops to Alqai, Soygetu and Taqai to advance towards Fenaket as vanguards. The Khwarazm side defense general, Iletqu Malik, opposed the Mongols with his 10,000 troops of Turks and Tajiks. After four days of fierce battle, Iletqu's defense troops were completely destroyed. Among the 30,000 citizens of Fenaket, only 150 industrial engineers, technicians, artisans, and 800 selected levies were saved. All the other male citizens were massacred. A levy was a laborer among enemy citizens who had little or no animosity and was very cooperative.

Juchi continued advancing, arriving at the riverside city Suqunaq, the population of which was about 40,000. In Juchi's war camp, there was a Persian man named Hassan Hajji. He was Jafa's friend and had once donated 1,000 sheep to Genghis Khan when he was in Lake Baljuna, hiding from Wang-Khan's attack, and joined to be one of the Baljuntus. Suqunaq was his hometown.

Hassan said to Juchi, "This is my hometown. My relatives and friends are still living here. I will try to persuade them to surrender."

Juchi sent him into the city as an envoy. Entering the city, Hassan began to persuade them in front of the crowd. However, among the crowd were hoodlums too. From the beginning, they would not listen to him; rather they agitated the crowd.

"Kill the betrayer of Allah!"

The crowd considered him a betrayer. They pulled him down from the platform and stoned him mercilessly. Hassan died on the spot. The mobs circled the marketplace, dragging Hassan's dead body.

They kept on shouting, "Holy war!"

Upon hearing of Hassan's death, Juchi immediately launched an attack. Their defense force collapsed immediately. Juchi issued an order of complete annihilation of the residents.

Before departure, Genghis Khan gave some guidelines and instructions on the war with Khwarazm to his generals and commanders:

- Disobedient and defiant enemy citizens should be annihilated. On the other hand, those that surrender should be saved.
- Defiant cities and their city walls should be completely destroyed and leveled, so that they cannot be used by the enemy for future bases to attempt a revival.

- Do not leave any possible force of future rebels behind when you are advancing.
- Try not to touch religious temples unless they are a base for the enemy.
- Leave the shahnas, or superintendents, in the surrendered cities.
- Save the industrial technicians, engineers and skilled artisans and send them to the Mongol mainland.
- If possible, save the women and children.

Genghis Khan left the independent power of decision-making and operations to his generals who were not under his direct commandership, as long as it did not violate the outline of his grand plan, because he had to cover a wide area with a relatively smaller number of troops. They did not need to report and get permission from Genghis Khan on every occasion.

All the people in Suqunaq were massacred. There was not a single survivor, and the city was completely destroyed and leveled. For many years, it remained as ruins. Later, when this city was rebuilt, Hassan's son was installed as the governor.

Juchi advanced farther south. When they arrived at the other cities, like Oskend and Barjigh Kant, the garrisons and residents gave up their resistance, coming out to meet them with bread and salt, the symbols of welcome. These two cities were saved without any slaughter. For these two cities, shahnas who had been selected from among the citizens were posted, and levies were picked from among the cooperative young citizens for labor. Once they had surrendered, they had to work for the Mongol troops, providing their labor and sometimes marching ahead of them. That was the meaning of surrender in the Mongols' interpretation. Surrender did not mean simply giving up resistance, it meant positive and active cooperation.

When Juchi's third army arrived at the city of Ashnas, they had to face fierce resistance. All the residents in this city were slaughtered and all the buildings, houses and walls were leveled. This news was conveyed to the city of Jand, with a population of 50,000. Qutlugh Khan, the garrison chief of this city, ran away with his close followers as the Mongol troops approached. Juchi dispatched Chin Temur, the Kara Khitai, into the city as an envoy to persuade them to surrender. Chin Temur tried, in front of the leading figures of the city, but some of them turned into a mob. Chin Temur had to make a false agreement with them to save his life.

Upon receiving the report from Chin Temur, Juchi sent his troops into the city. The city of Jand fell without any blood. About 200 rioters and uncooperative citizens were arrested and slaughtered, yet most of the rest were saved. Ali Khoja was appointed by Juchi as the shahna in this city and about 10,000 levies were chosen.

What about Jebe's fourth army, which was headed for the city of Khojent, a military strategic point?

Temur Malik, the garrison chief of Khojent, was a Khwarazm distinguished general. He put all the citizens into the citadel for their safety and built up the defense line at the diverging point of the Syr River, where the arrows could not reach from either side of the river. Then he built twelve large barges. These barges were large boats made of logs with flat bottoms and protective guardrails, with a maximum capacity of 200 soldiers. The guardrails were covered with felt coated with thick mud, protecting them from fire arrows. They had numerous, square openings, through which their soldiers could watch and shoot arrows. These barges were very efficient, so they irritated the Mongol soldiers coming and going from the lower and upper part of the river. The battle came to a lull.

Jebe contacted Juchi, who was occupying the lower part of the river. Juchi immediately sent out 50,000 levies for Jebe. Jebe began to embank the river with stones from nearby, using 50,000 levies. When the bank was close to the Khwarazm base camp, Temur Malik began to run away down the river, using seventy boats. Jebe contacted Juchi immediately. Juchi began to build a resistant line of iron chain and lined boats from one side of the river to the other to prevent Malik's ships from passing. With their boats stuck at the resistance line, Temur Malik and his soldiers had no other choice than to come onto land. They were slaughtered by the Mongol soldiers, who were waiting on both sides of the river.

Temur Malik landed on the west side of the bank and began to run away toward the west after mounting his horse, which he had brought on his boat. Three Mongol soldiers chased after him. Temur Malik's horse stepped into the desert area. Temur Malik's horse was an Arabian, which had long legs and was faster at a short distance. However, they were much weaker in long distances than the Mongol horses. The three Mongol soldiers kept chasing him. The gap between them became smaller and smaller. Temur Malik picked up one of the three arrows in his quiver and shot at them, and one of them fell from his horse. The two remaining Mongol soldiers did not give up. He shot a second arrow and another soldier fell down. The last Mongol soldier continued chasing. He picked up the last arrow; however, it was not for killing or hurting, it was for signaling, so the tip of the arrow was dull. His last arrow hit one of the eyes of the chasing Mongol soldier. However, he did not die. Instead, he was just wounded in one of his eyes. But he could not continue the chase.

This is the story of Temur Malik, twenty years later. After he escaped, for some time, he kept on fighting for the Khwarazm and then ran away to Syria. He stayed there for about twenty years and when everything became quiet, he returned to his hometown, Khojent. He missed his hometown so much and most of all, he wanted see his son. His son had become the governor of Khojent by that time, appointed by Ogodei Khan. His son willingly met the visitor from Syria, who was now an old man.

Being ushered in front of his son, Temur Malik asked him, "If you saw your father, do you think you would recognize him?"

The governor answered, putting his head a little bit to one side, "I parted from my father when I was a toddler. I do not even know whether he is still alive or not."

Temur Malik told his son, "I am your father."

Astonished, the governor summoned his father's old servant to confirm. The old servant found his master's face in the middle of a thick gray beard and mustache. The old servant told the governor, "I think he is your father. However, to be sure I need to see his right shoulder. Your father had a scar on his right shoulder."

Temur Malik took off the upper part of his clothing and showed his scar. The father and son embraced.

A while later, the son raised his head, with tears in his eyes and said, "Father, I am a subject of the Mongol Empire. I pledged my loyalty a long time ago. There is only one way left. You have to go and see Ogodei Khan for a special pardon. The Mongols never forgive their enemies, even after a long period of time."

Temur Malik stayed with his son for several days and then left for the Mongol mainland to see Ogodei Khan. However, he was unlucky. On his way, he was captured by the soldiers of Qadaqan, Ogodei Khan's sixth son. He was taken to Qadaqan. Qadaqan stared at him for a while and then gave an order to his men to bring the record book about him. In there, his past and previous activities were recorded in detail.

Temur Malik, the garrison chief of Khojent at the beginning of the war. One of the leading figures of the opposition force. After escape from Khojent, he rejoined the enemy side. Attacked the Kent region, killing the shahna there. Afterwards activity unknown. Some witnessed that he had escaped to Syria.

Those were the key points. After confirming his records, once more he stared at him and said, "Your son has rendered distinguished services to the Mongol Empire. Your past activity as the enemy to the Mongol Empire could be canceled out by your son's merits. However, your criminal activity in killing the shahna, who was representing the Mongol khan in that area, cannot be forgiven. I will confirm one more time, if you are really Temur Malik."

Qadaqan ordered to summon the Mongol soldier on the record, who had chased after him until the last moment. Of course, he was still alive, and, by that time, he was a commander of 1,000 soldiers. The commander, who now wore an eye patch, after face-to-face questioning, confirmed and witnessed he was Temur Malik. Temur Malik was executed by being shot with an arrow. Nobody could escape from the punishments of the Mongols, regardless of time or place.

The Fall of Bukhara and Otral

Genghis Khan's first Mongol army headed for the north, by passing the city of Oral and then suddenly, turned to the southwest. As the troops crossed the Syr River, the vastness of the Kyzil Kum Desert came into sight. The distance from the northern end to the southern end of this desert was about 400 miles and it was full of snakes and scorpions. Of course, there was no water in this area and the temperature varied dramatically between day and night. It was hell. Sultan Muhammad considered this a natural defensive barrier that the Mongols would never be able to cross. He built his defense strategy based on this supposition. However, Genghis Khan's troops prepared an enormous amount of water and stepped into the desert. Water was needed not only for drinking, but also to minimize damage from the scorpions. Before setting up their tents each night, the people in this area poured boiling water into the small holes that surrounded them, killing the scorpions within. The venom from this creature was deadly. Once a person got stung, he would suffer from a high fever and severe swelling and then die within twenty-four hours.

The Mongol troops mainly slept in the daytime and marched at night. This was because the scorpions were active in the nighttime. The soldiers were told to sleep with their boots on, because the insides of their boots were a favorite hiding place for the scorpions.

The Mongols' first army successfully crossed the desert. They finally stepped on the fertile soil of the Transoxiana. They continued marching towards the south. Genghis Khan's first target was Bukhara.

Bukhara was a backward city, about 150 miles to the west of Samarqand, the capital city of Khwarazm. Bukhara was an important intermediate city between Samarqand and their western territory. Genghis planned to surround Samarqand by seizing Bukhara.

To get to Bukhara, Genghis Khan had to pass through a few small and intermediate cities. One of them was Jarnuq. After surrounding the city, Genghis Khan dispatched an envoy into the city. The citizens were shocked at the unexpected and sudden appearance of the Mongol troops, and fear threw the whole city into confusion and chaos.

Genghis Khan's envoy, Danishmand, shouted in front of the crowd, "My name is Danishmand. I am a Muslim and my father and my ancestors were all Muslims. I am here to save you from the annihilation and whirlpool of destruction as the khan's envoy. The war has finally arrived. If you resist, this city will be leveled within half a day and an endless river of blood will flow. If you listen to my advice with sense and wisdom, you will surrender and promise to obey him. Then at least you will save your lives."

The aristocrats and leading figures of city of Jarnuq gathered and discussed. They all agreed to surrender. They opened the gate and showed up in front of the Mongol troops in a group, presenting bread and salt, the symbols of surrender as well as welcome. As promised, Genghis Khan did not touch the people but disarmed the garrison and broke down the citadel and the city wall. It was a preventive measure so as to make the city unusable by the enemy in the future. About 5,000 levies were selected from this city.

The Mongol troops continued marching. Genghis dispatched Tayir Bagatur as the vanguard to the next city, Nur. Genghis tried to conceal his movements until he reached the first-phase destination, Bukhara. Genghis advised Tayir Bagatur to make a surprise attack at night, to take control of their garrison. Tayir ordered his soldiers to cover their bodies with leafy tree branches, one in each of their hands. They did not use horses and marched at a very slow pace.

In the city of Nur, there was a strange woman. They called her Zarqa of Yamama, which meant "woman with blue eyes." She was being treated as a lunatic or possessed woman. This Persian woman used to walk around the city murmuring things that nobody could understand. She used to shout in the marketplace, gazing into space with eyes without focus.

"The day when the forest moves, a big calamity will fall upon this land! The mountains of human heads and the rivers of human blood will be everywhere. Be aware of the day the forest moves!"

People shook their heads listening to her silly shouting. They clucked their tongues in sympathy and turned away from this insane woman.

"How can the forest move?"

However, her words turned out to be true. That night, Tayir's surprise attackers approached the city like a moving forest. It was a dark night, without a single gleam of moonlight. Upon arriving just underneath the rampart, the Mongol soldiers crawled up the rampart wall using the ladder and ropes. Crossing over the wall, they took control of the garrison. The next day, the citizens of Nur surrendered to Subedei, who arrived early in the morning with his large troops.

Because they surrendered, Genghis spared their lives and allowed them to keep their livestock. However, the citadel and the rampart were leveled and the people were evacuated. In addition, the leaders of this city had to make a contribution of 1,500 dinars. Later, Genghis appointed Il Khoja, the son of the former governor, the ruler of this city.

Genghis Khan marched towards Bukhara. Bukhara was a big city on the riverside of the Oxus, or Amu River, with a population of 400,000 inhabitants. Bukhara meant "center of learning," and as the name implied, there were numerous schools, libraries and Islamic temples. Bukhara was also the industrial and trading center. The woolen textile industry, using wool from sheep and camels, and the leather industry, producing leather garments, belts and boots, were highly developed. Their Persian carpets were the best in the world at that time.

The city was always crowded with caravans from the Mediterranean, Persia, India and China.

As the city of Bukhara was drawing near, the picturesque images of the onion-shaped Muslim mosques and the observatory towers covered with red brick walls came into Genghis Khan's view. Genghis stopped there and sent out the scouts to reconnoiter the outskirts of the city. The Bukhara garrison commander, Kok Khan, was stationed along the Amu River with his 30,000 troops. He had outstanding Turkish and Persian generals like Khamid Bur, Sevich Khan and Keshli Khan. Ironically, Kok Khan was Mongolian. After he had been orphaned as a small boy, he followed the caravans into this area. He was recognized as an outstanding warrior as he was growing up, and finally became a high-ranking general in the Khwarazm army. Kok Khan, who was presumed to be a descendant of the Taichut, and his 30,000 troops, clashed with the Mongol expeditionary forces on the Amu riverside, only to end up being completely destroyed within half a day. All 30,000 garrison soldiers were killed, along with Kok Khan, who had been shot by about ten arrows.

Their blood stained the river and their dead bodies covered the riverbank endlessly.

The news that the garrison troops had been destroyed put the city into a state of panic. Some citizens hid themselves in the citadel and others just sat there and waited for their destinies. To minimize the victims, they opened the city gate wide and welcomed the Mongol troops. Genghis Khan entered the city side by side with his son Tolui. The roads inside the city were wide and clean, and big buildings like palaces were lined up along the street on both sides. Those buildings were covered with shiny, milky tiles, which were reflecting the mid-afternoon sunlight, creating dazzling rainbows.

Some citizens hid themselves in buildings and some others came out onto the streets and watched the Mongol horse soldiers marching in. Some of the Mongol troops went into the city, and some others were stationed outside the city. Genghis Khan gathered the city leaders and asked them to bring a list of the rich men in the city. They discussed this together and brought a list of 280 rich men. Among them, about 180 men were natives and about 90 were from outside, including India. Genghis Khan made them pay 200,000 dinars of war compensation money. They brought gold coins and jewelry in that amount. Genghis gathered all the citizens in the open ground in the center of the city. He stepped on a high platform made of marble stairs and shouted at them. Next to him were two interpreters who repeated his Mongolian in Turkish and Persian.

"I am the punishment of God! I am not here simply to invade another land and loot. Your leader has committed a serious crime. God is enraged. Because of your leader, you, too, are paying the penalties. From now on, you will have a new order, a new world and a new era. Join us and cooperate with us! That is the only way you can save yourselves and allow yourselves to prosper. Otherwise, you will perish from this earth! That is the will of God and the will of me. Here, I am making it very clear to you that you will have freedom of religion. This is my promise."

Next, Genghis Khan attended a welcome party arranged by the citizens. Some of the citizens brought him Persian honey wine; however, Genghis refused it and drank kumis that his soldiers had brought. Musicians played their musical instruments and several woman singers came out and sang their songs. Some time later, the Mongol soldiers who were sitting around the open ground, putting their arms around each other's shoulders, sang their military songs at the top of their voices, swaying their upper bodies.

Genghis did not stay there too long. Before leaving, he gave instructions to Tolui.

"Do not leave this city to be the possible future base for the rebels. Try to save the women and children."

Genghis returned to his camp outside the city. The next morning, Tolui attacked the citadel on the outskirts of the city with his troops. The 50,000 rebels inside refused to surrender. The Mongol troops began to shoot rocks and flames, using catapults and naphtha flamethrowers. They also used the battering ram to break down the gate of the citadel. After a few days of battle, the citadel was taken and all the men and male youngsters were massacred, while the women and toddlers were spared. Mountains of dead bodies were made, and a river of blood flowed. The women and toddlers were sent to the Mongol mainland as slaves.

Next, Tolui picked 50,000 levies from among the citizens. He ordered the evacuation of the whole population from the city. They had to move out of the city. After opening the warehouses for food and taking everything out of there, Tolui issued an order to burn the city. Since most of the houses were made of wood, the city was wrapped in flames quickly. The city of Bukhara burned for several days. The sky above the city was stained red, and it could be seen from over 100 miles away. Six days later, the city was reduced to ashes. Nothing was left except the heaps of ashes, a destroyed rampart and half-burnt palaces and temples made of bricks and marble. In the meantime, the defiant citizens hiding in every corner of the city were forced outside by the heat and killed one by one. The surrendering citizens and their family members waiting outside the city were provided with livestock, food and minimum necessities, and were advised to find their own way to survive until the completion of the conquest of Khwarazm by the Mongols. Afterward, it took thirty years to rebuild the city. Yalavachi and his son, Masud, were installed as governors, one after another. A Persian poet expressed scorn like this, after he had seen the fate of Bukhara:

Fate is a stick,
And life is a ball.
The stick toys with the ball!

Fate is a gale,
And life is a grain of millet.
Who can resist from blowing?

Fate is a hunter,
And life is a lark.
Who can hide from his keen eyes and arrows?

In the meantime, in Otral, the battle was still going on. The city of Otral was devastated after five months of Mongol attacks. Most of their houses were burned down by naphtha flame attacks and the streets were covered with dead bodies. At the beginning of the war, they buried the dead bodies, but as time went by, there were too many. The air stank, and the swarms of flies from the dead bodies never stopped bothering those who were still alive. Though food was still available, water gradually became scarce. In a normal situation, they used the water from the nearby river for everything. However, in this situation they had to depend only on the water from the wells inside the city. Of course, they had prepared for a long war, digging additional wells, but those were not enough. Many horses died from dehydration. Besides all this, the most crucial fact they began to realize was that they were running out of arrows, which were definitely necessary to stop the approaching Mongol soldiers. Even in the face of all these problems, Inalchuq cut off the head of anyone who was talking about surrender, right on the spot, because he knew he would not survive even if he surrendered.

One day, after five months of battling, the Khwarazm general Qaracha, who joined Inalchuq with his 10,000 troops, could not tolerate it anymore and decided to escape. Without any notice or consultation with Inalchuq, he opened one side gate and made a dash to penetrate the encirclement with some of his troops. However, this trial was easily stopped and Qaracha became a captive and then lost his head. In this incident, the Mongol soldiers were able to take the gate successfully. The Mongol troops poured into the city. Inside the city, the dead bodies of the Khwarazm soldiers began to pile up. Losing the battle on the streets, the remaining Khwarazm soldiers sought safety in the citadel. Inalchuq held out in the citadel for another month with his 20,000 remaining troops. However, at the end of the month, his 20,000 troops were all dead and all he had were a few of his concubines. He had used his last arrow, and only one scimitar remained in his hand. He began to run to the top of the tower in the citadel with his concubines. Several dozen of the Mongol soldiers chased him. Genghis Khan's order was to capture him alive. When he reached the top chamber of the tower, which was used as an observatory, he was at the end. His concubines picked up some tiles from the roof and brought them to him. He threw the tiles toward the Mongol soldiers, who were ascending the spiral stairs and approaching him. He was captured alive there. Iron chains were put on his hands and feet and he was put into a mobile one-man prison made of iron bars. After destroying and leveling the city of Otral, Chagatai and Ogodei advanced towards Samarqand with their second army group. It was February of 1220.

Afterwards, all four army groups of the Mongol force, Genghis Khan's first, Chagatai and Ogodei's second, Juchi's third, and Jebe's fourth, gathered at the outskirts of Samarqand. Genghis Khan handed Inalchuq over to Julchedai, who was well-known for his cruelty. He first put several lumps of silver into the smelting furnace to make it boil. He hanged Inalchuq upside down from a tree and poured the boiling silver into his nostrils and ear holes, little by little, in front of hundreds of spectators.

That was the last of Inalchuq.

The Fall of
Samarqand

Genghis Khan advanced towards Samarqand, the capital city of Khwarazm. Samarqand, a city with a population of 500,000, was not only a political, commercial, cultural and industrial center for the Khwarazm Empire, but also grand and magnificent. The buildings standing along the streets were built with red bricks and marble, and creamy tiles covered the brick to make it clean and bright. In the downtown area and marketplace, stores carrying luxurious foreign goods and merchandise from all over the world lined up endlessly and inns and theaters for travelers were everywhere. Blessed with warm and pleasant weather, neighboring areas of this city were filled with numerous varieties of fruits trees, including date palm trees, and the vineyards and watermelon fields were spread out endlessly. Watermelons, the specialty of this area, were highly popular because of their great sweetness and lower fiber than others. They exported large amounts of this product each season to satisfy the demand from faraway countries. When exporting to faraway places, they put these products into wooden boxes filled with heat-resistant and shockproof materials.

The Persian poets praised this beautiful city:

Samarqand!
The jewel of the east!

Full of the grace of God,
It is the hometown for angels.

Sweet wine rains,
And the wind is full of fragrance.

The earth is musk,
And the gems are rolling everywhere.

Where is the Garden of Eden?
It is Samarqand!

Samarqand was guarded by 60,000 Turks and 50,000 Tajiks, totaling 110,000 men. They were the elite troops of the Khwarazm Empire. Their generals, Alper Khan, Shaik Khan and Bala Khan were the best among them and were major role players in building up the empire.

One evening, a man was galloping his horse at full speed toward the main gate of Samarqand. His hair was disheveled and his clothing was torn to ribbons. He was the Tajik soldier who had escaped from Bukhara. He was one of a few survivors of the garrison there. He was ushered in front of Sultan Muhammad. Panting, he told him what had happened in Bukhara.

"They burned Bukhara! The city was leveled and the garrison was destroyed completely!"

Sultan Muhammad was shocked. He thought the Mongols could not break the Syr River defense line so easily and even if they did, it would take a long time for them to get to Samarqand. Now that Bukhara was in their hands, he was surrounded! He was in danger of losing the supply line from the west. He was still intent upon repairing the rampart of Samarqand and it was not over yet! He decided to escape to the west with the excuse that he had to bring more troops. His transparent lie left only one man who could dare to resist his escape plan, and that was his son, Jal-al-Addin. He was one of only a few heroes of Khwarazm. However, he also had to flee to the Hindu Kush once his father had left there.

Genghis Khan's first army arrived at Samarqand with 70,000 levies in front of them. All the while, Genghis Khan was in close contact with the other three army groups and knew their exact locations, movements, and situations. Only a half day after his arrival, Chagatai and Ogodei's second army also arrived and joined him. Chagatai and Ogodei's second army brought 20,000 levies. For a day, Genghis looked around the outside of the city, and the following day he created a complete encirclement.

In the city of Samarqand, they had enough stored provisions for 600,000 people, including the garrison, to use for several years. They thought they could resist and hold the city for at least a year. However, it fell to the Mongols just five days later!

First, Genghis had the levies fill the deep moat around the rampart. The levies completed their job using dirt and rocks from nearby. On that first night, the moat was completely filled and the Mongol troops commenced a surprise attack. The rocks shot by the catapults began to break down the buildings and houses, and the naphtha flames lit the city up like daytime. As the Mongol troops were approaching the rampart with their 3,000 ladder carriers, the Khwarazm soldiers greeted them with showers of arrows. However, the ladder carriers were designed and equipped with an anti-arrow system. The Mongol soldiers began to climb the rampart using the ladders once they got there. The garrison soldiers tried to push away the approaching ladder carriers with long logs, yet some of the Mongol commandos were already on the rampart. After fierce man-to-man fighting on the rampart, the Mongol commandos successfully occupied one of the main gates. Knowing that they had lost one of the main gates, the leaders of the Khwarazm garrison tried a full-scale counterattack. They opened the other gate and came pouring out of the city with twenty armed elephants in front of them. However, it turned out to be a stupid tactic. Attacked by showers of arrows, the intolerant elephants stepped back or turned around, trampling on their own soldiers. The Khwarazm soldiers who were pouring out of the gate fell down in great numbers, like winged insects swarming to a fire. The dead bodies of Khwarazm soldiers covered the field outside the city, making it hard for the Mongol soldiers to move around.

The following day, the leaders of the city gathered, discussed and decided to surrender. The citizens of Samarqand were not loyal to Sultan Muhammad, who deserted Samarqand quickly for his own safety. The Mongol troops broke down the rampart first and then attacked the citadel where the defiant Alper Khan and his 30,000 troops were hiding. Three days later, the citadel was taken and the 30,000 troops were annihilated. At the last moment, Alper Khan tried to escape with his 1,000 suicide soldiers. However, most of them were massacred and only he and a few survivors made their way to the west.

Genghis Khan issued an order of evacuation of all citizens from the city. They needed to be screened. The whole population of Samarqand was evacuated to the field. The Mongol soldiers entered the city and killed tens of thousands of disobedient people who were hiding in the ceilings or sewers in spite of the evacuation order. Then, the Mongol officials began the screening and selection of the citizens. The first group of people selected were leading figures connected to the Mongol Empire and cooperative officials, and second were engineers, technicians and artisans. Their numbers came up to 50,000. Among the rest, 30,000 levies who pledged their allegiance to the Mongol Empire were selected. Next, women and children were selected. Among the rest of the male population, all the defiant, disobedient ones and some who had refused to convert were executed. The selected citizens were imposed with 200,000 dinars of war support money, and two men, Siqa-al-Mulk and Amid Buzurq, who had pledged their loyalty to Genghis Khan, were installed as the chief administrative officials. Genghis appointed Yalavachi as the governor of Samarqand and left several shahnas there.

Genghis Khan organized the pursuit of Sultan Muhammad, who had fled before the fall of Samarqand. For this mission, 30,000 elite troops were selected and two commanders were appointed, Jebe and Subedei. They were ordered to chase down Sultan Muhammad to the end of the world. Next, he dispatched his three sons, Juchi, Chagatai and Ogodei, to take Urgenchi, a city located at the southern shore of the Aral Sea, where the Amu River meets it in a triangular basin. It was a city for the aristocrats and rich people. In the city of Urgenchi, luxurious mansions were lined up along the streets, and rose gardens and water fountains were everywhere. The houses facing the shoreline had beautiful views of the Aral Sea.

However, the dispatched Mongol troops began to have internal trouble. Juchi and Chagatai clashed on the issue of commandership of the troops. Juchi claimed that he should be the commander because he was the first son. On the other hand, Chagatai insisted that he was the right one because after the occupation of Urgenchi, their father, Genghis Khan, had promised him that he would be the ruler of this area. They could not agree and their arguments continued on and on. The garrison of Urgenchi took advantage of this and reinforced the defense system in the meantime.

Bogorchu, who was with them, could not tolerate this and sent an urgent messenger to Genghis asking for a solution for this problem. At that time, the structural system of the Mongol troops was that the nominal commanderships were given to the descendants of Genghis Khan, butthe tactics and battle plans were made by the experienced generals.

Upon receiving Bogorchu's report, an enraged Genghis Khan scolded his two sons severely and gave the commandership to Ogodei. This outcome made Juchi very unhappy, causing him to remain in the Kipchak, the Russian steppe, which his father gave him, and refusing to return to the Mongol mainland.

First, Ogodei sent his envoy into the city, to persuade them to surrender. However, Khuman Tegin, the garrison commander, refused him, cutting off the envoy's head. The Mongol troops commenced an attack. Since the Mongol soldiers could not find rocks around there, they had to cut the mulberry trees to use in the catapults. The 50,000 levies, specially transferred from Jand for this operation, filled up the moat with soil. The Mongol commandos went up the rampart using the ladder carriers and then opened the gate for the main troops. The Mongol horse soldiers began street fighting and soon the dead bodies of the garrison were strewn across the streets. Before long, the city was enveloped in flames. The Mongol soldiers at last seized every corner of the city. The fiercest battle was on the arch-shaped bridge on the Amu River, which flowed through the western outskirts of the city. On this bridge, a great number of garrison soldiers were killed and fell into the river. The Amu River was stained with blood and filled with dead bodies. The Mongol soldiers cut the heads off 100,000 men from this city, leaving skilled technicians, women and children alive.

Genghis Khan spent the spring in the suburbs of Samarqand and moved to Nakh Shab (Karsh) plain as the summer approached. He spent the summer there, giving a rest to both the men and horses.

In autumn, he began his movements for the conquest of the southern region. Genghis headed for Tirmiz, the city located to the east side of the Amu River, from the north. This city, with a population of 100,000, was protected with a well-built fortress, and the garrison was fully equipped with defensive and offensive weapons, including a mangonel, which was similar to a catapult. Genghis Khan dispatched an envoy persuading them to surrender by breaking the fortress and citadel by the citizens of Tirmiz themselves. However, they not only refused to surrender but also opened the gate and commenced an attack, believing that their fortress was invincible and they had more than enough weapons. After eleven days of battle, the city fell to the Mongols. The whole population was taken out to the field and massacred. There was not a single survivor in that city. The city was burned and leveled as an example to others.

Before the departure for Khwarazm, Genghis had strongly emphasized to his soldiers that the war with Khwarazm was not for mere retaliation. The Mongols had a mission to establish a new order in the world; they were not simply to destroy, kill, plunder and leave. They were to conquer, remove, rebuild and govern. The Mongols had to conquer a large area and had to deal with large numbers of enemies with a small number of troops. They could not leave possible future enemies behind. However, Genghis treated well the people and their descendants who had surrendered from their hearts. The Mongols always posted shahnas, or basqaqs among their people, in the cities or regions that had surrendered. They were empowered to govern the city or region on behalf of the Mongol khan. Usually they were given an official letter from the khan, written on a sheepskin roll, with an official seal. On the ivory or jade seal, this was written in Mongolian letters: "God in the heaven, Kha-Khan. The power of God on the earth. The ruler of mankind."

Genghis Khan crossed the Amu River. From there, it was Khurasan. Genghis Khan's troops headed for Balkh. Balkh was an industrial city with a population of 150,000 and, in the past, it was called the "eastern Mecca" by the Persians. Genghis was informed that Jal-al-Addin, Sultan Muhammad's son, was there, trying to recruit and gather the troops. Jal-al-Addin was the hero of the Khwarazm side. He crossed over the Hindu Kush Mountains and actively moved around, gathering troops in the area of Khalaj and Peshawar, the area bordered by India and later called Afghanistan.

At the same time, he dispatched his envoy to the caliph in Baghdad, asking for military support. However, his request was turned down immediately: *Genghis Khan has a policy of religious freedom. This cannot be a holy war!*

The Caliph and Sultan Muhammad were enemies. Genghis launched an attack on this city. He already had the information that many of the residents in the city had joined Jal-al-Addin, and most of the people were cooperating with him. After seven days, the city fell to the Mongol troops. Before the fall, the chief of the city showed his intention of surrender, but it was not accepted. The entire rampart, large houses and the palace were completely destroyed and all of the 150,000 residents were taken out to the field and beheaded.

Genghis gave 30,000 troops to Tolui to conquer the farther western region of Khurasan. In Khurasan, numerous small and large cities were spread out over a large area, and among them, Merv, Nishapur and Herat were the largest.

After sending Tolui to the other Khurasan area, Genghis himself advanced toward Talaqan. Talaqan, with a population of 100,000, was near the Hindu Kush Mountains. Since this city was pro-Jal-al-Addin, all the garrisons and residents were massacred. From there, Genghis received information that Jal-al-Addin had amassed a large number of troops in Khalaj and Peshawar. Genghis immediately dispatched 5,000 suppression troops under the command of Sigi Qutuku. However, when Sigi Qutuku and his 5,000 suppression troops arrived at Peshawar, they were ambushed by 50,000 Jal-al-Addin troops. Genghis was embarrassed when Sigi Qutuku lost the battle and came back with only half of his troops. That was the only defeat the Mongol troops experienced among 800 small and large battles, from the time they stepped into Khwarazm territory until they went back to their homeland. Genghis did not punish him, as he was like his adopted son and made a great contribution to the administrative side.

"Qutuku is full of ideas for winning the battle. However, he did not have the chance to use those ideas because of his lack of experience. Now he has experienced the difficulty of battle, and from now on, will have great victories that will cover the loss and more."

Genghis immediately set out to chase down Jal-al-Addin.

CHAPTER EIGHTY-ONE

Misery at Merv

Tolui, who had advanced towards the heart of Khurasan, conquered the small and medium-sized cities one by one. It was acknowledged that Tolui had inherited most of his father's disposition as a warrior. He was brilliant, valiant and decisive, and yet considered too cruel. What he had done in Khurasan, while he was conquering those areas, clearly showed that. While he was on the way to Merv, one of the largest cities in Khurasan, he leveled almost all the cities he passed through, massacred the residents, and left only a small number of survivors:

Avivard, population 80,000, no survivors

Nisa, population 100,000, no survivors

Yazir, population 70,000, no survivors

Nuqan, population 60,000, no survivors

Jajarm, population 60,000, survivors: 1

Sabzavar, population 70,000, no survivors

Baihaq, population 50,000, no survivors

Khaf, population 60,000, no survivors

Sanjan, population 110,000, no survivors

Zurabad, population 90,000, survivors: 1

Sijistan, population 70,000, no survivors

Sarakhs, population 50,000 (surrendered and very
cooperative), all survived

However, the death toll from a single city in Khurasan was
higher than all the numbers above, combined.

Merv was one of the largest and richest cities in Khurasan and
was the hometown for the aristocrats and the chiefs. The original population of this city was 450,000, but by the time Tolui's
Mongol troops arrived, it had swelled to 1,200,000, due to
refugees from other areas retreating there since the beginning
of the war. The number was increasing every day. The Persian
poets praised this city:

> *Attractive city, generous ruler.*
> *Soils emit fragrance of musk.*
> *Once you step in,*
> *Its own beauty of the name,*
> *Will never let you go!*

Sultan Muhammad stopped by this city on his way to escape. Before leaving to go farther west, he appointed Baha-al-Mulk as the governor and garrison chief of this city.
However, finding that the conditions of the city rampart,
fortress and citadel were not at their best, he simply ran
away like his ruler. After this, the leaders of this city divided
into two groups, and they clashed. One group insisted on

surrendering, and the other insisted on the opposite, fighting to the last.

Upon receiving the report, Sultan Muhammad sent his favorite general, Mujir-al-Mulk as the new governor and garrison
chief. Mujir-al-Mulk was his son. Mujir-al-Mulk's mother was
originally a concubine of the sultan. The sultan gave her to
one of his generals who had rendered a distinguished service.
However, at the time of the transfer, the concubine was already
pregnant. The sultan knew she was pregnant and acknowledged Mujir-al-Mulk as his son.

Mujir-al-Mulk was highly ambitious and wanted to be the
next sultan.

The first thing he did after his arrival at Merv was remove
the moderate group who were pro-Mongol. After Sarakhs, the
neighboring city to Merv, had surrendered to the Mongol troops,
many of the moderate group moved to that city and the remain-
der in Merv were in close contact with them. The moderate
group thought that Merv could not stand against a Mongol attack and so they thought the right thing to do was to surrender
to save the city and the people. If that was not possible, they
wanted to save the remaining members of the moderate group
in the city by giving the list of their names to the Mongols before
they took the city.

Sheiks-al-Islam, the governor of Sarakhs, secretly had one of
his relatives who was a cadi, or low judicial officer, infiltrate
Merv to get the list. He successfully acquired the list, but failed
to get out. He was taken to Mujir-al-Mulk, who took the list
and ordered him stabbed to death. His dead body was dragged

around the marketplace, pulled by his two legs, with his face down. Next, the 700 remaining members of the moderate group on the list were taken out to the open ground and beheaded.

Baha-al-Mulk, the runaway former governor, at last surrendered to the Mongol troops. Upon facing Tolui, he said he would try to persuade Mujir-al-Mulk to surrender. Tolui did not count on him, but gave him a chance. Baha wrote a letter to Mujir, and seven envoys were dispatched to Merv with a letter:

> *God of fate is with the Mongols.*
> *I am already with them.*
> *They put deadly blows on Nisa and Bavard,*
> *Making them cease to exist.*
> *Do not cast yourself into the whirlpool of destruction,*
> *Or the swamp of ruins,*
> *And save yourself and your people.*

After reading this letter, Mujir nodded and asked many questions of the envoys, asking about the size of the Mongol troops, their equipment and present location, etc. After he got the answers, he ordered his men to take the envoys out to the field and cut their heads off.

Upon receiving the report that the seven envoys had been beheaded, Tolui was enraged and cut Baha-al-Mulk's head off.

Next Mujir attacked Sarakhs, the city that had surrendered to the Mongols, with his 2,500 troops. They captured Shams-Addin, the shahna who had Genghis Khan's letter of appointment and the official seal. Mujir handed him over to the son of Pahla-van Abu-Bakr Divana, who had been killed by the moderate group, who stabbed Shams-Addin all over the body to death.

Merv was in a mood of celebration. They played music and had drinks as if they had already won the war. Good news and excitement were continually brought to them. Ikhtiyar Addin, who used to be the Malik of Amuya, joined them, and Shaik Khan, one of the garrison commanders of Samarqand, arrived with his man Ogur Hajib and 2,000 troops. On their way, they ambushed the 800-strong Mongol scout corps and took 60 Mongol captives. The 60 Mongol captives were dragged through the streets and then killed by having metal wedges hammered into their ears. One by one, they were taken out in front, and the crowd shouted in joy each time they saw the tip of the metal wedge popping out through the victim's ear on the other side, having been hammered through their skulls by the executioner.

The city of Merv was guarded by 70,000 Turcomans, a tribe from Persia, who had set up a base camp at a nearby riverside outside the city. Tolui picked 400 commandos and dispatched them as vanguards. Tolui knew that 12,000 garrison troops were patrolling the city each day, and at dusk, they were retiring to their base camp. The Mongol commandos hid in the forest near the return to their camp. It was a dark night, without a single gleam of moonlight, and all their faces were painted with tar.

When the Mongols surprise-attacked them, the garrison troops were completely destroyed in a very short time. They were killed by spears and scimitars and many of them were drowned in the river. The Mongol commandos, who had destroyed 12,000 garrison troops, now attacked their main base camp. First, they broke down the fences and released the troops' horses into the field. Then the Mongols fell upon the camp. A garrison with tens of thousands of troops was like sheep driven by the wolves and fell like autumn leaves in front of a gale. Many of them managed to escape into the fields, but were then killed one by one by Tolui's main forces, which were encircling the area. Thus, a garrison of 70,000 men was demolished by a handful of Mongol commandos. There was not a single survivor. Tolui did not accept prisoners.

Merv, with no defense force, was doomed. The following day, Tolui took a look around the city. After six days of planning and preparation, the Mongols launched an attack. Led by Tolui, the Mongol troops took the two main gates of the city. However, they did not enter the city. Mujir-al-Mulk tried to surrender after losing the main defense force and the two gates. He dispatched Jamal Addin, the chief imam, to Tolui to talk about surrender. Tolui pretended that he was willing to accept their surrender. He asked for the list of rich men in Merv. Mujir-al-Muik responded with a list of 200.

They were asked to make the reparations. After that, the Mongol troops entered the city. Tolui issued an order of complete evacuation of the residents. All the people on the streets and in their homes were driven out of the city to the fields. It took four days and four nights for the complete evacuation. The Mongol soldiers began to set fire to all the houses and buildings in the city, which had been changed into a ghost town with no trace of humans. The flames shot up. In a very short time, the city was enveloped in flames. The people began to cry out at the scene of their houses and city burning. The wives wept with their faces buried in their husbands' chests and the parents hugged their children tightly, covering their children's eyes with their hands. However, that was nothing but a prelude to the tragedy. The Mongol troops began their selection. They picked only 400 of the most superb artisans. A special unit of 4,000 executioners was organized, composed of the Mongol soldiers and levies. Most of the levies were from the surrendered neighboring city of Sarakhs. The executioners divided the people into three groups: men, women and children.

> *Oh! How many wives like nymphs struggled and writhed*
> *not to part from their husbands' bosoms?*
> *Oh! How many children like dolls struggled and wriggled*
> *not to lose their parents' hands?*
> *Oh! How many brothers and sisters had their hearts torn*
> *with sorrow to say good-bye to each other?*

That was how Persian poets described the situation. The levies from Sarakhs mocked and humiliated their fellow Muslims. The order of execution had arrived. It included women and children. Quotas were laid out to each of the executioners: 300 to 400. The first one who was executed was the chief of the city, Mujir-al-Mulk. He was kicked to death surrounded by ten levies. The execution lasted half a day. The vast field was covered with dead bodies in a short period of time. Levies made pyramids with human heads. Three pyramids of human heads, men, women and children, rivaled the nearby hills. The field around the area became muddy with human blood.

Next, Tolui ordered them to destroy the rampart and brick buildings that had not already been burned. The city was leveled and fell into desolate ruins of ashes and heaps of stone. The Mongol troops left.

A few days later, the survivors crept out of the sewers and deep dugouts in which they had been hiding and opened up the piles of ashes and heaps of stone. However, they were not safe, because the Mongol rear-guard troops came back to handle them. Five thousands of them were killed. They lived merely a few more days.

There was a man named Izz Addin. He arrived at Merv several days after the tragedy. He was shocked and stood with his mouth agape at the horrifying scene of three huge pyramids of human heads and dead bodies endlessly spread over the vast field.

"Ah! I see what I should not have seen. This horrifying scene will torment me in my dreams, all through my life, until the last day. This should be recorded in human history." After murmuring this, he began to count the number of dead bodies with several helpers. After fourteen days, he had the number of dead bodies and it was 1,300,000.

CHAPTER EIGHTY-TWO

Tragedy at Nishapur

If all the cities on this earth are stars in the sky,
The brightest one will be Nishapur.

If the mother earth is the body of the human,
The eyes, the gateway for the spirit, are Nishapur.

The Persian poets praised Nishapur in many ways. The city of Nishapur, located 150 miles southwest of Merv, was the most popular stopover for caravans traveling between Baghdad and Samarqand. It was the commercial, cultural and religious center for that region. The markets were busy, the streets were lined with luxurious mansions and the Islamic temples were beautifully covered with creamy tiles. Normally, its population was 400,000. However, having taken in refugees from other areas, the number swelled to over a million.

Sultan Muhammad stayed in this city for a while on his way further west, running from the Mongol pursuers. The city of Nishapur was guarded by a garrison of 30,000 troops, who were armed with 3,000 crossbows and 300 mangonels. However, Sultan Muhammad had already lost his spirit to fight back against the surging Mongol troops. At one time, after conquering a large area with crushing power, starting from his hometown near the Caspian Sea, he had been called the "son of Allah" or the "second Alexander." Now he was leaving the stage of the world. He failed to get true support from the people he had conquered. He had had to face revolt twice, since he had occupied Samarqand. The direct cause was high taxes, but the real problem was the lack of an efficient administration system. It became very clear that he was not a rival to Genghis Khan as a military leader or strategist, as he had lost Samarqand.

Night after night, the same nightmare oppressed him. In his dream, a group of people with disheveled hair, scars on their faces, and wearing dark, dirty, worn-out condoler's suits, approached him in a mist. Some of them were holding their own heads.

"Who are you?" he shouted in his dream. They responded with horrible voices, looking at him with dead men's eyes.

"We are Muslims!"

He was torn from his sleep. He sighed deeply after wiping the perspiration from his forehead with his fist. He lamented:

How deceitful the human mind is, to itself!
When one is in the moment of victory,

One does not see the other side of defeat.
Anytime, anywhere, the one who sees both,
Shall be the last victor!

Sultan Muhammad escaped from Nishapur after he was informed that the Mongol chasing troops were near. Before he left, he summoned four chiefs, Umar Rukkhi, Nizam Addin, Katib Jami and Arid Zuzani and told them to defend the city.

"I will send Saraf Addin soon. Together with him, do your best to defend the city!"

However, Saraf Addin, who was the newly appointed governor, as well as the garrison chief, died suddenly on his way to Nishapur. Umar Rukkhi, the oldest chief, took the position of regent temporarily, on behalf of the dead governor. At this time, Jebe's chasing corps arrived at a place near Nishapur. Jebe dispatched a vanguard of 1,000 troops to advise them to surrender. Umar Rukkhi voluntarily promised cooperation. He welcomed the Mongol vanguard with bread and salt.

He said to Jebe, who had arrived later, "I am temporarily ruling this city on behalf of the sultan. I am just an old clerk. You are chasing after the sultan. If you defeat the sultan, his empire will be yours and I will be your subject."

His remarks were foxy, but Jebe accepted them as a surrender and asked for cooperation.

Umar Rukkhi and the citizens of Nishapur supplied food, water and other necessities. Jebe selected three men as shahnas and gave them letters of appointment, written in Uighur characters. Jebe continued chasing, leaving Nishapur. It was June of 1220.

A few months later, a groundless rumor was circulating in and around Nishapur. The rumor was that the sultan's troops had destroyed the Mongol troops. Nobody knew who started it, but the citizens of Nishapur and the small and large surrounding cities began to get excited. They became resistant.

The devil of destruction laid eggs in their brains.

The Persians, afterward, described the situation like this: The first rebellious city was Tus. Tus had surrendered to Jebe before Nishapur. Siraj Addin, the leader of the rebellion in Tus, cut off the head of a shahna there and sent it to Umar Rukkhi in Nishapur. Encouraged, Umar Rukkhi began to incite the people. A large group of rebellious residents took three shahnas out into the open ground and cut their heads off, one by one. Each time a head fell to the ground, they shouted in joy and then put the heads on the tips of spears and posted them on top of the rampart.

In November, Tolui dispatched Toqcha as vanguard to Nishapur. Toqcha was the son-in-law of Genghis Khan. He was the commander of the defense corps of the Mongol mainland while Genghis Khan was in China. Toqcha led his 10,000 troops to attack Nishapur, which had already become a rebel city. On the first day of the attack, an arrow from the rampart hit him in his neck. Military surgeons tried to save him, but they were not successful. He bled to death immediately. Because of his death, the movement of the Mongol troops temporarily stopped. Tolui installed Nurkai as his successor and ordered him to continue operations in the nearby area until his arrival at Nishapur. At that time, Tolui was attacking Merv.

Nurkai first advanced towards Sabzavar and, after three days of fierce battle, took the city, killing all 70,000 residents. He further advanced towards the city of Tus, arresting Siraj Addin, the leader of the rebels and ruler of the city at that time. They beheaded Siraj Addin and massacred all the residents. The next stop was Nukan. All 60,000 residents there lost their heads. The fields in the area were covered with dead bodies. However, the big city of Nishapur remained untouched until the arrival of Tolui's main troops.

In the spring of 1222, Tolui arrived at Nishapur with his main forces after taking Merv. Nishapur was armed with 3,000 crossbows and 300 mangonels; however, their garrison and citizens had lost their spirit and willingness to fight. The news of the fall of Merv and what happened there put such fear into them that they had already lost the psychological battle.

Umar Rukkhi, the ruler of Nishapur, dispatched Rukn Addin, the highest cadi of the city, to negotiate the peace talks; but Tolui immediately stopped their attempts.

The next morning, Tolui issued an order of a full-scale attack on Nishapur. The Mongol troops broke down the rampart with catapults and 100,000 levies filled up the moat around the rampart with stones and soil. The battle started Friday morning and lasted until Saturday evening, completing the first phase of the plan. The Mongol troops took all the gates and the ramparts. The following Sunday was the last day for the citizens. The Mongol troops started street fighting. The bloody massacre began. The garrison soldiers and citizens sought hiding places in temples, palaces and mansions. Around noon, the resistance ended. The Mongol troops found Umar Rukkhi hiding in the sewer. The Mongol soldiers dragged him out into the open ground by his hair. He was stripped naked and then hanged from a tree upside down. His punishment was to be flayed alive. Among the levies, they chose a skillful butcher for the job. He specialized in flaying horses. The specialist opened Umar Rukkhi's head first, and then skinned his face, neck, chest and abdomen, step by step, just as he did with horses. The big red lump of human flesh hung from the tree and writhed for a while.

They took the entire population of the city out to the field. As at Merv, they beheaded all the residents, except 400 superb artisans. On the field outside Nishapur, they built three huge pyramids of human heads. The death toll of Nishapur and all the nearby cities was 1,747,000.

The Persian poets lamented:

On doomsday,
The dead will rejoice,
While those alive will lament.

The flames of calamity
Have fallen upon them,
Like the hail of April.

And the blackbird of death
Has spread its wings
Over the entire city.

An arrow of shallow wisdom
Cannot penetrate
The shield of impossibility.

And the stallion of will
Cannot take off his own reins of fate.

Oh! Merciful God! Close my eyes.
I have already seen
Judgment Day.

CHAPTER EIGHTY-THREE

The Final Battle at the Indus River

Genghis Khan set out to chase down Jal-al-Addin. It was late fall 1221, about the time when Tolui was attacking Merv. Genghis headed for Gurzivan from Talaqan. Gurzivan was a city located between the Hindu Kush Mountains and the Indus River, with a population of 70,000. Jal-al-Addin amassed a large number of new troops there. He strove hard to incite a holy war with the Mongols. He dispatched his envoys to the caliph in Baghdad, twice, and they were ignored both times. They concluded that the war with the Mongols was not a holy war. Sultan Muhammad had attacked the caliph many times in the past, as they were enemies. Almost all the people in the Khwarazm Empire were Muslim. However, they were not very loyal to the nation of Khwarazm and resisted the high tax policy. Although they were losing their mental and spiritual mainstay, their religion, they came out to the battlefield with everything they had. That was what Jal-al-Addin was going after. However, Genghis had already declared freedom of religion, and his taxes were lower than the sultan's were in the surrendered cities and regions.

"The Mongols are infidels! We cannot be ruled by infidels!" he shouted. He was the official successor of the Khwarazm Empire. He amassed 50,000 new troops. He traveled around the Afghan area and killed anyone who refused to join his troops. To raise the morale of his troops and to provoke hostility towards the Mongols, he had his men put metal wedges into the ears of 300 captives, and he beheaded twenty of them.

Gurzivan showed strong resistance. After the battle, which took longer than expected, the city was theirs and they slaughtered the whole population. Genghis found that Jal-al-Addin had left the city just a few days before the Mongol troops' arrival and headed toward the Indus River. Genghis kept on chasing.

The Mongol troops arrived at the city of Bamiyan, which was on top of a hill and covered by strong ramparts. Bamiyan was a key strategic point. The rampart of this city was not only tough, but was also on a high hill that was out of range of the catapults. Genghis had to send commandos to take this city. The Mongol commandos were greeted with showers of arrows and rolling rocks and logs, which made for a difficult approach. After the fall of this city, all the ramparts and buildings were leveled and the whole population was slaughtered. This city was never rebuilt and it disappeared from the map.

Genghis Khan's Mongol troops caught up with Jal-al-Addin's Khwarazm troops at the riverside of the Indus. It was November 23, 1221. Across the wide, winding Indus River were the vast plains of Punjab. Jal-al-Addin's 50,000 troops were stationed there because of the natural protection provided by the curved Indus River and high mountains on the other side. After careful observation of the enemy camp from his high ground, Genghis was struck with admiration for the superiority of their war camp.

"Jal-al-Addin is one who knows how to move his troops. His right side and backside are covered by the river and the other side is covered by the mountains. At first glance, it seemed that he was shut in, but the truth is the opposite. He can put concentrated power into one direction. This battle won't be easy," Genghis said to his sons.

Chagatai and Ogodei's troops joined Genghis Khan's main troops after they returned from taking Urgenchi. The number of troops on both sides was similar, 50,000 to 60,000. The Mongol troops surrounded the Khwarazm troops, making a half circle from afar.

The following day, early in the morning, the battle started. The Mongols could not easily defeat the Khwarazm troops, who were coming up against their opponents with desperate courage. It was an offensive and defensive battle for both at some points. However, suddenly a separate group of Mongol troops came pouring down the mountain, which nobody had thought such a number of troops could cross. This was characteristic of the Mongol troops: they showed up anytime and anywhere. The surprise attacker troops easily broke down one side wing of the Khwarazm troops. Just as a winged creature cannot fly very well with a broken wing, the Khwarazm troops began to be shaken. They lost. At last, in the late afternoon, the Indus riverside was covered with dead Khwarazm soldiers. Many of them drowned in the Indus River. Jal-al-Addin, who was leading his troops at the front line, was driven into the corner of the riverbank with his 700 surviving followers. He knew he was doomed. First, he had his men throw enormous amounts of gold coins and treasure that they had been keeping as war funds into the river. Next, he walked up to his family members. He drew his scimitar and cut off the heads of his two wives and seven concubines. He did not want his women to be humiliated by the enemy soldiers. The last woman left was his mother, Al Chichen. This Persian woman in her late forties was the most beloved concubine of Sultan Muhammad at one time. She was waiting with her eyes closed, shedding tears.

He walked up to his mother and said in a tone of sadness and agony, "Mother, forgive me!"

He cut off his mother's head with his scimitar, but left his two sons alive. He took off his armor and helmet and dove into the river, which was about twenty feet below. While the Mongol attackers were destroying the rest of the 700, he was swimming to the opposite bank. The Mongol archery unit discharged arrows, but he was already out of range.

Watching this, Genghis Khan admired, "Look! He is a real warrior! None of his men jumped into the lake to save their own lives. They all wanted to give him time to escape. A leader should have such followers."

The 700 Khwarazm soldiers fought to the last man and eventually Jal-al-Addin's two sons died, too. The Mongol divers retrieved as many of the gold coins and treasure as possible from the bottom of the river.

Thus the Mongols destroyed the last defense force of the Khwarazm Empire completely. After this, the Khwarazm Empire gradually disappeared from the stage of world history.

The following year, Genghis dispatched Dorbei Doksin to India with 20,000 troops to conquer some of the Khwarazm territory in India. At the same time, Dorbei had the mission of searching and collecting information about India. Doksin made several hundred large rafts out of logs to cross the river. After crossing the Indus River, he advanced towards the Nandana region, attacking and taking the fortress in that area. The 20,000-strong garrison, made up of Turks and Indians, was massacred and the fortress was leveled. Next, he advanced towards Multan and Lahore. Since they could not find rocks, Doksin's levies cut the nearby trees and replaced the rocks with cut timbers. Multan and Lahore fell to the Mongols, who completely destroyed and leveled all the buildings and fortresses. The Mongol troops found mountains of war booty there.

As the summer was approaching, the temperature in the area went up dramatically. The people in those areas had to live in houses that were specially designed and built to withstand the temperatures at the peak of summer. They even strictly restricted outdoor working and traveling. The troops could not stay there anymore. Doksin went across the Indus River again and joined Genghis Khan's main troops in Ghazna.

Doksin gave his report to Genghis. "The water is dirty and the temperature is too hot in the summertime. Those areas are not for human inhabitants."

Doksin's report was correct.

Meanwhile, Jal-al-Addin, who had successfully escaped death, went to Delhi. There, he was under the protection of the sultan of Delhi for a while, and then returned to Persia. For ten years, he continued to resist the activities of the Mongols, yet achieved nothing notable. At last, the Kurd warriors, who were under the rule of the Mongol Empire, captured him in Asia Minor, and he was beheaded.

CHAPTER EIGHTY-FOUR

The Last of Sultan Muhammad

Jebe and Subedei continued to chase down Sultan Muhammad with their 30,000 cavalrymen. It was April 1220. After the fall of Samarqand, Genghis Khan found that Sultan Muhammad had escaped. They organized the special chasing corps from the soldiers from each of the army groups. The commanders were Jebe and Subedei. Genghis usually put two commanders in a military unit with an important mission. They were told to discuss everything with each other when they had to make decisions; in case of a disagreement, Jebe was the final decision maker.

After crossing the Syr River, they began to sweep over area after area, with earth-shaking hoofbeats and roaring sounds, like a typhoon. It was the first step of the fantastic long march of 8,000 miles, which is unparalleled in human history and took three years.

The first city they arrived at was Balkh. By the way, Balkh was not a city of resistance at that time. The Mongol troops surprised and overwhelmed the city with their superior force. The city leaders cooperated with the Mongols and supplied food and water while the troops chased down the sultan. The people accepted without resistance three shahnas that Jebe installed. Jebe learned that the sultan had left a few weeks prior. Jebe selected several local guides and rushed to continue the chase. Later, this city turned to Jal-al-Addin and became rebellious, which drove them into the disaster of complete annihilation.

The vanguard of the chasing troops arrived at the city of Zava, which was on a vast field with three citadels built of dried mud. The residents began to shake in fear of the approaching group of men and horses coming from the east, making a huge cloud of dust rise into the sky. They closed their city gates firmly and were on the alert. The Mongol troops arrived in front of the main gate with earth-shaking hoofbeats and urged them to open the gate and surrender. The leaders of the city had an urgent meeting and decided against surrender. Since the Mongol troops were in a hurry to chase the sultan, they had only intended to pass through. However, when the last cavalryman holding the banner had just passed their gate, the people began to hoot and ridicule, hitting big drums and tabors, small hand drums. They invited their own tragedy. They humiliated Genghis Khan's banner! The returning Mongol troops attacked the three citadels. After three days, the city fell to the Mongols. The entire population was slaughtered and the citadels and ramparts were leveled. The city was burned down and nothing was left. It was the first blow of the chasing troops and it was fierce.

In June 1220, Jebe and Subedei's troops arrived at Nishapur. Jebe urged them to surrender by sending an envoy into the city. Nishapur too, as described earlier, was cooperative in accepting Jebe's demand. Jebe left three shahnas in this city with the rolled-up, written decree and an al tamgha, or official seal. The decree was this:

> *You monarchs, aristocrats and commoners, must know this.*
> *From God,*
> *The land from the sunrise to sunset*
> *Was given to me.*
> *The ones who accept this,*
> *Will survive with their wives and children,*
> *And the others will perish from this earth.*

The Mongol chasing troops hit Juvine, Tus, Radkan, Khabushan, Isfarayin and Adkan, one by one. Shahnas were left in the surrendered cities, and the others were completely destroyed, along with their entire population.

Jebe and Subedei's troops arrived at the city of Damghan, which was located at the eastern end of the Elburz Mountains, around the southern end of the Caspian Sea. The Mongol troops entered the heart of the past Persian Empire. Having known of the Mongol troops' arrival, the aristocrats and leaders of the city fled into Girdkuh, the strong fortress nearby. The fortress Girdkuh was on top of a high mountain.

It was one of the strongholds of the Assassins, one branch of Islam.

The Assassins were a group of Shiites who rose in revolt, declaring religious reform. Since they were not yet accepted in mainstream Islam, they retreated into the mountains. They built fortresses on top of high mountains in many places and retired there, waiting out their days. They dealt with their enemies not by routine warfare, but by individual hit men or a team of them. In normal times, they contemplated life, raised sheep and goats, drank grape or honey wine, wrote poems, painted and danced to music. They called their leader "Hassan Sabba," which meant "old man on the mountain." Hassan Sabba used to come down to the villages, tempting young ones ages twelve to twenty, taking them into the mountains to brainwash them. He used to tell them things after giving them hashish, a hallucinatory drug.

"All you have to do is kill. If you successfully accomplish your mission from God, you will go to Heaven. It is a place with 10,000 different kinds of flowers and various fragrances. There, you will find countless beautiful women who are waiting for you. You will live there forever without getting old or dying."

The young ones, under the influence of hashish, left there with only one short dagger in their clothing and committed murders. Their success rate was so high, many monarchs and religious leaders fell victim to their plots. The area under their influence was from Turkey to the east and Syria to the west, and the targeted monarchs and religious leaders even had to wear their armor to bed. They were called assassins because they committed murders under the influence of hashish. They could not be removed because their bases were located on top of mountains that other troops could not approach. Jebe and Subedei dispatched 3,000 commandos to take the Girdkuh fortress, while the main troops headed for Damghan. Damghan was taken after seven days of resistance, and all 50,000 residents were slaughtered. Meanwhile, the leader of the commandos, who was headed for Girdkuh, selected 500 mountain war specialists out of the 3,000, and let them climb the mountain at night. They all successfully reached the top of the mountain and crossed over the rampart with a rope ladder. They opened the gate for the main troops and took control of 2,000 garrison troops. All the members of the Assassins and the garrison were beheaded, and all the aristocrats from Damghan, who were hiding there, were arrested. Among them, those who were cooperative and provided valuable information were saved and the others were slaughtered.

The Mongol troops continued on to take Samnan and Khuvar, massacring all the residents there, and proceeded to Ray, the biggest city in this region. The city of Ray, or Tehran in later times, was not only the biggest, but was also the industrial center of that region, especially for pottery and ceramics. This city was also completely destroyed and a great number of the residents slaughtered.

From there, the Mongol troops learned that Sultan Muhammad had fled to Hamadan, the city between Ray and Baghdad.

The Mongol troops advanced towards Hamadan. Ala Adduala, the ruler of Hamadan, opened the gate and surrendered to the Mongols. He supplied food and clothing and accepted the al tamgha, Genghis Khan's seal. Jebe installed three shahnas there, yet they did not find the sultan there.

Ala Adduala said, "He escaped to Mazandaran about three weeks ago. His family members and concubines are staying in Mazandaran. However, on the way to the city, about 30,000 of his loyal troops were stationed there to guard the city. The name of that spot is Sujas."

Mazandaran was a city located close to the southwestern end of the Caspian Sea and about 200 miles from Hamadan, to the north-northeastern direction. At the time, when Sultan Muhammad was escaping from Samarqand, he dispatched urgent messengers to the city of Urgenchi, where his family members and concubines were staying, and moved all of them to Mazandaran. Mazandaran was in the westernmost territory of the Khwarazm Empire and close to the border with Shirvan (now Azerbaijan).

The Mongol troops clashed with the sultan's 30,000 troops at Sujas. The sultan's last defense line was broken down. Dozens of arrows coming from the Mongol archery unit were responsible for the deaths of the two commanders of the defense troops, Beg-Tegin Silahdar and Kuch-Buga Khan, and their troops were completely destroyed. The Mongol troops advanced toward Mazandaran, stepping over the dead bodies of the Khwarazm soldiers that were strewn across the field.

Upon receiving the news that the last defense force had been destroyed, Sultan Muhammad summoned Nazil Addin, the governor of Mazandaran, as well as his loyal servant.

"Take my family members to the two fortresses of Larijan and Ilal; put half of them in each. Kill all the hostages we are keeping."

In Mazandaran, they were keeping about 150 hostages who were taken by the sultan while he was conquering many different areas. They were sons or brothers of the monarchs of the various areas he had conquered. Nazil Addin, the loyal servant of the sultan, tied the hands and feet of all the hostages and threw them into the river. As the urgent report came in that the Mongol troops had arrived outside the city, the sultan hurriedly left the city, after asking Nazil Addin to take good care of his family and concubines.

Before leaving, he accepted some advice from Nazil Addin.

"Sultan, change your clothing. You never know if the Mongol spies are already in the city."

Nazil Addin brought him a set of dirty, lousy clothes that he had taken from a beggar. The sultan, after looking at the tatters, nodded and changed his gold embroidered silk garments to those of the beggar's. He also changed his turban, which was decorated with gems and peacock feathers, to that of the beggar's. He hurried out of the city with only two servants. His escape was immediately reported to Subedei by his spies. Subedei rapidly dispatched a chasing unit. When the Mongol chasing unit arrived at the seaside of the Caspian Sea, the sultan, in a small fishing boat, was rowing away from shore with his two servants. Galloping along the shoreline, the Mongol soldiers chased him, shooting arrows as they went; however, the fishing boat was already out of range.

Nazil Addin rushed out of the city with about 400 of the sultan's family members and concubines and put them into the two fortresses, Larijan and Ilal. Subedei immediately chased them and surrounded the two fortresses. Since the fortresses were firmly built on a high mountain, Subedei reinforced the encirclements instead of attacking directly. They held out for two weeks. However, since they were running out of drinking water and began to die of dehydration, Nazil Addin gave up. He descended the mountain and surrendered.

Sultan Muhammad's sons and grandsons, about 60 of them, were all beheaded. About 200 of his wives and concubines and about 50 of his daughters were sent to Genghis Khan in Talaqan, after all sorts of humiliations. Among them was the sultan's old mother, Terke Khatun, who at one time was considered a heroine in their world. After they were taken to the Mongol mainland, they were forced to live the lives of slaves.

As for Nazil Addin, he was flayed alive by a skillful butcher, and his flayed skin was used to cover a dummy made of barley straw. The troops returned to Mazandaran with the dummy with human skin in front of them.

At the same time, Jebe took the city of Mazandaran, the last stronghold of the Khwarazm Empire, beheading 100,000 of its resisters. This meant the complete fall of the Khwarazm

Empire. But what happened to Sultan Muhammad? After he left Mazandaran, he escaped to a tiny island in the Caspian Sea. It was an uninhabited island, with only rocks covered with seagulls' droppings. The sultan's two servants made a hut out of small pieces of wood and dried weeds that they collected. After they used up all the food they had brought, they had to fish to survive.

He held out there for some time. However, he fell into intense grief when he heard the news from a nearby fisherman who had come across to the island that all his male descendants had been killed and his wives, concubines and daughters had been taken to some other place after many humiliations. After all that, he died a few weeks later of a disease, possibly acute pleurisy, caused by emotional hardships and malnutrition. The man who at one time had an empire with vast land, more subjects than stars in the sky and hundreds of concubines, died in his beggar's rags, in his hut on a tiny island where the cold wind never ceased to blow.

Before he died, he shouted with his two eyes staring into space, "Ah! Where are all my subjects? Where is my great land? Now I don't even have a piece of land for my own body!"

His two servants tried to bury him, but they could not dig a hole deep enough to bury his body, because after a few inches of digging they hit rock. They left the island after covering his dead body with gravel and small stones. It was January 1221, nine months after the Mongol chasing troops had been dispatched.

The Long March of Jebe and Subedei

That winter, they experienced very heavy snow. The great plain of Mugan, which was close to the western shore of the Caspian Sea, was covered with white snow. From there, they could see the faraway horizon of the great Caspian Sea. On the vast plain covered with snow, countless yurts, the Mongols' unique dome-shaped felt tents, were spread out, forming a city. Jebe and Subedei passed the winter there. Neither men and horses could move freely, due to the snow piled up to human height. In the meantime, they sent mountains of war booty to Genghis Khan in Talaqan. They were not to leave there until they confirmed the death of Sultan Muhammad.

In February, the two servants who had been with the sultan until his last moment were captured. The death of the sultan was confirmed through them. Subedei dispatched an urgent messenger. The "Arrow Messenger," the nickname of the urgent messengers of the Mongol troops, ran the distance of 1,200 miles in seven days, arriving at Genghis Khan's main camp with Subedei's letter. Subedei was reporting to Genghis the complete conquest of western Khwarazm and the death of Sultan Muhammad. At the same time, he was reporting the political climates of those areas, including the activities of possible supporters of Jal-al-Addin, who was still alive at that time, in the remaining Islamic world. He also stated his opinion about the future movements of their troops and asked for approval. The great general, Subedei, had sharp eyes, and his judgments were quite accurate. He was already looking to the far distant future of the Mongol Empire.

Genghis Khan's answer was this: "Advance to Russia!"

In the spring of 1221, Jebe headed for Iraq. In the region of Ardabil in Iraq, a man named Ai Baba organized troops, then attacked and took Hamadan, the city that had previously surrendered to the Mongols, and killed three shahnas there. Ai Baba also imprisoned Ala Adduala in a small castle in Girit. Jebe surrounded Hamadan again, attacked and successfully recaptured the city. The head of the rebels, Ai Baba, tried to surrender, but Jebe did not accept his offer and ordered Ai Baba and several hundred of his followers beheaded. Next, Jebe advanced towards Ardabil, the place where the revolt began, and completely destroyed and slaughtered the whole population. Ala Adduala was reinstalled as the governor of Hamadan, and the Mongol supremacy was recovered.

Jebe and Subedei headed north from the southwestern region of the Caspian Sea. They crossed the northern border of the Khwarazm, stepping into Shirvan. The Mongol troops took Maragha and Nakhchivan, massacring the resistant residents. As the Mongol troops surrounded Tabriz, their important

city, Ozbeg, the atabeg, or ruler, of Shirvan, came up to surrender. He sent tuzghu, the symbol of their ruler, a great amount
of gold and treasures, ten of his envoys and twenty of their
beauties.

Upon facing ten of their envoys, Jebe drew his scimitar and
cut one of their heads off, which fell to the ground. Since they
could not be fully trusted, it was an example and warning.
Ozbeg's request for surrender was accepted, and Tabriz was
saved. Ozbeg became the last king of Seljuk Turkey.

The Mongol troops advanced towards Arran (now Armenia). From there, it was a Christian world. The Mongols took
Bailaqan, the capital city, and installed three shahnas there, letting them know it was the new Mongol territory. The Mongol
troops continued advancing, stepping into Georgia, another
Christian kingdom, which was located just south of the Caucasus Mountains. At that time, Georgia was at the peak of its
power and wealth, and its knights were known to be invincible. Their knights were wearing protective metallic tunics
and coifs and on top of that, they wore metal armor. Once
they put on their armor and helmets, and shut the visors for
the eye opening of the helmets, not even a single arrow could
hurt them. They were armed with long heavy spears, swords
and huge battle-axes.

The Georgian king, Giorgi IV Lasha, faced the Mongol troops
with his invincible armored cavalry. The knights, 10,000 of
them, in their protective armor and helmets, proudly marched
toward the Mongol troops. They even had heavy coverings
on their horses. Behind them, about 20,000 foot soldiers were

following like their shadows. They faced each other at the field of Tiflis.

After careful evaluation of the enemy power and situation, Subedei discussed with Jebe.

"I think we need to separate the knight troops and foot soldiers first."

Jebe agreed. For a brief moment, they made their battle plan. The battle began. The commander of the Georgian troops, Giorgi IV, thought the Mongol troops, whose main weapons were bows and arrows, could never defeat his knight cavalry who were protected by arrowproof metal armor. After their commander's charge order, the knight cavalry dashed towards the Mongol troops like a huge rolling rock. Subedei, who was acting as the vanguard, immediately ordered his troops to retreat. For a while, the knight cavalry chased the Mongol troops, however, their horses could not catch up with them because their horses were carrying very heavy armor and armored soldiers. Once the knight cavalry passed a certain spot, they were suddenly attacked by unknown troops from the side. They were Jebe's Mongol cavalry. At the same time, Subedei and his troops turned around and began a counterattack. It was a hand-to-hand fight. The knight cavalrymen in heavy armor could not move as fast as the Mongol soldiers, who were wearing very light, leather armor. The Mongol soldiers used the spears with hooks or lassos to take them down and once they fell to the ground, they could never remount their horses. Subedei's cavalrymen destroyed the 20,000 enemy foot soldiers that were following their knight cavalry. After laying down the entire 20,000 of them, Subedei's troops returned and again joined Jebe's troops to handle the knights one by one. They took off the knights' helmets and hit their heads or faces with battle-axes or maces. Georgia's invincible 10,000 knight troops and 20,000 foot soldiers were all slaughtered. Thus, the kingdom of Georgia fell to the Mongols.

Jebe and Subedei crossed over the Caucasus Mountains through the gate of Dorbent. Now they were in Europe. Jebe and Subedei's eyes met with magnificent images of the vast steppe of Kipchak. It was February 1222 and the field was still covered with snow. The beating sound of their horses' hooves on the vast ground dispersed through the snow, which absorbed the noise. The sky of deep-sea blue, the land with horizons in all four directions; nothing was different from their homeland on the Mongol plain.

Now it had been two years since they began their mission and their expedition. Their strong life force, their traditional culture that any place could be their home once they set up their yurts, and their philosophy that they wanted to die on the battlefield all contributed to their strong mental immunity against the stresses of a long march. Most important was the thousand-year-old traditional philosophy engraved in their bones, that a man is born in a yurt but should die on the battlefield. This was their mental background as warriors and directed their movements and actions. Their best friend and companion, the Mongol horse, which had extraordinary toughness, resilience and a life force like its owner's, threaded its way through the battlefields with them and stepped over immensely long distances. The Mongol horses, which did not need particular feed, unlike others, could eat snow and ice and had instincts to find their own food.

Jebe and Subedei's expedition troops met with the coalition army groups of four different tribes who declared they were the owners of the lands on the Russian steppe. They were Alans, Lezghians, Circassians and the Turks in the Kipchak. They stood face to face against the Mongols with their 50,000 troops. They formed a union, and yet the cooperation among them was not very smooth. Subedei decided to use a trick tactic. The Alans, Lezghians and Circassians were the natives in that area; the Turks were different. Their original homeland was central Asia and their ancestors had immigrated to this area. The Mongols and the Kipchak Turks even looked alike. Psychological warfare had begun and the pacification unit was formed. It worked. They lost their motivation to fight, because the Kipchak Turks were also foreigners to the other three tribes.

The Mongols destroyed the Alans, Lezghians and Circassians, one by one, and lastly, they completely annihilated the Kipchak Turks, who were the strongest and had become very uncooperative with the other three tribes.

Jebe and Subedei arrived at the coast of the Black Sea. They marched along the coastline, looking at the dark-blue Black Sea, and arrived at the northern area of the Crimean Peninsula. The Mongol expedition troops stayed there for a while.

One day, Subedei had a visitor who was a Venetian. The Venetian was ushered into the visitor's tent and served tea.

Subedei asked him the purpose of his visit. At that time, the Venetians were in a conflict with the Genoese for commercial supremacy. The visitor explained the situation and asked Subedei to attack the city of Sudak at the southern end of the Crimean Peninsula, which was occupied by the Genoese.

Subedei eyed him very carefully and asked him a question.

"If I grant your request, what you can do for me?"

The Venetian gave a deep bow, twice, and answered, "I will do whatever you ask, if it is within my power."

Subedei opened his mouth slowly, again after a careful look, "I need a detailed, accurate map covering all of Europe. I also need information about all the kings and their lineages, and the size of their troops. Do you think you can bring those to me?"

The Venetian gave another bow and answered, "It won't be an easy job. However, it is not impossible either, for people like us, merchants, who are traveling around all the time. If you can give me three months, I will bring you an answer."

An agreement was made between Subedei and the Venetian. Three months later, the Venetian brought the information, and even more than Subedei asked. He brought not only the most detailed map of Europe at that time, but also all the information about the kings of each nation, their relatives, lineage, present and possible maximum number of troops and even their personalities and hobbies. Subedei was satisfied. A new long-term spy network was built with the Venetian as the leader. As promised, Subedei attacked and destroyed the city of Sudak, obtaining enormous amounts of war booty.

At that time, Russia was divided into eight principalities. Each principality was ruled by its own duke, and they were independent of each other. The eight principalities were Kiev, Chernigov, Galich, Smolensk, Rostov, Suzdal, Novgorod and Vladimir.

The news that the Mongols had stepped into the Russian territory and destroyed the coalition troops in that region, including the Kipchak Turks, was passed on to Mstislav, the grand duke of Galich. His wife was a daughter of the chieftain of a certain tribe of the Kipchak Turks. The dukes of the eight principalities gathered and had a meeting. They agreed to punish these formidable invaders with their troops.

"They are not simple invaders! They are trying to conquer us, all of Russia! We can tell by what they have done so far. If we fail to destroy them right now, we will be ruled by them."

Mstislav's eye was accurate and his judgment was correct. Together, they made a coalition troop of 80,000. They marched to the south, along the Dnieper River, with their 80,000 troops and met the Mongol troops, whose number had been reduced to 25,000, at the Kalka riverside, an estuary to the northern side of the Black Sea. They stood face to face on the vast plain of Kipchak.

At this time, some of the dukes, encouraged by their superiority in numbers, dashed toward the Mongol side. The Mongol vanguards turned around and began to run away. The chasing Russian troops could not catch up with them and began to get tired. At that moment, from both sides of the hills they were passing, flames of naphtha went shooting up into the sky and a thick smoke covered the area like a veil. The runaway Mongol vanguards disappeared into this smoke. At the same moment, showers of arrows fell upon the chasing Russian troops. The disorganized Russian troops tried to turn around and retreat, but they simply ended up sending themselves into more chaos, colliding with their own surging troops. Several minutes of this uncontrollable chaos was enough time for the Mongol archery units. The Russian troops were completely destroyed in just one day. The plain of Kipchak was covered with dead Russian soldiers, and survivors were very few. It was May 31, 1223. Later, the three captured Russian dukes were put into leather bags and suffocated to death. That was the last stand for the Russian aristocrats.

Jebe and Subedei were on their way home. They went across the Don and Volga Rivers. After crossing the Volga River, they met with the Bulgars. After losing the battle, the Bulgars surrendered to the Mongols. The Mongol troops faced the Qangli Turks again after crossing over the Ural Mountains. They were easily destroyed. After that, there was nobody in front of them. Finally, they joined Genghis Khan's main force around Balkhash Lake, closing their 8,000-mile long march, which had taken them more than three years. It was the longest cavalry march, unparalleled before or since.

CHAPTER EIGHTY-SIX

The Meeting with Chang-Chun

"Tao is the creator of all things in the universe. Tao creates the sun, the moon, the stars, the earth and all living things—animals and plants and even humans. Tao is the creator, not only of the visible things, but also the invisible, like the spirit and soul. People talk about the greatness of God, but few people acknowledge the greatness of Tao. Some people think Tao is the same thing as God, but that is not true. Tao is not like the God people think of, that is a personified God who thinks, talks, listens, gets angry and is happy. We then arrive at one last question, 'What is Tao?'"

Chang-Chun was giving a lecture in front of about 300 people. It was the summer of 1222, at Genghis Khan's main war camp on the mountainside of the Hindu Kush heights. Tens of thousands of camps were spread out from the mountainside to the vast plain below and the supreme headquarters was at the northernmost part. In a huge tent, with a capacity of 300 to 400 people, all the important figures of the Mongol Empire, including Genghis Khan himself, his sons, generals and high-ranking officials, gathered.

The lecture continued.

"What is Tao? Tao is a kind of energy that is very hard to describe. There are no limitations to this energy because it is limitless. It is free from time and there is no end. All things in the universe are simply different manifestations of this energy. This energy changes its manifestation, or form, moment to moment. When we burn firewood, the wood becomes ashes after changing itself into flames, smoke and heat. What that means is that the original shape and contents of the firewood have disappeared. However, through the eyes of someone who understands Tao, nothing has been changed. It is a simple change of the original energy in the wood into a different form. The energy never dies or disappears. We named this energy Tao, because it constantly moves. This energy accumulates in one place, creating a solid mass, and so looks as if it does not move at all, but that is not true. This energy constantly moves. The only difference is the speed of the movements in each form or manifestation. All of life's phenomena and forms, our thinking, emotions, feelings of happiness, anger, love and hate are flow, or movement, of this energy. The original meaning of Tao in Chinese is the way it moves."

Two different interpreters interpreted Chang-Chun's lecture into Mongolian and Persian, and Yelu Chutze, in the front seat, put it down in writing.

Chang-Chun continued.

"Since I went into the monastery when I was fourteen, for sixty years I have studied and researched this movement of energy. The movements of energy are very complicated and unpredictable and it is hard to find its original pattern. I could only find a very small piece of it. Movements of energy happen not only within a single entity, but also in between or among many other things, for example, the man and the earth, the man and the sun, or even star to star. Then, someone will ask me the question, 'What would be the benefit for us to know this thing called Tao?' He is right to ask. If we do not get any benefit from these hard-to-find rules of the movements of energy, there is no meaning in what I am doing. However, I declare clearly in here, in front of you, the person who discovers the complete structure of the rules for the movement of energy, is the one who has found the truth of nature and the universe. If he uses just a small fraction of the truth for himself, the result would be enormous. It is just like a boatman who knows the direction of the wind; if he takes advantage of it, he can get to his destination more safely and easily. If not, he will suffer and eventually might get shipwrecked."

Chang-Chun had left the monastery in his hometown, Shantung, two years prior, with his fourteen disciples, after receiving Genghis Khan's courteous invitation. Actually, he received the invitation in the spring of 1219, more than three years before his arrival. One day, two men came to see him in his monastery in Shantung. One of them was Genghis Khan's Chinese herbal doctor, Liu Wen, and the other was the darughachi of northern China, Chingai. Liu Wen came as an envoy from Genghis Khan and was carrying his letter of invitation. He was wearing a rectangular golden tablet the size of an adult's palm connected to a leather strap around his neck. There was an engraved tiger head on the top of the tablet and, just underneath that, was an engraved message: "The holder of this tiger tablet has been given the privilege and all the freedoms, just as if I am there." That was the proof that he was Genghis Khan's envoy. He had delayed his departure for a year, but at last, he left the monastery with his fourteen followers. He crossed the Gobi Desert after stopping by Zhongdu and went to Samarqand by way of the Mongol mainland and the Uighur Kingdom. From there, he went to the Hindu Kush, where Genghis Khan stationed his main war camps. He had traveled 4,500 miles over two years. During the journey, one of his followers had died of an endemic disease, and another one had given up.

Genghis Khan was exhilarated when he faced his guest who had traveled so many miles, over so many months.

"I appreciate you greatly and highly value your sincerity and good faith, coming from such a far, distant place, spending more than two years traveling! I am also very elated by your acceptance of my invitation, since you have never accepted the same from other monarchs and rulers."

In response to Genghis Khan's welcoming remarks, Chang-Chun bowed deeply.

"I am just an old person hiding in the mountains. I am greatly honored to be recognized by my humble name and invited by the great lord."

This is how they started their dialogue.

Genghis asked Chingai how others addressed him.

"Some address him as 'adept,' some others simply call him 'teacher' or 'Shin-Shien,' which means the enlightened one."

Genghis Khan called him Shin-Shien, or holy one. Genghis Khan ushered him into his tent and offered him some tea. Genghis Khan asked him, with a smile on his face,

"I have heard many people say that Shin-Shien has found a secret for health and long life. Is that true?"

At this question, Chang-Chun answered, after deeply bow-ing again, "I know I have been exaggerated and flattered by many people. I simply have a tiny bit of knowledge that could help protect life. That's all."

Genghis let out a loud guffaw, and said,

"Shin-Shien, I like your answer. If you had said you had found a secret, I might have been disappointed."

An officer who had faced Chang-Chun in Zhongdu described him like this: "At first glance, I acknowledged he is not an or-dinary man. Unlike other seventy-four-year-old men, his sitting and standing postures were like those of a young soldier. His body looked as strong as a tree and his movements were like a gale. Nobody would believe he is a seventy-four-year-year-old man. When I talked to him, I realized that he was a man with enormous knowledge in every field. I felt like he had already visited the other side of the sacred clouds, where nobody had gone before and seen the original, primitive darkness of a long time ago. I could clearly understand why the great conqueror invited him. The great conqueror needed a great philosopher."

Chang-Chun gave four lectures in total. While he was with Genghis Khan, he had many chances to talk to him individually.

Chang-Chun's lecture continued.

"I said even all the human emotions, including gladness, sadness, fear and anger, are the movements of Tao. Based on my study, all animals have emotions, too. The only difference is that theirs are not developed in detail. The trees do not have emotions. Many trees live up to hundreds or thousands of years. However, with animals, that is impossible. The trees do not let the Tao out from their body through emotions."

He continued.

"Every living thing has two basic instincts: the instincts of preservation of self and species. All this happens because of one simple nature of the energy of Tao. The energies of Tao tend to get together and accumulate. All things in the universe are created because of this nature of energy of Tao. In another words, once the energies of Tao get together and form an entity, they tend to remain there.

"One time, I made a careful observation of mulberry trees. The ones that I had in my backyard were the short kind. One day I noticed my goats were eating up the leaves of these plants. Can you imagine what happened the following year? The mulberry trees began to grow taller. At last, several years later, the mulberry trees became so tall that the goats could not reach their leaves. However, the same kind of mulberry trees, in a different location, without goats, remained unchanged. As I said, the energy of Tao tends to remain in the same entity it created. The power of Tao made them grow."

One time, Chang-Chun said this: "While I was researching the movement of the energy of Tao, for my convenience I created names for the directions of the movements. When the energy moves from something in an outward direction, it is called yang energy, if the energy moves in an inward direction, it is called yin. Yet, the yang energy and the yin energy are the same, after all, only moving in different directions. So, the yang can be changed into yin in the blink of an eye or can remain unchanged for a while. All things in the universe are the production of the teamwork of these two energies. Their variety is unlimited. Some productions are quickly disappearing and some others remain unchanged to eternity. Some of them can be seen by the human eye and some others cannot. Some of them are very light compared to others that are very heavy. The heavy ones are grouping together, eventually making a big mass. The sun, the moon, the stars and this earth are all made in this way."

He continued.

"The soil and water belong to yin Tao. On the other hand, the light and heat belong to yang Tao. The combination of these two particular energies created life on this earth. Once life is born, it can be changed into many different forms, because of the unlimited nature of Tao. The creation of new lives and changing into many different varieties happen all the time without interruption."

He said this too:

"I told you before that even the emotions of humans and animals are the result of the movement of energy. The emotions of anger, hate, fear, jealousy and excitement make your energy come out from your body; on the other hand, hope, good dreams, love, passion, and appreciation will make energy move into your body. The best condition of a living thing is achieved when the yang and yin energies are balanced. Let me put it this way: if you sprinkle water on a wood fire, the fire becomes weak. If you keep on sprinkling water, the fire becomes weaker and weaker and will eventually die. That is because the yang energy in the fire moved to the yin side, the water. One woman is enough for one man. This ratio is best in the viewpoint of yang and yin balance. If you have more than one, it is like unbalancing the yang and yin energies, and so you cannot keep yourself in the best condition."

After these words, there was a general stir among the audience, many of whom had five to six wives and sixty to three hundred concubines.

Chang-Chun put much stress on the ideology of respect for life, moderation and temperance. Chang-Chun personally advised Genghis that he would be better to reduce the number of hunting expeditions, better to sleep without a woman at least one month per year and better to avoid pleasure. After that, Genghis had many individual meetings with Chang-Chun, and talked on many topics and shared opinions.

After several months, Chang-Chun bade farewell to Genghis Khan. On his departure day, Genghis and many other people went out several miles to see him off. In return for his visit, Genghis granted the privilege of exemption from taxation to his many students in China. Even after his departure, Genghis frequently sent out his envoys to make sure everything was fine with his return journey. He never forgot to let him know of his warm heart towards him.

Holy one, how was your journey during last spring and summer? I know it is not an easy one. Did you have all the daily necessities and transportation without much trouble? Did the officials in each area provide you appropriate accommodations? I am always grateful to you. Please, forget me not. Chang-Chun returned to his monastery in Shantung in the spring of 1224.

CHAPTER EIGHTY-SEVEN

Punishment of the Shisha Kingdom

Genghis Khan stayed in the Khwarazm territory for some time to consolidate his conquest. The most tragic bloodbath during his expedition in Khwarazm occurred at the city of Herat, which was about 250 miles to the south of Merv. At one time, they had surrendered, but then suddenly they revolted. Genghis dispatched Alchidai. Alchidai, after retaking the city, slaughtered rebellious residents down to the last one. During this deadly event, which lasted about a week, two million people died. After this, the people in the Khwarazm territory completely lost their spirit of resistance.

This happened about three months before Genghis Khan's meeting with Chang-Chun. After seeing off Chang-Chun, Genghis began to review the return route to his homeland. The first possible route was to return by way of India and the Tangut territory. However, this route was not considered the best choice because of rough roads, many forested areas and dirty water. After considering his options, Genghis Khan chose the same route by which he had come.

In the fall of 1222, Genghis crossed the Amu River. He stayed in the suburbs of Samarqand until the spring of the following year. During this period, he spent his time hunting, and his two sons Chagatai and Ogodei went out to a faraway place called Qara Kol, which meant black lake, for swan hunting. It was a place with many lakes and endlessly stretching swamps. Every week, they sent Genghis Khan their captured game on fifty camels with full loads.

In the spring of 1223, they had a large-scale khuriltai in Fenaket, the riverside city of the Syr River. At this meeting, Genghis Khan appointed Yalavachi as the viceroy of the newly conquered Khwarazm. For the darughachi of the most important city, Samarqand, he appointed Yelu Ahai. Yelu Chutze organized the detailed administrative system.

This was about the time Genghis Khan's concept of "ulus" was born. Ulus was the ruling system of the conquered lands and the whole Mongol Empire, by which the lands were divided and each of his sons received a portion and then they and their descendants would rule their given land. By this concept, the Aral Sea and the land north of the Caspian Sea, east to the Irgiz River and west to the Volga River, including the great Kipchak plain, were given to Juchi and his descendants. Central Asia and the area of the Kara Khitai were given to Chagatai and his descendants. From there to the east, the area of the Irtish River, the Altai Mountains and the land to Lake Baikal were for Ogodei, and the heart of the Mongol mainland was given to Tolui.

In the spring of 1223, Genghis headed for the Mongol mainland. The caravans carrying the war booty formed a line from one horizon to the other, and the line of slaves was endless. In 1224, Jebe and Subedei's troops joined Genghis Khan's main force after they had completed the conquest of the enormously large area that included Russia. They brought 1,000 Russian grey horses and also 1,000 Russian slaves, men and women, with blue eyes and blond hair. Above all, the most valuable thing they brought was a huge amount of information about Europe. Based on Subedei's report, it was estimated that it would take eighteen years to conquer all of Europe.

Juchi did not go back to the Mongol mainland. He headed for the great plains of Kipchak with his ordu. He was sick and tired of the disharmony with his brothers. He really liked the great plain of Kipchak. Genghis tried to recall him many times, but he did not respond. Genghis Khan's mind was mixed with many different feelings.

In the fall of the same year, Genghis heard the news of Mukali's death. As viceroy of northern China, Mukali had continued the war with the Chin, taking many other cities and regions. However, the Chin retrieved some areas after his death. Genghis appointed Jafa, the Muslim merchant, as the darughachi of northern China.

In 1225, Genghis Khan returned to the Mongol mainland. It had been exactly six years since his departure. He stayed in the Black Forest, alongside the Tula River. Now, from Zhongdu to the Volga River, nobody could escape from terror upon hearing his name. Genghis let his soldiers and horses rest for a year.

In the fall of 1226, Genghis set out to punish the Tanguts of the Shisha Kingdom. Actually, punishment for their breach of the agreement for military support was not the only motivation. While Genghis was out on the conquest of Khwarazm, the Tanguts had increased their military power dramatically. Since their previous king, Li Anqan, had died, and his son, Li Tsun Hsiang, acceded to the throne, he devoted all his might to building up their military power. He not only strengthened his troops from 150,000 to half a million, but also made a new mutual defense treaty with the Chin.

A deed is not glorious until it is complete.

This is what Genghis used to say to his sons.

Before his new war, Genghis Khan summoned his son Juchi, who was staying in Kipchak. However, once again, Juchi did not respond. He always had excuses, mainly of sickness. Genghis issued another summons, and yet he still did not comply. Genghis had a good reason to summon him. There was a rumor going around that Juchi was planning to be independent from his father and make a separate policy. That was what Genghis feared most, the disunion of the Empire.

One day, Genghis saw a traveler, a man of the Mangkud tribe, who had come through Juchi's ordu. Genghis Khan questioned him about the condition of Juchi's sickness, and he replied, "I don't know about his sickness, but I saw him going out hunting."

Genghis was enraged. If he could go out hunting, he was not sick at all. Genghis had a feeling that his son, Juchi, was cheating him.

"He became a traitor, disobeying his own father's order! I will remove him after the Tanguts, without seeing his face."

Genghis mounted his horse again. One hundred fifty thousand troops were mobilized for this war against the Tanguts. His third son, Ogodei, and fourth son, Tolui, joined him, and Tolun Cherbi was the chief of staff. Genghis Khan took a different route from the one he had used seventeen years earlier. He did not feel comfortable. In this war, his second wife, Yesui was accompanying him. His eyes met the vast image of the Gobi Desert. The sea of sands, the endlessly stretched out land of mixed mud and sand with dried shrubs and bushes like an old man's beard, which made lonely moon shadows at night ... that was the Gobi Desert. How many times did he cross this route?

When he arrived at the middle part of the desert, a huge group of wild horses moving around, making clouds of dust on the far distant horizon came into view. Genghis decided to camp there overnight. It was close to an oasis. Genghis went out hunting with only a few close men. The group of wild horses was moving this way and that, changing their direction all the time, like a swarm of bees or a school of fish. Genghis approached them with only a lasso in his hand. He galloped at full speed to catch up with the moving wild animals. His favorite horse, named Josotu Boro, was a swift one. The group of wild horses was galloping on the desert land, flapping their manes and making thunderous sounds with their beating hooves. The moment the loop of his lasso was about to cover the neck of one of the animals, something unexpected happened. The group of wild horses suddenly changed their direction. The hundreds of wild horses dashed toward him. His horse, Josotu Boro, was surprised by the huge surging tide of animals. Neighing in a high tone, Josotu Boro suddenly reared on his hind legs. Genghis fell from his horse. The group of wild horses, after running over his body, disappeared into the far distant horizon like an ebbing tide.

Genghis moaned all night due to a high fever. His body was swollen and bruised, and his muscles were very hot.

He was walking toward the end of the world. The earth was covered with mist and the mysterious dark-blue sky was touching the faraway horizon. Genghis, who had turned back into the nine-year-old boy, Temujin, was walking on the earth covered with mist without knowing where he was going. From the faraway horizon, two tiny objects were approaching him, and they were becoming bigger and bigger with every minute. At last, when they were near, they showed their clear image. They were Yesugei and Ouluun, Genghis Khan's father and mother. For a moment, they watched Temujin with eyes full of worry and then disappeared into the horizon without saying anything. Temujin tried to follow them, but he could not. His feet were too heavy.

"How do you feel, my lord?" Yesui, who had stayed overnight next to Genghis's bed, asked him, casting a worried look when he opened his eyes. Genghis looked around. He was in the war camp in the middle of the desert. He tried to move, but there was unbearably sharp pain all over his body, as if he had been whipped.

Tolun Cherbi gave his opinion in an urgent meeting with all the generals, including Ogodei and Tolui.

"The khan's condition is not so good; we had better retreat and come back later, when he is better."

Nobody disagreed with his opinion. They let him know their agreed opinion.

Genghis said in a quiet voice, "Give them the chance to surrender."

By the order of Genghis Khan, a group of envoys was dispatched. However, the envoys who came back a few days later brought the return message from the commander-in-chief of the Shisha Kingdom, Weiming Linggong:

"Our war camp covers the ground endlessly, in great numbers. The countless amount of treasure, which would be our war fund, is stacked in the warehouse. Take it if you can."

Upon this return message, Genghis was enraged. It was clear that Weiming Linggong was counting on his half a million troops.

"How can he talk big like that? I will surely annihilate them on this earth! The everlasting blue sky will watch this!"

Genghis Khan's order to advance was issued. The Mongol troops were taking the important cities of the Shisha Kingdom, one by one, including Kanchou and Suchou. In December of the same year, the Mongol troops surrounded the city of Lingchou, which was located eighteen miles from their capital city of Chunghing and was considered a strategically important defense point. Weiming Linggong, the commander-in chief of the Shisha, came out to save Lingchou with his 300,000 troops. Genghis Khan ordered his troops to retreat to the frozen Yellow River. Some of the main forces of the Shisha began to chase after the Mongol troops. However, when the Shisha troops reached the middle of the wide Yellow River, Genghis Khan's immediate order of counterattack was issued. A fierce battle on the thickly frozen river followed.

What happened next was amazing. The horses of the Shisha cavalry began to slip and fall on the ice. The Shisha horses, with their metal horseshoes, could not balance well on the ice; on the other hand, the Mongol horses had no shoes. The Shisha horses fell down on the ice, with their riders. A great massacre began on the frozen Yellow River. While the remaining Shisha troops on the riverbank were watching this in astonishment, a separate unit of the Mongol troops came to attack them from the side. The Shisha troops were completely destroyed. They lost their main force in this battle and numerous arrows killed their commander, Weiming Linggong, making him look like a porcupine. Some of their survivors escaped into the city of Chunghing. The Mongol troops took Lingchou and then surrounded their capital city, Chunghing.

While Genghis was stationed near the city of Chunghing, an urgent messenger arrived from the west with news of Juchi's death. Juchi had not been faking his illness. It was true that he was planning to go hunting several days before his death, but once he realized something was wrong with his body, he gave up and returned, leaving the hunting to the other generals. He died several days later. He was forty-one. Genghis Khan fell into intense grief. He blamed himself harshly for misunderstanding him and treating him wrongly, even though it was only for a short time. He ordered the Mangkud traveler be found and beheaded for giving him this misinformation, and yet he could not be found anywhere. For three days, Genghis stayed in his war tent. He did not want to show his image of great sadness to his soldiers. It was February of 1227.

Genghis divided his forces into three groups, used one group for the encirclement of Chunghing, and swept over the whole nation with the other two. Almost the whole population was massacred, except for a fraction who had escaped into the deep forests in mountains and caves.

Chunghing was an impregnable fortress. Based on their previous experience, they installed and built many new systems in their city against the invasion tactics. Knowing that the whole nation had been devastated except the city of Chunghing, the Shisha king, Li Tsun Hsiang, tried to surrender. He came out to see Genghis Khan with several of his senior officials, leaving his son, Li Hsien, in the city. He brought with him a golden Buddha statue, nine gold and silver ritual utensils used for their ancestral memorial ceremony, nine boys and nine girls, nine white camels, nine of his best geldings and many other treasures. He arranged all these things in front of Genghis Khan's war tent and waited for his answer on his bended knees.

Nevertheless, Genghis Khan's war tent was never opened. Genghis gave an order to Tolun Cherbi, who came into the tent to report this.

"They have already surrendered before. Surrendering twice should not be allowed! Remove him!"

By the order, Tolun Cherbi drew his scimitar on the spot and cut off the Shisha king's head.

CHAPTER EIGHTY-EIGHT

The Iron Man's Last Wish

L i Hsien, the son of the beheaded Shisha king, Li Tsun Hsiang, continued resistance because their surrender had not been accepted. Genghis did not loosen the encirclement. It was the beginning of summer, and the weather was getting hot. Genghis realized his illness was getting worse. His medical team, which consisted of Persian, Uighur and Chinese doctors, tried many ways to restore his health, but they were not successful. He moved his headquarters to the middle part of a high mountain to avoid the heat. It was an area named Lungto and, in later days, was called Ping Liang.

Genghis saw Juchi in his dream. He looked very peaceful. Juchi was the one whom he spent most of his time with on the battlefield, more than any other son. Genghis loved him very much. Juchi did not say anything. Without changing his peaceful face, he gradually disappeared into the mysterious, misty veil. Genghis awoke from his sleep in surprise. It was midnight. Under the dim light of the Baghdad lamp, he could see Yesui's image. She nursed him all through the night. He raised the upper part of his body. His whole body was drenched with sweat. He realized death was near.

He said to Yesui, "Yesui, call Ogodei and Tolui immediately!"

Genghis Khan's urgent messenger left for Ogodei and Tolui's war camp. It was late in the morning when his two sons arrived at his camp. His second son, Chagatai, had not joined this war. When Ogodei and Tolui stepped into their father's tent, they found him shivering in front of a small fire pot, with many wool blankets on his back.

Genghis Khan reminded his two sons of the stories he used to tell them, like the lessons of five arrows and the snake with two heads. He talked about harmonious brotherhood among his sons and if they were unable to reach agreements, Ogodei should be the one who made the final decisions. He also confirmed the division of the conquered lands for his sons. As for deceased Juchi's ulus, he subdivided it into two: one for Juchi's first son, Orda, which covered the northeastern shore of the Aral Sea to the Sari Su River, and the other one for his second son, Batu, which covered the northern shore of the Caspian Sea to the Volga River and the Irgiz River. Northern China was given to Ogodei. Ever since then, Orda's ordu has been called the "White Ordu" and Batu's was called the "Golden Ordu."

Genghis also told them to keep his death secret until the fall of the city of Chunghing and the complete conquest of the Shisha Kingdom.

In the late evening of that day, Genghis Khan passed away in the presence of his two sons, his second wife, Yesui, all the other royal families who had joined this war and his first comrade, Bogorchu. Borte, his first wife, could not be at his deathbed, because she was in the mainland at that time. He died on the battlefield, in accordance with the last wish of the Mongol man and their tradition.

Before his last moment, Genghis said, "Life is too short to fulfill one man's dream. I have been thinking of only one thing, the glory of the Mongols. Conquer the whole world! Build up an empire of one thousand years with no wars!"

It was August 18, 1227, and he was sixty years old.

After the opening of the main gate of Chunghing the Mongol soldiers learned of the death of Genghis Khan. The Mongol soldiers killed every living thing in that city. Genghis Khan's last battle was flooded with blood. The whole population of the Shisha Kingdom, presumed to be about seven million, was slaughtered and a nation with 200 years of history, with ten kings in each generation, disappeared from the earth forever.

Ogodei immediately summoned the funeral specialists of the Khitans, Uighurs and Persians for preservative treatment of his father's body. At that time, the Khitans had the most highly developed embalming skills. Since the weather was so hot, preservation of the dead body was most urgent. Ogodei also ordered immediate construction of a golden coffin and a golden cart to carry it. Genghis Khan's dead body, in his golden coffin on the golden cart, was sent on a long journey back to his homeland. Everyone who accompanied the body on its voyage kept silent. Everyone, men and women of all ages, whom they encountered on their funeral procession was killed to keep the secrecy of his death and burial site. When the cart with Genghis Khan's dead body arrived near Mountain Muna, the area later called Ordos, the wheels stuck in the mud and would not budge. The Mongols summoned a spiritual communicator and let him find out if this setback was related to a certain revelation.

The spiritual communicator prayed for a long time and finally opened his mouth.

"Genghis Khan's spirit wants to be buried here."

However, it was considered very important to his descendants and to the rest of the Mongols to bury his body on the Mongol mainland.

All the royal family members, of all ages, gathered and began to pray, *The great Khan's spirit, circling in the sky of the Mongol land! Please protect your descendants and all the Mongols.*

After the long prayer, the cart began to move again. Ogodei gave this a little thought. He buried Genghis Khan's underwear, boots and the carpet from his own tent there. In later days, Genghis Khan's descendants built eight chomchogs in that region, which were specially designed white yurts used as shrines. After that, the area was called ordos, which meant multiple chomchogs.

Genghis Khan's dead body arrived on the Mongol mainland. Once there, his dead body was laid in state in a temporary chomchog for three months. This was to give time for all the royal family members, kings of the conquered lands, monarchs and heads of the nations to visit and pay their respects.

After that, his dead body was carried to Burkan Mountain, which was a holy place for the Mongols and the playground of Temujin's early childhood. To keep the secrecy of the burial site, a very limited number of people were allowed to attend, and all the religious people who prayed for his spirit were selected from the blind. In addition, 1,000 slave laborers who were brought for the construction of the tomb were killed after the burial. The burial site and its vicinity were off limits for a long time.

Genghis Khan's tomb, built in the Mongol tradition of being on flat land with no tombstone, no mound and no structure, leaving no trace due to newly grown grass and trees before the turn of the generation, was engulfed by the great steppe.

A Postscript

According to legend, Ogodei, who became the kha-khan two years later, offered sacrifices to his father of forty maidens and forty horses for his afterlife. The forty fairest maidens were selected from the daughters of the aristocrats of the conquered lands, and forty of the best horses were chosen to be buried alongside him. Later, the Mongols named seven other mountains in different areas "Burkan Mountain" to strengthen the secrecy of his tomb.

A Brief Mongol History After Genghis Khan

After Genghis Khan's death, Tolui was entrusted with the position of regent for about two years. In the spring of 1229, they had a grand scale khuriltai at the Kerulen riverside. At this khuriltai, the Mongols elected Ogodei as the kha-khan, carrying out the intention of the deceased Genghis Khan. Ogodei, who was crowned on September 13, 1229, reinforced the administrative system of the empire with Yelu Chutze and in 1235 built up the capital city in Kara Korum.

Ogodei, who was forty when he became the new kha-khan of the Mongol Empire, set out to conquer the whole world, honoring the intention of his deceased father, Genghis Khan. In the year 1230, he gave 30,000 troops to Chormaqan to re-conquer some parts of Persia and the area west of the Caspian Sea, which were in a state of anarchy, and at the same time remove Jal-al-Addin, who had revolted in the area of Shirvan in a dream of resurrection. Chormaqan dashed out to the city of Tabriz in Shirvan at lightning speed, destroyed the rebel groups there and chased down the escaped Jal-al-Addin. Jal-al-Addin wandered from one place to another in flight, and was at last captured by Kurd warriors and beheaded. His head was presented to Chormaqan. Chormaqan stayed on the great plain of Mugan and imposed military rule there for ten years.

Baiju, who was the successor to Chormaqan, destroyed the Seljuk Turkish troops led by Kai Khosrau and conquered those areas, which connected the Mongol territory to the Mediterranean Sea.

In the fall of 1231, Ogodei gave 6,000 cavalry to Saletai to conquer Korea. Saletai, after crossing the Yalu River, took Kaesung, the capital city of Korea, in a few months. Korea moved its capital city to Kang-Wha Island and continued fierce resistance for some time, but eventually surrendered.

Ogodei Khan, with Subedei, mobilized his troops and launched an attack from the rear on Kaifeng, the capital city of Chin, with silent approval and a little help from the Southern Sung. They took the city in May 1233, putting an end to the Chin Empire. Ogodei, in an acknowledgement of the cooperation of the Sung, conceded some part of the land in Honan Province. However, since the unsatisfied Sung began to attack Kaifeng, Ogodei declared war against them at the khuriltai in 1233. Thus the Mongol Empire started a war against the Sung Empire that lasted 45 years. Ogodei advanced toward Sung with his three army groups and reached the Yang-Tze River.

In the year 1237, Ogodei organized the an expeditionary force to conquer all of Europe. Batu, the second son of Juchi, became the commander-in-chief of the 150,000 troops. About ten of the direct descendants of Genghis Khan joined him, including his brothers Orda, Berke and Shayban; Ogodei's sons Guyuk and Qadaan; Tolui's son Mongke; and Chagatai's son and grandson, Baidar and Buri. However, the actual leader was Subedei, who was in his sixties now and the most experienced general in Europe.

In the spring of 1237, the Mongol troops destroyed the troops of the Turkish Cumans, who were holding areas on the Kipchak steppe. It was their first blow. The chief of the Cuman troops, Batchman, was cut in half by Mongke's scimitar. Kutan, the head of the Cumans, escaped to Hungary with his remaining 40,000 survivors.

In December 1237, the Mongol troops crossed the frozen Volga River. They laid siege to the fortress of Raizan, one of the eight Russian principalities, taking it and slaughtering the whole population, including the prince and his family. They took the eight principalities one by one and in February of the following year, the city of Moscow, which was a mere small town at that time, fell to the Mongols. In March 1238, at Sita, the Mongol troops defeated the troops of Yuri II, Grand Duke of Suzdal, which was the most powerful principality among the eight. Yuri II was beheaded after being taken captive.

In the beginning of 1240, the Mongol troops took the city of Chernigov and then Kiev also, which was essentially the capital city of Russia. Thus the Mongols completed the conquest of Russia.

Batu could not get along with Ogodei's son Guyuk and Chagatai's grandson, Buri. They disobeyed Batu's orders. Batu made a report of this to Ogodei, and he summoned the two, based on Genghis Khan's Yassa. Genghis Khan's Yassa clearly prescribed that once the expeditionary troops had left the khan's control, everybody had to obey the commander's orders without exception. This was the beginning of the disharmony between Batu and Guyuk.

Although suspicions of his illegitimacy prevented Juchi from being named kha-khan, his second son, Batu, eventually became the most powerful man in the empire. His ulus, the Golden Ordu, was the biggest compared to all others and he was the most influential and had a great impact on world history.

In January 1241, Batu's expeditionary force advanced toward Poland and Hungary. He left about 30,000 troops in Russia to handle the aftermath of the conquest. Batu gave 20,000 troops to Baidar and Qaidu to conquer Poland. To attack Hungary, he divided the rest of the main force into three groups. The three groups of the main force, commanded by Batu, Subedei and Shayban, crossed over the Carpathian Mountains.

Baidar and Qaidu's cavalry advanced toward Poland and took Lublin first, and then crossed the frozen Vistula River. After taking Sandomierz, they approached Cracow, the capital city of Poland. Duke Boleslaw of Poland had built up a defense line, but he was defeated at the decisive battle of Chmiernik. Cracow had fallen and was burned. The Mongol troops advanced towards Silesia. At the Wahlstatt great plain in the Liegnitz region, they faced the 30,000 Teutonic troops, the entire coalition troops of Europe, including Poland, Germany and France, led by Duke Henry of Poland. The European coalition was believed to be invincible. The coalition troops faced crushing defeat and Duke Henry lost his head. The Mongol soldiers cut off the ears from the dead bodies of the Teutonic knights strewn across the field, put them into nine huge leather bags and sent them to Batu as proof of victory. It was April 9, 1241.

At that time, the strongest troops in Europe were in Hungary. The Hungarians and the Mongols were descended from a common ancestor, the Huns. Attila was their ancestor. However, time had changed everything. Both groups had assimilated with neighboring tribes, so by that time they were different people.

Bela IV, the king of Hungary, proclaimed himself the protector of Europe. As refugees were flooding into his territory, he reinforced the defense system and put his troops on alert. The fate of all Europe was in his hands. First, he put a defense line on the Carpathian Mountains, but it was easily broken down by the Mongol troops. The Mongol troops advanced toward Pest, the capital city of Hungary. Finally, the two armies clashed on the stone bridge of the Sajo River, which ran between Buda and Pest.

At that time, the number of Bela's Hungarian troops was 100,000, and Batu's Mongol troops numbered 40,000. Bela thought the Mongol troops could never cross the bridge, which was so narrow that only three or four cavalrymen could pass over it side by side. However, the Mongol troops crossed over this bridge under the covering fire of highly efficient catapults and cannons and grenades developed by Chinese and Persian technicians. The Mongol troops pushed the Hungarians and at the same time, 30,000 Mongol troops led by Subedei crossed the river at the southern side with their own temporary bridge and launched an attack from their side. The Mongol forces surrounded the Hungarians the way Mongol hunters surrounded their prey. The Hungarians fell in crushing defeat. The Mongols cut off the heads of 60,000 Hungarians. It was April 11, 1241, and the last defense force of Europe had broken down. The Mongol soldiers chased down Bela IV advancing into Croatia and Dalmatia, but he escaped to one of the small islands in the Adriatic Sea.

Batu stayed in Pest for a while to give a rest to his soldiers and horses and then crossed the frozen Danube River on December 25, 1241. He took the city of Grand and also Neustadt, a suburb of Vienna. Now they were in Austria. There was no other force to stop them in Europe. However, in the beginning of 1242, Batu and Subedei received an urgent messenger from Kara Khorum of the Mongol mainland, who had galloped 6,000 miles. Ogodei had died on December 11, 1241.

Batu moved his troops back to Sarai, near the north of the Caspian Sea, in accordance with Genghis Khan's Yassa that all the princes have to attend the khuriltai and to exercise his influence over the election of the next khan.

After Ogodei's death, his widow, Toregene, was regent for four years. She made every effort to make her son, Guyuk, the next khan, and she was successful. The biggest opponent of Guyuk's election as the kha-khan was Batu.

In the spring of 1246, they had a grand-scale khuriltai at the shore of Koko Lake, near the upper part of the Orkhon River. All the other princes, the regional monarchs and the kings of the vassal kingdoms attended this meeting, but Batu did not. Guyuk became the kha-khan through this meeting.

Guyuk, the newly elected kha-khan, first removed the Ochigin Noyan, Genghis Khan's younger brother Temuge, whose loyalty was not trusted, and then marched toward Batu, his political enemy. However, Guyuk's secret plan was revealed to Sorghaqtani, Tolui's widow. She immediately dispatched secret messengers to Batu telling him to prepare. However, Guyuk died suddenly on his way, just two years after becoming the Kha-Khan.

After Guyuk's death, his widow, Oghul Qaimish, was the regent for about three years. For approximately nine years following the death of Ogodei Khan the Mongol Empire was stagnant, until the emergence of the new khan, Mongke, the first son of Tolui.

Mongke, who became Kha-Khan in 1251 at age forty-one, was energetic, reasonable and a fair man who restored Genghis Khan's Yassa. Being an outstanding warrior and an able statesman, he was supported by Batu at the election. After Batu's death, he took over the Golden Ordu which had a strong tendency toward independence, without any trouble. He reinstated the mission to conquer the world at the khuriltai held on the upper part of the Onon River in 1253. He gave 100,000 cavalry to his brother, Hulegu, to conquer Baghdad, Mesopotamia, and Syria. He himself set out to conquer the Southern Sung with his other brother, Khubilai. The northern half of the Chinese continent was conquered by many different people, but the southern half had never fallen. Mongke divided his expeditionary troops into three army groups. He led the first army group and attacked Hochow after taking the regions of Sensi and Szechwan. Khubilai's second army surrounded the city of Wuchow through Hopei. Urianqatai, the son of Subedei and the commander of the third army group, conquered Tibet and advanced towards Annam, taking the city of Hanoi, forcing their king, Tran Taitong, to surrender. He continued marching toward the Southern Sung, passing through the Tongking plain, and launched an attack on Changsha in Hunan Province, after taking Kweiling in Kwangsi Province.

Attacked from the north, west and south, the Southern Sung was a half-step from downfall, but the sudden death of Mongke brought a temporary end to all battles at the front lines. Mongke died of the endemic disease dysentery. It was August 11, 1259.

Meanwhile, Hulegu, who had advanced toward the Persian area, took the fortress of Almut, the stronghold of Assassins, which had never fallen before. After that, he launched an attack on Baghdad, which fell to the Mongols after a great number of killings. It was 1258. Thus, Hulegu put an end to the 500-year-old Abbasid caliphate and became the king of Persia in 1263, establishing the new Il Khan dynasty.

Khubilai, after defeating his brother, as well as political rival Arig Boke, became kha-khan in 1260 and continued the expansion policy. He conquered the Southern Sung and became the founder of the Yuan dynasty, ruling the entire Chinese territory. Later, he was recognized as kha-khan of the whole Mongol Empire. He reigned for thirty-four years, and those were the most powerful and prosperous years of the Mongol Empire. Later, he launched an attack on Japan and Java to open the trade route by the sea; however, it was not successful.

Thus, the descendants of Genghis Khan built up the largest empire in human history and ruled conquered people in every part of the world, opening new dynasties and a new era. Some examples of their long-lasting rule:

Russia, about 270 years

China, about 160 years (all of China, about 90 years)

Persia, about 120 years (including Baghdad area, about 80 years)

India, about 300 years (Babur, the founder of the Moghul Empire in India, was the distant descendant of Chagatai. He was the last conqueror who went out under the name and heritage of the Mongols. Moghul is the Persian pronunciation of Mongol.)

Sam Djang

His epic novel, *Genghis Khan, the World Conqueror*, was written after eight years of intensive research. During those eight years, he made a number of trips to Mongolia, Russia, China and related countries. He interviewed numerous people in those countries and read hundreds of articles and rare books in the libraries of Mongolia and beyond. Sam Djang testifies that his book, *Genghis Khan, the World Conqueror*, was written in the form of a historical novel, and yet 90 percent of its contents are based on the true story. Also, he believes that his book covers many facts that the majority of past historians failed to see due to their lack of understanding of the unique cultural, social, political, historical and geographical background of the people of Genghis Khan.